DES

The sentry was starting to struggle. Using the hand he had clamped on the man's face, he tried to knock his head against a rock, but the sentry resisted, and he managed not much more than a tap. Desperate, he dropped to the ground beside the target, wrapping one leg around him and wrapping his knife arm around the man's free arm. Of course, now he had the sentry somewhat restrained, but couldn't stab him.

The sentry was thrashing now, the desperation of his position getting through the drug-induced fog in his brain, clawing at the arm Dan had clamped around his chest. Dan held on tightly, keeping his off hand clamped over the man's face, while he tried to figure out what to do next.

He suddenly rolled on top of the sentry, letting go of the man's jaw just in time to keep from pinning his hand between the sentry's head and the tree root beneath them. He clamped that hand on the back of the man's neck, but now his knife hand was pinned beneath the sentry's body.

Taking a chance, he let go of the knife and yanked his arm free, putting his weight on the other hand, pressing the man's face into the mold and loam under the tree while he sank a knee into his back. Hastily switching hands, even as the sentry got a hand free and tried to reach back to claw at him, he snatched up the knife and plunged it into the side of the man's neck. He didn't want to slit his throat; he'd start aspirating air and blood through the wound and making a lot of noise. He just wanted to cut the blood vessels.

Hot blood pulsed out over the blade and onto his hand. His victim bucked and thrashed under him, and he shifted to pin the man's hands down with his knees, even while the sentry's feet scrabbled uselessly at the jungle floor, his soft shoes unable to get a purchase. He had to be running out of air, too, with his face mashed into the ground. Dan held on, keeping the man still while his lifeblood poured out over both of them. He'd hit the artery; it wouldn't take long.

Also By Peter Nealen

KILL YUAN

Peter Nealen

This is a work of fiction. Characters and incidents are products of the author's imagination. Real locations are used fictitiously. This book is not autobiographical. It is not a true story presented as fiction. It is more exciting than anything 99% of real gunfighters ever get to experience. Enjoy.

Chapter 1

A shout from the watchtower drew Nong Song out of his reverie. He looked up from the table where he had been cleaning his QSZ-92, to see Banh waving from the watchtower and pointing off to the southwest.

He grimaced. Nong didn't like most of the motley squad of Javanese and Malaysians he'd been saddled with, out here on tiny Pulau Repong. The scrawny, gap-toothed Vietnamese pirate, though, who liked to boast about the number of merchant throats he had slit dockside in Cam Ranh, revolted him. But *Shang Xiao* Yuan had put him on this flyspeck in the ocean for a reason, so he hastily reassembled the pistol, then got up and reached for his binoculars.

As he scanned the water, looking for whatever Banh had meant to indicate by that inarticulate yell, he thought, for the hundredth time that week, that there really was very little to like about this entire situation. He had put on the single bar of a *Shao Wei* in the PLA Navy only a year before, looking forward to a career that he hoped would ultimately end in command of at least a destroyer, if not one of the refit *Kuznetsov*-class carriers. He certainly hadn't expected his career to end less than a year later, resulting in him presently sitting on a tiny, miserable island in the South China Sea, commanding a band of pirates with only one other Han on the island. And Pan Jing was not the man he would have chosen to have with him. He was almost as bad as Banh.

It took a minute of scanning the horizon before he saw what the little Vietnamese was excited about. It was a yacht. A big one; his quick estimate put it at close to seventy-five meters or more. Sleek and silver, it looked very, very expensive. He ran to the tower and began to climb, while yelling to Pan, "Start getting the boats ready!" The big crewman looked up languidly, and started to get to his feet. If the target was as rich as Nong thought it was, Pan would shake off his lethargy in a hurry as soon as he found out. So would most of the rest.

The ladder leading up to the tower was as rickety as the rest of the structure, which had been hastily lashed together by men who had slightly more knowledge of knots than they had love for manual labor. It hadn't blown down yet, at any rate, but it creaked dangerously as Nong climbed. He was probably going to have to send Banh down when he got to the top, just to be on the safe side.

When he hoisted himself up onto the platform, Banh was staring

1

through the spotting scope at the yacht, muttering to himself gleefully in Vietnamese. Nong didn't speak a word of it, though Banh, along with most of the rest of the pirates except for a couple of the Javanese, spoke passable, if rough, Mandarin. Nong didn't speak, but simply jerked a finger toward the ladder. Banh hesitated, the look in his eyes suggesting that he was considering simply gutting the soft Chinese kid that was trying to give him orders, but then he stepped away from the spotting scope and started down the ladder.

Nong waited until Banh was already a good ten feet below before turning to the spotting scope himself. He'd learned early that trusting any of his fellow pirates was a bad idea, especially the ones who had been engaged in this particular occupation for much longer than he'd been a naval officer.

Banh already had the scope focused on the yacht, which was barely moving; it had hardly reached the edge of the optic's field of view by the time he put his eye to the scope. It took only the slightest of adjustments to recenter the yacht in the objective lens.

It *was* expensive. Nong didn't know anything about boat values, but he was guessing a price tag that no one he knew of short of the Central Committee could afford. As he focused the scope a little better, he could see figures on the bow. They were far enough away that it was hard to see, but he thought he could see several shirtless men and almost as many women in even less clothing. They were mostly light-skinned. Westerners. Probably Americans. Japanese were possible, but he thought he could just make out a flash of yellow hair on one of the women.

Whoever they were, they were obviously extremely wealthy, and just the kind of target that *Shang Xiao* Yuan would call a "target of opportunity." The majority of their targets were freighters or tankers, but the *Shang Xiao* wasn't going to pass up a juicy kidnapping, and this looked like it could be one of the juiciest.

Nong really didn't have his heart in this business, but he knew that the *Shang Xiao* would probably have his head if he passed up a target like the yacht. Worse, he'd probably just turn him over to Banh for sport. Not because Yuan held the Vietnamese pirate in any sort of esteem, but simply because he was the scum of Nong's crew. The *Shang Xiao* had a harsh imagination when it came to punishment. He wouldn't just take a man's life, he'd make sure that man lost all face before he died.

Abandoning the spotting scope, Nong started back down the ladder. Apparently, Banh had already started spreading the word. The pirates were stirring out of their afternoon stupor, though a few were still moving sluggishly, probably still either drunk on Arrack or stoned. The first few executions had curbed some of the harder narcotic use shortly after Yuan had consolidated his hold on the islands, but Arrack, Langkau, ruou, and marijuana were plentiful, and usually overlooked. Some of the

Malays and Javanese needed or wanted the liquid courage when they went after a ship, especially as more armed guards were getting posted on them.

"Is it true?" Pan asked as Nong reached the ground. There was an eager light in the big man's eyes that Nong didn't like, but that seemed to be the normal state of affairs anymore, ever since *Shang Xiao* Yuan had taken the *Zhaotong* and deserted to set up his little empire here in the Anambas.

He nodded. "It's true," he replied. "It is a very large yacht. It looks like tourists."

Pan grinned. He had very good teeth for a rating on a PLAN frigate. It didn't make the smile any prettier. "Rich tourists, then," he said. "It will be a big ransom. And they are probably too rich and spoiled to cause any trouble. Easy money. And maybe a little fun, too."

Nong carefully hid his disgust. Showing emotion in front of these men would be worse than losing face; they would descend on him like jackals. Like it or not, the only way to survive for now was to play his assigned role; to be a pirate. He pulled his pistol out of its holster and pointed it at the sky. "Let's go!" he shouted. With a roar of approval, the pirates swarmed to the armed speedboats partially hidden beneath overhanging branches that had been tied down to create some overhead camouflage.

The speedboats had belonged to the oil company that Yuan and his men had expelled from the islands. With the help of the local pirate bands that *Shang Xiao* Yuan had recruited or suborned, they had equipped them with a mix of Type 67s, PKPs, DShKs, and even a CIS . 50. They were attack boats now, and had seen use.

Even the drunks and the stoners made good time getting into the boats and getting ready for action. It wasn't often they got a target as enticing as an expensive yacht full of dumb Americans, or whoever they were. The women were an added bonus.

With a roar of outboards, the speedboats surged out of the little bay, quickly picking up speed as they raced toward the yacht. Nong was in the lead boat, as his position necessitated. These cutthroats might not be soldiers, but Nong was keeping to his training, as the *Shang Xiao* had admonished him to do before sending him to this shithole of an island. Only acting like soldiers was going to enable them to control this rabble.

He looked around at the rest of the boats. Their formation, if it could be called that, was a little ragged, with several of the boats racing ahead of the rest. He'd given orders that the machine guns were to be covered until they had the target surrounded, but Banh was in the bow of one of the smaller and faster boats, holding on to the CIS .50, grinning his gap-toothed madman's grin. Nong gritted his teeth, even as he reflected that he should have expected as much from the little *chusheng*.

But as they neared the yacht, it didn't look like the Americans

3

even noticed the gun. He could hear their music pounding even over the roar of the outboards, and a couple of the girls in bikinis on the bow were waving to the boats. One even lifted her top, flashing the incoming pirates with a whoop that was almost drowned out by the music. Nong momentarily felt a flash of resentment at these Westerners' arrogant stupidity; they would deserve just what his pirates were about to give them.

The pirate boats split, three swinging around the stern while Nong led the other two around the bow. In moments, they had the yacht surrounded, and Nong pointed at the bow. Jalak already had a grappling hook ready in his hands as Abdul steered the boat in toward the yacht's bow.

The stupid Americans still didn't see the danger. The big-breasted blond who had flashed the boats was leaning over the gunwale, waving to the pirates and yelling something that Nong couldn't understand in a high-pitched voice. A few more of the men had come to the side as well, all shirtless and carrying bottles of beer. One raised his bottle toward the boats with a gleeful shout.

Jalak was starting to twirl the rope with the grappling hook, preparing to throw it. Nong put his hand up and brought it down with a shout of, "Now!"

The covers came off the machine guns, except for Banh's. In a ragged volley, all five boats fired bursts into the air over the yacht.

Now the Americans got it. Screams erupted from the deck, and suddenly the partiers on the side were gone, a muscular arm hauling the blond away from the gunwale even as she screamed. Jalak gave the grapple a practiced heave, and it caught the gunwale on the first try. With a tug, Jalak made sure it was holding, then pulled, drawing the boat close enough to start climbing up.

Nong, true to his role as leader, made sure his pistol was in its holster, then grabbed the rope and started up, with Jalak and Soeprapto right behind him, each with a Type 63 rifle slung across his back. Jalak's even had its bayonet, which he liked to wave under crewmen's noses during a hijack.

Nong had not been the fittest of officers when he had pinned on his bars. He still wasn't; the diet of mostly rice that was all that was available out on the islands wasn't terribly conducive to physical fitness. But he was definitely leaner and stronger than he had been when he'd first set foot on the *Zhaotong*. That was by necessity. Just like the bravado and the pistol, being stronger than most of the pirates he was supposed to be leading was a survival trait. So, while his arms were burning by the time he got up to the deck, he still made the short climb quickly enough, and was able to launch himself over the gunwale at just about the same time that Banh came over from the other side.

The bow had emptied by the time the pirates got on deck. Nong caught a glimpse of a shapely rump in a bikini disappearing through the hatch beneath the helipad that was just aft of the bow. He followed, not so much out of lust, though he was sure many of his fellow boarders would have that foremost in their minds at that point, but because that appeared to be the best route to the bridge. While he really wasn't worried about much resistance from these spoiled rich Americans, there was always somebody who would try to be brave and stupid, and it was best to nip that in the bud by taking full control as quickly as possible. The bridge was the best spot to do that. He'd learned that on his first hijack, when Yuan had made him go along with Qiao.

The yacht's interior was a marked contrast to the freighters and tankers they usually attacked. Everything was very sleek, modern, and roomy. He stormed up the ladderwell into a wood-trimmed lounge with luxurious sofas and what looked like a well-stocked bar, before going through another hatch into a narrow passageway similarly paneled in what looked like oak. There were a couple of screaming, barely-dressed young people in front of him, who ducked into cabins on either side, but he ignored them for the time being. Once they had the bridge, they could sweep the yacht and gather all of the hostages on the top deck.

The bridge was two more decks up. By the time he got there, some of the heady thrill of the hijack was going to Nong's head. The yacht was one of the richest boats he'd ever seen. There was more money sunk into the vessel than anyone aside from a General or a Central Committee member could ever dream of having. Maybe, if he made a good enough showing, the *Shang Xiao* would be content with ransoming the hostages, and let him have the yacht. It was unlikely, he knew, but a man could dream.

He burst onto the bridge, pistol already in hand, and went straight to the man in board shorts at the tiller, who was still staring in shock at the pirates swarming onto the yacht's deck below. Nong pistol-whipped the man to the deck and stood over the crumpled body. "I am now in control of this ship!" he shouted, in passable English, or at least he thought it was. "Everyone down on the deck, now!"

He had been far too keyed up and absorbed with fantasies of owning the yacht he had captured to notice that the man had moved with the blow, instead of taking the full force of it. He also hadn't noticed the tattoos that crawled over the man's arms, chest, and ribs. Nor would he have necessarily recognized several of the insignias integrated into them, even if he had.

Most of the Americans had quickly dropped to the deck on command, though a brunette with slightly Asian features wearing short shorts and a red string bikini top was just standing there by the aft windows, staring at the pirates and shivering. Banh, who had been right behind Nong all the way up, now advanced on her, leering. His folding-stock Type 56 was slung on his back, and his knife was in his hand.

5

"I said get on the deck!" Nong shouted at the woman, as much to protect her from Banh's attention as to reinforce his command. Shaking like a leaf, she obeyed, as Banh stood over her, the same rotten leer on his face, thumbing the edge of his knife, both a promise of things to come. Nong looked away in disgust.

Gunfire suddenly erupted from below decks, a rapid, hammering series of reports that froze Nong's breath. He turned toward the hatch, sick with the sudden realization that he had just lost all control of his men, and opened his mouth to shout.

He never got the chance to yell. The sight of two large men, one black, one white, both dressed in shorts and t-shirts with plate carriers over them, rifles in their shoulders, made his brain go into lock. This was supposed to be a rich playboy's yacht, filled with soft, spoiled tourists. There weren't supposed to be any guns here aside from their own.

Before he could unfreeze his thoughts enough to act, an iron-hard leg slammed into his calves, sweeping his feet out from under him. He fell to the deck, striking his head on the tiller as he went down. He thought he heard three painfully loud *crack*s go by his head before everything went black.

When he came to, his head was pounding and he felt nauseous. As soon as he became aware of it, the nausea redoubled and he retched, bile dribbling down his chin and chest. He couldn't turn aside to keep it off of himself, which was when he realized that he was zip-tied to a chair, hand and foot.

He cracked his eyes open, squinting against the light, which only made the pain in his head worse. He could feel the knot in his skull where he'd hit the tiller throbbing. He felt sick, and only in part because of the concussion.

He was still on the bridge. There was another man at the tiller, and the faintly Asian brunette was now wearing a t-shirt and plate carrier, standing nearby with a rifle. She was standing over Banh's corpse. The Vietnamese pirate had taken a round to the side of the head, and the exit wound had blown a good chunk of his face off.

Nong realized that he'd heard the woman shout while he was puking his guts out. She turned toward the ladderwell that led up from below, where two men were now stepping onto the bridge. One was the man he had pistol-whipped, now armed and equipped just like the woman and the man at the tiller. The gash where the pistol had hit him just above his eyebrow had been closed with butterfly bandages and was still oozing a little bit of blood.

The other man, in the lead, was half a head shorter than his companion, with icy blue eyes and hair that was a dark brown shading to black. He unslung his rifle, leaned it against the bulkhead, then stepped over to Nong's chair, looking down at him for a moment. He loomed over Nong enough that it hurt to look up and squint at him.

Finally, the man squatted down in front of him, bringing his face about to eye level. "Do you speak English?" he asked.

It took a moment for Nong's aching brain to process the words. He didn't dare nod; it hurt too much just to keep his head still and upright. "Yes, a little," he replied.

"Good," the man said. "My Mandarin sucks. What's your name?"

Nong gulped, and didn't say anything for a moment. Old conditioning was reasserting itself. He might be a pirate now, and no longer in service to his country, but he was being questioned by what he could only assume was an American soldier. He couldn't bring himself to talk.

"Look, son," the man said calmly, "I'm being nice right now, because you've got a concussion, and you might have some information that we can use. If you piss me off, I'll turn you over to Lambert over there," he jerked a thumb toward the tattooed man with the cut on his forehead, "and he won't be nearly so nice. So let's try this again. What is your name?"

"Nong Song," he finally whispered, after it took a moment to gather enough spit to talk. His mouth and throat were raw with used stomach acid, and something tasted like blood. The man named Lambert laughed.

The dark-haired man glared at him for a second before turning back to Nong. "All right, Nong Song, here's how this is going to work. You're going to tell me everything you know about *Shang Xiao* Yuan's dispositions on the islands. How many men does he have? Where are his bases? What kind of defenses? Does he have allies on Borneo or mainland Malaysia that will come to support him if he's attacked?"

Nong shook his head painfully. It was hard to think, between translating the dark-haired man's rapid-fire questions in his head and the pounding agony and nausea of his concussion. "I do not know the answers to any of those questions," he said finally. "I was only a *Shao Wei*. I have been out on Pulau Repong for the last three months. The *Shang Xiao* does not tell me his plans; he just tells me to keep a lookout. I was to report big targets and attack smaller targets of opportunity."

"That would be an expensive yacht filled with scantily-clad tourists," Lambert added helpfully.

"No shit," the dark-haired man replied. "Shut up." He turned back to Nong. "Let me put it a different way. Is the entire crew of the *Zhaotong* part of the band? Or did some decline to become pirates?"

Nong thought about it for a moment. He honestly didn't think anyone had decided to object to Yuan's announced plan to desert and carve out his own little empire in the South China Sea. If anyone had, they had been dealt with quietly and permanently before any of the non-Chinese pirates had seen it. "I do not know," he muttered. "I do not think so."

"You don't think what?" the man demanded. "You don't think the whole crew went pirate along with you, or you don't think any decided they didn't want to play?"

"I do not think that any of the crew defied the *Shang Xiao*," Nong said thickly. "I was the junior officer on board. I think maybe the rest were already part of the *Shang Xiao*'s plans."

The dark-haired man looked up at the man called Lambert. Lambert shrugged. The man turned back to Nong. "All right, we'll assume that the whole crew joined. Do you know how many non-Chinese pirates there are?"

He tried to shrug, but couldn't. The zip ties were digging into his wrists. Only now that he was a bit more conscious was he aware of how cruelly tight they were. The pain had been eclipsed earlier by the throbbing agony in his skull.

"I do not know for sure," he confessed. "There are many. There are enough that only Pan Jing and I were put here to command these men."

"That's a lot, if the ratio holds," the woman said. "We're talking probably five or six hundred, minimum."

"I suspect that we'll find more of the Chinese closer to Yuan himself," the dark-haired man replied. "Presuming Nong Song here is telling the truth and he really is just a boot butter-bar who doesn't know shit, and got put out on the LP/OP because he's a boot and the Captain doesn't entirely trust him." Nong didn't understand all of that, but he got the gist. The dark-haired man turned back to him. "Where is the *Zhaotong* itself?" he asked.

"I do not know," he replied honestly. It had been at anchor off Pulau Matak the last he had seen it, but that had been three months before. "It has not come here since we were assigned to Repong."

"This guy doesn't know shit," the man called Lambert said. "Let's just off him, throw his corpse to the sharks, and quit wasting time."

A flash of irritation flickered across the dark-haired man's face, but he looked at Nong and said, "I hope you can give me more than that, Ensign Nong Song, because otherwise Lambert, as much of an asshole as he is, is right, and we have no further use for you. So, what's it going to be? Do you have something else for me?"

Nong felt a jolt of fear go through him like an electric shock. Looking at the man called Lambert, he could see his own death in the man's brown eyes. He felt another surge of nausea, whether because of the concussion or the imminence of his own demise, he couldn't be sure. He thought of the exultation he'd felt, in spite of himself, as he'd stormed

8

the yacht, watching the rich tourists run screaming from him. For a brief moment, he'd forgotten his nervousness and disgust at what he'd become, and embraced the savagery. Now all that was gone. He thought he felt his bladder let go.

"No, please," he stammered, trying to think past the befuddling pain in his head. There had to be something, some fact they didn't have, that might keep him alive for a little while longer. "I'm sure there is something, I just have to think of it..."

The dark-haired man studied him for a moment, his nose wrinkling as he noticed the urine stain on Nong's shorts. Finally, he stood up. "Two more questions, for now. Did any of your people get left on the island?" Nong hesitated. He honestly wasn't sure. He didn't think so, but he hadn't exactly taken a head count when they'd boarded the boats. He decided to say no; if there were still a few left, and the Americans didn't execute him right away, they might be able to get word back to *Shang Xiao* Yuan. He might even be rescued. Maybe.

The dark-haired man was starting to look impatient. He wanted an answer. When Nong shook his head in the negative, he continued. "Did you radio to the main base that we were here? Is anyone expecting to hear from you about the target you came out for?"

Nong's stomach dropped even further, if that was possible. He hadn't thought to report the sighting or his attack to Yuan's headquarters on Matak. He'd been too desperate not to let his motley band of cutthroats get ahead of him to even think about it. Slowly, he shook his head.

The dark-haired man nodded, satisfied. "Good. That gives us some breathing room. It gives you a longer lease on life, too. I'll have some more questions later. Think really hard about the answers." He looked at the woman. "Keep an eye on him." Then he turned and walked off the bridge.

Lambert started to follow him, but stopped at the top of the ladderwell, and watched the other man descend before turning back toward Nong. Nong didn't like the look he saw in the man's eyes as he paced back toward the chair.

"Lambert..." the woman began, but the man held up a hand toward her.

"Shut it, Cassy," he said, never taking his eyes off of Nong. He advanced until he was standing directly over him, looking down. It hurt, but Nong craned his neck to look up at the tattooed man.

For a moment, the man called Lambert just studied him with blank, dead, pitiless eyes. Then he drew his pistol. The woman started to say something, but without looking at her, Lambert said, "Get out." She hesitated. "I mean it. Get out." She still hesitated, her hands flexing a little on her rifle, and Lambert looked over at her. "You gonna shoot me to save a fucking pirate?" Lambert demanded. "Fuck off. Get out of here."

"Dan's going to hear about this," she said tightly.

"Sure he will," Lambert said. "But he won't shoot me for scragging a fucking pirate, either. Get lost."

With a glare, the woman planted her feet, defying him to force her to leave. "I can't let you do this," she insisted.

Lambert grinned humorlessly, then ignored her and turned back to Nong. "Some people are a little too good for this business, you know?" he said conversationally. "I know you're just wasting our time to try to save your worthless ass. You're just a clueless bootenant out of his depth, but you're going to string Dan along because he doesn't want to be the one to drop the hammer on you, all tied up like that. But as for me, I don't like having my time wasted. I think we could be doing better things than interrogating you. Plus," he added, reaching up to touch the bandage with two fingers of his off hand, "you gave me this. So fuck you." He dropped the index finger to flip Nong the bird.

The last thing Nong ever saw was the gaping maw of the pistol's muzzle below the coldest eyes he'd ever seen.

Chapter 2

Four Months Earlier

Amy and Tom were already outside on the curb waiting by the time Dan Tackett pulled up to the daycare center. It was already dark, and the clock numbers on his truck's dash shone accusingly at him. It was almost eight at night. Sandra Crawford was standing on the curb behind the kids, a stiffly impassive look on her face.

He parked the truck, grabbed the envelope off the dashboard, and got out. It was time to pay the daycare bill already, and he mused bitterly that every cent he made working extra hours was going into paying for those extra hours at child care.

"Good evening, Mr. Tackett," Sandra said stiffly, disapproval at his lateness in every word. "I trust you know what time it is." The Happy Circle Child Care Center was supposed to close at seven, and he was just getting there to pick up the kids at fifty minutes past that.

"Yes, Sandra, I do know what time it is," he replied tiredly. "Work went late tonight. I couldn't afford to pass up the overtime." He handed over the envelope, while turning to the kids. "Amy, Tom, you ready to go?"

"Sure, Dad," Amy chirped. Tom, younger than his sister by two years, just nodded. He had become a boy of few words ever since their mother had died in the crash. Amy grabbed her little brother's hand and pulled him over to the truck, pulling open the back door and helping the three-year-old into his car seat.

"You really should make an effort to spend more time with them," Sandra said, some of the lecturing tone gone from her voice. When he looked at her, he saw only concern in her eyes. "It's not good for kids to spend all day every day away from their parent."

He sighed heavily. "I'll take that under advisement when I can afford to pay all the bills," he replied, and started back toward the truck.

He got back in the driver's seat and turned down the music. Julie wouldn't have necessarily approved of the kids listening to the death metal that he'd taken to playing ninety percent of the time since her death. But he found that in his current state of mind, much else in the way of music just kind of ground on him, and both the news and talk radio just pissed him off.

"How was your day, Amy?" he asked, as he pulled away from

the curb. The little girl promptly launched into a detailed, if wandering and sometimes incoherent, story about the doings of the day in kindergarten and then at daycare. Dan couldn't really follow most of it, but it meant he didn't have to say much as his daughter chattered away. Tom was already asleep in his car seat; it was almost his bedtime already.

Dan clenched his hands around the steering wheel, Amy's description of the esoteric, made-up game she and several others had played that afternoon fading into slightly high-pitched background noise. *How am I going to maintain for another fifteen years?* he thought. *She's been gone for four months and I'm already losing it. The strain of not letting the kids see that Daddy is coming apart at the seams is just making it worse.*

It was a half hour drive to the house, where he gave Amy the keys to unlock the front door while he carefully lifted a sleeping Tom out of the car seat and carried him inside. Amy wanted to help take her little brother's shoes off before Dan put him to bed, but Dan did it himself, then tucked the little boy in. Tom barely moved or made a sound, just turning over on his side, his eyes still closed.

"Did you get something for dinner?" Dan asked Amy.

She nodded, her blond curls, inherited from her mother, bouncing. "Miss Sandra got us some food before you got there to pick us up." Good. At least Tom wouldn't be waking up *too* ravenously hungry. That was, of course, a rather relative measurement; the boy seemed to live to eat sometimes.

"All right, then, go brush your teeth, then it's time for bed," he told her. She nodded again, and bounced off to the bathroom.

It took another fifteen minutes to get Amy ready for bed, tucked in, prayers said, and the umpty-fifth reading of her favorite story gotten through, which Dan could probably recite word-for-word without being able to tell anyone what it was really about. He was running on autopilot by then, anyway, as the day's exhaustion started to weigh him down. He finally gave his daughter a last hug, then turned out the light and headed downstairs.

He'd ignored the mail sitting under the slot in the door when they'd gotten home, and he wanted to continue to ignore it. He knew what was there. The mortgage was due again, as well as the insurance bills. All of which would just about clean out what was left of the last month's wages. After standing over the pile of envelopes and unsolicited catalogs, he muttered, "Fuck it," and went into the kitchen. In the cupboard above the counter were several liquor bottles, and he grabbed one at random before heading for the back room that had been his study.

The place was as much of a wreck as most of the rest of the house. Part of that was because of the long hours he was working, and his corresponding lack of energy when he got home. Part of it was simply because he failed to see the point in trying to make it nice anymore.

He realized, as he popped open the bottle and took a swig of what turned out to be rum, that he was deep in a depressive episode, and had been pretty much ever since Julie had passed. She had been everything that was good in his world for six years, and then, in the time it took for a drunk not to hit the brakes, she was gone. Now he was struggling to keep himself together for the sake of his kids, unsure how to care for them the way she had, and feeling like he was drowning with every breath he took.

He sat down at the desk and fired up his laptop as he took another fiery gulp. He didn't know why he even bothered to turn the damned thing on. It never gave him good news.

But he did the same thing he did every night anyway. Once it was up, he logged onto Combatant Jobs and PMSCNET, and started scrolling through the listings.

I don't know why I'm doing this, he thought. *I'm just pretending there's a chance to get back in the action, make some good money and get a little bit of that combat thrill again. Those days are past. I'm just sitting here drinking, pretending that my life isn't over.*

"Listen to you, you self-pitying fuck," he growled out loud. "'Oh, woe is me, my life is over.'" He took another swallow. He should have been getting buzzed by now, but the fact that he wasn't didn't say anything good for his alcohol consumption habits over the last few months. "It better fucking not be. You've got two little kids you'd better stay alive for."

And now I'm sitting here drinking alone and talking to myself. That's real great, Tackett. Real good sign, there.

He wasn't really studying the job listings. Most of them he'd seen before; either State Department-sponsored training gigs in Africa, Stateside training contracts that were mostly tied up by one Good Old Boy network or another, or PSD assignments or static security jobs at big-box FOBs in Afghanistan. Those jobs were dwindling as the drawdown continued, though there looked like there were some new ones in Iraq. Of course, he was all too aware that most of the listings were from companies that didn't actually have the contracts in question, but were trying to get a stack of resumes built up so that they could tell the client that they had a ready-built crew standing by when they bid on the contract, six to nine months down the line. None of which made those particular listings of any immediate use.

Who am I kidding? None of these are of any "immediate" use to me. I'm a single dad with two kids. I can't just drop everything and go to Afghanistan for a year, certainly not for a measly...$65,000? You gotta be fucking kidding me. He'd been hearing for years that the glory days of contracting for $1200 per day were over, and his own perusals of the contract listings had borne that out, but if there were actually contractors settling for $65k a year in a war zone, it was worse than he'd thought.

He wasn't sure what made him click on the next listing. All it said was, "Sensitive High Risk Contract." It was just uninformative enough, and he was just drunk enough, that he had to check it out. He started skimming the description, then stopped and started over, setting the rum bottle aside.

MMPR Inc. is recruiting for a Sensitive, High-Risk, Counter-Piracy mission. Combat Deployment or Warzone Contracting experience required, minimum fourteen months on the ground. Candidates must be able to pass strenuous physical evaluation and training, as well as high-standard weapons and tactics training. Due to the sensitive nature of this contract, no details about operational location or the identity of the client can be included at this time, until the candidate has passed the pre-deployment vetting course. Training is expected to last two months. Actual contract is open ended, minimum four months. Beginning pay: $50,000/month. All resumes must be submitted no later than September 15. That was in two weeks.

Dan sat back and stared at the screen for a long time. He didn't even reach for the bottle. *Fifty grand a month?* That was astronomical, even back in the good old days. He suddenly found himself wondering how much he could pay off with two hundred grand. Four months would pay off the house, easy. That would be one huge Sword of Damocles no longer hanging over his head. With the house paid off, even if he went back to wrenching on Harleys and Gold Wings for a living, he wouldn't have to spend all the extra hours just to make ends meet.

Hold on, now, he thought. *If it sounds too good to be true, it probably is.* He read through the listing again. There weren't any overt red flags, at least not at first. The pay was high enough to raise some eyebrows, including his own, but the rest seemed to be pretty standard contract listing boilerplate. He studied the company name for a moment. *MMPR? Never heard of 'em.* A quick search turned up a company website, which was as sleek and generally uninformative as any contracting company website he'd seen. Companies with their fingers in the high-end, sensitive contract world didn't tend to advertise it on their front pages. If you could find it on their job listings, it would be couched in such esoteric, euphemistic terms that it would be next to impossible to know for sure what the job was or where it was.

He sat back in his chair again, the booze forgotten, and stared pensively at the screen. He'd opened this particular can of worms as an exercise in depressed, alcohol-fueled, maudlin pining after the glory days gone by, expecting, deep down, to do little more than fantasize about being a trigger-puller again. He knew it probably wasn't a good idea, especially with the kids to worry about, but that fifty kay a month was damned enticing. It would solve a lot of problems.

14

But Amy and Tom gave him pause. He would be away from them for a long time, at least six months to go by the listing. *Of course, how much time do I spend with them now? They're being raised by kindergarten teachers and babysitters, not their father.* Abruptly, he pushed back from the desk and left the room. He crept up the stairs to the kids' bedroom, eased open the door, and stepped inside, looking down at them.

Tom was still on his side, his knees pulled up, the blanket halfway down his torso, one chubby hand splayed on the sheet next to his head. Amy was lying asleep on her back, her golden curls splayed out on the pillow, breathing softly. For a long time, he just stood there, watching his children.

They'd be fine with Grandma and Grandpa, he thought. *Hell, probably better off than they are with me right now. And Julie's folks have offered to help time and again. I've just been too damned stubborn to take them up on it.* He felt a flash of guilt at the thought. He hadn't refused Roger's and Darlene's help because he bore them any ill will. He'd done it because he'd been too proud, too convinced that he had to take care of his kids all by himself. *And so instead I pay strangers to take care of them for me.* He turned to leave, the decision all but made. He eased the door shut, carefully turning the knob to latch it without making noise.

Back downstairs, he sat at his desk again, and picked up Julie's picture. *Please forgive me,* he thought. *I can tell your parents and anyone else who asks that I'm doing this for the kids, to make enough money that I can take better care of them. But I'd never be able to lie to you. The money's a bonus. I'm dying from the inside out, have been ever since I came home. I need this. I need something. I promise I'll come back and try to be a better father after this, once I've got enough of a nest egg to pay for the house, at least.* He hoped with every ounce of his being that he wasn't still lying.

He still hesitated ever so slightly as the pointer hovered over the "Apply" link. He still knew nothing about the company or the contract, and the promised paycheck was high enough to be as much of a warning as an enticement. *What the hell,* he thought, as he clicked the link and prepared to start filling out the application form. *It's worth a try. Probably just another resume farming operation, anyway.*

The next day went pretty much the same as the day before it had. He got up too early after going to bed too late, worked out until his headache was gone, then got the kids fed and off to kindergarten and daycare before going in to work. He tried to get back to pick them up from daycare earlier than he had the day before, and managed it. By a whopping fifteen minutes.

The entire day, he'd done his damnedest to concentrate on work and not think about that job listing. It probably was going to be just like so many others that he'd responded to before. He'd send his resume and then hear nothing. It wasn't like he was dead set on it.

But as soon as he got home and got Amy and Tom to bed, he went to the laptop, started it up, and went straight to his email. Nothing.

Well, what the hell did I expect? It's not like I've ever heard of a contracting company replying in twenty-four hours or less.

He had a couple more stiff drinks than he'd planned on and went to sleep.

Three more days went by. Dan kept working late, but he put the listing out of his mind. *If it sounds too good to be true, it probably is.* Then, on the fourth night after he applied, he checked his email to see a message from MMPR Inc.

Mr. Tackett,

We received your application for the Sensitive High Risk Counter-Piracy Mission we listed on Combatant Jobs. We are happy to say that you appear to meet all of our qualifications for a successful candidate. Therefore, we would like to invite you to attend our initial vetting course outside Naples, FL, from October 1 to November 30. Given the closeness of the date, we have attached your itinerary. Our chief instructor, Al Decker, will meet you at the airport and drive you out to the training facility. All required forms are attached, as well as a list of documents and equipment you should bring.

We wish you the best of luck at training, and urge you to bring your A-Game.

Respectfully,

J. Colton, Director of Recruitment and Training, MMPR, Inc.

Dan sat back in his chair and stared at the screen. His bluff had been called. Could he turn his kids over to Roger and Darlene for six months or more, while he went off to probably sit on a ship, waiting for nothing to happen? But even as he thought the question, he knew that it wasn't quite accurate. No company throws that kind of money around for glorified security guards on a freighter. There was something else going on. But for $50,000 a month, could he afford to care?

He thought for a long time, then grabbed the bottle, took what he determined was going to be his last drink for a while, and grabbed the phone to call Roger.

Three and a half weeks later, he pulled up to Roger and Darlene's house. Tom was excited to see Grandma and Grandpa, but Amy was a little more pensive. As he swung her down to the ground, she asked, "Why do you have to go away, Daddy?"

He knelt down in front of her and held her shoulders. "I got a new job, Amy," he said. "It's only for a while, and it's going to solve a lot of our money problems. I'll be able to pay off the house, and take better care of you and your brother. But to do it, I have to go away for a while, and I can't take you with me. So that's why you're going to stay with Grandma and Grandpa for a while."

"When are you coming back?" she asked. There was a little bit of a quiver in her lower lip. She had already been through the death of her mother, and now she was having to say goodbye to her father, less than five months later. It was a lot for a five-year-old girl to handle.

"It's going to be a few months, but I am coming back," he told her. "And when I get back, things are going to get better. I promise." *Please, God, don't let that be a lie.*

Amy was tearing up. This was not going well. Dan felt a lump hardening in his own throat. "I'm scared, Daddy," she said, her voice starting to get choked up. "What if you don't come back?"

He hugged her tightly. "I'll come back," he repeated thickly. "I promise. Grandma and Grandpa will take good care of you until I do."

Darlene intervened to collect her hug from her granddaughter, saving him a little bit of further heartache, but when he turned to get Tom out of the car seat, the little boy was already crying. He clung to Dan's neck tightly, sobbing. Through the sobs, he picked out that Tom didn't want his Daddy to go. His earlier excitement to see his grandparents had quickly faded when he'd picked up on his big sister's distress. Dan held his son for a little bit longer, murmuring reassuringly that it was only going to be for a little while, that he had to go, that it was going to make their lives better in the long run. He didn't know how much Tom understood or believed. At that point, he wasn't sure how much he believed, either.

But there isn't a great alternative, is there? I could call it off right here and go back to wrenching on bikes on overtime, letting strangers raise my kids while I struggle to make enough money to keep a roof over our heads, but then we'd be in the same boat, wouldn't we? I have to make this work. It's only for six months or so, and then I'll be able to stay home. He hoped he wasn't deceiving himself. He was afraid that he was. He knew the world he was about to go back into.

Darlene, cooing comfortingly, gathered Tom into her arms and carried him toward the house. The little boy was so miserable that he had completely forgotten his excitement at seeing his grandparents, and just kept bawling into her shoulder.

Dan watched his kids go into the house, his fists clenched, tears in his eyes, feeling like the worst father in the world. *I'm doing this for them, I'm doing this for them,* he kept repeating in his mind.

Roger, having stood nearby while Darlene ushered their grandchildren into the house, stepped over and put his hand on Dan's shoulder. He knew Roger understood; the man had done three tours in Vietnam, and later gone to Rhodesia, where he'd served with the Rhodesian Light Infantry. He had seen the elephant many times. Dan still couldn't help but imagine that his father-in-law disapproved of his running off to chase adventure, especially so soon after Julie's death. But the older man hadn't said a word of condemnation.

"It's always tough on kids," Roger said. "Fortunately, Darlene and I didn't have ours until after I'd already come back Stateside, but I've seen it enough times before." He looked Dan in the eye. "It's going to weigh on you. You're going to be sitting on the plane, going wherever you're going, and you're going to keep replaying Tom's crying and Amy's questions in your mind the whole time. Listen to me. You've got to leave that on the plane. If you're going somewhere risky—and for the paycheck they've promised you, I can't imagine that 'risky' quite covers it —you've got to have your head in the game at all times. For their sakes, you have to trust that we'll take good care of them, and just concentrate on getting your ass home in one piece. You hear me, son?"

Dan nodded, his throat tight, his eyes still wet and stinging. He finally met Roger's gaze. The old man was studying him with narrowed eyes.

"I hope so," Roger continued. "I worry about you, Dan. With this coming so soon after Julie passed...well." He paused, as if searching for the right words. "There was a kid who came to join the RLI, not long before the war ended. He was barely military age. He'd been out in the bush for a couple of days, and got home to find that ZANLA terrs had murdered his parents and his little sister. He crushed training, and when we got out to the bush, he was one of the most aggressive, ferocious fighters we had.

"But we could tell that he wasn't in it for revenge. There was a different look in his eye. One of the boys said he was, 'looking for a reunion round.' He was hoping to catch a bullet and see his family again." He paused again, as Dan looked at the ground. "I know you miss Julie, Dan. So do we. Not a day goes by that we don't still cry about her. But you can't go see her yet. Those little kids in there need their Daddy, even more now that their Mommy's gone. So if that's anywhere in your mind, you need to forget about that reunion round and concentrate on getting back to Amy and Tom."

Dan nodded again, and looked Roger in the eye. "I hear you," he said. "I'm not suicidal, Roger." *Are you being entirely honest, here?* a little voice asked in the back of his mind. *Shut up,* he thought. "I walked away from the mil contracting world five years ago, and I still remember why. I'm doing this strictly for the money." *Okay, that's not one hundred percent honest, but it* is *the primary motivating factor, so let's keep things simple.*

Roger just raised an eyebrow, as if to say, *I didn't fall off the turnip truck yesterday, kid,* but let it go. "That actually brings to mind another worry. I know, I sound like an old Jewish grandmother. But the pay...that's a lot of money, Dan. A shit-ton of money. Not only does it tell me that you're going to get dropped into some pretty horrific shit, but it's also the kind of money that people will go to great lengths to get their hands on. And I'm not just talking about your fellow contractors. Watch your back, Dan. Twenty-four seven, you need to be watching your back. As good as that paycheck sounds, it gives me a bad feeling."

Dan looked up at him with a raised eyebrow of his own. "You're thinking that if I'm dead, they don't have to pay me?"

"I've seen it before," he replied grimly. "Had a friend who was working contract in Afghanistan a few years ago. He said that he and his crew got ordered into an obvious ambush. He could never prove anything, but he's always suspected that his supervisor was trying to get rid of them because the company was having money troubles. Greed is an eternal motivator, and it turns people into monsters. Never forget that."

"Oh, I know," Dan answered. "I'm not new to this business, remember? I'm under no illusions that I'm anything but another monkey on the shelf to these people." He looked back toward the house. Amy and Tom were both in the window, watching, anguish in their faces. It looked like Tom was still crying. It was going to be a rough first few days in Roger and Darlene's house. He turned to Roger. "I'll be careful. Now, I should probably get going, while I still have the guts to go through with this."

Roger clapped him on the back. "Fair winds and following seas, son," he said. "We'll take good care of Amy and Tom. Call whenever you can. It's important. They need to know that Daddy didn't just leave and forget about them."

"I will." He turned and stepped into the cab of the truck. "I'll be back in a few months."

Chapter 3

The gear list hadn't been a long one, so when the plane landed in Fort Myers, Florida, he walked off with his carry-on and didn't even pause at the baggage claim. He headed straight for the ground transportation doors, his bag slung over one shoulder.

Spotting the group was fairly easy. Men in the contracting world have a certain look, and there were at least a dozen there on the curb who had it. All of them were of a certain age, fairly fit for the most part, short hair while still being outside of military regulation, some beards, jeans or khakis, collared shirts. Granted, some broadcast their "contractor" status more openly than others, sporting coyote tan backpacks, 5.11 shirts, tan desert boots, expensive Oakley sunglasses, and often worn, sweat-stained ballcaps in either tan or green, with velcro and patches on them. Those were generally the guys that Dan found he disliked. They were usually, though not always, more interested in projecting the tough-guy contractor image than in actually being professionals.

There were a few others hanging around that he suspected were probably there for the same job, but they looked even less professional than the ones decked out in "contractor chic." There was one guy with lots of tats, a screaming high-and-tight haircut, soul patch, and at least five earrings and a nose ring, wearing an old woodland BDU blouse. Another pair, who were standing over to one side, talking quietly, were both wearing black leather jackets and had shaved heads. He'd peg them for skinheads except that one was obviously Hispanic.

It was the girls dressed in the contractor starter kit that kind of threw him. There weren't a lot of women in the contracting world, largely because most contractors were former combat troops. He guessed that the times were a'changing, and that MMPR was going all equal-opportunity in their recruiting. He wondered again if this was a good idea; he'd yet to meet a female would-be combat soldier who could quite hack it. If PC was going to be the name of the game on this contract, this could get bad before it even got out the gate.

He tamped down his concerns, though. If the company was as serious as their emails had intimated about the strictness of their standards, it would all come out in the wash. Either the girls, if they really were there for the same reason, and weren't just gun bunnies going to one of the "tactical" training facilities that he knew littered southern Florida, would hack it or they wouldn't. Given the current political

20

climate, the recruiters may not have had any choice. It wasn't his concern. If it became a problem, he could always quit.

He didn't like to think that way, though. Quitting meant going back to the helpless nightmare that had been his life since the phone call that had summoned him to the county morgue to identify Julie's battered body. No, he just had to focus on meeting the training objectives and getting to work.

Three white, fifteen-pack vans pulled up to the curb, and a fireplug of a man with a shaved head got out of the first. He was wearing a skin-tight black polo shirt and khaki cargo pants, and he looked like he juggled barbells for a warm up. He stood on the curb with a clipboard and glared at the gathered wannabe contractors for a second before starting to call out names. As each individual rogered up, he just pointed with a knife hand at one or another of the vans.

So, that's how this is going to be, is it? Apparently, MMPR, or at least their training section, was going with the, "I don't give a fuck about you shitbirds, get on the fucking bus and do what you're told or get lost, we can always replace you" model of treating its contractors. He almost turned around to go get a ticket back home right then and there. In his experience, a contracting company that treated its contractors like boot privates or raw recruits generally wasn't worth much. They were likely to demand the contractors do something stupid downrange, and selected for Active Stupid in training, however much of it they actually offered.

But that fifty grand a month was still dangling there, enticing him with the possibility of paying off the mortgage and a lot of other bills, making it that much easier to raise the kids. And it was still just initial training. Things might develop. So he stuck around.

"Tackett!" the fireplug yelled.

"Here," he called out, stepping forward. The bald guy looked at him with all the warmth of a shark eyeballing its next meal, then pointed to the second van before going back to his clipboard, dismissing Dan as quickly as he'd noticed him. Dan didn't worry about it. It was annoying, sure, but he just kept that paycheck in mind as he climbed in. He was already starting to slip back into the detached mindset that he'd learned both during eight years as a Marine grunt and then another five in the contracting world.

He slid toward the back of the van, which was already occupied by two others. One was a linebacker-sized black man with close-cropped hair and a goatee, dressed simply in jeans and a plaid, short-sleeved button-up shirt. He watched Dan maneuver toward the back seats with cool appraisal in his eyes.

The other man was long haired, dressed in black cargo pants and a black t-shirt, with tattoos crawling up both arms and an earring in one ear. He looked like a hippy, except the tats were heavy on skulls, an American flag, and an infantryman's cross—a helmet atop an inverted rifle with a pair of boots at the base. Dan quickly reassessed his initial impression; the guy might look out of place otherwise, but unless he was a poser, those tats belonged to a grunt, at the very least.

Since those two were taking up the very back seat, he took the next seat forward, next to the window, placing his pack on his lap. A moment later, a fat, red-haired man with a patchy beard puffed his way into the seat next to him. "Boy, they're sure piling on the hard-ass routine early, aren't they?" the guy asked. Dan just nodded.

"Do you think they're going to keep it up through the whole training phase?" the red-haired man asked. He was still breathing a little hard, and looked sweaty. Dan wasn't sure what he was doing there; he obviously wasn't in shape, given the warning about strenuous PT standards, but then, they had women coming along too, so maybe the "strenuous PT standards" were only strenuous for some desk jockey who was looking at the numbers before writing the emails. Still, from the looks of the human fireplug out there, he wasn't sure. He still thought that the redhead's heart would probably pop if he had to run more than fifty yards.

In answer to the man's question, he shrugged. He wasn't feeling terribly talkative. Neither of the two men in the back seat seemed to be either, but that didn't deter the redhead.

"I'm Aldo," he said, sticking out a meaty hand. Dan shook it politely.

"Dan," he answered. Aldo proceeded to reach back to the guys in the seat behind them to introduce himself.

"Vernon," the black guy said, shaking Aldo's hand. "Glad to meet you."

"Trent," was all the long-haired guy said. He shook Aldo's hand, then leaned back and folded his arms. He was apparently not feeling particularly social, either.

"So, what do you think?" Aldo asked Dan. "Is this the way they're going to treat us? That seems kind of fucked up. I mean, we're not at boot camp here."

Dan *really* didn't feel like having this conversation, but didn't see a polite way to avoid it. He shrugged. "Maybe the job really is as dangerous as the email suggested it was, and they're trying to weed people out early. Good enough method."

"But why would they offer to pay us so much if they're just going to treat us like privates?" Aldo didn't seem to get it.

"I know, man," the bearded man wearing a tattered III% olive green ball cap in the next seat forward said loudly, "this is bullshit. We're professionals, we shouldn't have to put up with this motard fuckery."

"Then why'd you get on the fucking bus?" Vernon asked. "Ain't nobody holding you here at gunpoint that I can see."

The loudmouth looked back at him, but didn't seem to actually have an answer. He looked slightly nonplussed for a moment, then turned back front and continued haranguing the small Asian woman who had had the misfortune of sitting next to him. Dan heard enough to gather that it was mostly about how badass the man was, and that he wasn't going to put up with some bullshit contract trainer yelling at him like a drill instructor. After a moment, he put his head back against the window and tuned it out. It was the same thing he'd heard countless times, usually from people who weren't nearly as tough as they imagined they were.

After a few more minutes, the vans started to pull away from the curb. In a few minutes they were out of the airport and onto the highway. Few of the contractors talked, aside from the Three Percenter, who wouldn't shut up. Aldo tried starting a conversation a couple more times, but was met mostly with monosyllables, so he gave it up after a couple of miles.

Dan was somewhat more interested in where they were going. He was vaguely familiar with a few of the training facilities in Florida, and which one they ended up at was going to tell more of the so-far mysterious story of the contract. He was already questioning their training methodology just from the bald representative's attitude. If it turned out to be a professional outfit, it was good news. If it turned out to be one of the cheaper, loudmouthed, tacticool YouTube celebrity ranges, it might be a better idea to cut away and hope for another opportunity, regardless of the heartache he'd already gone through to get there.

They soon turned off the highway and onto a two-lane road that stretched off into the thick Florida pine woods and swamps. In moments, there was nothing to see outside but nearly impenetrable brush and trees on either side of the road. When they'd been driving for twenty-five minutes without a sign of a house or any other structure, he started to wonder how just far into the boondocks they were going.

After a about another thirty minutes, the vans slowed, then turned off onto a gravel road that led even deeper into the swamps. The road looked relatively new, built up on a levee with swampland and woods on either side. There was a lot of standing water back there under the trees, and Dan could already almost feel the itch of the mosquito bites. Sure, it was fall, but that didn't necessarily mean anything this far south.

They followed the gravel road for another fifteen minutes before coming to a blue-painted gate stretched across the road. There was a barbed-wire fence extending from either side out into the woods. There was also an armed guard at the gate. Dressed in khaki cargo pants and a black polo shirt, just like the human fireplug of a rep, though his shirt wasn't nearly so tight, he had an exterior belt on with a holstered Glock and four extra magazines.

The vans stopped just short of the gate, and the guard came out, pulling a small tablet out of his back pocket. He conferred briefly with the driver of the first van before walking back to the next one. Dan heard the driver list off the passengers, and the guard seemed to be checking them off of a list, before nodding and continuing back to the next vehicle.

"That's interesting," Vernon said from behind him. It was the first thing he'd said since he'd briefly shut the Three Percenter up.

"Seems like they're really particular about who comes in and who doesn't," Dan observed.

"It sure does," Vernon replied. "Makes me wonder even more about this gig."

"Wonder what?" Aldo asked, making Dan regret getting into the conversation. He had a feeling he could actually have a meeting with the minds with Vernon, but the fat kid was out of his element, and for some reason Dan found himself irritated at his question.

Vernon just shrugged, though. "Well, between the alleged sensitivity of the contract, the tough-guy approach that seems to me to be calculated to drive people away, and now the security, well, it raises questions. The listing I saw for this job suggested that training would be strenuous and the job high-risk. Add in the paycheck, and I am really starting to think that they understated the situation a bit. Whatever this gig is, it ain't the usual mall ninja job."

Dan had to agree, though he kept his thoughts to himself just to avoid talking to Aldo. He suspected he wouldn't be seeing the red-haired man for very long, especially if Vernon's suspicions were on the money.

The guard walked back up the little convoy of vehicles and swung open the gate. As they drove through, Dan looked out the window and saw a Heckler and Koch HK416 leaning against the cooler back in the guard's little shelter beside the gate. That was when he saw the second guard, who had stayed back in the shadows, wearing a vest and carrying his own HK carbine. They were not fucking around when it came to security. They also had to have some serious connections to get the HKs. Usually civilians could only get the neutered versions of HK rifles.

They continued trundling along the gravel road for another twenty minutes after the gate, and still didn't see any buildings, though Dan thought he caught a glimpse of what might have been a corrugated tin shed back in the trees at one point. Wherever this facility was, it was on some considerable acreage.

Finally, they came out of the thicker growth and into a broad, cleared area, probably about ten acres worth. Dan whistled.

Whoever was behind MMPR, they definitely had money. A lot of it. The brand-new, three-story brick barracks was the least eye-catching part of the installation. The far side of the compound was lined with ranges, running from five-hundred-meters to a series of one-hundred-meter bays. A rappelling tower rose next to the barracks, and what looked like three entire combat towns, purpose-built training villages, covered a lot of the remaining area. There was even what looked like a fifty-meter pool, with an extremely realistic facsimile of part of a ship's hull rising out of it, along with what looked like a partial superstructure. Three shiny Bell JetRangers were parked next to the helipad in the center of the open area.

"Well, that is rather impressive," Vernon murmured.

What have I gotten myself into? Dan wondered. While this certainly wasn't the crap training facility that he'd feared, its sheer expense only expanded the questions that both he and Vernon had been pondering. This was definitely not your standard security contract job. Certainly not your standard maritime security contract, which often as not just threw a bunch of guys who could sort of professionally handle weapons onto a ship with as little training as possible, often while the company assured the client that they were all twenty-year Navy SEALs. No, this was serious business, far more serious than he'd expected.

The vans rolled past one of the combat towns on the way to the barracks. As they passed, Dan studied the buildings. After the first two, he was fairly certain that they all had ballistic walls, which meant they were all for live-fire. That was rare enough, especially on a civilian facility.

The vans pulled up in front of the barracks. The bald man got out and stood there on the curb with his arms folded as doors were pulled open and the contractors started getting out. Apparently, not quickly enough for his satisfaction.

"Hurry the fuck up!" he bellowed. "We haven't got all fucking day! Get the fuck out and get on line, or you can stay in the van and go back to the airport!"

That got people moving a little more quickly, scrambling out of the side doors and around to the back to retrieve their luggage. Since Dan didn't have more than his backpack, he just got out and stood by the curb. The bald man stared at him for a second, then seemed to nod to himself and went back to staring at his watch.

With a frantic scramble that Dan hadn't seen since the School of Infantry, the men and women hurried to get into a ragged line on the curb, hauling their luggage along with them. Some of them had far more than Dan imagined they would need for an overseas deployment, never mind a training course. They were some of the last to get in position, and the bald guy looked decidedly pissed off as he watched them straggle in.

"Listen up, ladies and gentlemen," he said loudly. "You're going to have to do a lot better than that over the next eight weeks if you want a job here. We don't have time to play boot camp games, and we sure as shit won't coddle your asses. It looks like a few of you didn't read the full listing before you applied, but don't worry. We're going to sort that shit out in a hurry.

"You may call me Decker. I'm the chief training cadre here, which means I'm in charge of deciding whether you're going to be an asset or dead weight that needs to go away. I'm not your friend, I'm not your fucking mentor, and I'm not a nice guy that you'll want to have a beer with when this is all over. I'm a prick, I know it, and I will continue to be a prick for as long as you have the misfortune of knowing me. If you piss me off, you're gone, and I'm easily pissed off.

"All of you know that the job is going to be risky, and that it pays really, really well. I guess we'll see just how badly you want that paycheck." He pulled out his clipboard again. Dan was already starting to loathe it for some reason. "Now. Room assignments." He began calling off names and room numbers. If anyone took more than a second to roger up, he repeated the name loudly, with a rising note of anger in his voice.

He wasn't kidding about one thing, Dan thought. *He really is a prick.*

"Tackett! One oh seven!" Decker called out.

"Roger!" Dan replied, playing along. "One oh seven."

Decker got to the end of the list, and lowered the clipboard. Then he looked at his watch. "You've got five minutes to get to your rooms, stash your shit, and be back out here in PT gear. Starting now. Go."

There was another frantic scramble, with several of the recruits getting tangled up with each other and their luggage. Dan was finding that old habits were quickly reasserting themselves, and he hung back to avoid the worst of the press. He still got to his room while probably half of the class were lugging their bags down the hall or up the stairs, huffing and puffing as they tried to race Decker's watch.

He found his room quickly enough. It was spare, with cinderblock walls, a desk, a folding chair, a small private head, a twin-sized bed, and a rifle rack against the wall. He dropped his pack on the bed, dragged out his running shoes, shorts, and t-shirt, and quickly changed. He was one of the first ones back outside. Vernon was already out on the curb when he came back out, and Trent was on his heels.

Decker didn't appear to have moved. He was still standing there in his khakis and polo shirt, his arms folded, looking at his watch impatiently and tapping his foot. Dan hadn't bothered to check his own watch when Decker had started his time hack, but he gathered that the last few who came running out of the barracks, including Aldo and the Three Percenter, whose name was apparently Jon, were pushing the time limit down to a matter of seconds.

As soon as Aldo, already sweating and breathing hard, was in line, Decker simply said, "Let's go," turned, and started running toward the ranges. There was a moment's hesitation, as the contractors tried to figure out what was going on, then the line turned and started straggling after him.

He wasn't starting out with a nice jog. He had launched directly into what Dan felt was a slightly stiff distance pace, but which was obviously punishingly fast to a number of his classmates. After the time spent sitting in airports and airplanes on the way to Florida, he found he was sucking wind to start with, but he knew his own level of fitness well enough to be fairly certain he'd get his wind soon enough. Some of the others he wasn't so sure about.

Decker led the way down the five-hundred-meter range, keeping the same pace the entire way, then ducked behind the berm. Dan, about ten people back, lost sight of him, but as they came around the berm, saw that he'd stopped, and was now standing there, breathing normally, his hands on his hips as he waited. He pointed to the ground in front of him, facing back uprange, and the contractors started getting on line in front of him.

By the time the rest of the class had lined up, Dan was already breathing slowly and evenly, though he had a nasty suspicion that it wasn't a state of affairs that was going to last. The final arrivals, mostly the heavier contractors, though including more than a few of the women and a couple of the men who had *looked* halfway fit, were already obviously hurting, and they had barely gone half a mile. Aldo was already looking green around the gills and sweating profusely.

As soon as the last stragglers had stopped running, Decker rapped out, "Fifty burpees. Go." He proceeded to suit actions to words, and dropped to begin his own reps. Dan had to give it to him; Decker might be an asshole, but he wasn't going to demand they perform anything that he wasn't going to do himself. Still, there was a chorus of groans at the command, and Dan had to suppress his own. He hated burpees with a passion, but he dropped and started cranking them out.

Predictably, Decker was done first, though Vernon, Trent, Dan, and about a dozen more of the fitter-looking contractors were right behind him. Dan's breathing was labored, and his chest hurt a little, but it was no more than he expected after fifty burpees. *Damn, those things fucking suck*, he thought, as he fought to get his breathing and heart rate under control.

As soon as the last one finished, Decker simply turned and started running again, at the same pace as earlier. It was a little more painful this time, and Dan concentrated on stretching out his strides and keeping his breathing easy. This was going to be a long afternoon.

The trail led out into the woods and swamp, though fortunately it seemed to be mostly elevated, much like the road in had been, so they weren't running through the mud and water. Yet. Dan wasn't sure that it wasn't going to come to that. This was a hell of a way to start a training course, but as he thought about it, it seemed like an efficient enough way to weed out anybody who wasn't ready to be there, whatever the job ultimately turned out to be. He remembered the warning in the job listing about "strenuous" PT standards and thought, *They weren't kidding, were they?*

After another half-mile or so, they came to a mostly dry spot, with rows of pullup bars. Decker went to the farthest one and waited. Dan covered down on a bar and waited to hear how many he had to do.

It took even longer for everyone to catch up this time, and that was probably only going to get worse. Dan didn't mind; it gave him time to rest and even out his own breathing. Decker still didn't seem to be sucking much wind. He was still just as merciless, too. As soon as Aldo staggered to a stop, his hands on his knees and his head bowed toward the dirt, Decker called out, "Thirty pullups. Go." Again, he led the way.

Dan was feeling the burpees a bit, and had to get off the bar a couple of times to shake out his arms and hands, but he got his thirty knocked out, however ugly the last four or so were. Decker didn't bat an eye as he stepped away from the bar and let the next guy up.

It was ugly. A lot of the candidates weren't up to the task, and it was painfully obvious from the beginning. Aldo took three tries just to get his first, and was visibly weakening with every moment. Dan traded glances with Vernon. Depending on how Decker handled it, it was likely that they would see the last of Aldo, along with a number of others, sooner than they'd thought.

Finally, there were close to a dozen candidates still frantically kicking and kipping toward the bar, when Decker looked at his watch. "One more minute," he barked. "If you haven't gotten your thirty by then, get off the bar and wait here. Cadre will collect you and get you on your way back to the airport." His voice dripped with contempt, and he actually sneered as Aldo promptly dropped off the bar and stepped away, once again dropping his hands to his knees.

As soon as the minute was up, Decker led out again. He ran like a machine, keeping the same steady, relentless pace. After another mile or so, as the trail got rougher and wetter, they came to another cleared space, this one with thirty-five pound dumbbells lying on the ground. Dan suppressed a grimace. He knew what was coming next. Sure enough, once they had all gathered, Decker announced, "Forty renegade man-makers. Go." Dan dropped to the pushup position with his hands on the dumbbells, did a pushup, renegade row with the left, another pushup, row with the right, another pushup, then stood up and pressed both weights overhead. One down, thirty-nine to go.

And so it went, for what felt like the entire afternoon. Every half-mile or so, there would be another exercise. Kettlebell swings, rope climbs, ladder climbs, eight-count bodybuilders, more burpees, bear crawls, log lifts, log carries, casualty carries...it went on and on. When they finally ran back to the barracks, Dan was starting to stagger in spite of himself. He was so drenched in sweat that he felt like he'd been through a swim qual rather than any kind of regular PT, and every muscle ached. His lungs were burning, and his head was starting to hurt. It was beyond anything he'd done in years, as hard as he'd worked to stay in shape.

They hadn't actually lost that many more after the pullups. A few had fallen out from sheer exhaustion, but for the most part, about forty had hung in there. They had lost probably half of the women, and those who were still gutting it out were at the rear, but they were still pushing through, though they looked about ready to die.

Once everyone was back at the barracks, Decker finally slowed, and led an easy jog around the barracks and the closest combat town, then led them through a fairly comprehensive cool-down. When they were finished, standing there as the sun went down, he said, "Congratulations. You made it for today. Tomorrow we start Weapons and Tactics. Now get out of my sight."

A couple of hours later, after grabbing a rather insufficient boxed dinner from the small dining facility in the barracks, Dan was about ready to collapse into bed when there was a knock at his door. When he answered it, Vernon was standing there in the hallway.

"Hey, man, we didn't exactly get introduced," the big man said, sticking out his hand. "Vernon White."

Dan shook his hand. "Dan Tackett. Come on in." He waved Vernon to the chair and perched on the side of the bed. "What's on your mind?"

Vernon sat down. "What did you do before this?" he asked.

"I've been a mechanic for the last year, after my home improvement business went under," he replied. "Before that I did a few gigs with WPPS, and before that I was with 3/5 and 2/1. You?"

"First Ranger Battalion for six years, then WPPS and a few other gigs." He didn't elaborate on what the "other" gigs were, and Dan filled in the blanks without asking. "First time I've ever seen a setup like this since I got out of the Army, though."

"It's pretty wild," Dan agreed. "Can't say I've seen that method of weeding out undesirable candidates on contract before."

"Hell," Vernon said, "I've never seen this level of performance demanded on a contract before, and I've been on some pretty high-end ones. What do you think we're actually going to be doing?"

Dan shrugged. "The listing said counter-piracy. The only reason I can think of for going full-motard right out the gate would be if we're going to be less security guard on ships and a little more Executive Outcomes, if you know what I mean."

Vernon nodded. "Pretty much what I was thinking. And if that's the case, I think I'm actually glad that training is going to be hellish. I wouldn't want to go to actual combat with half the motherfuckers I worked WPPS with, but they could pass the standards."

"Yeah, I've known some awesome dudes in the business, and I've known some real turdbags," Dan replied. "What I'm wondering is how they're getting the clearance to do it if we really are going offensive? There hasn't been a company that's successfully done that since EO got shut down, at least not so far as I know."

"No idea, man," Vernon said, getting up and stretching. "But it's probably a question best left until later. Tomorrow's going to start early, and I know I'm going to be hurting in the morning after that death run this afternoon. Just wanted to make sure I properly introduced myself. See you in the AM."

"Cool," Dan replied. "Later, man."

Five minutes after Vernon left, he was asleep.

Chapter 4

Dan had to admit that this was the fanciest training setup he'd ever seen. While the initial impression of the compound had been eye-opening, the most sophisticated training modules weren't readily visible from outside.

He was presently standing on the deck of a small container ship. All around was sea and sky, with what looked like a green, jungle-cloaked island off in the distance. All of it was projected on screens that would recognize the laser light from the otherwise very real-feeling facsimile of a SIG SG 553 in his hands. It was the most expensive and sophisticated ISMT he'd ever seen. The freighter itself was a full-sized, complete mock-up, almost indistinguishable from a real ship, except that they had arrived in the trainer through a passage that led up through what would have been the hull, where he'd seen that it was in fact a purpose-built structure. If he hadn't, he might have believed that they had somehow moved an actual ship inland and buried it.

The entire trainer was underground; they had descended about ten flights of stairs to reach it. Patrone, another one of the trainers, a short, hairy Italian with a thick Jersey accent and Decker's attitude, had led them down, and was now presumably ensconced in some control center, watching.

The candidates had been split up into teams that morning, for the first time. It was only day four, and it had already been a whirlwind of a week. After the brutal introduction of the first day, they had started day two with another crushing PT session, then gone straight to the range, where they found their kit and weapons waiting for them. The vests were all identical, high-end London Bridge Trading Company plate carriers, all in Ranger Green. The weapons were all SIG; P226 pistols and SG 553 carbines. Dan had fired the P226 before, but never the SG 553. He adapted quickly, though, and it was a good thing, because the courses of fire kept getting more difficult and the time hacks shorter. Decker was merciless. It wasn't training; it was a sink-or-swim, pass-or-fail evaluation. If a candidate boloed a line, he or she got one chance to fix it. So far, they had only lost two more candidates to marksmanship failures on the range. Apparently, the day one thrashing had driven off most of the dead weight.

That morning, after another punishing hour and a half of PT, they had mustered in front of the barracks with gear and weapons, and Decker had called off teams. Dan had been happy enough to get teamed with Vernon, though he wasn't as sure of the other two members of his team. Tom Lambert was a fit, sandy-haired man with nearly as many tattoos as Trent. While he had so far said little, there was a certain arrogance to his demeanor that set Dan's teeth on edge. He had looked his teammates over with a critical glance that was almost contemptuous. When Dan had laid out the plan after Patrone had given them the scenario, Lambert's replies had been flippant, almost dismissive, as if he didn't give a shit about the plan because he knew what he was doing.

The fourth member of the team was a blond bombshell of a woman named Jenny Hagener. She was fine-featured and liked to wear low-cut shirts that showed off her considerable cleavage when not on the range. She also had the coldest, most calculating eyes Dan thought he'd ever seen. Not all the time; she could be very warm and engaging, but every so often the mask slipped, and he didn't much care for what he saw when it did. Though he had to admit that that very coldness might serve her well in the business at hand. Time would tell.

The scenario that Patrone had given them at the entrance of the trainer had been simple. "You are tasked with securing this ship. You are presently passing through waters known for pirate activity. Check over the ship and get into position as the team lead sees fit. You have twenty minutes to familiarize yourselves with the ship's layout before the scenario begins." With those words, he had shut the door and left them to their own devices. The "sink or swim" feeling of the whole course was only getting stronger in Dan's mind.

Now Dan was on the superstructure, scanning the simulated ocean, watching for the inevitable pirate strike. Vernon and Lambert were patrolling the forward section, and Jenny was on the stern. The *Daisy Duke* was small for a container ship, but it was still a little large for a four-man team to secure. Given everything else that had been thrown at them so far, Dan wasn't expecting a simple problem, either.

"Movement, one o'clock," Lambert's voice crackled over his earpiece. "Looks like we've got incoming from the island."

Dan's eyes snapped to the green hulk of the island, and quickly picked out the dancing pixels on the screen that had to be approaching boats. He corrected his assessment. They might be boats. It was probably best not to jump to any conclusions. It would be just like Decker's evil imagination to throw them a curveball right out of the gate.

As the specks got bigger, though, he became increasingly convinced that they were boats. At least three, possibly four. That was bad. They had the high ground on the ship, but four rifles against four boats was bad odds, regardless of any advantages they might have on the defense. If they concentrated in one spot to repel boarders, the other boats could move around to climb the hull in another spot that they didn't have covered.

He briefly considered falling back to one of the interior spaces, hardpointing and waiting for the pirates to come to them. He wasn't sure how the trainer would handle that; the pirates he could see were just pixels on a screen, after all. But he was fairly certain that Patrone had that eventuality covered, somehow, and he was forcing himself not to think of the scenario as a video game, but rather to approach it as he would a real-life combat action. He had a feeling that gaming the game would not go over well with this outfit.

"Hold your positions and keep a low profile," he sent over the radio. "Let them show their hand before we respond." How the pirates deployed would determine how they countered, he decided. If they didn't think they'd face resistance, they might concentrate in one spot to board the ship, and then the contractors might be able to spring an ambush. It seemed like a decent course of action given the disparity in numbers. If they could get the pirates bunched together, they'd have a better chance of taking enough of them out in one go to hopefully drive the remainder off.

He realized he was thinking in terms of combating real pirates rather than computer programs, that might not react the same way real human pirates would. He dismissed the thought as he studied the incoming boats. Patrone probably had a few more nasty surprises up his sleeve for them, and such scenarios were usually more about how to handle the situation on the fly than getting it exactly "right." If things went south, they'd just have to adjust.

As he watched the approaching boats from the superstructure, using the binoculars to magnify the images until they were big blocks of pixels instead of tiny dots, he started to think he saw shapes in their bows that might be machine guns. That wasn't good. It was hard to tell, since the images were still extremely pixellated, but he was fairly confident in the assessment.

"Be advised," he called out, "enemy boats appear to have machine guns in the bows. Looks like all four of them." He thought for a second. "All right, here's the plan. Everyone fall back toward the superstructure, but stay on deck, as concealed as possible. I don't want anyone visible from the water. I'll stay up top and observe until we can spot a boarding point. No one engages until I give the word. They've got us outnumbered and outgunned, so we're probably only going to get one shot at this. Hopefully, they'll decide the ship is undefended and board in one spot. When they do, we'll ambush them."

"And if they spread out and board at multiple points anyway?" White asked.

"Then fall back to the bridge," he replied. "We'll strongpoint there and call for support. If possible, we'll then push out to clear the rest of the ship from the bridge, situation depending."

He got clipped acknowledgements all around. He might have a vague bad feeling about both Lambert and Jenny, but he had to admit that they were pros, at least from what he'd seen so far. Hunkering down in his position atop the superstructure, he kept the binoculars to his eyes and watched the pirates approach.

They stayed in a loose formation as they closed in, and he was soon able to distinguish the pixellated figures of the pirates themselves. He counted five to six per boat, and there were definitely machine guns in three of the four. They looked roughly the size of military RHIBs, though they were nondescript speedboats that may or may not have had any real-world antecedents. Imagining that the coxswains and gunners would stay on the boats, that still left them with a good fifteen boarders to deal with. Not necessarily insurmountable, but at close quarters it made for very bad odds.

He briefly toyed with abandoning the earlier plan and opening fire at a distance, hoping to drive them off that way, but decided against it. Those machine guns had a lot longer reach than their carbines, and at the very least, could lay down enough suppressive fire to allow the boats in close enough to board and overwhelm them. No, if it had been Somali pirates in rickety wooden fishing skiffs, that would be one thing, but this was going to require a bit more circumspection.

The pirate boats spread out as they got closer, circling the freighter as if looking it over. Dan kept hoping that they'd examine their target, then mass together to board near the bow, but his hopes were dashed as they slowed, still encircling the ship, then started to close in from all directions, the machine guns pointed up at the gunwales.

"That's it, they're boarding at multiple points," he called. "Everyone fall back to the bridge."

He had considered the option to secure Engineering instead, since the pirates couldn't take the ship anywhere if the engines weren't under their control, but he'd decided that it would be easier to secure the bridge and then clear the ship from the top down rather than try to fight uphill through the narrow ladderways. Grabbing his carbine and slinging it, he headed for the hatch leading down into the superstructure, keeping low to hopefully avoid observation from the sea. It briefly flashed through his mind how ludicrous it was to be ducking to avoid being seen by a bunch of pixels, but he remembered that Patrone was watching everything, and would be judging everything they did or didn't do.

He got to the bridge a good thirty seconds before the rest did. "Cover down on the hatch, and stay away from the windows," he said. He had no idea how Patrone was going to handle CQB inside the ship; he hadn't seen any screens that might be ISMT trainers except for the outside screen. He'd let Patrone worry about that. None of the instructors had given the slightest indication that they were looking for canned responses to scenarios, so he wasn't going to assume that there was a canned drill that he was "supposed" to use. He'd play to his instincts and his own evaluation of the situation, and if they didn't like it, they could fire him.

He and Vernon got behind the console, their carbines pointed at the hatch, while Lambert and Jenny set up at opposing angles, keeping all four muzzles focused on the fatal funnel. For his own situational awareness, and with no little curiosity as to how things were going to play out, Dan glanced out the windows that faced down toward the deck, to see where the pirates were.

To his surprise, there were men clambering over the sides, equipped with rifles. It looked like hatches had opened in the screens around the base of the mock-up, and now there were real live OPFOR coming up over the gunwales. "Heads up," he said, "we've got company. Looks like role-players."

"How the fuck are we supposed to effectively shoot role-players with these laser-tag guns?" Vernon asked. "It's bad enough getting a role player to die when you hit him with simunitions."

"Don't know, don't especially care," Dan replied, turning his focus back on the hatchway. "I'm assuming that either that's been provided for, or else we're supposed to get overrun for some sadistic, judgmental reason that we'll probably never get explained. Let's just do what we'd do in the real world anyway."

"Fair enough," Lambert said, "but if I shoot one of these assholes in the face and he doesn't go down, I'm gonna buttstroke him until he does." Dan ignored the comment and waited.

They could faintly hear the sound of boots ringing on steel decking, as the pirates entered the superstructure. They kept quiet, waiting. Muffled voices rose from below. They sounded vaguely like orders being given, but they were too quiet and distorted by passing through the metal corridors for any of them to make out any words.

The assaulters were trying to stay quiet, but you can only walk so quietly on a steel deck. Dan heard them pause just outside the hatch and hissed, "Shut your eyes!" He suited actions to words, putting his head down and opening his mouth to try to reduce the impact of what was coming. A moment later, the flashbang hit the deck just inside the hatch and detonated with a deafening report and eye-searing flash that seemed to almost stab right through his closed eyelids.

The concussion had rocked him, even with his head down, but he immediately opened his eyes and got back on his rifle. Smoke from the bang was still roiling up from the deck, and the first assaulter was already in the hatch. The smoke was probably going to interfere with the ISMT rifle's laser, but since he'd been the one to say, "Play it like the real world," he wasn't going to wait.

The rifle *clacked*; the self-contained units didn't have the pneumatic systems that allowed for the more realistic noise and recoil of the bigger, stationary ISMT trainers. But something beeped on the OPFOR's gear, and he dropped to a knee, holding up a hand.

The man behind him, though, didn't slow down, and was already digging his corner as Lambert shot him, eliciting another beep, even as the OPFOR shooter's rifle barked, and a bright orange splatter pattern appeared on Lambert's vest.

A flurry of muted "shots" later, and it was over. All five OPFOR who had come through the hatch were down on a knee, their hands held up to indicate they were "out."

"Motherfucker!" Vernon was holding a hand to his forehead. When he took the hand away, a sizable welt was already starting to swell up, leaking a bit of blood. "You fucking cocksuckers almost put my fucking eye out!" None of them were wearing sim masks; they hadn't expected this. It wasn't the first time Dan had done sim training without them, but there was usually a serious effort made to avoid shooting the OPFOR in the face when that was done.

Before the OPFOR Vernon was bitching at could reply, a speaker in the overhead came alive. "White, you're down," Patrone's voice said. They waited for some further instructions, but that was all.

"So now what?" Jenny asked.

Dan shrugged, going through the motions of reloading. They'd been warned that each "magazine" was only good for so many shots before it had to be replaced. He wasn't sure what electronic wizardry led to that, but he wasn't going to take the chance of getting drummed out for having an "empty" weapon at the wrong time.

"I guess we clear the rest of the ship," he said.

"With three of us?" Lambert asked incredulously.

"I don't see any reinforcements rappelling in," Dan replied, "and it's pretty obvious the scenario's not over. I think they would have told us if it was."

"Fucking bullshit," Lambert muttered, but he also play-acted reloading his weapon, and stacked up on the hatch.

And he's right, Dan thought. *This is retarded. I guaran-fucking-tee this is just some sadistic, 'we want to see how you react,' no-win shit-show one of these fuckers thought up. Probably Decker.* For the moment, however, he wasn't quite ready to throw in the towel. So he joined Lambert at the hatch, waited for Jenny to get in position across from them, then kneed Lambert in the back of the leg. "With you."

Lambert launched through the hatch behind his rifle. He was still obviously pissed, though whether more at the ridiculousness of trying to clear an entire freighter with only three shooters or because he'd been shot in the plate with a sim round, Dan couldn't be sure.

The bridge took up most of the deck, with two small, easily cleared storage compartments aft. In seconds, they were on the ladderwell heading down.

The OPFOR can run circles around us in here, Dan thought. *There should only be ten left, unless the ones we just 'neutralized' get up and come around behind us.* That seemed pretty likely, under the circumstances. *No,* he thought after another moment, *they don't even need to do that to fuck us over on this scenario.*

Descending the ladderwell, they came to the next deck down, where the officers' quarters were located. Dan simply said, "Clear left." Lambert immediately turned starboard, pausing at the first hatch. As soon as Dan was behind him, he threw the hatch open and they went through.

The cabin was empty. This was where the attention to detail, not to mention the money, involved in this little trainer became even more evident. The cabin was fully furnished, just like on a real ship. It had to have cost a fortune to put this facility together.

Jenny, being the last one in the compartment, looked around for something to do for a second, before Dan impatiently pointed toward the hatch. She got the message and set up on the passageway. Moments later, they were pushing back out of the hatch.

Compartment by compartment, deck by deck, they made their way down toward the engine room. It was looking more and more like the OPFOR had gone for the bridge and the engine room, and ignored the rest of the ship. Which did kind of make sense. Secure power and control, and the rest just kind of drops in your lap.

Lambert was good, his movements, situational awareness, and weapons manipulation very smooth and practiced. He and Dan easily fell into a rhythm as they cleared compartment after compartment.

Jenny, on the other hand, seemed a little lost. She had the basics down, and her weapons manipulation was good, but she obviously hadn't had a lot of practice at CQB, and needed to be directed repeatedly. She also didn't have the smoothness of movement that either of the men did. She could handle her weapons, but her footwork in the confined spaces was awkward. Dan again found himself wondering just what she was doing there, given the decidedly non-PC standards they'd seen so far.

They hit resistance a deck above the engine room. Suddenly there were two muzzles in the passageway, spitting sim rounds at them. Jenny let out a piercing yell as she caught one in the neck. The three of them pressed forward, firing at the all-but-invisible OPFOR that were exposing little more than their rifles and one eye through the hatchways ahead. They all took a few sim rounds to hands and chests before getting right on top of their tormentors and practically pressing the ISMT guns to their chests to get the telltale beeps of kills.

By now, Dan was fuming. "Fucking assholes," he snarled at one of the OPFOR. This scenario had started out as challenging but professional, if a little unfair. Now it was just getting stupid, and it was pissing him off. But he still held out a hand to stop Lambert when the

37

other man looked like he was about to kick one of the OPFOR in the face. "Come on. Let's just finish this bullshit." Somewhat to his surprise, Patrone didn't break in to tell any of them that they'd been hit, even though all of them were now sporting bright orange splatters and nursing some decent-sized, stinging welts.

They pushed forward to the ladderwell that led down into the engine room. Dan suddenly had a thought, and motioned to Jenny to cover down the ladder, then went back to the hatches where the OPFOR had ambushed them. Crouching down, he started taking the flashbangs from the first guy's gear.

"Hey, what the fuck are you doing?" the OPFOR asked.

"Fuck you," Dan said. "You're dead. Dead people don't complain. So shut the fuck up." He shoved the man's two flashbangs into his cummerbund, then went to the other one.

"Fuck off, man," the OPFOR said. "You're not the last run."

"We didn't get the appropriate equipment for this evolution, so I'm *acquiring* some. Fork 'em over, or I hit you until you do."

"That's not cool, man."

"Neither is trying to clear a fucking ship with three people, with laser tag guns against simunitions," Dan snarled. "And don't get me started on the little stunt you dickbags pulled right here. Hand 'em over."

The guy just raised his hands. "Fine, man, take 'em." Dan obliged, yanking the stun grenades out of their pouches and stuffing them in his cargo pockets before starting to turn back toward the engine room. Then he stopped, reached back, cleared the sim rifle, chucked the magazine down the passageway, then did the same with the other man's weapon. "Because fuck you," he said. It was unprofessional, and his anger was quite possibly going to lose him the job that day, but the unfairness and just plain *cheapness* of the scenario had gotten under his skin.

Getting back to the ladderwell, he handed Lambert two of the flashbangs, then yanked the pin out of one of his and tossed it down the ladder. Lambert did the same a second later, then they raced down the ladder, weapons up and scanning for threats.

Apparently, the OPFOR hadn't quite been ready for their own flashbangs to be used against them. One of them was holding his ears, trying to blink the blotch out of his vision, just behind the ladder, when Lambert swung around and shot him. Just to make sure he didn't miss the beep, he then body-checked the guy into the bulkhead.

They weren't in the engine compartment itself, but in the engine control room, forward and slightly above it. So were most of the rest of the OPFOR.

Two of them were at the "controls," which were a reasonable facsimile of the green-painted control panels on an actual ship. The other four were bringing their weapons up toward the ladderwell. They'd taken some of the flashbang, but not quite enough to discombobulate them, at least not to the extent Dan had hoped for.

He sidestepped out of the ladderwell in order to clear Jenny's field of fire, and opened up, trying to put at least two rounds into each opposing shooter. He felt the impacts of more sim rounds on his plate but ignored them, many years of sim training and the conditioning to fight through the hits coming back even as he hoped that these clowns were professional enough not to aim at his unprotected face. Given what had happened to Vernon, that might be a forlorn hope, but there wasn't much he could do about it at that point.

A chorus of beeps announced that the OPFOR shooters were down. Jenny started to lower her weapon, and the last one, who had ducked behind the end of the control console, shot her. "Cocksucker!" she screamed, as she brought her own rifle up, but Lambert and Dan had already spread out along the bulkheads, and got shots at the OPFOR at almost the same time. His vest beeped and he dropped his rifle, raising a hand.

Jenny was fuming, her face tight and her teeth obviously gritted, but before she could say anything, Patrone's voice came over the PA system again. "Hagener, you're down."

"Fuck!" she yelled. "I hope you get fucking dick cancer, you fucking anal wart!" For a second, Dan thought she might actually throw her ISMT rifle. He traded a glance with Lambert, who just shrugged. This wasn't going well.

After a moment of catching their breath, trying to tune out Jenny's ranting, which had quieted down a little but not stopped, Lambert looked around. "So, what, the scenario's not over? Isn't this all of them?"

Dan shook his head. "We can't be sure. We've still got to clear the rest of the ship."

"With two of us. Fucking amazing." Lambert checked his kit. "I've got four mags left."

"Same here," Dan replied. He heaved a sigh. "No point in waiting around. Let's get this over with." He led the way, going through the hatch into the actual machinery spaces.

Like the rest of the ship, it was a remarkably faithful reproduction, a maze of pipes, condensers, giant diesel engine housings, and power transmission shafts. It took a long time to clear every nook and cranny where someone might be hiding, and there was the ever-present threat that if someone was back in there, they could easily stay ahead of or behind them. They had to be constantly on the alert, checking every corner, every angle, often above and below them, through the grated catwalks.

They came back up, out of the engineering spaces, and into the hold, which was full of cargo containers, stacked four high. It was another long, laborious process to sweep the deck, and they still couldn't be sure that someone wasn't playing hide-and-seek among the containers. Two men was just too few to effectively clear the hold.

But they played along, though Lambert's expression continued to sour as they went on. He apparently was highly unimpressed with the entire scenario, and Dan had to admit to himself that he was, too. If the whole course was going to be like this, it didn't bode well for the professionalism of the company, or the quality of the contract. *A couple hundred grand is a couple hundred grand, but you can't spend it on your kids if you're dead because your employer put you in an untenable position.*

At the bow, they paused for a moment before mounting the ladder leading up to the main deck. "We've got to keep low, below the gunwale, and see if we can take the boats out one at a time," Dan said.

Lambert nodded. "Of course, that's why they haven't called 'game over.'" He shrugged. "At least the ISMT fuckers can't hit me with sim rounds."

"I wouldn't put much past these fucktards at this point," Dan muttered. "We'll take the starboard side first, and work our way around clockwise. Cool?"

Lambert shrugged again. "Good with me."

Keeping close together, they mounted the ladderwell, coming up onto the weather deck. The gunwale only rose about three feet above the deck, so they had to stay crouched low. In real life, he doubted the steel would stop 7.62 rounds, never mind the heavier 12.7mm rounds the DShKs threw. For now, though, it would have to do.

The two of them crouched below the lip of the gunwale, facing each other. Dan eased one eye over the lip and spotted the "boat." The graphics were pretty crude, considering the sophistication of the rest of the trainer, but the targets were easy enough to pick out. The second on that side was back by the stern, looking quite distorted on the screen at that angle. Distance was impossible to judge, but he was hoping that the ISMT was set up for point of aim/point of impact. He ducked back down and pointed in the direction of the boat. "It's right over there. I think we can take it out and get back down before we get 'killed' by the other one."

"Fine," Lambert said. "Let's do it." He took a breath, then counted down. "One, two, three."

On "three," they rose up over the lip of the gunwale and opened fire. Knowing right where the boat was, Dan was on it in less than a second, and watched as the "pirates" jerked and stiffly fell off the boat to slide out of sight in the digital water. As soon as they were down, both men ducked back below the gunwale. Without a word, Lambert started duck-walking toward the stern. Dan followed.

They repeated the process with the other three boats. The ISMT's AI was not inventive, and not particularly responsive. None of the computerized pirates got a shot off. It may as well have been a carnival shooting gallery.

They paused after shooting the last pirates, but there was no input from Patrone. *Figures,* Dan thought. "Well, I guess we need to sweep back through the ship again," he said after a good thirty seconds of silence. "Scenario must not be over."

"Fuck," Lambert muttered. "This is fucking dumb."

"Yeah, it is," Dan agreed. His irritation was rising again, starting to override his thoughts of the money. He recalled the words of an old mentor, *It's easy to be hard, it's hard to be smart.* As unforgiving as the training program had been so far, its impressiveness was wearing off quickly as it became apparent that it was focused on being hard rather than being smart. He was really wondering what kind of smug douchebag had designed this scenario.

But they hadn't gotten ten steps before the screens around them went dark, and lights they hadn't previously seen in the ceiling came on. Patrone's voice came over the PA again. "All right, scenario's over. Meet me back at the entrance to the trainer."

They made their way back below decks to the hatch leading out of the ship. Jenny was still furious, her face pale and pinched above the swelling, livid welt on her neck. Vernon was just shaking his head, which was still bleeding a little.

Patrone was waiting for them on the other side of the hatch. He just pointed down the hallway. "Go down there, hand off your kit to the next group, and then go where Merchant tells you to go."

The others just nodded, but Dan couldn't stay quiet. "So tell me something, Patrone," he said, refusing to be intimidated by the little man's glare, "is this the way the the contract's going to go? Four motherfuckers to secure one ship?"

"You got a problem with that?" Patrone asked.

"Damn skippy I've got a problem with it," Dan retorted. *Is this guy fucking serious?* "It's fucking stupid. It's going to get people killed if bad shit happens. If that's the level of operations on this contract, I'll quit right fucking now."

For a second, Patrone just stared at him with that tough-guy look on his face, then his expression changed. It was subtle, but Dan thought he saw a bit of a smirk. "Noted," he said. "I'll just say this; the scenario as designed is a worst-case scenario. That ease your heartburn a little?"

Dan studied him for a moment, trying to see if the little man was jerking him around. "For the moment," he allowed, and turned toward the hallway. Patrone didn't say anything else, but just stood there with his arms folded, watching them leave.

None of them said anything as they passed their gear off to the next group. But Dan was thinking. *Was he just bullshitting us? Or might there actually be some brains behind the monkeys playing mindfuck games here?*

The rest of the day was depressingly boring. They were sequestered away from the groups that hadn't gone through the ship trainer, and set to work studying various ship schematics and videos of pirate attacks. One by one, the other groups joined them as they finished with the trainer, most of them visibly pissed off by the scenario. Dan was starting to suspect—and to hope, to some extent—that that was part of the point.

It was getting dark when they were summoned to form up in front of the barracks. Decker was waiting there, still in his skintight black polo shirt and khakis, his massive arms folded across his chest, watching them as they got in a ragged formation that would have had a drill instructor losing his mind but that was apparently about the best that MMPR and its trainers expected of them. They weren't there to drill, after all.

Decker stared at them for another moment after they'd stopped moving. "Well, what did everyone think of the ship trainer?" he asked, his tone strangely conversational.

Nobody spoke up. Dan expected that was because nobody wanted to tell Decker that they thought his training scenario was bullshit. He figured that he couldn't be the only one having second thoughts at this point.

"Nobody wants to say it was bullshit?" Decker said. "Because it was. And there are a couple of good reasons why. One, we wanted to see what you'd do if thrown into an untenable position in training. How badly do you want the job? A few of you essentially said, 'this isn't fair,' and quit. You might notice a few gaps in the ranks. Because we can't predict that things *won't* go badly pear shaped in the real world, and you can't just say, 'No fair!' and quit then. There's only so far we can take it in a training situation, but if you didn't game the game, you're already somewhat ahead.

"Now for the second part. Only one of you retarded monkeys actually had the foresight to extrapolate training to real-world deployment and the balls to call bullshit. Only one of you was thinking about whether or not we were going to throw you to the wolves downrange, like a number of contracting firms have done in the past. Fortunately for a lot of you, it's still early in training, and you've still got time to pull your heads out of your asses. Unfortunately for you, Tackett, you just skylined yourself. You're an operational team leader now, and provided you don't fuck it up between now and showtime, you will be when this goes real-world.

"Now get out of my sight and get some sleep. Morning comes early."

Chapter 5

Dan turned and looked behind him, barely able to see five meters even with the NVGs strapped to his head. He couldn't see Jenny behind him. Again. He turned back forward, waited until Vernon looked back, and then raised his hand to signal a halt. Vernon nodded, and sank to a knee in the muck; they were all soaked and filthy from the last four hours of slogging through the Florida swamp anyway, so it didn't matter.

Still making an effort not to make too much noise sloshing through the swamp, Dan started to work his way back to where Jenny had lost contact. He found her another ten yards back, stumbling over the roots in front of her. The Asian girl, named Cassy, was trying to hiss encouragement at her, but just from her posture, it looked like she was about all in. She was staggering, and making about as much noise as a baby elephant, her shoulders sagging under the weight of her gear and assault pack.

As he got closer, he could see her face, pale and drawn even in the sickly green tint of the NVGs. Her hair was lank and soaked with sweat, and all of her camouflage paint had been sweated and worn off. She looked about ready to collapse.

He touched her shoulder. "Ten more yards, then we'll take a halt," he whispered. She gulped and nodded, then slogged forward. He didn't even cringe at the amount of noise anymore. They were already screwed.

Cassy looked better as she passed him, though she still looked bushed. It hadn't been an easy movement for any of them, but the women were hurting. Which he could have predicted from day one, but nobody had asked him.

Lambert was coming up behind them, taking rear security. As soon as Dan saw that he was coming, he turned back to the front and worked his way up to where the rest of the team was waiting. He wound up right behind Cassy and Jenny, and followed them into the small perimeter that Vernon, Dave, and Max had already started. When they reached it, Jenny did a version of the rucksack flop, though her assault pack wasn't big enough to hold her up, so it was more of a collapse onto her back, with an audible splash. She lay her head back, panting, as Dan moved up next to her and Cassy.

"Are you going to make it?" he whispered. At first Jenny didn't say anything, but just lay there and gulped air. Cassy nodded as she took a gulp from her Camelbak.

"I think so," she added. "Jenny's hurting, though."

Dan took a deep breath. "We'll stay here for fifteen minutes, but that's all we can spare." It was actually more than they could spare, but at that point he didn't see that they had much choice. He moved over to Vernon and Dave. Dave was a short, hawk-nosed man with a nasty scar on his jaw that he said had been caused by shrapnel. So far, Dan had little call to disbelieve him; he'd performed well enough. You never knew in this business, though.

"Long halt, fifteen minutes," he whispered, as he took a knee. Dave muttered something that sounded obscene.

Vernon checked his watch, carefully shielding the green glow with his hand. He shook his head, the movement barely visible in the darkness. "It's going to start to get light in thirty," he whispered back, "and we've still got eight hundred meters to the assault position." He glanced back at the women. "This is the fifth halt in two hours."

"I know," Dan replied. "What do you want me to do? Leave her out here? We've got to make do with the assets we've got. She's a good shot, at least."

"Not going to make any difference if she can't even get to the fight," Vernon answered. He shook his head again.

Dan said no more, but took another thoughtful glance back at the two girls. Cassy was hanging in there better than Jenny was, but she was obviously exhausted, and she had barely passed the shooting quals. He had no idea how she had performed on the ship scenario, but she was hurting when it came to a light infantry mission.

Max was the other unknown quantity. At first glance, Dan had doubted he'd do any better than the women. He was overweight and pale, with a wispy, reddish-blond beard that he probably should just shave off. He looked like he should be sitting in front of a wall of computers and monitors, not out in the bush.

When he'd expressed this concern to Vernon, the other man had laughed. "Don't worry about Max," he had chuckled. "I've watched that fat fuck reduce lean, mean, greyhound-looking motherfuckers to tears, and laugh while he did it. He might not look like much, and he might not be the fastest man alive, but he simply never stops, never slows down. He's a fucking tank, and he's strong as a bull. He's also smart as shit. If it involves explosives and he doesn't know it, it's probably not worth knowing. He'll hang. And he'll probably embarrass a few of the hard-dicks in the process."

Dan had shrugged. "I'll take your word for it. Even though he looks like a basement-dweller."

Vernon had laughed again. "I was there the first time he tried to tan. After half an hour he came back inside, red as a lobster. Swore he'd never try it again."

Right at the moment, Max was on a knee, facing outboard, saying nothing. He'd certainly kept up, never falling behind, and so far, he appeared to be as tactically sound as Vernon had assured him he would be. Time would tell.

Vernon's concerns were more pressing, though. They were behind schedule. They were *way* behind schedule. They were supposed to be pulling off the target site by now. Instead, they hadn't even gotten into position yet, because Jenny, who had managed to make it through the punishing PT session of the first day, couldn't hang when it came to doing the real heavy, dirty, day-to-day infantry shit. A six-kilometer infiltration after a six hundred meter swim to shore with full kit was apparently more than she was prepared for.

Which, of course, raised the additional question of why counter-piracy contractors were training to do light infantry infiltration and assault in the first place.

Whatever. I'm still getting paid, and this is kind of fun. Or it would be, if it was going somewhat according to plan.

He kept watching the swamp around them, and glancing back at the girls. Jenny wasn't looking much better. But they didn't have the time to waste. "All right, halt's over. We've got to get moving. We'll push hard to the objective; the girls and Dave go on exterior security, the rest of us go in. It's going to have to be harder and faster than we planned for, because it will be light by the time we can jump off." *Damn, I'm glad we're not trying to coordinate this with another team. It's enough of a nightmare as it is. At least we've got sim guns this time instead of laser tag bullshit.* After a moment, he held up a hand. "Jenny, Cassy, hand your packs off. Max and I will carry them."

"Dan, no," Cassy started to say, but he cut her off.

"I don't like it either, but you two are the weakest links right now. We've got to make up some time, and we can't do that if you can't keep up. So drop 'em."

Cassy shed her pack reluctantly and handed it over. Jenny shucked the straps of hers without delay. Dan picked up Cassy's pack and slung it over the top of his own assault pack. It was awkward, and heavy, but he was still confident that he could carry it better than she could at that point. Jenny let Max come and get hers. The big man took it and slung it the same way Dan had Cassy's, what little was visible of his face expressionless.

Dave, who was on point, stood up without a word, and started forward. Dan stepped up behind him, with Max and Vernon following. He looked back in time to see the girls struggling to their feet, Cassy giving Jenny a hand up. They'd just have to keep up; there would be no more halts to catch their breath.

They forged through the swamp, making enough noise to wake the dead. Muddy, scummy water sloshed around their ankles and shins,

45

branches raked against gear and clothes, and the occasional stumble thanks to a root or a dip in the ground that was hidden beneath the foliage and mud all seemed like they gathered together to make about as much noise as a herd of elephants stampeding through the jungle. Dan was sure they had been detected, even before Dave plunged nearly to his crotch in a hole that he hadn't seen because it was full of water, spitting out a choked-off curse as he did so.

The night was noticeably giving way to gray pre-morning twilight when Dave suddenly put up a hand and sank to the ground. The rest followed suit, with another cringe-worthy splash in the back as Jenny flopped down behind a log.

Dan quickly saw what had prompted Dave's sudden halt. They were at the objective. Not the assault position, but the objective. The small group of tents and plywood buildings was right in front of them, maybe fifty yards away, and the nearest sentry was even closer than that. They'd gotten so focused on making up for lost time that they'd overshot.

"Fucking dammit," Dan muttered to himself. This just kept getting better and better. The sentry, an OPFOR role-player wearing tiger stripe cammies and a simunition mask, was already starting to move toward them. He had to have heard the splash, or maybe he'd just heard the racket they'd been making for the last three quarters of a klick. There was no time to deploy in any sort of formation, no time to make sure everybody was set. They had to go now. So he rose to a knee, shouldered his rifle, and shot the role-player in the facemask.

Even as the man swore, scraping at the orange splatter on his goggles, Dan bellowed, "Assault right, base of fire left!" Suiting actions to words, he got up and dashed forward toward the nearest plywood shack, hoping against hope that the team would react accordingly, and he wasn't about to turn himself into Leroy Jenkins.

Gratifyingly, he felt the impact as Vernon and Max hit the wall next to him. The faint snaps of sim rounds indicated that the base of fire had opened up, punctuated by a few noticeable *thud*s as the plastic rounds smacked into plywood. The role-players were yelling to each other, a few of them using the obnoxious pseudo-Russian accents favored by SERE instructors.

It was at that point that Dan realized the entrance to the shack he and the others had stacked up on was around the corner, exposed to the center of the camp, which was presumably filling up with hostile role-players. Even with the base of fire throwing paint in that direction, that was a no-go.

Can this op get any worse? he wondered. *Don't answer that.* He looked toward the opposite corner. "Max, on you!" The pudgy man simply nodded, eased his rifle around the corner, took two shots, and then followed the weapon. Vernon and Dan flowed after him.

A role-player was standing around the corner, his rifle held muzzle-down, a neat pair of orange splashes on his chest, his hand held up to indicate that he was "dead." Max moved up to the next corner, slowly easing around it while Vernon dashed to the corner of the next plywood shack to cover that direction.

Dan moved up behind Max, and peeked past his shoulder. There were about six role-players in the central part of the camp, mostly returning fire towards the base of fire out in the swamp, but a few were turning toward their position. Oh, well, time to throw caution to the winds. He stepped around Max, his rifle coming up, and opened fire.

The role-players had good cover against the base of fire, but not so good from the flank, and between Dan and Max, four of them were quickly eliminated. Two more ducked out of sight in the door of the third plywood shack.

"Cover that shack," Dan told Max. "Vernon, on me." As soon as he was sure that Vernon was behind him, he angled for the door in front of him.

The truth was, now that they were engaged, some of the suckiness of the entire situation was falling away, adrenaline flushing away the exhaustion and frustration. He felt alive, even if it was just sim rounds in a cheap combat town in the middle of a swamp.

He hit the doorway moving, button-hooking through to clear the deeper corners, Vernon half a step behind him. He could hear Max shooting behind them, hopefully taking out one or more of the role-players holed up across the camp.

The room was empty, nothing but a packed, muddy floor and four plywood walls spattered with blue, green, and orange sim impacts. As soon as he registered that there were no targets or hostages inside, Dan turned back to the door, Vernon already facing him across the opening. He briefly considered the possibility that, due to their lateness, the trainers had already removed the "hostages," just to fuck with them. He dismissed the thought. They still had to clear the objective, regardless.

With a nod, they burst back out into the clearing. More shots snapped, and Vernon yelled, "Fuck!" He'd been hit in the shoulder, a bright blue splash visible against his muddy cammies. "I'm good, let's go."

The two role-players were still trying to engage from the far shack; one of them had shot Vernon. Technically, they should clear the nearer shack, so as not to leave a potential threat at their backs, but Dan pressed toward the known threat, dashing toward the role-players' shelter, counting on Max's covering fire to keep their heads down. A few shots whipped by him from behind, reminding him that the base of fire was still back there, and hadn't necessarily gotten the word to shift fire. *Well, this was stupid.* But he made it to the wall without getting shot, unless he was now sporting a few new splatters on his back plate.

This was going to get tricky. The two role-players had definitely seen him coming, and there was no way he was getting through that door without getting shot. But the longer he lingered, the longer they'd have to get set to shoot him as he came through the door. Cursing his own stupidity, he charged through the door, thankful that Vernon had stuck by the crazy white boy running straight at the bad guys.

He button-hooked through the door again, this time running right into the role-player. They got tangled up, both falling to the muddy floor, while Vernon traded shots with the second guy, who had jumped backward to avoid the dogpile in the doorway. The guy under him was fighting him, both rifles out of play. So he got a knee under himself, heaved up off the floor, and then he and Vernon shot the last role-player at the same time.

They were the only ones in the shack. No hostages here, either. They didn't hear anymore shooting, but Max suddenly called out, "I've got the hostages!"

"Where the hell is he?" Dan gasped. Between the dash and the fight, he was a little out of breath. The movement of the night before was starting to take its toll.

"I'm guessing in that other shack," Vernon replied.

"By himself?" Dan looked out the doorway, to see Max standing in the doorway of the third shack. With another look around the camp to make sure there weren't any more role-players waiting to shoot them in the back, the two of them moved to join him.

"I know a one-man clear isn't the best option," Max said, in his nasal, high-pitched voice, "but when you guys went in there, I thought I'd better make sure there wasn't anyone in here waiting to shoot you in the back. Found the hostages instead." Behind him were three more role-players, two men and a woman, in shorts and t-shirts with bags over their heads. They were sitting on a tarp rather than the muddy floor, and appeared quite relaxed. Dan thought for a second, and recalled that there were only supposed to be three hostages. They had what they'd come for.

But there were still two tents out there, and he'd seen enough of Decker's evil imagination to expect a curveball. "We've still got to clear the tents," he said. "Hold here on the hostages." Since they didn't have intra-team comms, he stepped out into the center of the clearing, and circled his hand over his head, calling in the base of fire. They wouldn't be in a position to support effectively anymore; their fields of fire were shut down by the assault force's presence. Then he pointed to the nearest tent, waited until Vernon said, "With you," and dashed to the flap.

There was no stacking up on a tent; sims or not, it made no sense. He bulled through the flap, leading with his rifle muzzle.

Decker was standing in the center of the tent, his arms folded in front of his massive chest, dressed in his customary instructor uniform, glaring at his watch. "You're running late," he said.

Dan lowered his rifle. "Had a couple of hangups on the movement," he explained.

Decker just nodded. Then he reached into his back pocket, pulled out what looked like a firecracker, and yanked the string hanging out of it. It went off with a *bang*.

"An IED just went off in this tent," he yelled, so that Max could hear it. "Both Tackett and White are now casualties."

"Motherfucker," Vernon muttered.

"Both of you may as well lie down," Decker said. "You're not walking out of here."

They got down on the ground, Dan thinking about how completely fucked this entire exercise was. *There goes my team leader spot, I'll bet*, he thought. Decker just stood there, his arms folded again, and watched.

Lambert entered the tent with Dave and the women; Max was just outside the flap on security with the hostages. Lambert looked at the situation, then looked at Decker, who anticipated his question. "They are both alive, but non-ambulatory." He didn't ask what they were going to do, didn't prompt any action, but just went back to his baleful statue act.

"Shit," Lambert said bitterly. He looked around. Jenny was looking pretty peaked, and Cassy, while alert, didn't look like she was in the greatest of shape, either. "Dave, take Dan," he said. "Max, get in here and carry Vernon. Girls, sling the weapons. And you're going to have to take your packs back, too."

Dave grumbled as he handed his rifle off to Jenny, who slung it over her shoulders. Then he bent down and hauled Dan up into a fireman's carry. Dan helped as much as he could, without making it obvious enough to elicit a comment from Decker.

Max came in, passed his rifle to Cassy, and easily lifted Vernon to his shoulders, adjusting the weight slightly before crouching down and making his way out of the tent. Dave followed, with rather less grace.

"You might want to hurry up and get off the X," Decker offered helpfully. "OPFOR reinforcements are en route."

This just keeps getting better and better, doesn't it? Dan put his hand on Dave's back plate, trying to adjust his position so that his nuts weren't getting crushed. It was going to be a long movement. He was finding himself doubting that they were going to make it. Seven kilometers is a long way to carry a body, particularly through a swamp.

Lambert led out, taking point while Dave and Max followed, with the hostages next and the girls in the rear. They weren't going to make any better time than they had on the way in. In fact, it was probably going to be far worse on the way out.

The slog just kept getting harder, even for the guys being carried. While it may not be as stressful as walking, being carried fireman-style is not comfortable. The longer it goes on, especially as the carrier starts to get tired and stumble, the less comfortable it gets. Max was forging ahead, keeping up with Lambert without too much apparent difficulty, but after about five hundred meters, Dave was definitely falling behind, and starting to sag under Dan's weight. No surprise; Dan weighed about two hundred five pounds in his socks, never mind in kit and soaked, muddy cammies.

Finally, Dave staggered and dropped to a knee, almost catapulting Dan over his head. Fortunately, Max had turned to look back at that point, and signaled to Lambert that they needed to halt. Dave let Dan down, and stayed down on one knee with his head bowed to his chest, gulping air and looking like he was about to puke.

Under other circumstances, Dan would be tempted to cheat, and just get down and walk the rest of the way, but Decker was pacing them, about ten yards behind Cassy in the rear, so that wasn't an option. They were going to have to gut this out somehow. He just wasn't sure how.

Lambert came back to Dave and looked down at him, anger written all over his face. "Not even a klick, Dave? What the fuck?"

Dave looked up at him and snapped, "I don't see you carrying anybody, asshole."

"That's because I've got to get us where we need to go," Lambert retorted.

"I walked point in here, I can walk point on the way out while you take a turn," Dave pointed out.

"Yeah, and you damned near walked us right onto the objective without knowing it, too," Lambert said acidly. "Fine. I'll take a turn. You'd better not get us lost." He unslung his rifle and handed it to Dave, then bent down to pick Dan up. With a grunt, he swung him up into a fireman's carry, then, his voice sounding strained, said, "Come on, we've got to keep moving."

Lambert made it farther than Dave, but after about another kilometer and a half, he had to stop, sucking wind. He still shot Dave a venomous look. "Yeah, real hard to go a fucking klick."

"Will you knock it the fuck off?" Max said, speaking up for the first time. He was sweating profusely and starting to look a bit red in the face, but was still standing tall with Vernon on his shoulders. Vernon hadn't been kidding about the man's endurance. "We've still got too far to go to start bickering. You two want to go five rounds, you can do it back at the barracks. But we've still got five klicks to go, so save your breath and figure this shit out."

"I'll carry Dan for a little bit," Cassy offered suddenly. "I won't be able to carry him very far, but I'll try."

Lambert looked at her skeptically, and Dan couldn't help but agree. Cassy was not a large woman; she might be a hundred fifty pounds soaking wet. She might make it a couple hundred meters, and that would be slow and painful. Jenny didn't say anything or look at any of them; she was doing a convincing job of watching rear security.

Dave shook his head. "No, I'll take him. We'll just have to switch off."

"What about you, Max?" Cassy asked. "Are you doing okay?"

Max nodded. "I'm fine. Let's just get to the boats, shall we?" He turned back toward the beach and waited for Lambert to get back up to the point.

It took another couple of hours, all with Decker shadowing them silently, before they got all the way to the beach. Only to find that the boats weren't there.

Of course, they should have expected it. They were at least three hours late to extract. In the real world, extract wasn't going to hang out on a hostile beach for hours, they were going to scram within about thirty minutes. Which left them with a problem.

"Get the comms up," Lambert snapped. "We'll have to call for emergency extract." He glared out at the Gulf. "Which is probably going to give us a new RV point."

That wasn't going to go well. Dave was looking pretty strung out, and even Max had started to stagger over the last kilometer. Neither of the girls were looking that great; Jenny was noticeably dragging ass. If her rifle hadn't been slung around her shoulders, she probably would be dragging it along the ground.

"Delta Two-Zero, this is Gamma One-Four," Max called over the radio. It was a civilian job, though bigger than a Motorola handheld. Not as capable as a military green-gear radio, but still effective enough, and it could still be encrypted. "We are at the original extract point, requesting emergency extract."

"You're late, One-Four," came the reply. "Beach extraction is not possible at this time. You will need to swim twenty-five hundred meters west. The boats will come in and pick you up there." They were really being hard-assed about this. Twenty-five hundred meters was a long swim, and Dan had little doubt that Decker would insist that they tow the "casualties."

"Delta Two-Zero, be advised we have two non-ambulatory casualties and three hostages," Max sent. The answer was immediate.

"Good copy, One-Four. Rendezvous instructions remain the same."

"Fuck," Lambert snarled. "All right, let's dig up the fins and the UDT vests. Inflate the vests if you have to; this is going to suck." He glanced at Decker after saying that, but the big man didn't say anything, just still standing there and watching, looking completely unruffled. He didn't even look like he'd worked up much of a sweat following them through the swamp, which seemed impossible, given the humidity.

It took a few minutes to get geared up, then it was a dash across the open beach and into the water. Or an attempted dash; it quickly turned into more of a waddle, since Max and Lambert were once again carrying Vernon and Dan. Decker's hawk-like stare had dispelled any ideas of cheating and "fairy-dusting" the two of them mobile again.

It was a long, hard swim, with numerous stops, floating with the aid of inflated vests. It was made even slower by the fact that they didn't have fins for the hostages, so they had to breaststroke. It took almost an hour to get far enough out, and that was with the tide going out. Even once they were sure they were far enough from shore, it still took another fifteen minutes before they saw the boats coming in, and were able to signal for pickup. They crawled into the rubber craft and clung to the gunwales like drowned rats, soaked, exhausted, and miserable.

Back at the barracks, they were soon hard at work cleaning and drying their gear and weapons. The ocean had rinsed off most of the mud, but the salt still had to be hosed off, and everything had to be hung up to dry. Batteries needed to be replaced and magazines refilled. All of them were sitting on the benches in the sun, the men in trunks and the women in shorts and t-shirts.

Jenny had been one of the first to have her sodden gear and clothes off, and was sitting on a bench by herself, jamming her magazines. Dan looked across at her, then glanced over at Vernon next to him.

"She seems to have perked up quick enough now that the weight's off of her shoulders," he observed quietly. Vernon nodded.

"Watch yourselves around her," Cassy said, sitting down next to Dan. "She's evil."

Dan looked at her. "You know her?"

She shook her head. "No, but I know the type. She's hot and she knows it, and she'll manipulate everyone around her to get what she wants. Mark my words. If you stay team leader, she'll try to get into your pants sooner or later. That way she'll own you, and she'll get to do whatever she wants."

Lambert laughed. It had an ugly edge to it. "I'd fuck her and then slap her down anyway. Two can play at that game."

Cassy looked at him with distaste, then turned back to Dan. "I'm serious. Watch your back around her."

He nodded. "Thanks." He saw Max sit down on the far side of Vernon, and leaned out to address him. "Max, I owe you an apology."

Max just smiled. "No you don't. I know what I look like. Vernon can probably tell you that I have long owned the fact that I have been blessed with great strength, agility, and endurance, and cursed to possess them in a body that looks like a bag of mayonnaise and sounds like a squeaky chew toy."

52

Any further conversation was stilled as Decker walked in, alert and dressed in fresh clothes. He didn't look like he'd spent the entire night and morning after on a jaunt through the Florida swamps. "All right, hot wash time. Tackett. What went right, what went wrong?"

"We eliminated all the hostiles and got the hostages out without losing any of them," Dan said. "So much for the good news. Bad news, we got slowed down on the infiltration, and didn't get to the objective until it was already light. We got rushed and overshot the assault position, and just about ran right into the objective without getting set. Then I charged across open ground and past an open door to clear the second shack, instead of clearing methodically. Oh, yeah, then Vernon and I got blown up, but I'm not sure how we might have avoided that, since it was fairy-dusted."

Decker nodded. "Pretty good summation. Anyone have anything else to add?" When there were no takers, he just said, "All right, finish getting re-cocked and get some rest." He turned to leave.

Dan got up to follow him. "Decker?" he asked. The human fireplug turned to look at him. "Can I ask a couple of questions?"

Decker just looked at him for a second, then jerked his head and stepped out of the locker room. Dan followed. Out in the hall, Decker turned to face him, once again folding his arms. It seemed to be his default stance.

"Is this an evaluation course or a training course?" Dan asked. "Because it kinda seems like both."

"It is both," Decker replied. "While you are being evaluated every minute of every day, we do realize that none of you have worked as a team, so there are going to be things that need to be ironed out. There isn't a lot of time for a pre-deployment train-up, so that's why the grading is as harsh as it is."

Dan tried to keep his expression impassive, but something must have showed. "What?" Decker demanded.

"It's just that the 'harsh' grading seems to be on two different scales," Dan said carefully.

"You have concerns about the women," Decker said flatly. It wasn't a question.

"In a word, yes," he replied. "They can't keep up. Even the most hard-core of them."

"They're here for a good reason," Decker said cryptically. "Your concerns are noted." He looked at his watch. "Now, I suggest you finish getting your gear reset, get some water and chow in you, and get some rest. The Warning Order for your next scenario drops in eighteen hours." He turned without another word and walked away.

Chapter 6

As the weeks continued to go by, the scenarios got harder and more complex. They also covered more and more roles, until it became obvious to even the least aware of the contractors that they were being trained for less of a security guard mission and more of an offensive special operation. There were maritime and shore-side sniping missions, small boat handling, more hostage rescues, both ashore and afloat. There were raids with no hostages, where the mission was to kill everyone on the site and destroy everything. They spent an entire week working on demolitions; Max really shone during that week, further confirming Vernon's assertion of his abilities. In fact, several times the instructors just stepped back and let Max teach.

The conversations in the barracks got more and more speculative. Where were they going? Was all of this "just in case," or were they actually going to be expected to conduct offensive operations? Nobody had heard of a PMC doing that since Executive Outcomes in the '90s. There were a few who brought up Blackwater, but no one in the class had any first-hand knowledge to the effect that that particular company had actually conducted any direct action missions, much less on the level that they were presently training for.

Decker was no more forthcoming than he had been from the beginning, however. He still demanded performance, said little whether it was delivered or not, and simply passed down the next task. A few of the contractors mysteriously disappeared, their stuff packed and gone by the time anyone could ask any questions, none of which were ever answered. But the days were flying by and the end of the two-month training period was coming up fast. They had to get some information soon.

The day after a crushing, fifteen-hour raid-and-retrieval mission, they were awakened at 0800, well after the usual time. They hadn't gotten a warning order the night before, and Dave had muttered hopefully about the end date of the training phase getting close. But Decker just went down the hallway, pounding on doors, bellowing for everyone to meet in the conference room downstairs in ten minutes.

It was a bleary group that gathered around the conference table in the barracks basement. They'd gotten more sleep than usual, but that wasn't saying much. The last two months had been grueling, with hardly any breaks from the relentless training missions. If anything, the extra sleep had had something of a narcotic effect, if the fuzzy way Dan was feeling was any indication. He sat at the conference table, propped his elbows on the tabletop, and put his head in his hands.

He didn't have much time to try to rub the sleepy out, though, because a stack of papers hit the table next to his head. "Pass these out," Decker ordered. With a stifled groan, Dan picked himself up and started handing out the stapled packets.

When he was done, Decker stood at the head of the conference table, in front of a projector screen, and looked around the room. "I know all of you have been wondering and speculating as to exactly what you're here for. Why have we been training you like high-level infantrymen for a mere maritime security mission? Well, you're about to find out. But first, you're going to sign that NDA in front of you. Yes, I know, you already signed one on day one. But that was only to cover the training course. This goes a little more in-depth."

Dan started reading the document, and saw that, as usual, Decker wasn't kidding. The Non-Disclosure Agreement extended for seventy-five years, and strictly forbade any discussion or revelation of the mission they were being contracted for, on penalty of severe legal action and possibly prison. That alone suggested that the employer or client was somehow government, though there was no concrete statement to such effect in the paperwork.

Well, I've come this far, haven't I? He thought of Tom and Amy, and the handful of times he'd gotten to talk to them since this started. *The pay is still a hell of an incentive, and at this point I really don't want to have gone through all of this, and put my kids through it, for nothing.* He scrawled his signature in the appropriate blocks and pushed the NDA out toward the center of the table. Most of the rest were doing the same.

Decker waited until everyone had finished. As Dan looked around the table, it looked like no one had declined to sign the NDA. Apparently, everyone was either committed, or just saw things the same way he did; that they'd come that far, so they may as well see what it was all for.

Decker nodded, and turned on the projector. The image that appeared on the screen behind him was an overhead of a series of islands. Dan didn't recognize the shapes, but they were green enough that they were probably in the Pacific somewhere.

"As you may have surmised, this is not your typical maritime security mission," Decker began. "There is no specific ship that you will be securing. This is a far more kinetic mission than that." He clicked the controller, switching the view to a photo of a military vessel. "This is the Chinese PLA Navy frigate *Zhaotong*, captained by a *Shang Xiao* Yuan Wei. '*Shang Xiao*' is Mandarin for Captain, by the way. Anyway, about a month and a half ago, the *Zhaotong* was on patrol near several of the artificial islands that the Chinese have been building in the Spratlys to strengthen their territorial claims in the South China Sea. A week after she came on-station, contact was lost. Two or three days later, she showed up in the Anambas Islands, between Borneo and mainland Malaysia, turning her guns on the oil company installations there.

"Yuan has since taken over the Anambas, which are largely uninhabited, except for the oil companies. Technically, they are part of the Riau Islands, a province of Indonesia. But the Indonesians have enough difficulties patrolling the Pulaus closer in to Java and Sumatra, never mind the Anambas.

"In the last month, the word has gone out that Yuan has deserted, along with, apparently, the entire crew of the *Zhaotong*. He has reportedly reinforced his crew with a large number of Javanese, Malaysian, and Vietnamese pirates, and has begun preying on shipping passing by the Anambas toward the Straits of Malacca. As you can see, the islands are sited right on the primary north-south shipping lane through the South China Sea. At least three Japanese ships have been taken, and there are rumors to the effect that he has already formed ties with the Golden Triangle and several human trafficking organizations.

"Yuan is trying to carve out his own little empire in the South China Sea. Tensions are pretty high down there at the moment; the Malaysians, Vietnamese, and Filipinos are all getting really paranoid about the Chinese moves in the Spratlys and the Paracels. If Yuan really is a rogue, and not acting on orders from Beijing, then a Chinese response is expected in short order. However, the end result will be the same, with de facto Chinese possession of the Islands, well into Malaysian and Indonesian territory."

He changed the image again, this time showing what looked like a small town bordered by jungle. The caption in the upper right corner said, "Pulau Matak."

"Don't worry, though, it's not going to be our job to take on the People's Liberation Army. We have been hired to liberate the remaining oil company personnel still being held hostage. The client hopes that we can achieve this quickly, and hopefully return the islands to the status quo *before* the Chinese take a heavier hand to deal with Yuan. That's also why the training period was so rushed; time is of the essence on this job. For the moment, it is still a counter-piracy contract, albeit one that is rather more along the lines of an offensive PMC like Executive Outcomes than the usual shipboard security gig. It is not expected that the Chinese, or any other local player that might move against Yuan, will necessarily have the best interests of the oil companies or their personnel at heart. So the plan is to get in there and secure those people before they get caught in the crossfire."

He looked around the room. It was silent as the grave, as everyone there stared silently, either at him, the screen behind him, or the table. It was a hell of a mission statement. Doubtless a few people were having second thoughts right at that moment. Dan knew he was. *And how the hell can he guarantee that we're not going to be fighting the Chinese if we take this on? Can he guarantee their fucking timetable?* That raised another question. Just how good was their intel? If the implication that this was a shadowy government power play was correct, then they just might have some high-level information. That would explain the certainty that they wouldn't be fighting the PLA, but just the pirates.

"Now," Decker continued, "this is your last chance to back out. Bear in mind that even if you do, you've already signed the NDA. So any disclosure of this operation will be prosecuted just the same as if you go and then talk about it later." He straightened up, looked around the room, and then turned off the projector. "You've got an hour to decide. Then you need to get hurry and get packed up if you're going. The flight to Singapore goes wheels up in three hours."

Nobody decided to say no. The money was too good, and for those to whom it mattered, the mission appeared to be righteous. Who wouldn't want to really go pirate-hunting instead of sitting, bored to tears, on a ship? By the time the hour was up, everyone was already packed and waiting outside the barracks for the vans to the airport.

"Wow," Vernon said, as the bus came through the gate. "These are some serious digs."

Dan could only nod. He'd thought the training facility in Florida had been big money. This *had* been a multi-million—no, scratch that; multi-*billion*—dollar resort on the Desaru peninsula on the coast of Malaysia. MMPR had leased the whole thing for their base of operations.

While the resort had, until a couple of years before, been thick jungle, most of the undergrowth had been cleared away, while leaving most of the trees. The road meandered through the shade, past bungalows with golden light spilling from their windows in the early evening, toward the main buildings.

There were twelve three-story hotel buildings arranged in a pair of semicircles, facing the beach. Every cluster of buildings seemed to be built around a swimming pool. The grounds were immaculate; there wasn't even a stray leaf on the tennis court.

"Are we supposed to prep and stage out of here, or just lounge around the pool?" Dan wondered. "This seems way too fancy to be a base of operations."

Ty, a big, blond former Marine who had been assigned to Dan's team in the final personnel shuffle before they'd flown out, just shrugged. "Hey, if they want to piss their money away making us comfortable, I'm not going to complain. I'm still getting paid either way."

"Good point," Dan allowed. "I still think we're going to manage to break or scuff up most of this place before we're done."

Max laughed. It was a high-pitched, nasally sound that was rather unpleasant, at least until Dan realized that Max really couldn't help it. "Of course we are," he said, "and it can go on the company dime while we do it."

There was a general laugh in the bus at that, and a few hoots from some of the rowdier contractors, including Jenny, to Dan's complete lack of surprise. She definitely seemed the type. She was already on his list of those to watch carefully; he'd probably have to make sure she and several of the others on his team didn't let the appeal of fun on the beach interfere with the mission they were actually getting paid for. He'd seen it before, and he knew that living in this swank resort was going to be an enormous temptation for a lot of them. He suddenly found himself wishing they were living in tents in the jungle without air conditioning. It would help keep the looser ones focused.

But he wasn't making the call, and the company had decided to spare no expense. He really didn't give a damn about MMPR's finances; if they wanted to waste their money, he wasn't going to complain. He was more concerned with his fellow contractors being committed to the mission at hand, because if they were thinking of getting back to the fleshpots instead of concentrating on what had to be done downrange, it could very well get some of them killed.

The road didn't go straight toward the bigger buildings, but instead curved around behind them, coming out between the beach and the pools. That was where some of the illusion of the place being nothing but a fancy beach resort went away.

There were six pre-fab K-Span shelters up on the beach, with several big, utilitarian trucks parked around them, along with several trailers. One of them hadn't been unloaded yet; its cargo of two RHIBs, Rigid-Hulled Inflatable Boats, still strapped down to the long flatbed. RHIBs were preferred insert platforms for longer-range littoral operations where Zodiacs might not have the legs. They were also somewhat larger and more comfortable than Zodiacs, and could mount heavy machine guns.

The beach was lined with fairly utilitarian civilian boats, more like bass boats than speedboats. But out to sea, there were three yachts at anchor, all of them sleek, long, and looking very, very expensive. He nudged Vernon and pointed. "It looks like your theory about Trojan Horse ops might well be vindicated."

Vernon peered past him. "I really don't think there was any doubt," he said. "A few of those scenarios couldn't be anything but."

For a moment, Dan thought that Decker had somehow beaten them to Malaysia. But as the bus came to a stop in front of one of the K-

Spans, he saw that the short, thickset man standing there with his arms crossed in front of him wasn't Decker, though he could easily have been his brother. This guy was a little taller and a little thinner, though still massively muscled, and his face looked like he'd taken fewer punches to the nose. He also didn't have Decker's permanent scowl, either.

As the contractors filed down out of the bus, he spread his hands wide to encompass the entire resort. "Welcome to the Desaru Haven Resort, ladies and gentlemen, your home away from home. We'll be staging out of here. I'm glad you're here, because we've got a *lot* of work to do to get ready. The client wants operations to start soonest, and we're still getting situated here. Now, where are my team leads?"

Dan stepped forward, along with Sean and Will. The man shook their hands all around. "I'm Rex," he said by way of introduction. When Dan and Sean couldn't keep entirely straight faces, he rolled his eyes. "Yeah, I know. Blame my parents. It is my real name. Anyway, we do have a lot of work to do; this place isn't exactly set up as a military base, and I've had my hands full just making sure site security was set up. I haven't been able to get any of your gear broken out or ready to go, so you're going to have to get hopping with your people to get prepped to go out." He started to lead the way up from the beach, toward the little rec-center looking building just under the first trees. "Let me get you up to speed; Monica will get your teams to their living spaces and give them the current hard times."

The inside of the building was chaos. It looked like Rex and his people were trying to get a TOC set up; there were monitors, computers, and cables everywhere. None of it was up and running yet. A board tacked to the wall had maps and charts of the nearby waters and photo overheads of the target islands, with pushpins and sticky notes all over them. Rex evidently wasn't waiting around for the tech to get working.

"We've got a couple of containers full of gear and weapons on-site," he explained, leading them to a table near the map board. "But the ammo is at least twelve hours behind. I think they ran into some customs trouble, but I've been getting conflicting word on that. I do know we've got several local and American legal-beagles over at Customs to make sure everything gets smoothed out." Which probably meant a combination of political intimidation and large checks being passed to the right people. Whoever was behind this operation, it couldn't be entirely legal, particularly not in Malaysia. "The boats are getting sorted out, but you're going to need to make sure they get set up the way you want them."

He handed each of them a folder. "I'm sure you saw the yachts out there. Those are going to be yours; you're going to have a lot of work getting them ready to operate out of. They aren't going to be your exclusive platforms, of course; trying to run a ship-to-shore assault off of a luxury yacht isn't going to work all that well. But they'll do for reconnaissance at the very least, and possibly some Trojan Horse, pirate-baiting sort of work. I'll generally leave that up to you; you gentlemen are going to be the men on the ground, so you're going to have overall tactical discretion. I'm here to coordinate and facilitate, and pass on any intel I get. I would suggest, however, getting those yachts prepped, and taking them out as soon as possible. There is one vital bit of intelligence we haven't been able to get, and that's where the *Zhaotong* is."

"You don't have a location for her?" Sean asked incredulously. "She's a frigate; how the fuck do you lose a frigate? Don't you have sat recon to call on?"

For a second, Dan thought that Rex looked a little guilty, almost evasive. "*Nobody* knows where the *Zhaotong* is," he replied, which didn't really answer the question. "Even the Chinese don't know. Chinese comm nets have been frantic trying to locate it since Yuan went rogue. Whether he's got the ship moored and camouflaged, or sank it to avoid the higher profile, we do need to know where it is. So far, none of his pirates have used it to attack shipping, but if he's still got it, it may well only be a matter of time. So, as much as possible over the first week or so, you need to be keeping an eye out for that ship."

"What else do we know about their operation?" Dan asked, studying the maps on the board. "We got a basic rundown from Decker, but all the details were supposed to be here."

Rex turned to the map board. "Well, we know they've got camps spread out across the islands, with several on smaller Pulaus to keep lookouts for targets, and presumably for any naval assets coming after them. We have a few of these camps located already, and we believe that Yuan has set up his headquarters in the oil company town here on Pulau Matak…"

Rex hadn't been kidding. There was a *lot* of work to be done. The ammo got there late that night, but the contractors were so busy they couldn't even start jamming their combat loads before the morning. Gear had to be issued and shaken out, RHIBs needed to be set up, comms had to be set up, and the yachts had to be prepped so as to have all the comm and weapons they would need while still appearing like innocuous luxury cruisers to any observers or boarders. Several of the contractors had to take crash courses in piloting the yachts as well; driving a RHIB or a speedboat was one thing, but a seventy-meter yacht is something else altogether.

The first night, between the jet lag and the crushing workload, Dan didn't have to worry about any of his team deciding to have fun at the expense of work. They knocked off just before midnight, and then everyone crashed in their admittedly very plush hotel rooms almost immediately. The second night, however, was when the problems started.

Dan was jerked out of a deep sleep by someone trying to beat down his door. He squinted at his watch, and was disgusted to see that he'd only gone to sleep an hour before. He'd finally gotten a chance to call Amy and Tom, and it had kept him up later than he'd planned, but it had been worth it. He'd only gotten time to talk to his kids about six or seven times during the train-up, and it had been hard on all of them. He felt a little guilty that it had been harder on the kids than on him; he'd been too busy, too tired, and, he had to admit, too exhilarated to be getting back in the action, even if it was just training.

Dressed in his boxers, his P226 in his hand just in case, he went to the door. Peering through the peephole, he saw it was Vernon, looking tired and extremely pissed off, standing under the balcony lights. He swung the door open. "What is it?"

"Fuckery," was all Vernon said before he turned and led the way down the balcony. He was only wearing board shorts and flip-flops himself. "Some of our kids got into the booze already."

"Fuck. Hold on, let me get a little bit more in the way of clothes on." He started to step back into the room, but paused and looked back out at where Vernon had stopped to wait for him. "Do I need the gun?" He'd seen situations where he might, and with a few of these characters, and with alcohol involved, there was no telling just how out of control the situation might get.

"I doubt it," Vernon replied. "Bringing it might just make matters worse, come to think of it." Dan nodded, ducked back into his room, set the pistol back in the drawer of his nightstand, and pulled on his own cargo shorts before going out to join Vernon.

"All right, let's go." Vernon hadn't moved from where he'd stopped to wait, and simply turned and headed down the balcony again.

Dan could hear the yelling and carrying on already. He couldn't tell if it was just people being drunken jackasses or a fight. For all he knew, and he'd seen enough in the infantry and contracting worlds to know it was possible, it was both.

As they descended toward the pool, matters didn't become much clearer. That was largely because the drunks couldn't figure out what they wanted to do. There was a lot of yelling, a lot of cursing, and a lot of laughing. People were shoving each other around, but whether it was hostile or drunken horseplay was hard to tell.

None of which mattered much to Dan. He was already pissed off about having to wake up to deal with this. The irresponsibility of getting shitty drunk before they'd even started the real work actually enraged him.

Without a word, he waded into the chaos, found the first table full of halfway full bottles and flipped it over with a crash.

"Hey, what the fuck?" Lambert slurred, from where he had been in an animated, drunken argument with one of the other contractors from Sean's team about who had nailed more trim overseas. "What the fuck do you think you're doing?"

Dan didn't answer, but simply headed for the next table. One of Will's teammates, a skinny, tattooed kid with several nose piercings, started to get in his way, but he simply laid the kid out with an uppercut to the chin and continued on.

"Danny's just upset he didn't get invited to the party," Jenny said loudly. She was dressed in the shortest cutoffs Dan had ever seen, and a string bikini top that almost may as well not even be there. She draped an arm over Dan's neck and tried to kiss him on the cheek. "It's okay, though, you're here now. No need to be an angry-puss." She ran her hand down his chest. "Mmm," she purred. She was obviously drunk, and Dan shrugged her off.

"It's the first fucking night," he said, his hands on his hips, his voice loud enough to echo off the surrounding buildings around the pool. The noise didn't die down right away; it took a moment for the angry edge to his words to penetrate the alcoholic haze. "We've still got a fuck-ton of work to do in the morning, and we're moving out on our first recce in less than sixty hours. So what the fuck makes you idiots think this is a good idea?"

There wasn't an answer at first. Most of them were probably shocked at being dressed down for drinking, some of them probably hadn't understood just what he'd said. There was a lot of drunken incomprehension around the pool. Somebody laughed.

"Either you all get back to your rooms and go to sleep, or I start knocking you into the pool one at a time until you fucktards sober up," Dan snarled. "And rest assured, I'm going to be personally making sure your dumb asses are up at zero six tomorrow to work. Hangovers be damned. Now get the fuck out of here."

"Who the fuck do you think you are?" Jenny demanded.

He glared at her. "I'm one of the guys with his ass on the line if one of you stupid fucks screws it up in pirate country because you're hungover or still drunk," he snapped. "I'm also the guy who is going to talk to Rex in the morning and make sure anybody who is still in this fucking pool area in ten minutes is on a plane heading home tomorrow. If your booze is more important than fifty grand a month, you can pass up the money and go home to get shit-faced."

That seemed to get through. Jenny threw him a poisonous look and turned away. Slowly, the rest of the party started to break up. Lambert half-swaggered, half-staggered over and stood only inches away from Dan, staring him in the face. Dan returned the stare without flinching.

"Okay, big-shot," Lambert said after a moment. "We'll see how this works out." He turned away and started back toward his room.

Ty had been nearby, kind of hanging around Lambert. He didn't say anything, but he looked at Dan, then back to Lambert, with a sort of pained, confused look on his face. He dropped his half-empty plastic cup of beer in the nearest trash can and left the pool. Dan figured that Ty was feeling a bit like the little brother caught between his idolized older sibling and his parents. The guy was a decent enough teammate, but he wanted to be one of the cool kids. That was a weakness, one that some of the more unscrupulous were going to exploit.

Dan let out a long breath, finally looking over at Vernon, who had been standing to one side, ready to intervene if any of the other contractors had decided to make an issue of it. Only then did he start to feel a little bit of a post-confrontation shake. He'd agreed with Vernon that bringing a pistol in might have escalated things a little too much, but there had been no guarantee that one of the drunken contractors hadn't been armed. He'd seen worse things happen. Some people simply couldn't handle their booze. Adding weapons to the mix was potentially deadly.

"I'm going back to bed," he said. "Call me on the cell before you come to the door; I'll have it locked and bolted, with my gun close at hand. I don't trust some of these fuckers."

Vernon nodded. "I wouldn't either." He looked toward where Lambert had disappeared. "I think he's going to be a problem."

Dan followed his gaze. "I think you're right," he said tiredly. "But he's also one of the better operators in this bunch. Let's just hope we can keep a short enough leash on him to get through the mission."

Rex was nearly as frustrated as Dan, Sean, and Will the next morning. He reluctantly agreed to get the support staff on the task of locking up the liquor so that the operators could concentrate on mission prep. The team leaders proceeded to throw themselves into planning, while the teams, about half of which were hungover and surly, continued prepping gear and getting the yachts set up. There was a lot to do there; they had decided that concealed compartments were the best way to go to keep weapons and gear hidden and yet quick to access. That meant a lot of cutting, welding, and careful concealment.

Especially with the aftermath of the party the night before, the prep went longer than planned. They were still ready to go by midnight. The team leaders put their teams down for three hours of rest. They'd leave before sunup.

It was relatively cool as they loaded up on the yachts at three in the morning. Of course, that meant it was only about eighty degrees, and still humid as hell. The tourist disguise helped, as the men were all in shorts and t-shirts at most, and most of the women were wearing some form of swimsuit and shorts, mostly very short shorts. They still built up quite a bit of sweat getting the last of the weapons, ammo, and gear stowed, and getting the yachts ready to weigh anchor.

From the bridge of the *Mercury Quick*, Dan got on the radio with Sean and Will. They were using low-powered, encrypted sets to hopefully keep the Malaysians and the Chinese, whom Dan was sure had spy ships in the area, from listening in. "Good luck, gents," he said. "We'll see you in a couple of days."

"Likewise," Sean replied. "Try not to get too overzealous hunting scalps, Will. This is still supposed to be a reconnaissance. It's not a hunting expedition yet. Save some for the rest of us."

"I make no promises," Will laughed. "See you guys." They signed off.

Dan looked around the bridge. "Everybody ready?" There were curt acknowledgments all around. There was some tension in the air, but at the same time, every one of them was eager to start making things happen. This really was something of a dream job. "Alright, then. Let's go."

With a rumble of diesels, the yacht surged forward, its bow pointed northeast into the South China Sea.

Chapter 7

"Hey, Tackett? I think we've been spotted. Something's sure got 'em stirred up." Lambert had been cold but professional ever since the little confrontation a couple of nights before. Dan was pretty sure he was just biding his time until he could sink a knife, real or metaphorical, into his back; he'd seen the type before. But as long as his attitude wasn't getting in the way when there were pirates to kill, he'd leave it be.

He lifted his own binoculars and peered toward the island they'd been approaching since sunrise. Sure enough, the tiny dots that were people were scrambling around like someone had kicked an ant nest. They'd been spotted, all right. And if the pirates were even remotely on the ball, the *Mercury Quick* would be a big, juicy target that they simply couldn't pass up.

Assuming they were pirates, and that this was one of Yuan's outposts, and that it hadn't been taken by the Malaysians or the Indonesians in an attempt to push back against the pirates. Dan was hoping that wasn't the case; he neither wanted to engage Malaysian or Indonesian sailors or soldiers, nor did he want to pique their interest. Either case would be bad, although actually trading fire would be a lot worse.

"How do you want to play this?" Max asked. He didn't have binoculars, but he was watching the island anyway.

"Go low key," Dan replied immediately. "Draw 'em in if they're pirates, put 'em at ease if they're local counter-pirate naval forces."

"You're assuming that they're not one and the same," Lambert pointed out. "Or that Yuan hasn't already bought off the locals. Even if they're Malay or Indonesian Navy, they're still a threat."

"Of course they are," Dan said patiently, resisting the urge to add, *No shit*. "But if we smoke 'em, they're going to become even more of a threat, because then we won't just be taking on a frigate's worth of pirates, that everybody wants dead, we'll be taking on an entire country or two's military. Not on my list of 'Things To Do In Order To Live Long Enough To Spend My Fifty Grand A Month.'"

Lambert didn't look at him, but just shrugged. Dan was getting the impression that Lambert didn't really care about much, provided he got to occasionally get his violence on, got paid, and could get drunk and laid as often as possible. At the same time, he was beginning to suspect that that was an impression that Lambert was very careful to cultivate.

He grabbed the intercom. "We're getting in the horse, boys and girls. Bravo, you're on deck. Look as rich, dumb, and happy as possible. Alpha, we're going below and gearing up. Bravo, I know I don't have to tell you to keep close to a weapon at all times." Lambert just snorted as he moved to the tiller. Max and Dan went belowdecks.

The staging area for Alpha was all the way down by the keel, in the cramped machinery spaces. In contrast to the rest of the yacht, the machinery spaces were stark, utilitarian, and smelled of hot oil, diesel, and electronics. Every spare bit of bulkhead space was presently filled with plate carriers, ammunition, and weapons.

Dan was the third man down. He wove through the press of bodies to his kit. There wasn't a lot of room down there. He rapidly threw on the plate carrier and pistol belt over his t-shirt and shorts. It felt strange, wearing kit in what were essentially beach clothes, but there was no reason, for the moment, to go to full field uniforms.

He press-checked his pistol before holstering it, then did the same with his SG 553 before slinging it. He looked around at the other five men in the compartment, getting silent thumbs-ups from all of them.

Then it was just a matter of waiting.

They couldn't hear very much down in the machinery spaces. While they weren't underway, enough still had to be running to keep everything else on the yacht working. So there was too much noise to hear the approach of Nong's boats. They heard the machine gun fire, though. That was pretty unmistakable to men who had experienced combat in Afghanistan and Iraq.

There was a shift in mood, a ratcheting up of the tension in the compartment, even though nobody said anything. Eyes looked upward toward the overhead, even though no one could see anything of what was happening. Dan just put up a hand. *Wait for it.* If they moved too quickly, this could go pear-shaped in a hurry. Conversely, if they waited too long, it could get even messier.

The yelling was getting louder up above, though it was unintelligible over the noise of the machinery and through the deck. From the tone he could make out, though, Dan was pretty sure that everything was going according to plan.

A squawk box on the bulkhead chirped twice. They'd hastily wired it up for just this purpose. There was a switch on the console on the bridge that wouldn't look terribly out of place to a casual observer, but the number of times it was pushed would tell the ready-team just who was coming aboard. If it was pirates, it was two presses. If foreign naval personnel, it would be only one.

Still Dan waited for a few more seconds. He wanted the pirates to have the run of the yacht, determine that there was nobody aboard but a bunch of inebriated, scantily-clad Western idiots, and start to relax a little before he sprung the trap.

He reached out and tapped Max on the shoulder. The pudgy gunman immediately surged up the ladder, his rifle slung and his pistol in hand.

Dan stayed right behind Max on the way up. He took the risk of keeping his rifle in hand; Max was taking the right step in going through the relatively small hatch with his pistol, but Dan wanted the greater firepower right behind him.

The machinery spaces opened up on the galley, which was presently empty. The Bravo team had deliberately stayed away from the ready-team space, and it had worked. The pirates appeared to be concentrated where the hostages were, instead of spreading out through the yacht. Why would they bother, anyway? It was just a very expensive yacht full of a bunch of dumbass rich tourists, that were presumably good for little more than some sick fun and large ransoms. They could always strip the yacht for valuables later.

Max transitioned back to his rifle as Dan kept his own muzzle trained on the nearest hatch forward, leading toward the forward dining room. Then, the rest of the team up behind them, they started toward the bow. They'd push forward to the bow, then methodically clear aft.

There was a single, skinny pirate in the dining room, rifling through a bag someone had left there, an SKS or Chinese Type 63 lying on the table next to him. He was dressed in a dirty t-shirt and cotton trousers, with sandals on his feet and a cheap, canvas chest rig on. He looked up as they came through the door, his eyes as big as baseballs, and started to yell, making a grab for the rifle on the table.

Dan and Max shot him at the same time, the four reports blending together into a single blast of sound. Max had already demonstrated that he was a preternaturally fast shot; his second round was already on the way by the time Dan's trigger had reset.

Neither had aimed for a head shot, but four 77-grain 5.56mm bullets did a good enough job of pulverizing the pirate's vitals. Blood and bits of bone and tissue splashed out of a fist-sized exit wound in his back, and he fell straight back to hit the deck with a thud.

Now the game was afoot. There was no way the rest of the pirates hadn't heard that. It was now a race, just like any hostage situation, to clear the yacht before the pirates panicked and started killing the Bravo team. Of course, unlike most hostage situations, the hostages had teeth of their own, provided they could get the weapons out in time.

They moved quickly, pushing up to the sun deck on the bow. Dan pointed toward the stern, then pointed to Max, Dave, and Sam. Max nodded and led the way toward the conference room. Those three would start clearing the mid-decks, while he, Vernon, and Brad dealt with the machine gunners on the boats.

This would be tricky. They had to move fast, without exposing themselves more than necessary, and hope that the gunners didn't just start hosing down the yacht as soon as they thought something had gone wrong. He hoped that the presence of their compatriots on board would give them pause, but since they were pirates, and not necessarily all trained naval personnel, he couldn't discount the possibility of one of them panicking and deciding to strafe the yacht just to be on the safe side.

It felt a little like the training mission in the underground ISMT in Florida, except this time the bullets and the blood were real. Crouched low to stay below the gunwale, or at least far enough below to stay out of the line of sight from the boats on the water, they moved to the side and prepared to pop up and engage.

There was the slightest hesitation as he crouched there, across from Vernon. None of them had gotten eyes on the boats since they'd gone below, so they would have to acquire targets and engage as quickly as possible. They couldn't afford to spend so much time hunting for the boats that they got shot.

But they were in a race against the gunners' panic, so they made eye contact, traded a short nod, and rose up over the gunwale.

They were lucky. The first boat, with some kind of heavy machine gun mounted about amidships, was almost directly below them, barely thirty meters away. The gunner wasn't looking particularly alert, either; he must not have thought the gunshots were reason to be alarmed. He died quickly, as all three shooters put quick pairs of shots into his torso. The man at the tiller stared in shock as blood splashed against the side of the boat and his gunner dropped into the bottom, then he started to reach for the AK clone propped against the gunwale. He was too slow. Dan put his red dot on the man's head and squeezed the trigger. The rifle barked, and the pirate fell limply on top of his own weapon.

The roar of an outboard announced one of the other boats coming around to investigate. Either they'd heard the gunfire, or they had seen the men in the first boat die. A burst of machine gun fire, apparently unaimed, snapped by overhead, announcing that this one wasn't going to get caught so unawares.

Staying as low as he could, Dan leaned out over the gunwale, his rifle pointed toward the bow, hoping to get a shot at the oncoming boat just as soon as it came into view. Brad grabbed his kit, making sure he didn't fall overboard. That wouldn't just be embarrassing; it would be disastrous.

He didn't have long to wait. The boat was already surging up to full speed as it came around the *Mercury Quick*'s bow, and its bouncing motion on the gentle waves was throwing the gunner's fire all over the place. It was still dangerous, but Dan flicked his rifle to burst and squeezed off nine rounds, hoping to at least get enough metal in the same general space as the gunner to put him out of action. Most of the shots missed, but two rounds of the last burst caught the man in the leg and he crumpled, one hand still clenching the DShK's spade grips, convulsively mashing the butterfly trigger to send more rounds thumping into the sky.

More gunfire rattled behind them, as Max led the other half of Alpha through the yacht. Some of it was probably coming from the "hostages," as well. Dan just had to hope that the plan was going well, and that they'd gotten the drop on the pirates so effectively that this would be over in the next few minutes.

Brad suddenly sprinted across the deck to the port side. Dan wasn't sure if he'd seen something or just had a brain-wave, but he got to the gunwale and went straight over it, hammering half a mag out as soon as he did. Dan didn't have time to think any further about it, because another boat, with a PKP in the bow, was starting to come in from aft. He and Vernon both took it under fire; Dan ran his mag dry and smoothly reloaded as Vernon kept shooting. By the time Dan was back up, both the gunner and the coxswain were out of sight, either dead or maimed enough to hopefully be out of the fight.

Brad leaned out some more, but came back without shooting. "It looks like the last one doesn't want to play," he said. "He's just hanging back about a hundred yards from the stern. I can't get a shot."

"Up to the bridge, then," Dan said. "We can get a shot at him from there, and Max should be at least that far on the main deck already." There was no further conversation; all three knew how vital the next few seconds were going to be, as they made a beeline for the conference room and the ladderwell up to the bridge beyond it.

Jenny was holding security on the ladderwell, far enough back that she couldn't be seen from the top, still in the smallest bikini Dan thought he'd ever seen, but now with her SG 553 in her hands and trained on the stairs. She wasn't going to go up there without plates, but she could hold security. Dan and Vernon blew past her and started up the steps.

Dan saw a Chinese pirate, armed only with a pistol, stare wide-eyed at him for a second before Lambert swept the man's legs out from under him, slamming his head into the console. Dan stepped over the guy and put a round into the skinny pirate's head who was standing over Cassy, reaching for his rifle after dropping the long knife he'd been holding. The man's head jerked to one side, a red splash hitting the all-around windows before the bullet fragments cracked the glass. He fell on Cassy, blood pouring from his head onto her shoulders.

With a grunt of disgust, Cassy shoved the corpse off of her. "Fuck," she muttered. "Now I'm probably going to get the HIV."

"Just don't swallow any of it," Lambert said as he picked himself up off the deck. Cassy flipped him off.

Ignoring both of them, Dan pointed to the unconscious pirate. "Secure this asshole; I want to talk to him." He and Vernon moved to the back of bridge, looking for a shot at the fifth boat.

But it was already backing water, apparently having figured out that the expensive yacht had teeth. The gunner was frantically spraying fire at the yacht, though the movement of the boat on the water was throwing his rounds far wide of the mark. Vernon and Dan hesitated; there wasn't a good shot, but Lambert had grabbed his own rifle from its compartment under the bridge deck and was drawing a bead. He squeezed off five shots, none of which appeared to hit anything.

"Waste of ammo," Dan said. "Get back on the tiller and turn us around. We can run 'em down."

Lambert still took a couple more shots before turning back to the controls. Dan frowned. It had been unnecessary and wasteful, throwing rounds without a good possibility of hits. But he held his peace. They'd do a hot wash later, and it would definitely come out then, but for the moment, work took precedence.

The boat, however, was making tracks, heading back toward the beach and the small camp that they could now see on shore. Dan changed his mind. "Let 'em go, for now. Break out the long guns and make sure nobody leaves that island, at least on this side. We'll consolidate here, interrogate this son of a bitch, and then move in on the shore camp."

They were almost ready to go ashore when Cassy yelled at Dan that their prisoner was waking up. He hurried back up to the bridge with Lambert, to see what they could get out of him.

The prisoner was a scared kid. He'd been the equivalent of an ensign in the PLAN, was in over his head as a pirate and knew it, and figured that his life was over one way or another. Dan's pity was tempered by the fact that the kid had, in fact, gone pirate along with his Captain, deciding it was better to go along to get along than do what was right.

He kept the questioning short, both because they were pressed for time to clear the camp onshore before the remaining pirates scattered into the jungle, and because the kid was clearly concussed, and wasn't going to be at his clearest for a little bit. He didn't seem to actually know much, anyway, being, as Dan thought of it, "a boot butter-bar." Satisfied with what he'd gotten so far, he left the prisoner and headed down to the main deck to where the inflatable launches were ready to go ashore.

He had just gotten to the gunwale, where a collapsible ladder led down to the rubber boat already bobbing alongside, when he heard the shot. Everyone froze for a second; the shooting was supposed to be over. They had cleared the yacht carefully. There shouldn't have been any pirates left.

That was when Dan realized that Lambert wasn't behind him. "Motherfucker," he muttered, and ran for the ladder up to the bridge. He

70

thought he knew just what had happened.

He got up to the bridge just as Lambert started down. The other man's expression was as bland and unconcerned as it usually was, but Dan pushed past him, to see the Chinese pirate, Nong, slumped in his chair, his head lolling backward, a puckered red hole in his forehead, one eye slightly bulged out by overpressure, and a red splatter on the deck behind him. Cassy was standing back by the windows, looking simultaneously ashamed, disgusted, and horrified.

Dan turned back toward Lambert, who had stopped a couple of steps down the ladder. Wasting rounds on a boat that was trying to evade was one thing; that could be put off until debrief. This had to be addressed now.

"What the fuck did you do that for?" Dan demanded.

Lambert shrugged, the same look of blithe unconcern on his face. "Maybe he looked like he was getting loose."

Dan was a little surprised at the surge of rage he was feeling. He'd been a professional soldier in one form or another for a long time. He'd seen some ugly things done. Most of them could be put aside as the heat of combat. This, though, would be hard to justify as anything but cold-blooded murder. And, with a sick sinking feeling in his stomach, he realized that it had happened under his command, on his watch. "Bullshit," he replied. "He was zip-tied to a chair, and he had a concussion, that you gave him."

Lambert took a step onto the bridge. "You're not really getting ass-hurt over a fucking pirate, are you?" he asked. He pointed to the corpse. "He didn't know shit, and you damned well know it. And last I checked, we were getting paid to kill pirates, not take them prisoner. Have you seen any facilities for holding detainees? Have you seen any liaisons with Malaysian or Indonesian authorities to turn prisoners over? I'll answer that for you. You fucking haven't, because there aren't any. Face facts, Tackett. We're here to kill these assholes. I just cleaned up one of your loose ends before you were ready to."

Dan just looked at him for a second, his eyes narrowed. "That may be true," he said, "but don't try to justify this as being done out of pragmatism. You killed him because you wanted to."

Lambert stepped up close to him, a faint smile on his lips. The other man was about an inch taller, but they weighed almost the same, and had performed equally well at the physical evolutions in training.

"Prove it," he said quietly, then turned away and left the bridge.

Dan looked over at Cassy. She was watching Lambert leave, and there was fear in her eyes. She tore her gaze away from the ladderwell to meet Dan's eyes.

"He scares me," she admitted. "I should have done something, but I was afraid he'd shoot me too if I tried to stop him."

Dan just nodded. "This is going to have to be dealt with

eventually."

"How?" Cassy asked. "He's got a point. We don't have any facilities for taking care of prisoners. Do you really think that our employers are going to get bent out of shape over one executed pirate?"

Dan stared after Lambert for a moment, conflicting emotions raging. Both of them were right. More than likely, presuming that they weren't thrown under the bus for political expediency, this entire incident would get swept under the rug. A palatable cover story would be cooked up, or more likely it would never be mentioned outside of closed doors.

But Lambert's actions spoke of a greater threat to the mission and the team. Dan didn't think the other man was a psychopath, but he wasn't going to be moderated by any notions of justice or mercy. And furthermore, his very attitude was a challenge to Dan's leadership of the team. A challenge that could very well turn violent. Lambert's point about the lack of legal recourse for the pirates went double for the rest of them. They weren't operating with much of any oversight. If Lambert decided to make an issue of it, there was no one beyond the other MMPR operators to intervene. And even if it did come to legal action Stateside, it would probably be too late for Dan.

"I don't know yet," he admitted. "But I'll think of something."

"Just watch your back," Cassy warned him. "I have a feeling we all might need to soon."

Dan started down the ladder to go back to the boats. There was still work to do. But he checked the corners as he went through the hatch, just in case.

They didn't come straight in to the beach. That was definitely going to be a bad idea; while there probably weren't many pirates left on the island, the crew of that last boat would doubtless have machine guns trained on the beach. None of the contractors were interested in staging a replay of Inchon. They described a wide arc out to the west before coming in on an apparently abandoned stretch of beach about a quarter of the way around the island. It was still going to be less than half a mile to the camp. Pulau Repong was not a large island.

Beaching the boats, they bailed out quickly. They had changed from skimpy vacation clothes to the Kryptek Mandrake pattern jungle cammies that they'd been supplied with. Dan wasn't terribly impressed, but it seemed to generally do the trick in the shadows, particularly if the contractor wearing it was paying attention and moving properly.

The jungle was a thick tangle of branches, tree trunks, leaves, and vines from ground to upper canopy. Palm trees seemed to be some of the tallest, but there were more species than any of them could count. Not that they were concerned with the flora, aside from how it could conceal traps and ambushes. It also made movement a bitch. There was no clear footing, and the shooters of Alpha had to weave their way through the vines and broad, wet leaves carefully, trying to make as little noise as possible. Surprise was out of the question; obviously the pirates already knew they were there, and probably at least suspected they were coming. But they were probably pretty strung out, and Dan expected they would probably open fire at any odd sound they heard rather than take chances. None of the others had disagreed.

They were keeping a tight formation; there was no other option in the dense growth. Visibility was only a few meters at most. It was also steamy hot, and mist hung under the jungle canopy. Every one of them had been drenched with saltwater before they even hit the beach, but the jungle heat was adding sweat to their already sodden cammies and gear. Dan could feel his feet squelching in soaked socks in his lightweight hiking boots.

Vernon was on point, with the rest in a file behind him. He was taking his time, taking a step then pausing, looking around and listening, keeping his rifle up and ready, before taking the next step. It was terribly slow and laborious, but it was preferable to blundering into a mine, punji-pit, or ambush.

They could hear the pirates after half an hour, that had seen them cover just over two hundred meters. Nong had lied. There were still a few left; there was too much noise to just be the crew of the last boat. A babbling, bastard combination of Mandarin, Malay, and Javanese, they couldn't understand anything that was being said, but it was loud and scared. There was also the occasional gunshot, usually answered by a harsh *crack* that was probably from one of the AI AXMC .300 WinMag rifles on the yacht. At this rate, Dan mused, the pirates might all be eliminated from the yacht by Lambert and the other snipers before the ground team even got there, if they kept being dumb enough to take potshots.

He didn't signal Vernon to speed up, though. This kind of movement to contact required patience. Rushing was a good way to get killed, and none of them was interested in getting a shallow grave in the jungle in lieu of their fifty thousand a month.

When they finally broke out into the clearing that was the pirate outpost, though, none of the pirates were dug in waiting for them. Dan could see two crouched behind a fallen tree, facing the beach, and there was the noise of at least one more, possibly two, on the other side of a flimsy shack.

The six men quietly fanned out through the encampment. The place was miserable; a few nylon tents, a couple of fire pits, the shack, and a rickety-looking lookout tower were the only structures. There was trash everywhere, including a lot of liquor and beer bottles. There was still the faint, sickly-sweet smell of marijuana smoke in the air, as well. Somebody had been having a toke not too long ago.

Dan was hoping to take at least one of the pirates alive, if only to make sure that there weren't any more on the island, and that they hadn't talked to Yuan's people up on Matak over the radio. He kind of suspected that the radio was strictly controlled by the Chinese leadership, both of whom were now dead, but better safe than sorry.

But just as he was about to yell, "*Bu xu dong!*" Dave kicked a bottle.

It didn't make a lot of noise, but it was enough for at least one of the pirates, in spite of the sporadic gunfire, to hear it and turn around. He yelled something, whipping his Type 56 around, his finger tightening on the trigger.

He died before he could bring the rifle to bear, as did the other three. Dan had already had his red dot on the man's upper back, and simply squeezed the trigger as soon he started to swing around. Rifles barked, and blood and bits of tissue sprayed from exit wounds as the pirates all perished within a fraction of a second of each other. The bodies slumped in unnatural positions as they fell against the logs they had been using as cover.

The farthest one was still breathing, though with a sick gurgle in his moans that suggested he wouldn't be for long. Sam moved forward, slinging his rifle, until he was standing over the stricken pirate. The lean, hawkish man looked down at the mortally wounded pirate for a moment, then pulled a tomahawk out of his belt and buried the blade in the pirate's skull with a wet *thud* that seemed strangely loud in the clearing.

The act bothered Dan, as did the look in Sam's eye as he yanked the tomahawk head clear and wiped it on the pirate's shirt. While too many years of real-world operations against insurgents and terrorists had hard-wired a bit of the "don't leave a live one behind you" mindset into him, the intimacy of that particular killing seemed slightly obscene to him. He would have used a bullet. Still, dead was dead. He simply filed away what the act said about Sam and got back to work.

"Systematic clear and search," he said into the sudden quiet. "I doubt there's going to be a lot of useful intel here, but anything we can scrape together. And I know I don't have to say it, but keep an eye out in case there are more."

In pairs, tracing a clockwise circle around the camp, they checked the shack and the tents. They found nothing but booze, drugs, and porn. There was a radio in the shack, but it was powered down. There was no way of knowing whether a message had been sent, but they'd be long gone by the time Yuan could send reinforcements, presuming he was going to.

"There's got to be a good five large worth of marijuana and coke here," Dave noted. "What do you want to do with it?"

"Burn it," Dan replied without hesitation.

Vernon nodded. "Good call."

"You don't think some of ours would use the shit, do you?" Dave

74

asked incredulously. He was a little out there himself, but he seemed genuinely shocked at the thought. Of course, he hadn't been there at the drunken party the night before they'd set out, either.

"Let's just remove the temptation altogether, shall we?" Dan said diplomatically. Frankly, he was less concerned with use than he was with some of their compatriots trying to smuggle the narcotics back Stateside to sell. Neither was a good idea, but he could definitely see a few of their colleagues getting greedy, which would have far-reaching consequences for all of them. Five thousand dollars worth wasn't a lot, but it could still be enough to cause trouble.

In the end, they just set fire to all of it; the shack, the tents, the tower, the works. There was only the one boat that had run away from the yacht beached at the beach, and they shot it full of holes until it was awash. If there were any more pirates hiding in the jungle, they'd be marooned. It was a long, long swim to the nearest habitation on Pulau Jemaja.

Nobody said a word when they got back to the yacht, about the drugs or anything else. There was no new information, but they'd tested the pirates, and eliminated one of Yuan's outposts. Lambert looked in the boats when they got back, looked at the plume of black smoke ashore, then looked at Dan, but said nothing. Dan had the impression that Lambert had already figured out that they had indeed found something on the island, and elected not to bring any of it back.

Dan had had Lambert specifically in mind when he'd decided to burn everything rather than present any of the other contractors with the temptation of getting high or getting a little richer. He'd decided the other man, as good a fighter as he was, was a snake. Unfortunately, he was a snake that he was going to have to live with for a while.

Chapter 8

It was late when they got back to the resort. By the time they'd cleaned and stowed their gear, it was pushing three in the morning. Between the exhaustion of twenty-four hours awake, including a firefight, brief as it was, and the still looming weight of the incipient problems with Lambert, not to mention a few others who seemed to be Lambert's type, Dan dragged himself up to his room, locked the door, laid his pistol on the nightstand next to him, along with two spare mags and his flashlight, stripped to his skivvies, and dropped to the bed.

But if he was hoping to get the chance to pass out immediately, it was forestalled by a knock on the door. For a moment, he seriously contemplated just lying there silently until whoever it was gave up and went away, but he was the team lead. It might actually be a problem that he needed to address. With a groan, he sat up, snatched the pistol off the nightstand, just in case, and went to the door.

Whoever was at the door was standing off to one side, out of view of the peephole. With a grimace, and various creative curses going through his mind about people playing stupid games when he wanted to sleep, Dan unlocked the door and swung it open.

Jenny was leaning against the wall next to the door, stripped down to tiny cutoffs and the negligible bikini top she'd worn on the *Mercury Quick*. She turned to look at him standing in the doorway and smiled. "Mind if I come in?" she asked.

Dan squinted at her in the dim light. She really was stunningly attractive, and while he was pretty sure he knew what she had in mind, and knew that he really didn't want to get drawn into that trap, he was tired enough that he found himself actually appreciating the glints of lamp and starlight off her hair and the curves of her body. He had to remind himself of the other side of her he'd already seen; calculating, manipulative, and vicious when she didn't get her way.

"Can it wait until morning?" he asked.

"Not really," she answered, stepping away from the wall and into the doorway. She'd evidently showered and put some kind of perfume on before coming over; she smelled a lot better than Dan imagined he did. She stepped closer and kissed him, pushing them both back into the room as she did, pulling the door shut as soon as she cleared the threshold.

Dan stumbled back until he could lay the pistol down without dropping it on the floor, then carefully disengaged himself. "What do you think you're doing?" he asked.

She chuckled as she ran her hands over his shirtless torso. He grabbed her wrists to make her stop it. "It must have been a *really* long time for you," she said, amused. "I would think it would be obvious what I'm doing."

Still holding her wrists, Dan took half a step back. "No," he said. "We're not doing this."

"Oh, come on," she chided. "We're both adults. We had a good mission, and I feel like celebrating. And I feel like celebrating with you. There's no need for it to get weird. I won't let it interfere with the mission if you won't."

He shook his head. "Doesn't work that way, and you know it. Dipping your pen in company ink is never a good idea, even if I wasn't team lead."

"We're independent contractors, Danny," she pointed out. "It's not like we're employees or anything. What we do in our off time is our own business."

"That doesn't matter a damn," he replied. "Quit trying to pretend that this is anything but what it is. This is a combat mission, Jenny. These kinds of liaisons in a regular company can be disastrous. In a combat unit, they can be deadly. We're not playing this game. Go get some sleep; we've still got work to do in the morning."

He braced himself. He well remembered her searing outbursts when training scenarios hadn't gone her way. She could be very pretty and seductive, but there was a raging viciousness lying just beneath the surface. He could only imagine her reaction to having her advances rebuffed.

But she didn't scream, or hit him, or cuss him out as a pussy or a faggot, like he'd more than half expected. She just tilted her head a little, studying him, a little half-smile on her lips. Then she stepped back, and he let go of her wrists.

"Okay," she said, her voice even, even a little amused. "Fine. We'll give it a little more time." She smiled dazzlingly at him. "You'll come around." She turned toward the door, though it was more of a pirouette, calculated to draw attention to her ass as she turned. "I can be patient. I *always* get what I want, eventually."

Don't hold your breath, lady, Dan thought.

She opened the door, which hadn't quite latched, but paused halfway through and turned to look back at him. "Just a word to the wise," she said, in a more serious tone, "you need to watch your back. Lambert knows you burned the drugs that you guys found on the island."

"And?" Dan replied, his voice deadpan. He knew what was coming, but he wasn't going to give her the satisfaction of seeing much of any reaction. He felt that she was fishing for some angle, her attempted seduction having been rejected.

It was dim enough to make it hard to discern her expression, but her demeanor seemed to actually soften for a moment. "Some of the others are a little pissed about it. They think they could have made some extra money on the side. They'll get over it. But Lambert...he's thinking. He'll find a way to use it against you."

Which, frankly, was something that Dan had already had to consider with Lambert. The murder of Nong had been more than just indulging a violent whim. It had been a shot across Dan's bows, a warning that the other man wasn't going to necessarily play by the same rules. It was a challenge to Dan's leadership as well as a vision of things to come where Lambert was concerned. Dan was still determined to act like a professional soldier. Lambert was...something else.

When he didn't reply, she said, "Just...be careful, all right?" It sounded like some genuine concern in her voice. Then she was gone, and he stepped over to latch and lock the door.

He stood in the dark for a few moments, as weariness washed over him. Fighting pirates wasn't enough. No, there had to be assholes causing drama within the company. Dammit.

He dropped back onto the bed, but it still took over an hour before he finally dropped off to sleep. It would be far too early when he had to get up to call his kids.

Margaret Lawrence already wasn't having a good week. One of her case officers had skylined himself by getting pulled over by the Singaporean police for speeding. There was yet *another* fraternization blowup happening between one of the support personnel and a Diplomatic Security contractor. That was one that several of her people had tried to keep under her radar, but when a drunken confrontation in the Embassy canteen had threatened to turn violent, she couldn't help but become involved, because the Ambassador had gotten wind of it.

So here she was at her desk at nine in the morning, already nursing a pounding headache. And somehow she knew that when that phone rang, it wasn't going to be bringing her any more good news than it had the last couple of times it had rung.

It wasn't good news. It was the Ambassador. "Ms. Lawrence, could you come up to my office at your earliest convenience?" She didn't sound happy. The more pissed off Ambassador Amanda Telfried was, the more formal and clipped her speech got.

"Of course, Madam Ambassador," Lawrence replied. "I'll be up in five minutes."

"Thank you," Telfried said icily, and hung up.

"Crap," Lawrence said, digging her thumbs into her eyes. Hopefully it was just more screaming about the latest idiocy between her support people and the Embassy's contractors, and not another crisis that really had nothing to do with Singapore Station's actual mission. But she wasn't banking on it.

She checked her appearance in the small mirror that she kept at her desk for just that purpose. At any reasonably operational base, she'd be able to dress like a normal human being, but here at the Embassy, she had to be in "professional" attire at all times, in case the Ambassador wanted to consult. It was almost as bad as being back at Headquarters.

Satisfied that her suit and her makeup were in presentable condition, she headed upstairs to the Ambassador's office.

Of course, once she reached the Ambassador's office, she had to wait for ten minutes outside for the Ambassador's convenience. Of course it was a status game to make sure she understood her place; she was well aware of it, because she'd become well-versed in such status games herself in the course of her advancement with the Agency. It didn't make it any less irritating. The fact that she didn't know what she was being called on the carpet for this time didn't help matters. So she was feeling a bit testy when she was finally called into the office, though she was experienced enough to keep a lid on it. Further pissing off the Ambassador would not be a good idea. As Chief of Station, she was disposable compared to the political appointee behind the desk.

Telfried was sitting at her desk, her face looking as pinched and angry as usual. Lawrence still wondered how the woman could possibly have been made a diplomat; she still looked like she was searching for some reason to take offense even at the few diplomatic functions that Lawrence had attended with her. Of course, the fact that she'd made considerable campaign contributions to the right people had more to do with her appointment than any actual diplomatic acumen, but that tended to be the rule rather than the exception.

Telfried had a laptop on the desk in front of her, and frowned at it instead of looking at Lawrence. She pointed to a chair in front of the desk, which Lawrence took without a word. For a moment, neither said anything, as Telfried continued to glower at the offending computer. Then, suddenly, she swiveled it around so that Lawrence could see the screen.

"Would you care to explain, Ms. Lawrence," she began, "why there appears to be a major direct-action mission being executed right in our backyard, without either my knowledge or approval?"

Lawrence stared at the screen, which showed an overhead shot from one of the ISR drones that several agencies and offices of the intelligence community were now occasionally sending over the islands where the Chinese frigate *Zhaotong* had gone rogue. A renegade Chinese officer, with a sizable force of Chinese naval personnel and other pirates behind him, sitting right on the primary shipping lanes leading into the Straits of Malacca, was enough of a concern to everyone with interests in the Southern Pacific that the airspace was getting crowded with surveillance drones and reconnaissance aircraft.

Aside from Telfried's high-handed manner, what immediately angered Lawrence was that this was the first time she was seeing this.

The imagery was video, apparently from a US drone, either a Global Hawk or one of the ubiquitous Predators. It showed what looked like a high-end, very expensive yacht, surrounded by five speedboats. As the camera zoomed in, the operator apparently having just noticed this little hijack at sea, several tiny figures, that had to be pirates, swarmed aboard the yacht.

At first, Lawrence couldn't figure out what the issue was. It looked like a yacht full of rich tourists with more money than sense had gotten hijacked, that was all. There was nothing to suggest any Agency involvement, or "direct action." She began to suspect that Telfried had gone a little around the bend in her hatred for the Agency and its people.

Then all hell seemed to break loose. New figures came on deck, armed, and took the speedboats under fire. In moments, four of the five were drifting, their gunners and coxswains dead or incapacitated. The fifth started backing away quickly, heading back toward the nearby island.

Lawrence didn't say a word, but waited for the video to finish. It kept going, as a rubber raiding craft was launched off the fantail of the yacht, with what looked very much like light infantry troops aboard. The raft headed in to the island.

Most of the subsequent action was obscured by the jungle canopy, but the thick black smoke billowing up out of the jungle near the beach, where a little of what appeared to be a camp could be seen, strongly suggested another attack on land. Shortly afterward, the rubber boat returned to the yacht, which turned west, toward Malaysia.

The video came to an end, and Lawrence just sat there for a moment, staring at the now-blank screen, nonplussed. She wasn't sure what she'd just seen; if it was in fact an Agency op, it was one that she'd been completely cut out of, which, given that she was Chief of Station, was completely unacceptable. If it wasn't, even more questions arose, including who it was, and why the first time she'd heard of it was at the hands of Telfried the politically-appointed harpy.

"Well?" Telfried demanded. "I'm waiting for your explanation."

Lawrence fought to control her expression as she met the Ambassador's eye. "I don't have one."

An arched eyebrow. "Really? You're the Chief of Station, or you're supposed to be. What is Langley paying you for, if you don't even know what your own people are up to?"

Apparently they're paying me to deal with personnel issues because you like to find fault, rather than intelligence gathering, which is what I got sent here to oversee. Of course she wouldn't say that. That would be career suicide, talking back to an Ambassador like that, let alone *this* Ambassador. So she settled for a diplomatic, "I assure you,

Madam Ambassador, that no such operation is going through this Station. If, by some chance, it is an Agency or JSOC operation, it is not one I have been apprised of."

Telfried just stared at her with an expression of disgusted skepticism. "I'm sure you are quite well-rehearsed at that line," she said. "I expect a full report on my desk by this time tomorrow, or I am going to raise hell in Washington until this gets sorted out. And don't even try to bullshit me, or scrubbing toilets will be the best job you can hope to hold down at Langley for a long, long time."

Lawrence rose stiffly. "I'll see what I can find out, Madam Ambassador," she said tightly, momentarily desperately longing to tell this self-righteous sociopath what she thought of her. The implicit accusation that she was lying to the Ambassador was almost enough to make her see red all by itself, but Lawrence was an accomplished politician in her own right; one doesn't get to the post of Chief of Station without being able to play politics with the best of them. So she simply turned on her heel and walked out of the Ambassador's office, Telfried having already turned the laptop back around and gone back to whatever she did when she wasn't pissing everyone off around her.

It wasn't a terribly long walk down to the SCIF, and she covered it more quickly than usual. As she entered and looked around, she grabbed Hank Henson and told him, "Find Bogart and get him in my office, five minutes ago." Henson raised his eyebrows, then nodded and left.

While Henson was looking for Bogart, Lawrence got the SCIF hopping. She wanted *all* of the imagery from over the islands where the *Zhaotong* had been last seen, and she wanted it immediately. She wanted to know why she'd only just now found out about a firefight near Pulau Repong, and from the Ambassador at that.

They were still scrambling for the footage when Bogart stuck his head in her office. Bogart wasn't his real name, but he went by his callsign at all times around the Station, as did most of the rest of the small Special Activities unit attached to the Station. Their primary focus was Al Qaeda-affiliated groups in Malaysia, but if there was anybody with the training to pull off an op like she'd just watched, it was probably going to be them. Special Activities usually seemed to be on their own program, anyway.

"Were you going to deign to tell me about an op in the...Anambas Islands?" she demanded. She'd actually had to pause and double-check the name of the chain that Yuan had seized. Half of the Station just referred to them as the "Pulaus" even though that was actually the Javanese word for "island."

Bogart just blinked in surprise. He reached up and swept a hand through his long, brown hair to scratch his scalp. He actually looked nothing like Humphrey Bogart, but more like a California surfer. "The chain where that Chinese captain set up his little pirate kingdom?" he asked. "If we had an op running up there, you'd know. He's not really our bailiwick, anyway."

Lawrence frowned at him, not entirely unaware that she was now viewing him with much the same sort of distrust that Telfried had directed at her. She pointed to several stills of the fight at Repong, and what looked like a very similar operation to the north, near an unnamed island off the north coast of Pulau Jemaja. "*Somebody* sure just smoked a handful of Yuan's pirates. The Ambassador thinks it's us. I told her I knew nothing about it. I wasn't lying to her, was I?"

Bogart leaned over the laptop to study the stills more closely. He shook his head. "Wasn't us. It *might* be JSOC, but I doubt it; this isn't quite their style. They'd stage a team of DEVGRU guys off the *Antietam* and swoop in with Seahawks and SWCC boats, not do this Trojan-Horse thing." He frowned. "It *could* be the Malaysians or the Indonesians, or even the Vietnamese, though again, I doubt it. The Malaysians would be the most likely; the Indonesians are swamped just trying to patrol their closer-in islands. The Vietnamese have been building up a lot with Japanese help, since the Chinese keep pushing into their territorial waters in the South China Sea, but this doesn't quite feel like them, either."

"So you have no idea."

He shook his head, still looking at the pictures. "I don't, ma'am, I'm sorry. It wasn't us. It would be extremely hard to get a side operation going, too, given the sensitivity of the whole 'Chinese deserters' angle. Somebody might slip it into a terrorism brief, just because of all the lumping together of piracy and terrorism these days, and terrorism is an easy sell, but since none of Yuan's people bow down to Mecca five times a day, at least not that we know of, it's going to be harder to get anybody back at Headquarters to sign off on it."

She thought about it a moment, then nodded. "If you hear anything..."

"I'll let you know," he finished. "I'll keep my ear to the ground, and so will the rest of my team. We don't have a lot of assets out that way, but if we get any whispers, I'll be sure to pass it along."

"Okay, thanks, Bogart," she said. He nodded, and left.

She stared at the computer, rubbing the bridge of her nose. The headache had just gotten worse. The entire South China Sea was presently a powder-keg, and Yuan's desertion had only exacerbated an already delicate situation. If someone had already started shooting, it could get really ugly, really fast.

She had to find out who was behind this, and fast.

"*Shang Wei* Feng?" Feng Kung looked up from the equipment case he had just hauled in from the jeep. His team was still getting situated, and a lot of the gear and weapons still needed to be accounted for. *Shi Zhang* Shen Chao had just come out of their makeshift TOC, with a printout in his hands. "We just got this from the *Zhuhai*."

Feng straightened up and took the printout from his Chief Petty Officer and scanned it quickly. While the destroyer *Zhuhai*'s captain did not know all of the details of what this team of *Jiaolong* commandos was doing in Indonesia, he was eagerly sending them every notable update from his own ISR assets as quickly as he got them. Considering the mission, Feng appreciated it.

He skimmed the report, then stopped and read it more carefully. He frowned. "Have you read this?" he asked Shen.

"No, sir," the noncom replied. "What is it?"

He stared at the paper, as if it would reveal more than it said. "It says that two of the pirate outposts, one on Pulau Repong and another on an unnamed island north of Pulau Jemaja, were attacked and destroyed by an unknown force that appeared to camouflage its presence by traveling in high-end yachts."

Shen raised an eyebrow. Ordinarily the Chief was unflappable, especially as he was one of the few genuine combat veterans in the *Jiaolong*, or Sea Dragon, the People's Liberation Army Navy's special operations unit. He'd fought pirates in the Gulf of Aden, when one particular band of Somalis hadn't quite gotten the message not to trifle with ships flying Chinese colors. "Is there anything about the attackers' identity?" he asked.

Feng looked at him. Shen was trustworthy, but Feng was so far the only one to get the *full* briefing on the mission, including the history of all of the preparations Yuan had made before he'd deserted. And the implications of those preparations.

"At first guess?" he said. "I would imagine the Americans would have reason to try to intervene here, even if they don't know the full picture. It is what they do, after all. But we can't rule out a number of other players, either, at least until we know more."

"Russians?" Shen asked. While Chinese-Russian relations were generally good, both countries were ruthlessly pragmatic when it came to their interests. Feng would not be at all surprised to see the Russians sticking their noses into the situation with Yuan, *especially* if the SVR had caught wind of what Yuan had stolen before he went renegade.

But that couldn't be mentioned, not yet. "It's possible, though unlikely," was all he said. "Whoever it is, they have accelerated our timetable. We cannot have *laowai* taking down Yuan. He is Chinese, and he is our responsibility. Beijing will not take it well if we fail to kill or secure Yuan before anyone else does."

He handed the printout back to Shen and got back to work. There would be no sleep tonight. He hadn't been kidding when he had said that the timetable needed to be moved up. He would probably have to call for more direct support, as delicate as that might be. The

Changbai Shan amphibious warfare group was to the north, near the Spratlys, and he had authorization to call upon it if necessary. But Yuan had very carefully calculated his position; he had known that any further buildup of Chinese naval forces in the South China Sea was going to be met with protests and further hostility from the nearby nations, not to mention the United States. He had been banking on the delicacy of the situation to protect him, which was why the *Jiaolong* were there, instead of an entire naval task force. But Feng was determined that his cleverness would not save him. Feng and his men would kill or capture Yuan and the rest of his pirates, and they'd do it before the Americans could get their hands on either the *Shang Xiao* or what he had stolen.

He had sworn to *Zhong Jiang* Feng that he would accomplish his mission, and accomplish it he would. No matter what.

Chapter 9

Vernon may not have had the Zodiac's outboard engine opened all the way up, but Dan was still getting beaten up in his position on the gunwale, right at the bow. While Vernon had pointed out that Dan should probably be driving, he wanted to be the first one off the boat on landing. It was a tossup, between leadership as coordinator and leading from the front. Dan had gone with leading from the front. Vernon, along with everyone else on the boat, knew where to go.

The ocean was blacker than anything Dan thought he'd ever seen. No one on any of the four boats was showing any light; even the navigational compasses were shielded so that only the coxswains could see them, the dim light of the chemlights shielded so that they only illuminated the compasses themselves, without splashing any light back on the coxswains. Even through the twin-tube night vision goggles, Dan could just make out the darker blackness of the boats to either side, often enough only by the vague silhouette against the horizon that he could perceive from his position mere inches off the water. There was so little illumination that even the NVGs were struggling to resolve anything.

Pulau Airabu was now visible, albeit only as a black hulk blocking out the stars ahead. At least at first. As they got closer, a clump of several flickering lights appeared against the dark hulk of the island. That was the target.

The lights fell away to the right as the boats approached the beach. Coming dead-on to the objective was always a recipe for disaster, as several units had found out the hard way over the last couple decades. It had taken some detailed map study to pick out the landing site, and even then, they had set three alternates in case the one they'd picked turned out to be occupied or otherwise untenable.

The boat hit another wave with tooth-jarring impact, at least for the two shooters in the bow, then they were suddenly at the beach. It was too dark for Dan to see the bottom, and they ran the risk of hammering the outboard into the sand, but fortunately, Vernon judged the distance right, cutting the engine and lifting it clear of the water just in time before they glided in to scrape on the sand. Dan launched himself off the gunwale into knee-high water, his rifle already up and ready. For some reason, MMPR hadn't thought to purchase the SG 553s with rail systems, so there was no laser sight, but the red dot, dialed well down, was visible in the NVGs. Dan had been a little skeptical at first, but given the very real possibility that the Chinese pirates had some kind of night vision, flashing IR lasers around might not be the best idea.

The rest of the boats came in with the hiss and crunch of rubber on sand and rock, but little other noise. The rest of the shooters debarked in moments. Half, with Dan in the lead, moved up to the vegetation line, only a few meters away, and held security while the other half dragged the boats further up the beach, until they were nearly at the edge of the jungle. If the boats floated away, they'd never be able to show their faces again, regardless of how well the raid went. Of course, given that losing the boats would more than likely result in their deaths, that was immaterial, but it would still be a hell of a stupid way to go out.

Of course, they also weren't going to just leave the boats visibly on the beach. It took some extra effort to lift the boats and carry them off the sand and into the tangle of vegetation under the jungle canopy, but fortunately it was a narrow beach, so they didn't have far to go. The security cordon pushed deeper into the jungle, except for the two on the flanks, who stayed just inside the vegetation, watching up and down the beach, just in case.

It was still relatively early; Dan, Sean, and Will had been careful to leave enough time to make their way through the kilometer of jungle between the landing site and the target by 0300. It was still going to be a rough slog, even though the tide had been favorable, and they were actually a few minutes ahead of schedule. Jungle movement sucks at the best of times; at night it gets even worse.

The jungle wasn't exactly quiet; there were all sorts of nocturnal animals and insects making a cacophony of buzzes, clicks, shrieks, and hoots in the darkness around them. While the NVGs were hard-pressed, with so little illumination for the optics to amplify, to resolve much more than a few shapes and movement, Dan thought he could make out a few of the closer animals moving through the trees and the undergrowth.

The ambient noise of the jungle was masking a lot of the thrashing around as the contractors cut down undergrowth to camouflage the boats. It was starting to get quieter, though, as a lot of the animals heard and smelled them and either hid or fled the area, but there was no sign that any of the pirates were close enough to hear or notice anyway. Dan was still on edge about it. The noise was unavoidable, but a klick was pretty damned close to the objective, in his experience.

Finally, the boats were camouflaged, and Dan felt the tap on his shoulder as Vernon signaled that they were up and ready to go. Dan moved forward to tap Dave, who smoothly came to his feet and led out.

It was slow going. The foliage was thick as hell, and Dave had to carefully move a step at a time, picking out where to put his foot before carefully setting it down, trying not to snap too many twigs or get caught in the wait-a-minute vines. He would take a step, stop, look around and overhead, then find where to take the next step. It was laborious and painstaking, and Dan was right behind him, doing the same thing.

It was swelteringly hot. Even the night hadn't relieved the heat much. The salt spray from the approach might be evaporating away, but it was impossible to tell, as it was being immediately replaced by sweat. Dan's cammies were drenched. Each step had to be accompanied with a sort of swimming action to get through the undergrowth without thrashing through it like a herd of elephants. He was hoping that they would still have at least thirty minutes at the rally point just shy of the objective to catch their breath before launching the attack just before dawn. He *really* didn't want to have a repeat of that first swamp assault in Florida.

Being the jungle, there were other things to look out for beyond possible hostile patrols and making too much noise in the vegetation. Ahead of him, Dave suddenly looked up, then pointed at a tree branch above and changed course to move around it. As he followed, Dan looked up. It took a moment for him to see the snake coiled around the branch. The jungle has many ways to kill anyone stumbling into it unwarily, and it can still get even the wary. Dan passed the signal to Max, a few feet behind him, and continued on, still trying to see everything around him in the dim green glow of his NVGs.

They halted often, both to rest from the heart-pounding exertion of the slow, careful movement and constant vigilance, and to listen carefully for any sign that they had been detected. It seemed unlikely; pirates weren't generally given to lots of military training and the drugs they'd found at the Pulau Repong outpost suggested that they'd probably all be drunk, high, or some combination of the two during the night, and possibly during the day as well. But Dan wasn't inclined to chance it. He'd seen the tragic results of complacency about the opposition before. It was part of what made him so angry about the attitudes he saw in a few of the other contractors.

They finally reached the designated assault position, a small knoll that might have gone otherwise unnoticed in the tangle of jungle growth if not for a very careful study of the overhead imagery beforehand. Dave had navigated to it unerringly, even in the pitch blackness beneath the jungle canopy.

They carefully worked their way up the knoll, looking out for Sean's team, which should be close; they had planned on parallel routes through the jungle, but the darkness and the foliage were both so dense that they hadn't seen any sign of the others since leaving the landing site. Finally, Dan signaled Dave to halt there, and they circled up, shoulder to shoulder in the steamy heat, rifles trained outward.

Dan's earpiece chirped, the first noise it had made since landing. "One, this is Two," Sean's voice hissed over the net. "Coming in."

"Bring it in," he replied. He kept his eyes up, looking for the signal from Sean's pointman.

After a few seconds, he saw the IR flash, very briefly. They were all still nervous about the possibility that the bad guys might have NVGs. For years, the idea had been met with contempt, the opposition being mostly low-tech Arab guerrillas who largely didn't like to operate at night, but the involvement of actual Chinese military forces with the pirates made the likelihood of IR being spotted if not used very, very carefully much higher. So linkup signals were very brief, to hopefully prevent detection.

He returned the signal with an equally brief flash, and a few minutes later, Sean's team, looking rather alien with the twin tubes of their NVGs protruding beneath ball caps and bush hats, came out of the sea of greenery to join them. Dan's team adjusted their perimeter so the two teams could form a single, tight circle just below the crest of the knoll, surrounded by towering trees and thick fronds of whatever the predominant lower growth was.

Sean found Dan and sank to the damp ground beside him. "That was a hell of a movement," he murmured, just above a whisper.

"The jungle sucks," Dan agreed, even more quietly. For all the racket the local fauna was making, sound has a way of carrying after dark, and the bad guys were only a few hundred meters away. Dan could still hear the last of their nightly debauchery going on, which threatened to make him question why they were working so hard to stay stealthy instead of just swooping in and leveling the place.

He reminded himself that this hit could turn out to be a turkey shoot or it could go horribly, horribly wrong. Just because the bad guys were making a lot of noise didn't mean they wouldn't have sentries out, and numbers can count for a lot, drunk or not.

He keyed the radio one more time. "Three, One. Advise when you're in position." Three was Will's team, working its way over to the support-by-fire position. They had a longer route, and it would probably be at least another half an hour before they were set.

Based on how the Florida training had gone, Dan had deliberately left Jenny and Cassy back on the mainland, manning the COC. While none of the team leaders had consulted about it, both Sean and Will had done the same with the women on their teams. It was a matter of making sure everyone in the team could keep up.

It felt like a very long time, sitting there in the steaming, dripping jungle, soaked to the bone in their own juices, feeling every bit of vegetation that had worked its way into their cammies, not to mention the biting insects of every variety that were finding every bit of exposed skin, bug juice or no, and some bits that weren't exposed. Dan's watch said it was almost dawn, but it was still pitch black under the canopy when Will's voice whispered over the net. "Three in position. I have eyes on the objective. At least fifteen armed guards are visible from here, and they appear to be mostly alert. There are tents for the workers, and permanent structures for guards and management. There also appears to be a large, armed boat moored at the beach."

Dan looked over at Sean, who nodded that he'd heard. "Good copy," he sent back. "We're moving. Ten mikes."

Both team leaders rose and started going around to their teams, making sure everyone had heard and was read-in on what Will had sent. It was vital that they know as much as possible about what they were about to go into. It also served to get them more alert and ready to roll.

In a few minutes, the word had been passed to everyone, and they were up and moving, spreading out into a line abreast as they moved toward the pirates' camp.

If anything, the final approach to the target site was even more excruciating than the initial movement. Stealth and alertness were even more vital at this point. Take a step. Look and listen. Make sure you're not getting ahead of the rest of the team. Make sure you're not about to walk into a snake or a banana spider web. Look for the next place to put your foot that's not going to snap a branch. Repeat.

Slowly, the undergrowth began to thin, and the camp came into view, dimly visible through the fronds, lit by several work lamps and the growing lightness in the sky, no longer blocked out by the canopy where the jungle had been cleared to build the camp. Dan could see movement near the shelters, though there was still too much foliage and too little light to make out details. The lights were also threatening to wash out his NVGs, even though none of them appeared to be pointed out at the jungle.

With Max and Dave to either side of him, Dan crept to the very edge of the clearing. The site had been cleared by crude hack-and-slash, leaving several blackened stumps from the towering jungle trees jutting out of the dark earth. Most of the shelters were equally crude, mostly consisting of bamboo poles holding up roofs of corrugated sheet metal and palm fronds. Whether the fronds were intended as camouflage from overhead observers or had just fallen on the roofs was unclear. The entire place had a rough, "don't give a fuck" quality to it. Even the shacks that must have been for the guards weren't very well made, being mostly just more corrugated sheet metal slapped over a frame, with open windows and doors. A generator throbbed next to the larger shack, keeping the work lights glowing, though not well; they were brightening and dimming rhythmically with the rising and falling noise of the generator.

He started to pick out the guards. A group of three of them were standing next to one of the shelters, smoking. Two were carrying AKs, while the third had some kind of bullpup. The huddled forms at their feet suggested that was where the workers slept. Dan took note of the fact

89

the guards appeared to be watching the workers, rather than the perimeter.

As he scanned the other groups, all similarly armed, he started to get the idea. The guards were mainly there to keep the workers in line, and make sure that nobody was stealing any of the drugs that were being either processed or sorted here. At least most of them were; he got the impression of slightly higher level of professionalism from the group of five that were near the boat, a large fishing boat with a heavy machine gun mounted on the bow. He began to suspect that the boat held more of Yuan's own people, while the majority of the rest were the rag-tag local pirates he'd recruited.

It was time. Dan lifted his rifle, slowly took off the safety, and centered his dot, simply a brighter green in his NVGs, on the pirate standing by the heavy gun. That one was farther away from him, but he was more concerned with keeping that gun out of action than any of the rest, and initiation was on him. Letting out his breath, he squeezed the trigger.

The rifle's *crack* split through the noise of the jungle and the muttered conversations of the guards. The man standing beside the heavy machine gun staggered with the impact, but didn't go down. Dan's follow-up shot was drowned out by the roar of three teams opening fire at once.

Muzzle flashes lit up the darkened jungle, as bullets ripped through shacks, guards, and bamboo shelters. In seconds, every armed man in the camp was down, dead or dying. The four on the boat had tried to return fire, but had been cut down quickly. Two more came running out of one of the corrugated metal shacks, only to be immediately shot full of holes, collapsing on their faces at the door.

No more guards appeared, and the gunfire fell silent, replaced by the screams and moans of the wounded and the terrified screaming of several of the workers, who had awakened to gunfire and carnage. Several got up and tried to run. Dan tensed, waiting for the gunshot. While he was fairly confident in most of his contractors' target discrimination, there were a few, Lambert included, that he wasn't so sure of. But nobody shot the fleeing workers, and he relaxed, just a little.

"This is One," he sent over the radio. "Moving on the boat." He was still nervous about that heavy machine gun; until it was secured, the assault force was still vulnerable. The clearing might have gone quiet for the moment, but the entire site wasn't cleared yet. There could be all sorts of nasty surprises waiting for them, especially if Yuan's people had put two and two together after the strikes a few days before.

He carefully rose to his feet, his team following suit. They stepped into the clearing, though they were careful not to get too far into the open, allowing them to dash back into the concealment of the jungle if things went hot again.

The boat was only a couple hundred yards away. They still didn't run to it, though a few of the contractors, including Lambert and Sam, looked frustrated at maintaining the slow, careful pace that Dan and Dave were setting. In Lambert's case, Dan had little doubt that the man could probably switch back on in moments, but not everybody had Lambert's reflexes or undeniable skill.

Dan looked left, toward the shelter closest to the beach, and spotted one of the guards, not yet entirely dead, tugging a pistol out of his waistband. He slowed, pivoted, and snapped his rifle up. The first shot was hasty, the dot just below the man's ribcage as it broke. The wounded guard jerked at the impact, but kept trying to draw the pistol, so Dan carefully put the dot on his head and fired again. This time the man's head snapped back, bouncing slightly with the impact, and he was still.

As he turned back toward the boat, Dave suddenly dropped to the ground in front of him. For a moment he thought that they had taken fire, masked by the sound of his own shots, and Dave was hit. But the pointman just yelled, "Cover!" even as muzzle flashes erupted from two of the boat's portholes.

Dan felt the *snap* of a round passing less than a foot from his head, and dove for the dirt. For a split second, the only thought in his head was to get the hell away from the bullets. But he was still on open ground, and there wasn't any cover between him and the boat.

Fighting the NVGs that were dragging his head down, he craned his neck to get a shot at the boat, getting the dot somewhere in the vicinity of the muzzle flashes before opening fire. He wasn't too worried about accuracy at that point. It was time to suppress and get to cover.

Dave and Max were hammering shots at the boat while still trying to get as small as possible. Rounds were starting to impact in the dirt around them, sending up little geysers of grit and mud as they hit. They had to get out of there.

The fire from the boat seemed to be getting a little wilder, a little more sporadic. Then the support by fire team opened up on it.

The noise drowned out the moans and screams from the wounded and dying, bullets shredding the air with hard, painful *crack*s. Dust and splinters started to fly off the boat and the fire coming from the portholes slacked off to nothing. The engine started to chug suddenly; they were trying to get off the beach and away.

"On me!" Dan yelled. Scrambling to his feet, and careful to stay out of Will's team's cone of fire, he started running for the boat. He did *not* want that boat getting off the beach and back to Yuan, or whoever had sent it. That had been agreed early on. The more they could keep the pirates guessing, the better. It made it less likely that they would be adequately prepared for the next attack.

He made a mad dash for the boat, nearly seventy yards away. It was a long way to run in a firefight, and if he'd really thought about it, he might not have done it. But whoever was on the boat had stopped shooting, and Will's guys were hammering the hell out of it, so he took the chance.

And almost lost his head. Will's team's fire suddenly slowed, as too many of them ran dry at the same time and hastily reloaded. It was all the opening the gunmen behind the portholes needed. A muzzle flash seemed to erupt like a baseball-sized fireball right in front of Dan's face, and he felt the rounds snapping past his head only inches away. "Fuck!" He dove for the ground, hitting the dirt painfully, a fiery pain going through his knee as he landed on it badly. He nearly drove the breath from his lungs with the impact, and for a split second, everything was a painful haze. He had enough presence of mind to wrench his rifle around and crank ten shots off at the boat as fast as he could pull the trigger, though whether he was hitting anywhere near the gunmen shooting at him was questionable.

The gunfire from the boat didn't subside, but fortunately still wasn't that accurate. He'd already be dead if the pirates had been good shots. They were spraying and praying just as much as he was at that point. But they didn't have to be good, just lucky, and he was close. Bullet impacts were smacking dirt and mud into the air around him already.

The base of fire got their shit together a second later, and the covering fire intensified, blowing more jagged holes in the boat's hull. The shooting from the portholes dropped off, and Dan scrambled to his feet.

Dave wasn't moving. He was lying face-down in the dirt, blood and brain matter leaking out of the hole in the back of his skull. The pirates had gotten lucky.

Dan had been in enough firefights over the years that he'd long since learned to compartmentalize. There would be time to deal with Dave's death later. Right now it was time to drive forward, kill the pirates on the boat, and stay alive.

"On me!" he shouted to Max and Vernon as he sprinted for the rickety quay where the boat had tied up. Or he tried to sprint. After his abrupt impact with the ground, it started off as more of a pained hobble.

Black smoke was belching from the engine at the stern, and the water started to churn as the prop spun in reverse, starting to draw the boat back off the quay. The lines were still tied, but the quay was built of logs and rough-cut planks, and looked like it would simply tear itself apart rather than keep the boat in place if it applied any serious power. The gangplank was even still leading up to the gunwale. Dan pushed hard, his breath coming in hard gasps as he pounded for the gangplank before the boat could make any headway and knock it off.

The bamboo planks bent under his boots as he hit the plank half a stride ahead of Max and surged up toward the deck. The covering fire had all but ceased as he got closer to the boat, Will's guys unwilling to shoot that close to his team. As he cleared the gunwale and hit the deck, it stopped altogether.

The sudden cease fire left the deck eerily quiet, aside from the chugging thrum of the engines. Dan didn't relax; he wouldn't until he knew that every pirate on the boat was dead. He moved away from the gangplank, clearing the way for Max, Vernon, and Lambert behind him, rifle in his shoulder and pointed back toward the pilothouse, just aft of midships. It was getting light, so he flipped his NVGs up, bending back the brim of his bush hat.

Movement caught his eye from inside the pilothouse. The structure was riddled with bullet holes, the windows shattered and the white-painted wood splintered and smashed. He brought his rifle up, keeping his eyes just over the Aimpoint, the muzzle pointed at the side of the pilothouse, just waiting as he moved forward as smoothly as the boat's slight rocking would allow.

With a lunge, a gunman dropped out of the pilothouse at deck level, bringing a short, black, bullpup rifle to bear, his finger already tightening on the trigger.

Dan didn't even have to move his muzzle. He dropped his head to his sight, the red dot just settling on the man's upper chest, and stroked the trigger three times, as fast as it would reset. The rifle roared, flame stabbing from the short barrel in the early morning dimness, and the shots tracked across the smaller man's upper torso, ripping bloody tracks through his heart and lungs. The bullpup clattered to the deck as he slumped, blood pouring onto the wooden planks.

Dan kicked the rifle away as he stepped over the body, quickly swiveling his rifle to clear the pilothouse. Another corpse was slumped beneath the tiller, a gaping hole in his throat and another bullpup, which the analytical part of Dan's mind identified as a Chinese QBZ-95, still slung around his neck.

He snapped his muzzle aft, toward the hatch leading below, just as Max blasted out a hammer pair, the muzzle blast slapping Dan in the face as he turned. He caught a brief glimpse of movement as whoever Max had been shooting at fell back down the hatch. The glistening crimson spray on the hatch coaming suggested that the man wouldn't be coming back up.

The four of them closed on the hatch, rifles trained on it. There wasn't anywhere else for the pirates to come up on deck. Conversely, there wasn't any other way down.

"I really don't want to go down there," Vernon admitted, as they paused above the hatch, staying just far enough back so that they couldn't be shot through it.

"Neither do I," Dan replied, "but they can still shoot us through the deck if they think of it. The only safe way to go here is to clear this damned thing out." He momentarily wished for a frag, but shrapnel would probably go through the deck just as easily as bullets. He stepped to the hatch, keeping his muzzle trained down it, watching for any pirates waiting for him to silhouette himself. Aside from the corpse at the base of the ladder, its head bloody and deformed by Max's bullets, there was no one in sight.

"Fuck it," he muttered. "Let's do it live." Quickly slinging his rifle, he grabbed the ladder and slid down, hitting the lower deck with a jarring impact, dropping to a squat as he desperately scrambled to bring his weapon back up.

A shot cracked loudly in the dim hold, and Dan was sure he was dead. But he was still breathing, and quickly swung the rifle up, zeroing in on the pirate slumped against the hull beneath a shattered porthole, struggling to bring a Type 56 AK clone up. He apparently couldn't use one arm, so he was trying to shoot the rifle unsupported. It was too dark to see very well, but his chest looked wet, and there was dark fluid around his mouth. Dan put the red dot on his forehead and squeezed the trigger. The rifle's report was painfully loud in the enclosed space, and the pirate's head jerked back, red spattering across the broken remains of the porthole.

He had stepped forward as he fired, and that kept Max from flattening him on the way down. He waited a second for the big man to get his rifle back in the fight, then moved forward, leaving the aft section to Vernon and Lambert.

The hold was packed, pallets of packages of white powder stacked close together. It didn't take a rocket scientist to figure out what they were hauling, especially considering the fact that the intel had pointed to the site as being a drug processing hub. Exactly what connection Yuan had with local drug trafficking was unclear, but that there was a connection was pretty obvious.

"Heroin, you think?" Max asked as they worked their way forward.

"Probably," Dan replied. "The Golden Triangle ain't that far away." There was another corpse lying beneath a smashed porthole, the hull so torn up with bullet holes that he could almost see through it. There was no room for anyone else forward. "I suppose it could be coke or meth or something, but heroin seems to be the most likely option."

"We could always cut one open and taste it," Max suggested. "They always do that on TV."

Dan shot him a *I hope you're kidding* look. "I don't fucking know what heroin tastes like. Do you?"

Max grinned. "Nope. At least now I know that either you don't either, or you're a good liar."

Dan just shook his head, turning back down the other side of the stacks of drug pallets. Vernon and Lambert were waiting for them by the ladder. Vernon gave a thumbs-up. The boat was clear. Dan pointed up the ladder, and Vernon started climbing.

Lambert was looking at the pallets. "I'm guessing we're going to burn the boat or something?" he asked.

"Yeah," Dan said flatly. "You have a problem with that?"

Lambert just shrugged, meeting Dan's eyes evenly, only the faintest hint of insolence in his gaze. "I think it's stupid," he acknowledged. "This is one motherfucker of a payday, and we haven't got the USG looking over our shoulders to make sure we're not 'illicitly profiting.' There are any number of ways we could dispose of this and take home a fuckload of cash. But hey, you're in charge, not me."

Dan looked at him for a moment, trying to get a sense for what the other man was thinking. But Lambert was good at masking what was going on behind those cold shark's eyes of his. Before he could decide, Sam yelled down the hatch for him. "Hey, Dan! You might want to see this."

Turning away from Lambert's too-steady stare and faint smirk, Dan started back up the ladder. He could feel Lambert's eyes on him the whole way up.

Sam was holding a chart, that had been extensively marked up with pens and grease pencils. The annotations were all in Chinese, but one of them was definitely the island where they were presently standing. Most of the rest were still in the Anambas.

Except for one. That one was on the island of Borneo, right on the Malaysian/Indonesian border. There was a lot of extra writing around that one, too. Dan squinted at it, as if concentration might force the Mandarin characters to give up their secrets. "I don't suppose you read Mandarin?" he asked Sam.

"Sorry, bud," the mustachioed man replied. "I specialized in Dari. East Asia hasn't been a huge focus of effort, at least not for trigger-pullers, for a few years now."

Dan checked his watch. "Bag it. We'll get it translated later. We've got another thirty-one minutes before our surveillance blackout ends, and I want to have everything we can snatch up on the Zodes and this place burning in twenty."

He should have expected something to happen. Lambert had folded on the drugs too easily.

"Really?" Sam demanded as he walked up to Dan on the quay. "We're just going to torch a couple million dollars on your say-so, without consulting any of the rest of us?"

Dan looked past him toward the camp. Lambert was watching, the faintest hint of a smirk on his face. *I see how it is, asshole*, he thought, before turning his eyes back to Sam. "Really?" he echoed.

"We're going to do this now?"

"Back at Desaru after the boat's burning is kind of too late, don't you think?" Sam retorted.

Dan looked him in the eye. "The boat's gonna fucking burn," he said stonily. "We're getting paid enough not to get mixed up in this shit."

"Oh really, fucking Boy Scout?" Sam snapped. "No issues with making money killing people, but making money on drugs, oh, that's too fucking far!"

"There's a bit of a difference between pirate hunting on contract and turning into drug traffickers, don't you think?" Dan retorted. "If you can't see the difference, I don't think I can help you."

A couple of the others were starting to gather around the altercation now. Ty looked uncomfortable, but spoke up from behind Sam, where he'd been hanging back a little. "I don't think he's talking about trying to get the stuff back to the States," he said. "Just find a local middle man to sell it to, make a little extra."

"No fucking difference," Dan replied, still looking at Sam. "It's still fucking drug trafficking. And even if I didn't have any moral objection to it, it'd still fuck us if we got caught. It's not worth it. *Especially* given what we're getting paid for this job. Getting greedy is just going to invite trouble."

Ty frowned and shifted his feet. He really looked like a kid caught between siblings having a spat. He was a nice enough guy, and certainly competent enough tactically, but he was more than a little naive, and therefore an easy mark for the less scrupulous among them. Dan was pretty sure Jenny had turned him into her boy toy, and Lambert had him following him around like a puppy half the time.

Sam was still glaring at him, but the glare had lost a little bit of its force. Dan could see the wheels turning behind his eyes. He was calculating, and Dan thought that maybe what he'd said was getting through, at least a little.

Then the other man's eyes hardened again, and he stabbed a finger at Dan. "Doesn't fucking matter," he snarled. "You made that decision by yourself, without bothering to bring it up to the rest of the team. This ain't the fucking mil anymore; you're not a fucking officer, and I don't give a flying fuck what line of authority bullshit you've got going through your head. You don't get to make these decisions without talking to the rest of us."

Cary had come over from the bow of the boat, where he'd been on lookout for any other pirate boats coming in. "Hey, guys, come on," he said. "This ain't the time or the place." Cary had, so far, demonstrated a willingness to follow along and not say too much, though he was always cheerful and friendly when he did say anything. He wasn't the most stellar performer on the team; a little out of shape, without Max's preternatural endurance, he was somewhere in the middle or back of the pack most of the time. "Dan's right, this stuff may as well be radioactive. But the point is, we've got to trust each other, and that means we've got to trust that Dan knows what he's doing."

"Shut up, Skinny-Fat," Sam snapped. "Nobody fucking asked you." He turned back to Dan, then looked over his shoulder. Something in his eyes changed, and he took a deep breath, then looked back up at Dan.

"Fine," he said, still sounding a little bitter. "You may have a point. I still think it was fucking shitty to make the decision without us." He stabbed a finger at Dan. "Next time, you'd better lay it out for the team, or we're going to have problems." He turned and walked away, going back out to the perimeter. Ty stood there for another moment, looking like he wanted to say something, then changed his mind and followed Sam.

Dan looked over at Lambert again. The sandy-haired man was still watching, that same ghostly look of triumph and amusement on his face.

He turned around, to see Max and Brad standing behind him. Max just shot him a crooked half-smile before heading back off the boat, giving him a solid punch to the shoulder as he passed. Brad, as always, was silent and expressionless. The man made "morose" seem happy. Dan had no idea what his deal was; he never talked unless he had to, and then never about himself. But he'd apparently lent the weight of his presence, at least, stand behind Dan.

He followed Max off the boat. They still had work to do, interpersonal problems or not. Those problems worried him, though.

It wasn't that he was on an authority trip, like Sam seemed to think. At least he didn't think he was. He was just trying to get through the job with his life, and those of his teammates, and sense of honor mostly intact. Guys like Max and Vernon seemed to accept that. The job was dangerous enough, without a power play within the team.

But that was starting to look like what he'd have to deal with. Pirates weren't enough, apparently.

He had no idea.

Chapter 10

"*Shang Wei*?" the pilot called out as he pointed. "Look over there."

Feng looked up from his chart, craning his neck to see out the cockpit windows. The Harbin Y-12 had passenger windows, but they didn't provide the kind of view he needed.

He didn't have to ask what the pilot was talking about. The column of greasy black smoke rising above the unnamed Pulau was obvious enough. He looked back down at his chart. "Interesting. Surveillance suggested that there was some activity there, though no one in the Second Department could say for certain if it was Yuan's people or not." He looked back out the window at the black tower of smoke. "Take us lower, to get a better look."

The pilot and copilot shared a look. "If there are hostiles down there..." the pilot began.

"If there *were* hostiles down there, they are probably dead," Feng snapped. "If they aren't, they probably wish that they were. Fly lower, or we will return to Singapore and I will find a different pilot."

The pilot hesitated for a moment, then, without a word, dutifully banked toward the billowing smoke, losing altitude with the turn, spiraling down toward the island and the fire.

The plane descended in silence, then did a long, slow circle above the site of the fire. From the lower altitude, Feng could see that there were in fact several fires, that were beginning to spread to the surrounding jungle. There had been several structures in the camp, all of them now burning. A fishing boat was smoldering at a makeshift quay. There was a lot of smoke, but the wind off the ocean was blowing it inland enough to make out some details. Details that included several of the bodies lying on the ground.

Feng scanned the scene without a word, cataloging what he saw and trying to fill in some of the blanks. Finally, after the third circle, he decided that he'd seen as much as he was going to from the air. "Take us back to Singapore," he said. He moved back and strapped himself into a seat behind the cockpit without another word. He started working up the plan for the ground reconnaissance in his head.

By the time the *Jiaolong* team got to the island, the fires had pretty much burned themselves out. They had moved in to the beach on the motor launches from the *Xinjiang*, a freighter whose captain had been informed in no uncertain terms that he would cooperate with Feng and his men, or face serious sanctions if and when he returned to China.

All of Feng's men were in khakis that couldn't be immediately identified as Chinese military uniforms, generic chest rigs, and SAR-21 rifles in place of the standard QBZ-95s. Feng was taking the low-key nature of this mission seriously. The SAR-21, a Singaporean bullpup not all that dissimilar from the Chinese QBZ-95, was far more widespread in Malaysia and Indonesia than the Chinese weapons.

Their hands were on their weapons, heads up and alert as they landed, but it was obvious that any opposition forces were long gone. Scavengers had already set in on the bodies, and even the ruins had stopped smoking except in a few places. Still, without any unnecessary words, Feng signaled to his teams to push out and form a perimeter. Shen and his squad he kept close, as he started up the slight slope toward what looked like it might once have been a sizable solid structure. Unlike some officers he knew, Feng carried the same loadout as the rest; rifle, magazines, and all.

The place stank of smoke, chemicals, rot, feces, and death. Feng had to breathe shallowly lest he break into a vicious coughing fit. He stepped around a corpse that looked like it had been chewed on by several varieties of jungle life, that was still swarming with flies, a black, writhing mass glistening red and gray between the clumps of insects. He noted the brass cartridge casings scattered in the mud around the site. This had definitely been a raid. Not that there had been any doubt before.

There wasn't much left of the shack. Feng stood there for a moment, his rifle slung and staring at the jumble of charred timbers and collapsed, blackened tin sheeting. With a gesture, he got the squad to work clearing the crumpled walls away.

Feng watched the work, his eyes moving to scan the rest of the encampment from time to time. Even burned to the ground, the shelters where the workers had slept and processed and sorted the drugs were identifiable as such. If there had been anything there of importance, it would have been in the hard shelter.

Shen stepped up to him. "*Shang Wei*," he ventured, "may I ask a question?"

Feng simply nodded.

"Our objective is to kill or capture *Shang Xiao* Yuan, is it not?" When Feng nodded again, he forged ahead. "Then I fail to see what we are doing here. No intelligence I have seen suggests that Yuan is here, or ever has been. Every bit of information points to him staying on Pulau Matak."

"So it does," Feng agreed. "But Yuan is not the *sole* objective here." When Shen looked puzzled, he looked around at the squad sifting

99

through the wreckage and stepped away. "Walk with me."

He led the way back down toward the beach until he was confident that he was out of earshot of the rest. "I received a separate set of orders from *Zhong Jiang* Feng before we departed," he explained. "They were for my eyes only, but under the circumstances, I believe that you should know." He took a deep breath. "Yuan stole more than just the *Zhaotong*. He must have had this in mind for a long time; he had help. Help that came from some of the highest levels of the information warfare forces.

"Before he deserted, taking an entire frigate with him, Yuan stole a great deal of extremely sensitive information, information which could do a great deal of damage to China's interests abroad if it were to become public. I have heard from reliable sources that he has been using these files to attempt to blackmail the Central Committee into leaving him alone to carve out his little kingdom here in the South China Sea. We are here because that cannot be allowed to happen."

He glanced over at the shack, which was almost completely cleared. "Yes, Yuan is almost certainly on Matak. Surveillance satellites believe that the *Zhaotong* is there as well, though he has been strangely effective at hiding the ship, enough so that some are beginning to suspect that he has been informed of surveillance schedules. While Yuan is the primary target, we *must* ensure that he has not disseminated the stolen information for release in case he is captured. That means that we cannot simply strike at the head of the snake. We must investigate every outpost he has, which means disassembling his network."

"Just as our unknown rivals appear to be doing," Shen observed.

Feng frowned at the carnage around them. "Indeed. This presents an additional complication."

"Who do you think it is?" Shen asked. "The Americans?"

"They would seem to be the most likely candidates, yes," Feng agreed. "But I spoke to *Zhong Jiang* Feng after the last incident, and while he agrees that it is probably Americans, he needs proof. We could accuse them of interfering in our affairs in this matter, only to have them deny it, unless we have solid evidence."

"So, we want to capture some of them?"

"Ideally, we will accomplish our mission, neutralize Yuan, retrieve the stolen data, and be gone before that becomes necessary. Directly confronting the Americans about this situation could be nearly as damaging as losing the stolen files to them. If we succeed, and they fail, this sordid situation need never see the light of day." He grimaced. "The Americans will certainly never admit to having forces in the area if those forces failed their task. It will become an embarrassment that their politicians will eagerly sweep under the rug, lest one of them take the blame."

"So," Shen said, as the squad leader approached, shaking his head, "we are in a race."

"Indeed we are, my friend," Feng said. "A deadly one." He stepped forward to meet the squad leader.

The man had good news and bad news. "There is nothing of any intelligence value in the wreckage, *Shang Wei*," he said. "There were a few papers, burned beyond legibility, and the remains of a tablet, but nothing is readable."

Feng's lips tightened at the news. The tablet being left behind suggested that it hadn't held the stolen files, presuming the Americans, or whoever they were, even knew about that aspect. There was, unfortunately, no way to know if there had been other computers on the target that had been taken. At least, there was no way to know until he was recalled, to be sent to a labor camp or simply shot, because the information had appeared in public.

He stared at the wreckage of the camp for a moment, then turned and started toward the motor launch at a brisk walk. "We will move up our timetable," he decided. "We also need to take steps to disrupt or neutralize our mysterious rivals."

"Whoever these guys are, they either have some serious backing, or some amazing luck," Henson said, as he laid a file on Lawrence's desk.

She looked up from her computer to look at the file, then up at him. "Explain," she said. She had enough on her plate already without having to decipher Henson being cryptic.

He motioned to the file. "There was another hit on a suspected Yuan holding, this time a camp on an island just off Pulau Airabu. Strangely enough, the hit just so happened to go down during a down period in surveillance over the area."

That got Lawrence's attention. She ignored the email on the monitor and reached for the file. "How the hell did that happen?"

"Like I said," Henson replied, as she skimmed the file, noting the overhead imagery, "they're either very lucky, or they're getting support from somebody who knows our surveillance schedule, and was able to tell them when we wouldn't have eyes in the sky over the target area."

Lawrence raised an eyebrow. Henson didn't need to elaborate why that was serious news; she was well aware of the implications. Whether or not Bogart was telling her the truth about having no knowledge of the operation—and he damned well better be, or she'd see him destroyed so thoroughly that if he managed to avoid a lengthy stay in Federal prison, he'd be standing on a streetcorner with a cardboard sign for the rest of his life—*somebody* high up was running an op on her turf without her knowledge. And that was utterly unacceptable.

The file was a combination of reports and overhead imagery, both before and after. The reports were as dry as always, setting the known facts out as tersely as possible. The anomaly had been spotted once drone coverage had come back on-line, after a down window of approximately ninety minutes.

"Anomaly" was a rather euphemistic term, Lawrence thought, as she picked up the "after" imagery. What had been a camp that saw fairly regular traffic from what appeared to be fishing boats, but were almost certainly smuggling craft, had turned into a blazing inferno belching thick, greasy, black smoke skyward. What looked like one of the smuggling boats was tied up at the quay, also burning.

"And we got no imagery of the attackers on the approach or on the way out?" she demanded.

Henson shook his head. "The surveillance was focused pretty tightly on the camp, since until recently, our entire interest has been in Yuan's activities. If they came from anywhere outside of a roughly one-kilometer bubble, the drone wouldn't have seen them."

"What about satellite?"

"Again, we're dealing with tasking," Henson said patiently. "Yuan has been viewed as something of a side problem, especially considering the Chinese' increasing aggressiveness with the *Antietam*, up north."

Lawrence grimaced. That rather summed up the entire situation. Her station had far more pressing worries than some unknown factor killing pirates and drug traffickers on some flyspeck islands in the West Pacific. Most of the station would probably be cheering the killers on, depending on who they were. But the possibility of an illegal American operation was diverting attention that was better suited dealing with the PRC's expansionism in the Spratlys and Paracels, or Jemaah Islamiyah in Indonesia. It was pissing her off that she had to deal with this at all, much less that she had the Ambassador breathing down her neck about it.

She looked up at Henson. Even though the man was a soft-bodied geek through-and-through, he returned her gaze steadily. He was good at what he did, knew it, and refused to be intimidated by superiors, even Station Chiefs who could destroy his career with a word.

"We still have no solid indications as to who is behind this?" she asked quietly.

He shook his head again. "Nothing. Honestly, if it's any of our people, they are doing an unusually admirable job of keeping their mouths shut about it. Usually an op like this would have been leaked *somewhere* by now."

"Is it possible that it's a JSOC op, and General Taylor is playing turf wars with the Agency?" she asked.

Henson frowned. "Doubtful. I don't know enough about Taylor to say for sure whether or not it's his style, but I'd think that our operations and JSOC's would be too tightly intertwined by now. Besides, if it *was* JSOC, that would mean SEALs for this kind of profile, and the nearest platform for them to operate off of would be the *Antietam*." He shook his head again. "There simply haven't been any indicators of JSOC's presence in the area. No helos, no SWCC boats, no naval platforms to base off of. Anything this low-profile, JSOC has always 'sheep-dipped' their personnel to the Agency. It just doesn't fit."

"With this kind of effectiveness, who else could it be?" she asked, looking back at the overheads. "They were in and out in less than ninety minutes, apparently neutralized everyone and burned the place down. That certainly doesn't say 'Indonesians' to me."

"Not to me, either," Henson agreed. "They can barely police the closer-in islands, much less getting out into the Anambas to go after the biggest pirate gang in the region. It's too far from the Philippines..." He thought for a moment, visibly hesitated, then suggested, "What if it's the Chinese?"

That was a thought. Not a pleasant one, either. In general, the Chinese had been fairly circumspect in their interventions abroad, preferring to work quietly, taking advantage of other nations' military adventures and chaos to benefit economically. But with the proximity to the growing pressure-cooker of the South China Sea and the fact that Yuan was a high-ranking Chinese officer who had absconded with an entire frigate and its crew, would they be willing to step out of their usual modus operandi to deal with him more directly?

It would be a definite shift in Chinese policy. And it could have pretty far-reaching implications.

Lawrence sat and stared at the imagery, thinking it over. None of the options looked very good. Whether it was a rogue American operation or a Chinese paramilitary clean-up crew, it demanded attention in a part of the world where resources were scarce enough, thanks to the focus on the Middle East, that the Spratlys and the Paracels were sucking most of them up. Meanwhile, this little sideshow could quickly get out of control, especially sitting on a major shipping lane the way that it was.

"See if you can put some more feelers out," she said, handing the file back to Henson. "And get 24/7 surveillance coverage over the Anambas. I want to know when the next attack happens, and I want to know where the hitters are coming from."

Hu Jian's tea shop was a small affair for how popular it was. Of course, the fact that Hu was something of a facilitator for all sorts of business deals across Southeast Asia had more than a little to do with the shop's popularity. Most of the men and women who crammed into the tiny shop were only very peripherally interested in the tea.

Feng fit right in in that sense. The tea was good, but he needed to get to see Hu himself, and the fat man was very busy. Unfortunately, as much as he might like to, Feng couldn't simply barge in front and threaten either Hu or his present clients with grievous bodily harm and/or imprisonment somewhere as close to Lop Nur as he could manage if Hu didn't shut up and deal with him right then. No, this called for more subtlety, and while he had received enough training in tradecraft to know that and know how to practice it, it still went against the grain.

So he waited his turn, sipping tea and trying to look as bored and disinterested as possible, while Hu held court in a small corner booth of the shop. In a way, it was an interesting exercise, watching who came to talk to the little man. There were *laowai* and Han both, men and women, all well-dressed. Some rather too well-dressed for the neighborhood. While Hu hadn't exactly set up in a poor section of Singapore, he had his reasons for fronting his operation with a small, traditional tea shop rather than a large, glass-fronted office building. Not all of his clients were entirely aboveboard, and even those that were often had enough concerns about industrial espionage that a high-profile meeting place was the last thing they wanted when making arrangements through Hu.

Of course, that meant that the shop was packed to the gills with the same industrial espionage agents that the businessmen were worried about. Hu had been operating his network for long enough that anyone interested knew that his shop was the place to hear interesting things.

Feng knew he would have to ensure most of those people were out of earshot when he spoke to Hu. His concerns were rather more dire than who had an interesting new business deal that they wished to keep secret from their competitors.

Finally, his turn came. The beefy mountain of a Malaysian bodyguard, who had to be taking some serious steroids to be that size, waved him forward.

He slid into the booth across from Hu, and folded his hands on the table in front of him. He looked across at Hu. The photo in the man's dossier was obviously old; he had more gray in his temples, and seemed to have grown an extra chin since it had been taken. He wore a suit but no tie, his collar open to allow his chins some extra room.

He knew what Hu saw. A fit, hard-eyed young man, his hair cropped short, in an inexpensive but impeccable business suit. He probably looked like any number of ambitious young corporate sharks looking to advance themselves no matter what.

His next words gave the lie to that impression. "Good afternoon, *tongzhi* Hu," he said in Mandarin. "How is our grandfather faring?"

The fat man's eyes snapped into sharp focus, and his chins quivered a little as he started. It must have been some time since he heard the code phrase. He stared at Feng for a moment, then snapped his fingers. The Malaysian bodyguard leaned over to listen to his hastily whispered instructions before straightening and announcing that the shop was closed for the remainder of the day. He and several of his fellows immediately began ushering the loudly protesting patrons outside.

Hu watched them, and leaned forward over the table when he

was confident that none were close enough to hear. "I do not know you," he hissed. "If *tongzhi* Liao had business for me, why would he not come himself?"

"That doesn't matter," Feng said coldly. "What matters is that I am here, and that *is* the correct passphrase. Your protocols have not changed. Can I expect your cooperation, or do I need to report to Liao that you have apparently decided to no longer perform your patriotic duty to the People's Republic?"

Hu glared at him. "I fought the Vietnamese in 1979, before you were even born," he snapped. "I have been performing my patriotic duty to the People's Republic for longer than you have been alive. Do not presume to belittle my service because I am now old and fat." He straightened. "Now, who are you and what do you want?"

Feng didn't relax, though he did allow his tone to become more polite. "I am *Shang Wei* Feng Kung of the *Jiaolong*," he introduced himself. "I am here on a sensitive mission, and I need your intelligence support."

Hu didn't move or change expression. "What sort of intelligence?"

"There is a paramilitary force operating somewhere between here and Borneo," Feng explained. "They are not ours. My suspicion is that they are American, but I have no proof of it, nor do I have the information I need to counter them. They present a risk to my mission. I need to know who they are, and where they are based."

Hu raised an eyebrow. "What do you know about them?"

Feng thought for a moment before answering. Technically, while he had been given Hu's bona fides and activation signal, he had not been given clearance to read the man in on his own mission. But if he was going to get the information he needed, he was going to have to give him *something*.

"They appear to be targeting the interests of former *Shang Xiao* Yuan Wei," he said.

"Ah, I see," Hu replied, folding his hands over his expansive belly. "And the risk you are worried about is that they will get to the deserter and his men before you do."

He should have expected Hu to see through to what was going on quickly. No one could build the kind of business network that he had without being extremely perceptive, as well as lightning quick at putting the pieces of a puzzle together. The sleepy-eyed, open-collared fat man was deceptive. Of course, that was also what made him useful to the Second Department.

"Do you have a particular area I should have my people start looking?" Hu asked.

Feng shook his head. "Unfortunately, no," he replied. "Though I suspect they may be based somewhere near Singapore. It would provide much of the resources they might seek to obtain locally."

Hu nodded. "And how do I reach you?"

"I have all of the points of contact Liao set up with you," Feng said. "You may contact me using any of them."

"Good," Hu said, nodding again. "I will have some information for you soon. Now, if you do not mind, I wish to try to salvage some of the business you interrupted, while there is still time left in the day."

"I don't know," Decker said. He had shown up in Desaru with another fifty contractors the day before. "The office might see it as a distraction from getting Yuan himself."

"Are we trying to shut this operation down," Dan demanded, "or just get a trophy to put on somebody's wall to make them feel better about 'doing something?' Because I thought we were being paid to burn this fucker's whole rodeo down. He's obviously got contacts with the larger underworld in the area; there's no way in hell that he could build the operation that he has overnight without 'em. This is the first solid indication we've gotten of any of those contacts. If we can start cutting his connections with the locals, he might start to wither on the vine. Then we can move in and pick him off when he's weakened."

Decker sighed impatiently. "You're right, the entire mission is to shut down Yuan's operation. *Yuan's* operation. The office is going to have some serious second thoughts about okaying an op in Indonesia or Malaysia proper. They'll say that there's no sign that this site on Borneo is in any way run by Yuan or his people. The Anambas have become enough of a no-man's land that we've had a fair degree of latitude operating there, and that's fine with the client. But going into actual sovereign Malaysian or Indonesian territory is going to be another matter."

Dan snorted. "Don't give me that shit," he replied. Any fear of Decker's position from training had disappeared after the last two ops in combat. "Show me the agreement with the government of Singapore to let us operate out of Desaru. Show me the agreement with Jakarta to go into the Anambas. Legalities are meaningless on this operation, and you and I both know it, so let's cut the crap. This site is right on the Malaysian-Indonesian borderland, and obviously neither country has seen fit to do anything about it, if they even know it's there. There ain't shit on the imagery—granted, it's almost a year old—so it can't be that big. Considering it's probably all drugs, guns, and human trafficking, I doubt anybody is going to shed any tears about the place getting burned to the ground and all the scumbags shot in the face. If they really need more of a justification, tell 'em that Yuan is using this as a transshipment point for drugs he's bringing in from the Golden Triangle and slaves he's probably taking off of ships he's interdicting. Shutting it down will definitely put a crimp in his operation; how is he supposed to reap the rewards of his piracy if he can't sell what he steals?"

Decker stared at him across the map for a moment, with the same blank, dead-eyed, appraising stare that he'd worn during the train-up. Then he cracked a slight smile and shook his head.

"I knew I picked you as a team lead for a reason, Tackett," he said. "For what it's worth, I agree with you. This could not only help further isolate Yuan, but it just might get us some additional intel about who he's working with. I'll send it up. But don't be too surprised if it gets kicked back. The office is just as full of the same sort of soft-suited political assholes as any other client you've ever worked for. If one of them gets the heebie-jeebies about this, it'll be off."

He stood up. "In the meantime, get your planning process started. We're going to be stepping the tempo up soon, now that we're almost at full strength, so we won't have time to fuck around getting prepped if the 'go' comes through from the office."

Dan grinned. "Way ahead of you," he said. "We've already started."

Chapter 11

Holy hell, Dan thought. *We just might have bitten off more than we can chew.*

He had expected the trafficking hub to be a relatively small affair, another camp buried in the jungle to hide it from prying eyes. Google Earth still didn't show anything but triple canopy rainforest at its location. What he hadn't been expecting was the small city that had been hacked out of the jungle in a relatively short time.

Somebody had put a lot of thought into it, too. Concrete slabs formed most of the roads and walkways, between surprisingly well-laid out buildings. Granted, the buildings were mostly made of hasty frames covered in corrugated sheet metal, and the whole thing looked like it could be torn down in a few hours, but it was a far cry from the anticipated tiny jungle camp of tents and rude lean-tos.

Not only was it big, it was teeming with people, most of them armed. Dan had started to develop an eye for the ethnic differences in Southeast Asia over the last couple of weeks, and he could see Javanese, Malays, Chinese, Vietnamese, Japanese, and even a few Filipinos. Most of them moved in groups generally broken up along ethnic lines. He was pretty sure most of the Chinese were from one or another Triad; more than one was present, just judging by the general hostility he saw between a few of the groups. The Japanese, well-dressed and favoring handguns, as opposed to the more heavily-armed groups, had to be Yakuza. He knew that the traditional Japanese mafia had a major hand in human trafficking, and this was as good a place as any to pick up more slaves.

More striking were the Arabs. He first spotted a group of them, mostly wearing the kind of tracksuits that had been identifiers for insurgent gunmen in Iraq over ten years before, armed with mostly AKs and a few ARs, surrounding a man in a traditional white thobe and keffiyeh. They were a long way from home, but considering the taste a lot of Arabs seemed to have for Indonesian and Filipino forced laborers, that shouldn't have been all that surprising.

"This is very, very bad," Vernon said from the passenger seat. They had gotten a couple of diesel Ford Rangers, a Suzuki Equator, and a Kia van when they flew into Sematan. It had been a long drive, but the camp was far enough from the coast that they didn't want to risk an amphibious assault, nor did they want to land and use the same port at

Temajuk that the pirates used. Now it was looking like the port might make for the only proper exit plan they might have. "This is like riding into Darra Adam Khel with a platoon to try to shut that down." The Darra Adam Khel was an ancient, massive arms market on the Afghan-Pakistan border, famous for being utterly lawless and a bad place for foreigners.

"Who would have thought they'd have something this big built in less than a year?" Dan asked. The latest imagery they had was almost a year old. He blew a sigh past his nose. "I think we need to wave off. Especially with so little ass." Decker hadn't been joking about the tempo going up. He also hadn't freed up any of the new arrivals, or Will's or Sean's teams. This was all Dan's show, and he had far too few people to pull it off. They might manage a quick snatch of a few slaves, maybe get a little more intel on Yuan's involvement with the local drug and slave trades, but other than that, they weren't going to make so much as a dent in this place. Certainly not if they were going to walk away from it. The most support Decker had authorized had been one of the yachts sitting offshore with four Zodiacs on standby to extract from the Malaysian coast.

What really bothered him, aside from the fact that no matter what he tried to do, this target was going to go relatively unscathed, was the fact that he knew Lambert was going to make hay out of this, one way or another. After the incident with the drugs, he'd heard from several people that Lambert was starting to openly spread discontent through the team and with the other teams about Dan's leadership. This wasn't going to look good for him any way it came out. The fact that he'd made the call to push forward on the intel they had wasn't going to be good enough for Lambert. Worse, he was sure that Lambert would be just as pissed that he didn't get a chance at any "grateful little brown fucking machines," to use the man's own choice of words.

He'd been sorely tempted to just shoot Lambert after that conversation. It had already become abundantly obvious that the man was as amoral as they came, and several whispers suggested that he was gunning for Dan. He no longer trusted the man at all. He was sleeping with the door locked and his rifle in the bed with him at this point; he fully expected Lambert to make an attempt on his life eventually. He was cunning enough to hold off until a fight made it plausibly deniable, but Dan had no doubt that Lambert would murder him and sleep like a baby afterward.

But if Lambert didn't have a conscience, Dan still did. He couldn't justify killing one of his own men in cold blood. So, while he dreaded what the man might do without supervision, he kept his distance as much as possible. Which was why Lambert was presently in the Suzuki, a few blocks away.

He shook off the reverie. However badly his reputation and

109

position was going to suffer from getting all the way there and calling off the op, there was no other choice. No other survivable choice, anyway. He reached for the radio to call the recall.

Before he could press the transmit button, however, the radio crackled with Max's voice. "We've got a problem."

He snatched up the handset and asked, "What's going on?"

"Some of the locals seem to have decided they don't like our looks," Max replied. His voice was calm, but Dan could just hear yelling in either Javanese or Malay; he couldn't tell which. Needless to say, the yelling didn't sound friendly.

"Can you reverse out?" he asked.

"Negative," was the reply. "They've got us boxed in. We'll need support here shortly. And by 'shortly,' I mean right fucking now."

"Motherfucker!" Dan swore, punching the steering wheel as he stomped on the gas, startling a wizened Javanese man hawking what looked like marijuana on the corner. The little man waved a fist at the pickup truck, yelling imprecations at the foreigners disturbing the peace. It would have been funny if the situation wasn't so dire.

The place might not be a regular city, but it was just as congested as any city Dan had seen in the Third World. Granted, it was a good bet that at least ninety-five percent of the people on the streets were criminals, terrorists, or a combination of the two, but that wasn't going to make it any easier to get through; shooting their way through was just going to make the entire camp descend on them, Black Hawk Down style.

He wove through the narrow thoroughfares, trying to avoid the knots of heavily armed men, hookers, drug dealers, and the hundreds of vehicles, ranging from rickshaws and bicycles to technicals and expensive new SUVs. In the seat beside him, Vernon was already pulling plate carriers and rifles out of the gear bag crammed beneath the dash at his feet. This was probably about to go loud.

"We're starting to attract attention," Vernon warned. Dan could see that already. They were moving a lot more quickly than was normal, and they had already come dangerously close to plowing into one group of Malay pirates, dressed in loose t-shirts and headbands, toting a variety of rifles from AKs to brand-new looking SAR-21s.

"Do we know what we're going to say to try to defuse this little situation?" Vernon asked, bracing himself against the dash as Dan whipped around a corner and nearly collided with an overloaded rickshaw that was blocking half the road. "Or are we just going to go in shooting?"

"I'm still hoping to get out of here without shooting," Dan replied. "I'm hoping that the sight of the roundeyes having backup might get the locals to back off a little. I can only imagine that this kind of confrontation is actually a fairly regular occurrence around here. It *is* an outlaw border town, after all."

"Here's hoping you're right, buddy," Vernon said. "Because this could get real ugly, real fast."

"No shit," Dan answered. The first shot fired was going to wake up the hornet's nest. They'd be lucky to get anybody out intact.

The next turn brought Max's van into view. The situation was worse than Max had made it sound.

The van was solidly boxed in. Several tires had been rolled behind it, and a pickup truck with a CIS .50 mounted in the bed was almost touching the front bumper. If the gunner got twitchy, everyone in the van was going to be hamburger in seconds.

The lane was narrow, with tin shacks crowding to a few feet on either side of the van. One side of the street was lined with short, skinny gunmen, aiming a motley mix of rifles and submachine guns at the van.

"This is even worse than I expected," Vernon commented. He'd already shouldered into his plate carrier, and was bringing his SG 553 up onto his lap as he handed Dan his own rig. "Are any of the other vics close enough?"

"They're not going to be able to get in here," he said. "This is about as perfect a fire-sack as they could have set up. If I didn't know better, I'd think this was a deliberate ambush."

Vernon looked across at him. "You think maybe it was?"

"I doubt it," Dan said as he hastily got his plate carrier fastened around his ribs. "Let's leave discussion for later."

At that moment, one of the scrawny, gun-toting men on the side of the lane seemed to notice the pickup that had just pulled up behind the cornered van. The little man's eyes widened as he saw two large, armored Westerners in the truck, and his mouth opened to yell as his rusty AK started to rise.

We're all going to die, Dan thought, as time seemed to slow down. *We're all going to die in this miserable back alley for absolutely nothing, and it's my fault.*

Even as the thought flashed through his mind, he was bringing his rifle up and over the steering wheel. He'd be damned if he went out without a fight. He wasn't looking at the little man with the AK, though; Vernon was closer and had a better shot. He was focused on the .50 gunner.

While the thin-skinned vehicles they were in wouldn't even slow down the AK's 7.62 rounds, that .50 could go through both trucks long-ways. It was the worst of a slew of lethal possibilities, so he hoped to at least take the gunner out before getting torn to shreds by rifle fire.

He was close enough to see the look on the gunner's face as the man realized that things were about to go loud. The man tensed, even as Dan's Aimpoint settled high on his chest, just above the heavy machine gun's receiver. Desperate to get the first shot off, Dan slapped the trigger as soon as the dot hit the gunner's torso.

The sound of the shot was painfully loud in the cab of the truck, and Dan's ears were ringing immediately. The windshield spider-webbed around the bullet hole, obscuring his view of his target, but he was gorilla-gripping the forearm to hold the rifle locked against the top of the steering wheel, continuing to dump rounds through the disintegrating glass at the gunner, hoping he was either hitting or at least keeping the man's head down.

Vernon had started shooting a split second behind him, dumping a mag as fast as he could squeeze the trigger, tracking the barrel along the line of gunmen on the side of the street. Flame and shards of glass were exploding from the van's windows ahead of them, as Max, Jenny, and Bill opened fire on their own. Dan had momentarily forgotten that Jenny was in the vehicle; she had doubtless been agitating to start shooting as soon as they'd been stopped.

The windshield finished shattering with a cascade of broken glass pouring over the dashboard. There was no sign of the .50 gunner; either Dan had killed or seriously wounded him, or he'd ducked out of the line of fire. The CIS .50 was pointed uselessly at the sky. Most of the gunmen on side of the road were down, having been caught by surprise by the sudden fusillade from their flank. A few were still moving feebly, and it looked like a couple had ducked behind the building, but there were no gunmen still on their feet within Dan's line of sight.

Dan grabbed the handset, keeping his rifle up on the steering wheel with his firing hand. "Bail out and get back here to the truck!" he yelled over the ringing in his ears.

No sooner had he said that than a bullet snapped straight through the cab, hitting the dash with an audible *bang*. Dan jerked his head back to look behind them, to see at least a dozen ragged gunmen pouring into the lane from a few houses down. "Disregard," he sent, before Max could reply. "We have contact rear. Bailing out, moving to the west."

Vernon had already twisted around in his seat, not an easy thing for a man of his size, wearing a plate carrier, and was already shooting back, his 553 braced against the door frame. Rapid shots sprayed brass inside the vehicle, one of them painfully wedging itself inside Dan's plate carrier before he could flip it out. The gunmen on the street scattered, trying to avoid the bullets shredding air, dirt, and corrugated metal.

Dan kicked his door open, even as he saw Max, Jenny, and Bill scramble clear of the van. Jenny and Bill got out on the right side, which was where the gunmen had been lined up; not the best choice, but the sliding door was on that side. Jenny apparently decided to make up for it by spraying a full mag at every body she could see, giving the corrugated metal building a couple of bursts for good measure. *Damn, that is one bloodthirsty bitch.*

Bill was visibly limping, one leg of his khaki shorts wet with blood. He almost had to drag Jenny back around the van to where Max was covering over the hood.

Dan took it all in with a glance as he went out the door, then focused down the lane, toward the gunmen who were trying to get shots off at them. In the distance, he could hear someone start yelling in Javanese over a loudspeaker. He couldn't make out the words, but it sure sounded like they'd just kicked the hornet's nest, and the hornets were starting to swarm on them.

A shaggy-haired man wielding an AK popped out from behind a pile of tires and trash, ripping off a wild burst in their general direction. Dan squeezed off two rapid shots, catching the man in the throat and then under the chin as he jerked backward from the impact. He fell half in the street, blood pouring out of his shattered skull onto the concrete.

Behind him, he heard a crash as Max or Jenny kicked the door to the shack on the west side of the street open. Max's voice yelled at them both over the hammering of gunfire. "Turn and go! On me!"

The last syllable was nearly drowned out by gunfire. A stuttering roar of automatic 5.56 fire split the air from the far side of the pickup, as Vernon flipped his selector to "auto" and ripped off the rest of his mag down the street at the gathering gunmen, and more fire echoed from behind Dan, as either Max, Bill, or Jenny shot at some of the survivors of the first group.

Vernon pounded past behind him, gasping out, "Last man!" Dan put another few rounds down before turning and following him the few paces into the shack.

It really was a shack, little more than a rough frame with sheet metal walls nailed onto it. It provided no cover, only concealment. It was going to have to do for the moment; Dan had no intentions of trying to hard-point there anyway. That was just a good way to get surrounded and overrun. They may as well just shoot themselves in the head.

"Bill, where are you hit?" he asked, as he rocked a fresh mag into his rifle.

"High in the ass cheek," the lean, hawk-like older man replied, as dry and deadpan as ever. "Missed the femoral, and didn't hit bone, near as I can tell. I'll limp a little, but I'll be fine." Considering that the former Ranger was sporting a few old bullet scars, Dan trusted he knew how to differentiate a flesh wound from a life-threatening hole.

"Anybody else hit?" he asked. When he got all negative replies, he grabbed the radio again. "All stations, this is Tack. Bonfire, I say again, Bonfire. Rendezvous at Rally Point Omega." He briefly considered calling the other elements in to provide more firepower to break out with, but that would mean staying in place for longer. Judging by the rising noise he was hearing outside, that was going to be a very bad idea.

Without waiting for further acknowledgments, he hefted his rifle and looked for a back door. There wasn't one. *Easy enough to fix*, he thought, as he lifted a booted foot and kicked one of the sheets of corrugated tin right next to one of the support posts. With an ear-splitting screech, the nails holding the sheet metal up tore through, and the sheet flapped free, or at least free enough to get a body through.

"On me," he said. "We're moving." His rifle in his shoulder, he pushed through the gap and into the alley beyond. Vernon was right behind him, wrenching the panel completely free as he bulled through to cover Dan's back.

The alley looked pretty much exactly like the street they had just left; narrow, dirty, and lined with similarly flimsy shacks. Even as Dan got his footing and found a pile of refuse to take a knee behind, a knot of five men burst out of a shanty about a hundred yards ahead. They were all armed to the teeth, and one of them was pointing in their general direction.

They might not have seen us yet, Dan thought. *Better hold fire until we have to; every shot is going to draw more attention from this point out. The less they can pinpoint where we are, the better odds we've got.*

Jenny apparently did not share his opinion. She dropped to a knee next to him, lifted her rifle to her shoulder, and ripped off a burst before he could caution her not to.

What the fuck is going through this chick's head?! he thought furiously, seriously regretting bringing her along. He'd needed the extra gun, though, and there hadn't been much foot-slogging expected. So much for trying to slip away while the locals tried to figure out just what had just happened. Granted, the odds of the group ahead being an innocent neighborhood watch were pretty slim; this was an outlaw town devoted to smuggling the worst sorts of human misery and slavery, after all. But if you go looking for trouble, you're going to find more than you can deal with, and they were already up to their necks in it as it was.

She hadn't even hit any of them that he could see, and now she had their full and undivided attention. They scattered across the narrow lane, ducking into gaps between shacks, and started returning fire. Bullets *crack*ed past, building to a crackling roar as Jenny's mag ran dry and she started scrambling to reload.

Leaving recriminations for later, Dan rose above the pile of refuse, rifle in his shoulder and seeking a target. Just as he rose up, he caught a glimpse of a head disappearing behind a pile of tires; he might be able to shoot through them, but he was generally leery about shooting at targets he couldn't quite see. Even as he started to take up the slack on the trigger anyway, movement in his peripheral vision drew his gaze. Another man was leaning out from a narrow gap between shacks, his SKS in his shoulder, and apparently pointed right at Dan.

114

His heart racing, he snapped his barrel over toward the new target, the trigger breaking almost just as the dot crossed the man's shoulders. The shot missed, punching through the sheet metal behind his head, but it was enough to make him flinch off-target. It bought Dan the split second he needed to put a pair of shots, so close together that the reports sounded like a single blast of sound, into the man's upper chest. The man staggered back, dropping his rifle, and Dan shot him four more times, until he fell to the ground.

By then, Jenny had her rifle back up, and was firing at the rest of the men down the street. Unfortunately, there were more of them coming, and if they tried to kill everyone coming after them, they'd never get away. Grabbing Jenny by the shoulder strap of her kit, he spun her around and shoved her back toward Vernon. "Fall back, dammit!" he snarled, as he hammered pairs of shots at anyone showing themselves down the street.

More fire began to snap down the street to his left, far too close for comfort, but after a second, he realized that it was coming from behind him, and Max was bellowing at him to move his ass. Ducking below the refuse pile, he looked back to see the pudgy, pale man pressed against a shanty wall, ripping shots off to cover him. Getting his feet under him, he surged up and sprinted along the opposite wall, heading for Bill, Vernon, and Jenny, who were pushing forward just beyond Max.

He pushed just about ten yards back before turning to take up the fire, giving Max cover to bound back. Max yelled as he passed, "Turning right!" Dan ripped off another ten shots before turning to follow the rest, who had ducked down a cross-street, or alley, or whatever the hell it was. It was just like every other lane in the town; narrow, filthy, and a complete fucking nightmare to fight in.

For the moment, at least, they weren't taking any fire, though that could change at any second, if the enemies they'd just been trading bullets with pursued them fast enough, or sent word ahead to cut them off. They were still a good mile of twisting, turning, narrow lanes short of the edge of the camp. It was going to be a long haul.

Vernon had taken point, with Bill and Jenny close behind him, Max and Dan bringing up the rear. Jenny looked spitting mad, as if she was offended that these little bastards had dared to shoot at her. Max was just sweaty. Bill was bleeding, but moving gamely in spite of it.

Vernon wasn't taking a straight path; that would make it too easy for whichever faction they'd run afoul of to head them off. Dan was really wishing he knew more about who all was operating there; if they could get two or more of the factions fighting, they might be able to slip away unnoticed in the chaos.

There was a lot of shouting, some of it over loudspeakers, and some shooting going on around them. It was hard to tell for sure if all of it was about them; there were at least ten different languages in play, and

English was not one of them. There was definitely some shooting going on that wasn't close enough to be directed at them. But that didn't mean much. There were no friendlies there. They had to keep moving, and assume anyone they met along the way was an enemy at this point.

Unfortunately, they didn't have a map of the town, and after a few more twists and turns, Dan wasn't sure if they were really getting any closer to getting out, or if they were just going in circles. They'd taken a few potshots, and returned fire, but they were going to run low on ammo soon, and if they weren't out before that happened, they were probably dead. Actually, they were almost certainly dead in that case.

No sooner had that thought crossed his mind than they ran across a slightly wider street, just as a large group of gunmen, looking a little better kitted out than the rag-tag outlaws that they'd traded shots with already, came around the corner, running behind a crudely up-armored technical.

Any hope that they could duck out of the street before being spotted was quickly dispensed with as the gunner on the technical opened fire. He was free-gunning the machine gun, so the rounds went wild, smacking into the ground, the shacks on either side of the road, and probably several people downrange, but weren't even close to hitting Dan or the rest of the team. It did increase the pucker factor, but considering that they were all pretty much shitting diamonds at that point, that wasn't saying much.

The men on foot, mostly wearing black with green canvas AK chest rigs, were a little more accurate, though they were still spraying bullets down the lane without bothering to do much aiming. The sheet metal side of the shack sounded like it was in the middle of the world's heaviest hailstorm, as rounds smacked through the thin walls with a series of loud *bangs* that blended together into a vicious, rattling roar. Dan dove for the ground, pumping half a mag blindly back through the wall at their tormentors. Hopefully that got a few heads down. At least the fire slackened slightly, and he scrambled to his feet, almost running into Max, who seemed to be pausing to shoot back himself. Dan shoved him after Jenny, Vernon, and Bill. "Keep moving!" he snarled. "If we stay in one place, we're dead."

Max didn't say a word, but glanced once at the opening they'd just run through, then turned and moved on. Dan realized that Max had probably stopped to make sure he wasn't hit, but this was not the time to worry about having yelled at him for the wrong reasons. Now was the time to stay alive. He could apologize later.

Vernon immediately led them through several more turns, though whether because he had become aware of their new pursuers or simply out of good practice, Dan neither knew nor cared. Unfortunately, the latest group seemed to be a bit more tenacious than the first.

He could still hear sporadic gunshots and shouts from behind them. If the camp hadn't already erupted into a cacophony of shouting and shooting, he was sure he'd be able to hear footsteps pounding behind them. They didn't seem to be gaining any ground.

Even after weeks in Malaysia, training and getting acclimated to the sopping heat, the run and the fight was starting to sap his strength. He was soaked with sweat, especially under his plate carrier, and his breath was coming in great gulps. Only the nearness of death kept him from slowing down.

Jenny was doing better than she had in the Florida swamp, but not by much. She was starting to slow down, her hair lank and dripping, her rifle starting to dangle on its sling as her breath came in heaving gasps. She wasn't falling out yet, but she wasn't going to be able to keep the pace that the men were for long.

Dan yelled up to Vernon, "We're going to have to grab a vehicle. We're not going to get clear on foot."

Vernon just nodded as he paused at the next corner, easing an eye around to reconnoiter the next street.

Even in that split second that they weren't moving, two of their pursuers rounded the last corner they'd turned, spotting them at the same instant that Dan turned back to check six.

He started shooting a fraction of a second ahead of Max and the two gunmen. Both had had their rifle muzzles low as they came around the corner, giving him a fractionally shorter distance to bring his muzzle down to cover them. At barely fifty feet, it wasn't much of an advantage, but it was an advantage.

He felt a round burn along his support arm, while another snapped past his head, even as he hammered two rounds into the man on the left before transitioning to the man on the right. He dumped that one with five rounds to the upper torso and throat before snapping his rifle back to a third man who was sticking his AK around the corner. While all that was visible of that one were his hands and his rifle, Dan blasted six more rounds through the flimsy walls of the shack he was using as cover. The AK clattered to the street, and a wet, gurgling scream came from around the corner.

Max had cleaned up the first man he'd shot; the gunman was lying on his back, red spreading across his chest, staring sightlessly at the sky. Max was continuing to put more rounds through the corner to discourage further pursuit, as he yelled, "Go!"

Dan turned and ran after the other three, who were already moving out onto the next street, Vernon bellowing, "With me!" He went just far enough to drop to a knee at the corner to cover Max. The pursuit was too close behind now to just turn and run.

Not trusting anyone's hearing at that point, Dan fired two shots past Max. Max got the message, immediately turning, checking where Dan was, then sprinting toward him. While he was as sweaty as the rest of them, Max was still showing no sign that his extra weight was slowing him down at all.

Dan spun and followed as soon as Max passed him. They burst out onto the street only a few feet behind Jenny and Bill. Vernon had apparently found their way out.

"What the fuck?" Dan blurted. He had no idea what a G-Wagon was doing in the middle of this shithole, but there it was, painted black with tinted windows. It was probably too much to hope for that it was up-armored, but it was wheels, and would probably be able to power through most obstacles the locals could throw at them.

Vernon was already yanking the door open, while Bill ran to cover the front from the passenger side. Jenny piled into the back seat immediately.

Max promptly reached in and yanked her out, shoving her toward the front on Vernon's side. "Get up there and cover Vernon before he gets fucking shot," he barked, though with his voice it sounded a bit more like a yip.

She shot him a venomous look but complied without a word, her face pale with anger. Max didn't appear to notice, simply taking up a position covering down the long axis of the street on the vehicle's six o'clock. Dan had noticed all of this on his way to take a knee behind Bill, covering the alley they'd just come out of.

The G-Wagon roared to life a moment later. Vernon, who had been bent down hotwiring the vehicle, sat up in the driver's seat, yelling, "Get in, get in, get in!"

Jenny, Bill, and Max immediately piled in. Dan was about to, when he saw movement down the alley where he and Max had smoked the three pursuing gunmen. Without waiting to see more, he flipped the selector to full auto and ripped the rest of the magazine down the alley, just to discourage pursuit. Only then did he squeeze into the back seat, reloading and colliding with Jenny, and yanking the door shut as he yelled, "GO! Fucking go!"

Vernon floored the accelerator, and the G-Wagon surged down the street, knocking several barrels and piles of rubbish out of the way in the process. Dan started cranking the window down.

"What the fuck are you doing?" Jenny demanded.

"This ain't ballistic glass," he pointed out. "So if we're going to avoid getting shot full of holes on the way out of here, firepower is going to have to take the place of armor." Suiting actions to words, he stuck his rifle out of the window, and started looking for targets.

There weren't many, though they were definitely taking fire, rounds smacking into the SUV with loud *bangs*. Vernon was driving like a madman, the close-crowded shack walls blurring by as he made as close to a straight-line course toward the edge of the camp that he could. Dan had to pull his rifle back to keep it from getting smacked out of his

grip as they got particularly uncomfortably close to a corner. They were
going too fast to be able to reliably ID targets, but he squeezed off a few
rounds anyway, just to give the locals something to think about.

Suddenly, they were on the edge of the camp, and Vernon had to
yank the wheel and slam on the brakes to keep from hitting a tree. They
weren't on the cleared side, where a carpet of rice fields led down to
Tamjuk and the ocean; they were at the edge of the jungle, looking up at
the hills to the south. The interior of the camp had been so disorienting
that Dan hadn't realized they'd gotten turned around to the south.

"Everybody out!" Dan yelled, kicking open the door and
dropping out of the SUV, turning back to see if there was anyone behind
them. There were; about four or five men were running down the street,
blazing away on automatic as they came. They were mostly firing from
the hip, and none of them were using their sights, which was the one
saving grace.

Dan dropped to a knee and shot the lead man in the lung, right
about at the same time that another shot *crack*ed from the far side of the
G-Wagon. The man fell on his face, his AK flying out of his grip, and
the others scattered.

"Move!" Vernon yelled. The four of them hammered more shots
at their pursuers, making sure they didn't get too enthusiastic about
following into the jungle. Then they were up and running, the camp
disappearing behind the foliage behind them. The noise didn't fade, with
more shots going overhead and smacking into trees, but the shooters
behind them couldn't see what they were shooting at.

They plunged into the greenery, thrashing through the
undergrowth in a more or less straight line to the southwest. They were
just trying to put some distance between themselves and the camp before
slowing down and making for the shore. It almost got Vernon killed.

Dan nearly ran into Max as they piled up behind Vernon, who
had suddenly stopped dead. Dan stepped around only to see what had
held them up.

There was a king cobra coiled not a meter from Vernon, its head
up and its hood spread.

Dan glanced back toward the camp. So far, their pursuit might
not actually have a fix on their location; a gunshot would change that.
They would come toward the noise, instead of fanning out to search the
jungle. But it was only a matter of time before that snake bit Vernon, and
then they were in a world of hurt.

Bill beat him to it. The older man stepped around to Vernon's
other side, drew his pistol, and blew the snake's head off.

Vernon breathed again as the snake's body twitched and thrashed
on the ground, then he was moving again, albeit slightly more slowly,
watching carefully for any other nasty surprises. The jungle can kill a
man just as easily as a bullet.

Dan was about to direct Vernon to turn west, but didn't have to; after the report of the gunshot that had killed the cobra, he evidently was about as eager to stay in the same area or to keep moving in the same direction as Dan was. He immediately started along the slope of the hill, aiming toward the beach. Behind them, Dan could hear yelling in Mandarin and Malay. They weren't out of the woods yet.

Six hours later, crouched in a hole beneath a gigantic fallen tree, Dan thought they could risk moving again.

They'd made another half a mile before they had had to go to ground. The locals knew the jungle; they didn't. So they found the fallen tree, squeezed into the hole, and pulled as much foliage over themselves as they could while still making it look a little natural.

He hadn't heard any movement or voices, aside from the usual wildlife, for over an hour. It was too dark to see, though he pulled his NVGs and their harness out of his go bag and strapped them on as soon as he was out of the hole.

No sign of company in the green-on-green image. "Let's go," he whispered. Hopefully the boat was still offshore. They hadn't been able to afford to call on the radio while the hunters were that close.

Now he gave it a shot, turning the radio on and calling, "Extract, this is Tack. Are you still on station?"

For a long, heart-attack-inducing moment, there was no reply. Dan's guts sank into his boots. Lambert had doubtless argued that they were dead, and they'd been written off. But then the radio crackled to life.

"Tack, this is Extract. Affirmative. Though we were about to leave in the next five minutes."

Dan took a deep breath, a sigh echoed by the other four. "Roger. We are still about three klicks from rendezvous; it's going to be a little while before we get there."

"Good copy," came the reply. "Now that we know you're alive, we'll stick around. Call us when you're five hundred meters from the beach, and we'll meet you there."

Dan pointed to Vernon, who now had his own NVGs on. Vernon nodded, and led off.

Dan tried not to think too hard about the repercussions of this little disaster, and focus on getting off Borneo. There'd be trouble enough when they got back to Desaru.

Chapter 12

Decker was waiting at the entrance of the makeshift CP in the rec center as they walked up. He pointed to Dan, made a "come here" gesture, and waved the rest away. Dan turned to the rest of the team. "Go get cleaned up and get some chow. Stay close, though." He got a series of nods in response.

He couldn't help but notice the faint smirk on Lambert's face. He forced himself not to react, even as the other man made a point of locking eyes with him before turning away. He waited for the rest of the team to head up the path toward the hotel-turned-barracks before turning back to Decker.

The bald man just inclined his head toward the door, and stepped into the CP. Dan followed dutifully.

They actually hadn't done much with the room; it was still a large, open room with a fairly decent carpet, fabric-covered walls, and a number of folding tables and cheap, if fancy-looking, chairs. Of course, now the carpeted floor was littered with taped cables, the walls had charts, photos, target dossiers, and maps plastered all over them, and every bit of table space was taken up with laptops, comm equipment, and monitors. It wasn't loud; most of the contractors monitoring comms had headsets on. In fact, few even seemed to notice the two of them walking into the room.

Decker led the way to a small cubicle toward the back where he'd set up his office. It was the same place where Dan had convinced him to green-light the disastrous Borneo mission only a couple days before. Dan wasn't sure if that was an ominous sign or not. Or, rather, he wasn't sure just *how* ominous it was. Nothing about his current position was particularly good.

Decker ushered him into the cubicle, then sat down at the desk, which was still littered with maps and printed reports. He leaned back in his chair and folded his arms, looking across at Dan with a blank expression and hooded eyes. The man was very good at concealing what he was feeling or thinking.

"So," he began. "Tell me what happened."

Dan laid it out. "Our intel was bad. We went in expecting a dirty little jungle camp like the drug processing site we hit to get the lead in the first place. We found a fucking city." He looked down at the map. "My mistake was in trying to reconnoiter the place on the ground, to see if there was anything we *could* accomplish, instead of just calling the whole op off as soon as I saw the size of the target. We got cornered, fingered as outsiders, and then it all fell apart. We had to shoot our way out."

Decker nodded. "That's about what I gathered from the comm traffic." He studied Dan for a moment. "So, judging by the Eeyore face, you're figuring that I'm getting ready to fire you for this."

Dan didn't respond, except to raise an eyebrow as he waited for Decker to continue.

"I'm sure, judging by the message I got from Lambert as soon as you landed, that he at least would be happy to see that happen," Decker went on after a momentary pause. "However, there are two problems with that. One: you can't be blamed for shit intel. You acted on the intel you had, and it turned out to be a bust. Now, I would tend to agree that you should have called an abort as soon as you saw the scale of the thing. Riding around an illegal smuggling hub with a bunch of obvious ugly Americans was probably not the best idea you've ever had. While I liked the aggressiveness you displayed in pushing to cut Yuan's exterior ties, you let it go to your head. Honestly, if somebody *had* been killed because of it, I very well might have you on the next thing smoking back to the States.

"But under the circumstances, you got everyone out in one piece, and you admit that you fucked up. As long as that fuck-up didn't cost any lives, and you learn from it and don't let it happen again, I'm willing to keep you where you are.

"Two: right at the moment, I don't want to encourage Lambert any more than absolutely necessary."

Both of Dan's eyebrows went up at that. Decker just nodded. "Oh yes, I've noticed that he's a problem. I'd have to be completely blind not to. The man is a functional sociopath, and he's a perennial discipline problem. You should see his service record. He's just too good at the job to get rid of. He is also smart enough to keep his misbehavior below the threshold where I'd have to do something about it.

"But while I might not be able or willing to fire him at the moment, that doesn't mean I trust him with the team lead spot he wants so badly."

Dan couldn't help but let out a bit of a sigh of relief. He did his best to keep it small, but Decker noticed. The other man was so difficult to read most of the time that Dan could never be entirely sure what he noticed or ignored, never mind what he was thinking about any particular situation.

"That doesn't mean that you're entirely off the hook, however," Decker continued. "You're going to have to step up your game after this, and not only for the sake of my confidence level. The other contractors are going to be watching how you react to this, and how you move forward. If you want to keep that team lead spot, you're going to have to step up and make it abundantly clear that you deserve *their* confidence. If I notice, or start hearing, that you've either let this start to paralyze you, or that you start going overly gung-ho to try to make up for it, well...you'll be on the next thing smoking. Am I clear?"

Dan nodded. "Clear as crystal."

"Good," Decker replied, and sat up. Apparently that subject was done with. He swiveled his laptop around so that Dan could see the screen. "What does this look like to you?"

Dan studied the imagery. At first glance, it only appeared to be a Harbin Z-9, the Chinese version of the French Dauphin helicopter, landing in a clearing hacked out of the jungle. The next shot showed three men getting off and walking toward the vehicles parked next to the edge of the LZ. The third zoomed in on the three.

Dan squinted at it for a moment. "Is that Yuan?" he asked. The center man seemed to be wearing some kind of uniform, though it definitely wasn't a PLAN uniform.

"We think so," Decker replied. "This was taken on Siantan about thirty-six hours ago. He hasn't budged from the place since; we're pretty sure he's sticking."

"I thought his base of operations was on Matak," Dan mentioned.

"So did we. Like you just found out the hard way, intel can be sketchy. Keep scrolling."

The next series of shots followed a motorcade of three vehicles moving down the island's one major road. They didn't appear to be headed for one of the small coastal settlements on Siantan, but were heading north, into the jungle-swathed heart of the island.

The final series showed their destination: a fortified camp in the middle of the jungle.

The pirates had been busy. A large swath of jungle had been cleared away, down to the mostly reddish dirt. The center of the roughly triangular camp was occupied by several red mounds that could only be bunkers. More tents were scattered around the bunkers, but the fortifications were considerably larger. Dan guessed that a lot of the trees that had been cleared had gone into building the bunkers. There were deep trenches running between the bunkers and the outer defenses. The outer defenses were a network of dug-in, sandbagged fighting positions, and looked like they might have some serious heavy weapons in them.

"That's going to be one hell of a nut to crack," Dan commented.

"That's a no-shitter," Decker agreed. "Our eggheads think that with the pressure we've been putting on him, hitting his outer installations, Yuan's going to ground, holing up in his fortifications until either he can find out who we are and deal with us, or we come to him

123

and get slaughtered trying to storm that place."

"So what's the plan?" Dan asked.

"We're going to take that camp," Decker replied, "and take out Yuan and at least a good chunk of his pirates. The theory is that Yuan is the one holding the whole shebang together. We get him and the bulk of his crew, and the rest will atomize to the point that local forces can probably deal with them."

"But you just mentioned getting slaughtered trying to storm this fucking place," Dan pointed out.

Decker nodded, leaning back in his chair again. "And that's why we're not launching tonight. I'm getting some pressure from the office, but we're going to run some infiltration exercises for a couple of days, until we can work out how to get in close and avoid having to engage those heavy weapons from a distance. In the good old days, we might have just called in air support and then gone in to pick up the pieces, but that's not an option here, so we're having to go a little bit more old-fashioned. Think Vietcong old-fashioned."

Dan grimaced. Not at the idea itself; he thought it had a lot of merit. No, his concern was actually trying to train some of the contractors that way. If he'd been able to hand-pick his people, there might be some more hope. But few Americans had trained that way in decades; they were used to big, combined-arms assaults. He didn't think this was going to go well, even with two days to prepare and rehearse.

Decker seemed to read his mind. "Don't worry," he said. "We'll make it work. For now, go get some rest. We'll be starting first thing in the morning."

"I still don't know for sure when I'll be home," Dan told Amy. "But it shouldn't be much longer. Are you being good for Grandma and Grandpa?"

"Yes, Daddy," the little girl replied. There was still a little quaver in her voice; Daddy had been gone for almost three months already, and the same questions had started to take on greater and greater urgency every time he called. *When is Daddy coming home, and is he going to come home at all?*

It hurt Dan's very soul when she asked. Tom was still too little to think much about it; he was vaguely aware that neither Mommy or Daddy were there, but he loved Grandma, and he was happy enough. The pain of parting had disappeared into a murky past that he wasn't all that aware of anymore. But Amy was all too aware that Mommy was gone and wasn't ever coming back, and Daddy had left to go somewhere dangerous. She was already scarred by her mother's death; the fear that her father was going to disappear the same way was one that, according to Roger, had her waking up crying in the middle of the night on a regular basis.

124

Just a little while longer, and we'll be set for a good long time, he told himself, wondering in the back of his mind if he wasn't lying to himself, never mind his in-laws and his kids. This job had gotten thorny as hell, and he was starting to wonder if he or any of the rest stood any chance of getting out of it alive. *I should have known it was too good to be true.* The pay was fantastic, but he was starting to get the heebie-jeebies about the mission, never mind some of his fellow contractors.

But he couldn't say that to his kids. He couldn't even bring himself to admit it to Roger. He still remembered their last conversation before he'd left quite vividly. Even if he didn't say it outright, Roger would be thinking that if he was that worried about the mission and the men, then he needed to cut away and make his way home. That his ultimate responsibility was still to Amy and Tom.

He knew it. But he couldn't just walk away, not yet. As much as he was worried about both higher management and the likes of Lambert and Jenny, he couldn't just leave Vernon, Max, and the others behind. The bond of brotherhood had been forged already, and he couldn't turn his back on them. Not yet.

There was a knock at his door. He glanced toward it; he'd set his desk up so that he could keep his back to the wall, and his P226 was lying next to the laptop. "Amy," he said, "I'm sorry, but I'm going to have to go." Whatever this was, he definitely didn't want his daughter to hear or see any of it. "I love you, and I'll be home as soon as I can, okay? I promise. Be good for Grandma and Grandpa, and take care of your little brother."

"I will, Daddy," she sniffled. "I love you."

Another knock sounded at the door, more insistently, as he ended the call and shut the laptop. Picking up his pistol, he went to the door and peered out the peephole.

Vernon's bulk almost completely blacked out the view, but he could see that there were at least a couple more people with him. He relaxed a little, and opened the door.

"We need to talk," Vernon said as the door swung open. Behind him, Max, Bill, and Cassy were also waiting.

Dan stepped aside. "Come on in." He was only wearing a t-shirt and shorts, but none of the others were exactly over-dressed, either. It was hot.

As he closed the door, he turned to his four friends, who were standing in an awkward circle in the middle of the room. "Let me guess," he said. "It's about Lambert."

He got nods all around. "He's running his mouth about what a complete fucking disaster the Borneo op was," Max said. "And he's making no secret of the fact he thinks that it's entirely your fault. Says that you've been timid the entire time, and when it started to look like you might not have a job anymore because of it, that you went off half-cocked and fucked up the preparations for Borneo."

Dan blinked. The bald-faced lie was a bit more than he'd been prepared for. He'd come to expect that Lambert would try to undermine him; they'd butted heads over ethics and contraband too many times already. But this was a level of dishonesty that frankly surprised him. He'd expected Lambert to be a little more subtle than that.

"He hasn't said what he'd have done differently, of course," Cassy put in quietly. "But that's not the point. The point is to drag you down, so he can step into your place. And as much as I hate to say it, a few are listening."

Of course they were. Lambert would appeal to greed and envy, two of the strongest motivators among the contractors, particularly those who were just there for a paycheck and some action. *Which actually sounds a hell of a lot like what I signed up for*, Dan mused. But there were definitely those with stronger moral compasses than others, and many of them were currently standing there in the room with him.

"Fortunately," he replied, "I talked to Decker earlier, and whatever Lambert tells the teams, management hasn't decided that I'm enough of a fuck-up to fire me yet. So Lambert's just going to have to wait."

"And if he doesn't?" Bill put in. Dan looked at him. He'd never talked much with his teammate; Bill was older, in his late forties, and didn't mix or talk very much. When he had spoken, it had mostly been business. Dan knew next to nothing about the man or his background outside of his time as a Ranger, yet he apparently had decided that he was on Dan's side in this particular case. "I've seen his type before. The only thing holding him back is the possibility that he gets caught and punished if he moves too soon. He's starting to think that this entire situation is fluid and lawless enough that he might just be able to get away with fragging your ass." The older man looked like he wanted to punctuate the statement by spitting, but there wasn't anyplace to spit in Dan's hotel room. "His bullshit is calculated to mentally prep everyone else to just shrug and turn to him once you're out of the picture. Whether he can get you fired or get you killed is immaterial to him."

"Look, Dan," Cassy said. "We're with you, and we don't want anything to happen to you. We just want to make sure you're watching your back."

Dan chuckled bleakly. "I've been watching my back since I got here," he replied. "Or did you think I answered the door with a pistol in my hand just because?"

Cassy started, as if noticing the drawn SIG for the first time. The other three just nodded.

"We just wanted to make sure all of us are on the same page," Vernon said, looking around at the others. "I know you and I have talked about Lambert before, but what we just heard downstairs makes us all a

126

little more concerned." He folded his arms. "We're going to have to deal with him, sooner or later."

"Permanently," Bill said coldly. "And sooner is better than later."

"Believe me, I've thought about it," Dan said, even as Cassy looked ready to say something. She looked like she'd picked up on the subtext of Bill's comment, and didn't like it. Which was fine; Dan didn't like it, either. Which didn't mean he didn't think it might become a necessity. "And if I think he's about to try to kill me, believe me, I'll end him in a heartbeat. But I'm a TL. I can't afford to just off one of my guys because he's a violent, amoral asshole. Whether justified or not, it would still be murder, and I'm not ready to cross that line yet. Sorry."

"We're not talking about killing him outright," Cassy started to say. Bill snorted.

"Speak for yourself," he said acidly.

"That's enough," Vernon said, beating Dan to the punch. "Dan's right." He looked Dan in the eye. "We've got your back, brother," he said. "As long as you're okay with watching and waiting, we'll go with your play. Just don't watch and wait too long."

"I won't," Dan assured them all. "I've got a couple kids to get back to. I have no intention of going back to them in a box because of fucking Lambert."

Apparently satisfied, he got another series of nods. Max was slightly grim, Cassy looked pretty upset, and Bill's mouth had thinned; he apparently still thought that a proactive approach was better. Vernon was just as calm and composed as ever.

As the other three left, Vernon lingered. "Do I have to worry about Bill now?" Dan asked him.

Vernon shook his head. "Nah. He's solid. He thinks you're being dumb, and I gather that he really, really wants to put a bullet in Lambert, but he'll hold his fire until either you give the word or he decides there really isn't any other option anymore." He glanced after the other three. "Though I wouldn't put it past him, if you don't give the word, to go ahead and let you get yourself killed. He'd probably think you deserved it for being an idiot."

Dan just shook his head. "What the hell did we get ourselves into?"

Vernon gusted a sigh. "A job that seemed too good to be true," he said. "And that's part of the problem. You remove some of the restraints we had before, and you get more people like Lambert. Even if he passed every selection criteria MMPR set to try to avoid it, even if he was a straight arrow before—and I don't believe that for a second—the temptations inherent in being this far off the reservation, with as little oversight as we seem to have, have got to be overpowering for some people."

"What about for you?" Dan asked, genuinely curious.

Vernon just shrugged. "You've got kids. I want kids someday. I want to be able to tell them that their Daddy's not a bad man." He looked a little sheepish. "Maybe that's not much, but it's been enough for me so far."

Dan just nodded. In a way, he understood that. "It's getting late," he said, "and we've got a lot of work ahead of us in the morning."

"Yeah." Vernon turned back to the door again. "You think this is gonna work?"

"It'll take a miracle," Dan admitted. "But if the team really nuts up over the next few days, we might be able to pull it off. Personally, I think we'd be better off backing off for a while until Yuan gets comfortable again, and then try to nab him while he's moving, but I kind of suspect the office doesn't want to pay us these rates that long."

"You're probably right," Vernon said. "'You can have it fast, cheap, or good, but not all three,'" he quoted. "See you in the morning, bro."

"Later, man," Dan replied. He shut the door after Vernon, locked it, then stripped off his shirt and laid down on the bed, his pistol within arm's reach.

Clasping his hands behind his head, he stared at the slowly rotating ceiling fan. Getting to sleep was going to be a bitch after that conversation.

Feng had been waiting at the restaurant for exactly four minutes when Hu walked in and gestured for him to follow. A hostess immediately fell in behind the overweight facilitator/intelligence agent, and followed them to the table, where she poured drinks, apparently without having to be told, and then bowed out. Hu must be a regular here.

The older man made a show of sipping his *baijiu* and studying the menu, even though the kitchen staff was most likely already preparing his meal. As near as he'd been able to tell, Hu was a man of routine and habit; his sheer predictability serving to disguise his work for the PRC. He was too boring to be a spy.

Feng waited patiently. He'd gotten the message at their last encounter. Rushing Hu would not gain him anything. If the facilitator had asked for a meeting, he had something of value. He was not a man who wasted time, nor liked to have his time wasted.

The hostess returned, and Hu ordered his food. Feng followed suit, considering that to do otherwise would be out of place, and would likely anger Hu because of it. Only once the woman had left did Hu actually look across the table at him.

"I believe that one of my sources has located your mysterious interlopers, *Shang Wei* Feng," he said, taking another sip of the warm

128

liquor. "There is an entire resort on the Desaru peninsula that has been rented out indefinitely to a Western company." Feng listened closely, concentrating on committing everything Hu said to memory. This wasn't information he wanted to write down. "The company, MMPR, has tried very hard to obfuscate its nature, but I have enough sources to have determined that it is an American security contractor, not unlike the late and unlamented Blackwater.

"They have instituted a considerable security presence at the resort, and my source was unable to see very much from the inland side; however, he was able to get close enough in a fishing boat to see what looked a great deal like paramilitary preparations and equipment on the beach. There also were two very large, very expensive yachts moored there, which may have been used in one or more of the operations you mentioned against the defector and his pirates.

"He estimated that there are between one and two hundred people presently on the site. As I said, the security is considerable. It will not be an easy place to take by force."

"Did he provide any details about the external security?" Feng asked.

Hu shook his head. "He is not military, so he lacks much of the experience and vocabulary to do so," he replied. "If you are that interested, I can provide you with the exact location of the resort in question, so that you might make your own reconnaissance."

"I would appreciate that, *tongzhi* Hu," Feng replied. "As will my superiors."

Hu waved a hand dismissively. "As I said during our previous conversation, *Shang Wei*," he said, "I do my duty to the People's Republic. Reporting on American activities in our sphere of influence certainly falls within that bailiwick." He glanced over at the waitress, who was already approaching with their food, confirming Feng's earlier suspicion that they had started preparing Hu's order as soon as he had walked in, though how they had fixed his so fast was another question. "Now, let us eat."

Chapter 13

The sun was rapidly dipping toward the horizon as the small flotilla of yachts, fishing boats, and trawlers began to converge on the coast of Pulau Siantan.

Dan was already kitted up, back in his Kryptek cammies and chest rig, his rifle presently slung across his back. He really didn't want it knocking around his knees while he manhandled the Zodiac into the water. Most of the rest had followed suit.

He'd broken the team up into elements again, and once again, he'd assigned Lambert to the other element. He'd gotten the same knowing smirk from the other man when he'd read out the assignments. He actually felt a little guilty leaving Lambert with Bill, Sam, Brad, and Cary, but under the circumstances, he figured it was less risky to keep the man in his own element. Keeping him close would only give him a better shot at his own back in a firefight. Lambert was competent; there was no question about that. What he wasn't was trustworthy.

He put any further thought on the matter out of his mind as he, Max, Vernon, and Ty shoved the Zodiac off the back of the *Mercury Quick*. The girls were staying behind again; there'd been some heated words over the matter, but Dan had put his foot down. As far as he was concerned, neither of them was physically up to a long infantry operation, and Jenny's performance during the fiasco on Borneo hadn't instilled any more confidence in him. He wasn't going to risk the op for the sake of inclusiveness. They were staying aboard the yacht and running comms. Jenny had been furious, though Cassy had taken it relatively calmly. Decker had taken Dan aside to question him about it, but when Dan had stayed firm and stated his reasons, the other man had simply listened, nodded, and said, "It's your team."

The boat hit the water with a splash. It didn't have far to go; the yacht's fantail wasn't all that high above the water. That also made it an easy matter to jump in after the boat and swim to the gunwale. In a matter of a couple of minutes, they were all aboard and Dan had the motor started. Turning the tiller, he steered toward the beach, joining the swarm of similar landing craft heading in toward the island. He looked over at the other boat that had launched just before, where Lambert sat at the tiller. The other man met his gaze coolly, and simply nodded.

The sun hadn't quite set yet, and Dan was feeling pretty exposed out on the water, looking toward the dark green hump of Pulau Siantan.

It did help that the sun was setting almost directly behind them, and they would have the maximum amount of darkness to make their infiltration prior to the assault, but somehow he didn't find that all that comforting. All it would take would be a single LP/OP looking out to sea and paying attention, and they were going to motor right into an ambush. And given Yuan's apparent recent nervousness, he'd be surprised if the man *didn't* have extra lookouts posted.

For the most part, the boats held water while waiting for sunset, though a few of the more eager elements started drifting closer to the shore. When sunset finally came, with the briefest of green flashes, darkness descended abruptly, leaving only a faint line of lighter blue at the western horizon. Only then did Dan open the throttle and start the Zodiac moving toward the dark bulk of the island ahead.

It was a ragged line that advanced over the water, with some boat crews opening the throttle more than others. Dan kept the Zodiac's outboard running at a dull rumble, trying to keep the noise down. It meant getting to the beach a few dozen yards behind the more enthusiastic crews, but he figured most of them were the newbies that Decker had brought in. Rex was taking almost all of the new guys on the diversionary attack, anyway, so they could actually use the extra time, provided there weren't crew-served weapons sited in the jungle, zeroing in on them as they approached.

But as they got closer, his NVGs showed only the near-impenetrable darkness under the jungle canopy. No movement, no starlight on equipment, nothing. No muzzle flashes or tracers, either. Either the pirates on Siantan were a *lot* better disciplined and camouflaged than any of the rag-tag bastards they'd killed on the outer islands, or they weren't covering the beach. Or, apparently, the entire west shore of the island.

Even in the dark, the water was clear enough that Vernon and Ty, up in the bow, could tell when they were shallow enough, making quick chopping gestures to signal that they were about to go aground. Dan yanked the kill lanyard on the motor and quickly lifted it clear before it rammed into the sand, and a moment later, Vernon and Ty were out and pulling the boat up onto the beach, alongside the other four boats of the main assault teams.

They dropped the boat as soon as it wasn't going to float away on its own, rifles coming off of backs and up to scan the surrounding jungle. A line of black rubber boats, glistening in the starlight, was drawn up for five hundred yards along the rocks and white sand of the beach, as more dark shapes carrying guns and packs leaped out and moved up to the treeline.

It took another fifteen minutes to push the beachhead perimeter out far enough that Decker was finally satisfied that they weren't about to get hit by a pirate ambush waiting in the jungle. He still didn't risk the radio, instead circling one hand above his head where he crouched at the edge of the beach. It took Dan a few seconds to see what he was doing; even with the NVGs, it was dark enough by then to make picking out hand and arm signals at any kind of distance difficult.

Dan finished making sure that his team was set in its defensive position before moving back to join Decker and Will. Decker was leading the assault element, while Rex was already taking the diversionary element into the jungle to the north, leaving the boats for the assault element to draw up into the vegetation and conceal. Which was according to plan, though if Dave had still been around, he'd probably be bitching about it the entire time.

Dan took a knee next to Decker and Will in the sand. Sean came up to join them a moment later. All four of them looked rather alien, black NVG tubes poking out from under boonie hats. Decker checked his watch, carefully covering it to keep the brief green glow from being seen very far.

"We're mostly on schedule," he whispered. "We've still got to get the boats off the beach and concealed; after that, we'll check the timeline again. We might still have to burn a few minutes to give the diversionary element the time to get in position and get prepped." Those guys not only had farther to go, they were also lugging heavier ordnance, and needed to be able to dig in; they were going to draw a lot of hostile attention as soon as they opened fire.

Dan had asked Rex where they'd gotten the heavy weapons. The company's handful of Ultimax 100s had already been a little eyebrow-raising, given the apparently unofficial nature of the mission, but he was damned sure that the mortars, RPG-18s, and RPG-32s were probably in violation of *somebody*'s version of international arms trafficking regulations.

Rex had simply tapped the side of his nose and said, "Ask me no questions and I'll tell you no lies." Dan had let it drop.

The team leaders parted to get their teams working. It was backbreaking work, especially since they still had to leave several of the shooters on security on the perimeter. That left about eighteen men to drag all the boats up and get them camouflaged with hacked-off foliage in the jungle. It took the better part of an hour and a half, all told, to get the entire small flotilla off the beach. Everyone was already sweating profusely by the time the team leads got back together with Decker.

"Still good on time," he said. "We'll step off in five minutes, so everybody at least gets a breather before we tackle that." He pointed up at the slope above them. The island rose fairly steeply from the western shore. It wasn't going to be fun, though again, Dan was glad he wasn't trying to lug a mortar up it. "I'd rather we had a little bit more flex time on the final infil, if we're being honest."

The team leads nodded their acknowledgments, then split up to go pass the word to their teams. By the time Dan had given everybody a quick rundown, it was already time to step. So much for a breather.

"If I am to be frank, *Shang Wei* Yiti," Feng said, as the two officers stepped away from the briefing platform aboard the amphibious warfare ship *Changbai Shan*, "I would rather not use your men at all."

Shang Wei Erkan Yiti frowned. While they were the same age, the hawk-nosed PLA Marine officer looked a decade older. He'd come from a hard life before joining the People's Liberation Army Marine Corps, and advancing through the ranks as a Uighur and a Muslim hadn't been easy. "The situation is truly that sensitive?"

Feng nodded. Yiti knew him well enough not to think that this was a matter of *Jiaolong* ego-tripping. The two men had attended officer training together, and had become unlikely friends, even though grown somewhat distant by the necessities of duty and politics. Yiti, after all, did not have a father who was a *Zhong Jiang*, and had not thereby earned a slot with the *Jiaolong* commandos.

"The Central Committee would prefer not to draw any further attention to this affair," he confirmed. "Yuan's defection is enough of an embarrassment, especially considering the fact that he took an entire frigate and its crew with him. With the overall situation here in the South China Sea being what it is, Beijing does not wish it to become wider knowledge that Yuan is considered anything more than a nuisance. It weakens our position with the other powers in the region." Of course, that wasn't the only reason, but Yiti did not need to know the rest.

He still thought that he could have dealt with the pirates on his own, slowly whittling down the network of outposts and camps throughout the islands, isolating Yuan until it was time to finally close in and eliminate him. He had resisted calling for the *Changbai Shan*'s support for as long as possible.

But with the reports of the Western mercenaries in Malaysia, corroborated by Hu's information, his superiors had insisted that the situation be resolved as quickly as possible. Guo had been ordered south, whether Feng liked it or not.

Yiti nodded his own understanding. Feng suspected that the other man read enough between the lines to perceive that there was a lot more going on beneath the surface than Feng would or could say, and let it go. He had spent his entire career understanding, accepting, and driving forward. "So, you would rather we stayed on the perimeter?"

"Yes," Feng replied. "You may have to whisper in *Shang Xiao* Guo's ear to make sure that happens." He had kept in close enough touch with his old friend to know that even though Yiti was only a company commander in his battalion, and unlikely, given his heritage and religion, to rise much further, he had demonstrated enough tactical competence, and political circumspection, that *Shang Xiao* Guo Pan valued his

133

insight.

"He will not like it," Yiti said unnecessarily. "He is already annoyed at having to take directions from a *Shang Wei*, even a *Jiaolong* commander, no matter how well-connected you are."

"No doubt," Feng answered, glancing at the lined, glowering face of the battalion commander, across the briefing room. "Though he would be rather more upset if the *guobao* locks him up along with half of his Marines for overstepping his bounds."

Yiti's expression didn't change, though there might have been a flicker of reaction in his eyes. Of course, he'd lived his entire life with the prospect of being declared an enemy of the state hanging over his head. "I will do my best to help him see the truth of the situation," he said diplomatically.

"I hope that you can, my friend," Feng said. He checked his watch. "Now, if you will excuse me, I need to prep my own men. We are launching soon." He shook hands with Yiti and left for the hold his team had taken over on the *Changbai Shan* for their team room.

He hoped that this would be the final strike, and that he could report back to *Zhong Jiang* Feng that Yuan had been neutralized and the situation dealt with. He would much rather be working on securing Chinese interests against the Vietnamese, Japanese, or the renegades on Taiwan than negotiating this minefield.

The movement sucked. There was no other word for it. Covering only a couple kilometers took hours of fighting the thick jungle growth and the terrain, all while trying to watch for any number of poisonous fauna that was prowling around the undergrowth or the canopy after dark. Vines and branches caught on kit, snagged on NVGs, and grabbed at rifles. Within a short time, the sweat that drenched everyone had been joined by what Dan figured was probably several pounds of vegetable matter, bits of leaves and branches that had worked their way into collars, belts, and socks to chafe and itch.

He didn't even want to think about the bug bites. Which meant he couldn't ignore the ferocious itching and burning from several of them.

They had reached the rally point, sited above a waterfall that now overlooked the cleared section of jungle where Yuan had placed his fortress, after about three hours of miserable hiking. They were still a good fifty minutes ahead of the pre-planned timeline, for which he was thankful. From what little he could see of his teammates in the dark, so were the rest of them. Vernon and Max seemed to be in the best shape. Bill was sucking wind, muttering something about getting too old for this shit when Dan checked on him. Cary had struggled getting up the mountain; he'd kept up, but only barely. Lambert and Sam hadn't voiced a word of complaint, maintaining their hardassed exteriors, though he was pretty sure he'd seen both shooting disgusted glances at Cary during the movement. Brad and Ty had just given him thumbs up when he'd checked, neither displaying a great deal of either enthusiasm or exhaustion.

Dan was smoked. He hated to admit it, but he had to stifle a grateful sigh of his own as he sank to the jungle floor, leaning his assault pack up against a rock. He was soaked to the skin in his own juices, and had felt a little light-headed a couple of times toward the end. He didn't dare show it to Lambert or Decker, but he was glad for the better part of an hour to catch his breath before beginning the assault.

Decker himself hadn't shown any signs of fatigue, and was presently on a knee in the middle of their little perimeter, his pack at his feet and the handset of the small VHF radio held to his ear. Distance and the necessities of coordination meant they had to risk comms at this point. Not that they were all that worried about Yuan's people having signals intercept capability; that was unlikely. But talking this close to the objective was a risk. They were fairly sure that the majority of the pirates in the fortress were Yuan's Han crew, and could be prudently expected to be somewhat more disciplined and well-trained than the local pirates that they'd encountered out on the outposts. They could be expected to have a more alert watch on guard, and so noise discipline became paramount. So Decker's voice was pitched as low as possible, to where his words were barely a murmur only a couple of yards away.

He finished quickly, most of the conversation having gone on in brevity codes to further decrease the amount of talking, and moved over to Dan. "Okay," he whispered, barely audible over the gurgling of the falls, "we've got an extra thirty minutes to work with. The other element had a harder time getting the heavies over the hills than expected."

Decker's voice was flat and matter-of-fact, but Dan could hear an echo of his own thoughts underlying it. *Apparently some of the newbies are a little out of shape, too. I wonder how many corners the company cut to get them out here so fast?*

"We'll hold tight for an hour," Decker went on. "I want an LP/OP pushed out to get eyes on the objective until we're ready to step off again. Pick two and send them out. I'll have Will and Sean put flankers out."

Dan nodded, considering who to send out. The obvious choice would be Lambert and Sam. *How much am I thinking that just because I want to keep Lambert as far away from me as possible?* Still, they had weathered the movement better than at least half the team, and however much they might both be fairly amoral, sadistic fucks, they were still professionals when it counted.

Fuck it, he thought. *Decker already knows all there is to know about my little battle of wills with Lambert. Let him think that I'm picking him because of it. I'll know better.* He silenced the little voice in the back of his head that wondered if he wasn't lying to himself. He shouldered out of his pack and heaved himself up onto his feet, moving over to Lambert and Sam. "You two push out to get eyes on the target," he told them. "LP/OP until we're ready to move out. It's going to be about an hour."

Lambert made a point of making eye contact, even though there was little to see in the dark. He was just going to be a dick about everything Dan told him to do. But he nodded, after just a little too long a pause, got to his feet, and started out toward the very top of the falls. Sam followed without looking back.

Dan returned to his pack, though instead of sitting back down, he knelt next to it and started pulling his camouflage out. In the US military that had trained most of them, ghillie suits were for snipers. But they were following a bit of an older model of infantry combat this time, so each one of them had a ghillie suit in their assault pack. They were going to have to get very close without being detected.

The Lightweight Assaulter's Ghillie was actually designed with this kind of stealthy assault in mind. It wasn't as bulky or heavy as a classic ghillie suit, but still broke up the outline enough that they should, with the right vegetation, look like clumps of weeds crossing the relatively open area leading up to the fort's outer perimeter.

He didn't start tying vegetation into the attachment points yet; that would wait until closer to showtime. But he threw it over his kit anyway, and touched up his camouflage face paint as best he could in the dark. Better to be as ready to go as possible. Once it was on, and he was satisfied that the rest of his kit was ready for the attack, he moved up to Vernon to relieve him so that he could get his own gear and camouflage ready.

By the time he'd gone around to the rest of his teammates to make sure that they were ready to go, their wait time was almost up. He had picked up his pack again when Lambert and Sam came back in from the LP/OP. They were a couple minutes early, which Dan couldn't help but see as another challenge from Lambert, but he didn't comment on it. Not the time, nor the place.

Finally, Decker made eye contact with each of the team leaders, and pointed down into the valley. It was time.

Going down wasn't much more pleasant than climbing up had been. The undergrowth was just as thick, especially as they were trying to avoid moving along the bed of the river, and the climb down worked an entirely different set of muscles than going up had, awakening an entirely new set of aches and pains. None of them were necessarily all that young anymore.

They paused again right at the edge of the cleared ground. The fort was clearly visible; Yuan must not have been all that worried about light discipline. The rumble of several gas generators could be heard even over the nocturnal racket of the jungle, and several floods were set up near the center of the camp. Some of them even silhouetted a few of the fighting positions on the berm. Dan could see one in particular right in front of him, sandbagged up and with what looked like a heavy machine gun, just by the size, pointing out at the jungle.

No further words were necessary; they'd extensively planned, briefed, and rehearsed this part. While trading off to maintain security, they started tying vegetation, mostly grass from the edges of the clearing, into their LWAGs' rubber netting. While the jute string helped break up the outline, without local vegetation it just looked like a pile of jute string.

Once everyone was freshly camouflaged, they spread out into a rough line, got down on their bellies, and started to slowly crawl out into the clearing.

Fortunately, it wasn't just perfectly flat grassland. They'd never have been able to avoid being spotted, even at night, if it was. While there was still ash under the growth, from when Yuan's people had slashed and burned the jungle away, there was just no keeping the rampant growth of the tropics down. Tall grass and leafy shrubs were already cropping up all around the dug-in fort. With care, the growth provided plenty of concealment.

Of course, Siantan being the island that it was, there wasn't just undergrowth. There were a *lot* of rocks, ranging from the smaller ones that dug into ribs like claws to clumps of large boulders that had to be negotiated while simultaneously providing some extra cover and concealment between the crawling assaulters and the defenders on the berm.

For the moment, Dan was, for all intents and purposes, alone, negotiating the infiltration without being able to see any of his teammates on either side. The growth was just too thick. It meant he didn't have to skull drag all the way, and he could hear the rustling of the others to his right and left, but it still lent a feeling of uneasy isolation as he worked his way across the field in the dark, his rifle in one hand, his pack dragging by one strap looped around the other arm. Caching the packs had been suggested, but it had been decided that it was a better idea to bring them along, just in case.

The cleared ground was only about three hundred meters wide. It felt more like thirty miles. Crawling is never all that easy, especially dragging a rifle and pack along. But Dan reflected, as he dragged himself through the damp grass, that he'd probably rather be doing this than running upright across it, trying to do the "I'm up, he sees me, I'm down" for three hundred yards, probably with body armor.

Almost sooner than he'd expected, he found himself up against the berm. Checking his watch, he saw that it had still taken almost an hour and a half to traverse the killing field. *So far, so good.* Nobody had started shooting yet, so they appeared to have made it without being spotted.

He peered up at the berm, but his sense of direction hadn't been too off. He'd aimed just to the right of the emplacement he'd seen on the berm, and now he could just see it, the edge of a couple of sandbags and the muzzle of what looked like a DShK sticking out, pointing up toward the jungle-swathed hillside.

More shrubs and grass rustled faintly, and he watched, pressed up against the berm, as Vernon, Max, and Bill came out of the undergrowth and up to the berm, faint, dark shapes against the slightly lighter earth. So far, nobody had come up under the machine gun emplacement.

He eased his pack onto his back and took his rifle in his hands. The berm was only about seven feet tall. It would still present a formidable obstacle, but it wasn't as bad as it could have been. Especially since the enemy should be looking the other way any minute now.

Right on cue, a series of faint, metallic *pops* echoed across the valley. Moments later, a whirring sound started to increase in pitch, and Dan got flat against the berm instinctively, desperately hoping that the mortarmen were on target. He knew of a few too many blue-on-blue incidents with mortars.

They were. Whoever MMPR had recruited as mortarmen, they were either really lucky, or they knew their stuff. With a series of earthshaking *krumps*, the mortar rounds screamed in to hammer the north side of the triangle, fountains of dirt, smoke, and flying metal rising into the night sky, lit from underneath by the brief, actinic flashes of detonations.

A moment later, almost drowned out by the mortar barrage, several machine guns opened fire from the treeline, and RPG-32 rounds started to hit, sounding like the world's biggest rifles firing moments before the thunderous explosions as the rounds spent their fury against the northern defensive positions.

As soon as they were reasonably sure they weren't about to have a mortar round drop on their heads, Dan and his teammates started up over the berm.

The berm was steep, but not all that well-compacted. It was a hands-and-knees scramble to get up to the top, where Dan flattened himself on the top of the berm, his rifle up and searching for targets. Ideally, they wouldn't have to engage until they were well inside the camp, maximizing the element of surprise. As long as the pirates' attention was on the guys out in the jungle raining fire on them, the ground assault still had that advantage.

The camp was in full scramble, but, just as planned, the pirates' entire focus seemed to be on both getting to cover and moving to repel an attack from the north. The emplacement they'd just flanked actually appeared to be empty, the gunners having either run toward the sound of the explosions or toward the nearest bunker.

Dan looked to either side, made sure that at least most of his team was with him, then started down the inside of the berm. Now he was feeling the absence of body armor, but plates would not have been a good idea during the approach. They would have to concentrate on maintaining stealth, surprise, and quickly get absolute fire superiority when they inevitably made contact.

He glanced back at the berm, to see that somebody—he couldn't see who—had actually commandeered the DShK and turned it around to face the inside of the camp. So they'd have somewhat more direct fire support when the time came. He felt a little better, even as he pointed to Lambert and pointed him toward the nearest group of tents on the left, which on closer inspection were actually semi-permanent shelters with canvas roofs. It wouldn't do them any good against indirect fire, as was being brutally demonstrated on the north side, but they weren't quite as flimsy as they had looked on the overheads.

The tents weren't their primary focus, anyway. Their little team of analyst eggheads was sure that Yuan was in one of the bunkers. They had some distance still to go to get to the nearest one.

Moving carefully from shadow to shadow, though less worried about noise thanks to the miniature Armageddon going on to the north, Dan slipped toward the center of the camp. A few bone-shaking *thud*s sounded nearby, and canvas roofs flapped into the sky, shredded by shrapnel and overpressure as grenades rolled inside went off. So far, it still just sounded like a bombardment, rather than an assault. Nobody but the machine gunners in the jungle had fired a shot yet.

After ten minutes of pounding, the bombardment lifted, as planned. A few long bursts of machine gun fire continued to rake the northern side of the triangle for a handful of seconds before they, too, went silent.

The silence lasted for mere moments, and even then, it only seemed silent in contrast to the thunder that had preceded it.

Moans and screams from the wounded rose into the night sky, competing against shouts in Mandarin as a few of Yuan's officers tried to rally the pirates to repel the anticipated assault. A few moments later, the relative quiet was shattered again as some of the pirates got back up onto the cratered, smoking berm and opened fire with a ragged roar of automatic weapons fire, pouring a sloppy mad minute into the killing zone and the treeline to try to stop the imagined assault cold.

There was enough noise from the weapons fire, even as Dan concentrated on penetrating deeper into the camp, still unnoticed, that he almost missed the other sound that was steadily getting louder.

The snarl of helicopters.

Chapter 14

"*Shang Wei*?" the pilot called back on the Z-8's intercom. "The pirates appear to be already engaged with someone else."

Feng looked up, standing to get a better look out of the helicopter's windshield. It was easy to see what the pilot was talking about; the entire north side of Yuan's fortified camp was wreathed in smoke and dust, and muzzle flashes flickered all along the berm, with some green tracers easily seen flashing into the treeline.

Either our timing is perfect, or the entire operation is about to disintegrate, he thought. *It would appear that our mysterious rivals are on the ground already. Perhaps we can neutralize the mercenaries and the pirates at the same time. Two hawks, one arrow.*

"Noted," he said to the pilot, then switched to the overall air net, addressing the entire formation, though primarily aimed at the Z-10 attack helicopters on the flanks. "All stations, be advised that there are two factions fighting on the ground. Both are to be considered hostile. Fire support, begin prepping the landing zone, concentrate fire on the treeline as well as the camp."

He got crisp acknowledgments from each pilot in turn, and the wasp-like silhouettes of the Z-10s dipped down toward the jungle, looking for their prey. In moments, rockets were streaking down toward the treeline and the camp's fortified wall, as the lumbering transports circled above, waiting for the enemy to be suppressed enough to descend and disgorge their cargoes of Marines and *Jiaolong* commandos.

This ends tonight, Feng thought.

Dan froze as the first salvo of rockets streaked down from the sky to slam into the northern berm and the treeline beyond with a series of savage detonations that rivaled the earlier mortar barrage.

Now, we are fucked, he thought. He briefly thought that somehow Yuan had gotten his own air support, but in a moment it became clear that the pirates were under fire, as well. Granted, that was small comfort. If the helos were hitting any source of gunfire they saw, that meant the support-by-fire positions in the jungle were getting hammered, too.

Glancing back, he saw the DShK on the berm, that had been turned around to provide fire support for the assault element, turn skyward and start firing at the growling shapes spitting death down on

140

the camp. Flame belched from the bell-shaped muzzle brake, the heavy *thud-thud-thud* of the 12.7mm all but drowned out by the renewed cacophony of the aerial bombardment.

It was also the gunner's death sentence. One of the helicopters banked hard, coming around and launching a four-rocket salvo at the berm. The helo gunner was dead-on. The DShK position disappeared in a blast of fire, smoke, and dust. Dan wasn't sure who had been manning the gun; all he was sure about at that point was that he had Max, Vernon, Bill, and Sam near him. The rest were spread out through the camp. They had objectives and rally points. The requirements of stealth had precluded much more coordination than that.

The camp was now a hellstorm of smoke, dust, explosions, and gunfire. In a way, it wasn't that different from what had been happening only a few minutes before, except now the situation had just flown right out of the mercenaries' control.

Dan and his teammates held their position. For the moment, they were still undetected, as near as he could tell. But that could change any second. He had to decide what to do, and decide fast. Try to complete the mission under cover of the shitstorm falling down around their ears, try to go to ground and lay low—not a good option if there were troops coming in behind the attack helicopters—or try to get the hell out.

Decision time was momentarily pushed back as a small knot of pirates suddenly ran in front of their shadowed concealment. One of them happened to glance toward the violent death of the heavy gun emplacement, and spied the ghillied-up shapes crouching next to one of the shelters. He let out a yell, that got strangled as Dan brought up his rifle, the Aimpoint's red dot a bright green pinpoint in his NVGs, and rapped three rounds into the man's upper torso and throat. The pirate fell backward, knocking into the man behind him. Whether or not they'd heard his yell or the sound of the shots over the rest of the noise, one of their own going down was enough to get their attention. They turned toward the nearer threat, rifles tracking toward Dan's muzzle flash.

The rest of the mercenaries were ready for them, however, and a stuttering barrage of gunfire cut them down, the rifle reports sounding like little more than *pops* in the roar of destructive noise around them. So much for staying undetected.

A hand clapped down on Dan's shoulder. He whipped his head around, thinking he was dead, but it was Decker, his cammie paint streaked with sweat, dirt, and blood; he looked like he'd taken a little frag to the scalp. There were a few other figures behind him, but it didn't look like anything close to the entire twenty-nine man element they'd come over the berm with.

"We can still get Yuan," Decker barked over the thunder. Another attack helicopter was making a pass, rockets streaking from its stubby wings even as its cannon roared, kicking up fountains of dirt and pulverized rock along the berm and into the camp. There was more fire going skyward now, as the pirates that had survived the initial onslaught rallied to fight back. Of course, that wasn't necessarily working out all that well, as the helo gunners retaliated quickly, and with greater firepower. Rockets and tracer fire lit the night. "We get that bastard, and the job's done."

Dan wasn't so sure. Somebody else sure wanted Yuan out of the picture, and now the contractors were pretty well caught in the crossfire. But Decker didn't wait to see what his response would be. He just did a "follow me" wave and started toward the nearest bunker.

It was kind of the last thing that Dan had expected out of the man. Decker had seemed entirely jaded and cynical about the job, the employer, and the entire situation. Yet here he was, leading a charge through the fire and smoke like some gung-ho officer who'd read too many war stories.

"Fuck!" Decker might be a humorless bastard, and some of the decisions he had enforced had made his judgment a little doubtful, but Dan couldn't just stay back and watch him run to his death. He got up and followed, trying to stay as low as possible. The rest followed, getting into a sort of rough wedge as best they could in the increasingly narrow confines of the camp.

It took a second for him to realize that there were fewer explosions and less cannon fire going on around them. Whether it was due to a lack of targets or because the birds were running out of ordnance, he didn't know. Either way, they didn't have to worry as much about getting smoked from the air, but at the same time, they had less chaos to conceal their movement. There was still plenty of smoke and dust in the air, but he still fully expected that whoever had sent in those helos was going to be sending in ground troops soon, and then they really would be between a rock and a hard place.

One of the central bunkers loomed up out of the darkness and smoke ahead. It stood only about five feet above the ground, a thick, solid structure of logs, stones, and packed dirt. There were burning generators and toppled, smashed floodlights around it, but the bunker itself looked like it hadn't even been scratched. The entrance was a darker square in the side, and that was what Decker was making for, now at a dead run.

Which was exactly what the pirates inside had been expecting any assaulters who might have made it inside the perimeter to do.

The dark rectangle of the entrance suddenly lit up with a blazing ball of white-hot flame, and machine gun fire just about tore Decker in half. His momentum kept his corpse moving forward, but he sprawled on his face in a welter of blood, mud, and his own shredded intestines spilling from his midsection.

142

Two of the others who had joined them along with Decker went down hard in the same instant. Dan threw himself to the ground and behind the nearest somewhat solid object he could find, which was the wreckage of one of the shelters. There were some timbers that might act as cover for a few moments before they were chewed to splinters, but he had to get something between him and that gun's kill zone.

He found Vernon, Max, and Sam had come with him. He wasn't sure where Bill was, but he was afraid he was one of the bodies still getting chewed up out in the lane.

"We've got to get the fuck out of here," Max said into his ear. "This situation is officially fucked."

Dan couldn't agree more. But with the helos circling overhead, making a run for it would probably only get them gunned down before they could cross the kill zone outside the berm. Their options weren't just limited, they were damned near nonexistent.

He lay there in the meager cover of the collapsed shelter, breathing in the smoke and dust and the shit-smell of death, and an eerie calm settled over him. He'd experienced it a handful of times before, usually in very dangerous situations where life or death balanced on a knife-point. Everything around him seemed strangely clear, even through the haze and darkness. Peering up over the timbers, he could see the entrance of the bunker, that had been turned into a hasty firing position, and several other firing ports around the flank, shored up with sandbags. Even without the sudden arrival of the air strikes, that would have been one hell of a nut to crack. If they'd managed to creep close enough undetected, they might have managed it. Now, it was completely hopeless.

Another attack helicopter snarled by overhead. The rocket fire had all but stopped, and only the occasional burst of cannon fire roared in response to any fire from below. Dan briefly wondered how many of the contractors were still alive, lying low and trying to play dead like them, hoping the gunners didn't decide to make certain of the thermal signatures down below with a few well-placed cannon shells. It certainly seemed like the pirates were done.

A hulking shape dipped toward the camp, its rotors churning the smoke into fantastical whorls, lit by a few ground fires. The downdraft hammered at the wreckage of the soft shelters beneath, as fast ropes dropped from the heavy transport helo's rear ramp.

Something drew Dan's eyes back toward the bunker. A hatch seemed to have opened in the roof, and three figures were crawling out, drawing several long tubes with them. It took him a second to realize what he was looking at. In that time, one of the crouched figures had brought a tube to his shoulder and aimed it at the helicopter.

Oh, shit, he thought. *Nobody said anything about the pirates having SAMs.*

The first troops were already on the fast ropes when the MANPAD fired, the initial *hiss* of the ejection charge quickly drowned out by the *bang* of the missile's main engine firing. It didn't have far to fly before it slammed into the helicopter's flank with a catastrophic, ear-splitting crash. Flames spat from the engine and fragments whickered through the air, including several large sections of the aircraft's rotor. The helo spun halfway around as it plunged the sixty feet to the ground, where it hit with a tooth-rattling impact, the still-spinning remains of the rotor biting into ground and wreckage and ripping into smaller bits of flying metal and fiberglass that could easily tear a man apart.

The night just wasn't going according to plan for *anybody*.

Feng felt his guts clench as he saw the lead Z-8 take a close-range hit from what could only be a shoulder-fired SAM or heavy RPG and go down. There was a slim chance that there might be survivors, but it had hit hard, and the Marines, along with a squad of his own *Jiaolong*, had been already deploying. The likelihood that any of them had been sufficiently braced for the impact was pretty low. At least thirty men were probably dead, just like that.

The helo pilots were already reacting, even before he could say anything. The Z-10s were trying to take the launch site under fire, but they had already expended most of their munitions, and another MANPAD rose up out of the murk, reaching for the attack helicopter that was just starting to make a gun run. The pilot tried to jink, but if there wasn't much space for the missile to correct its course, neither was there much for him to evade it in the split second between launch and impact. The warhead detonated just behind his tail rotor, and the Z-10 limped away, smoke pouring from its tail.

His own pilot was already pulling hard for the nearest ridge, trying to get some terrain between his bird and the deadly missiles below, hitting the flare dispenser several times along the way, spitting white-hot magnesium out into the sky to try to spoof the SAMs before they could zero in on the heat pouring from the helicopter's engines. Feng wanted to tell him to set down and let his men out, but the pilot wasn't even acknowledging him; the safety of the helicopter came first.

Feng held on as the evasive maneuvers threatened to throw him across the Z-8's passenger compartment, trying to think of how to salvage the situation. He still had three platoons of Marines and three squads of *Jiaolong* remaining. If he could get them on the ground close enough, they could still move in overland and take the camp. Both the pirates and the mysterious Westerners had to have taken a thorough beating. They could still take Yuan down and finish this.

But his radio crackled with Yiti's voice. "Abort, abort, abort," the Uighur *Shang Wei* called. "All callsigns, take evasive action and return to base."

"Negative!" Feng snapped, as soon as he could reach his transmit switch. "We will move to a secondary landing zone and deploy on the ground."

"The air support is nearly out of ordnance, and fuel is becoming an issue," Yiti replied emotionlessly. He was right; in the interests of trying to maintain some illusion that this was not a major operation, the *Changbai Shan* was nearly at the limit of the helicopters' range to the north. "And we have just lost a quarter of our assault force. We need to regroup and re-attack, instead of attempting to salvage the attack now."

Before Feng could respond, a new voice came over the radio. "This is 200453," *Shang Xiao* Guo Pan said. "All units abort and return to 20045."

That was that. Feng raged behind a blank face. He might have been the one tasked with neutralizing Yuan, but even he could not disobey a direct order from a *Shang Xiao*. The pilot, without even turning back to look at him, banked the helicopter back to the northwest to swing wide around Pulau Matak, heading back to the *Changbai Shan*.

Dan watched the helos retreat, the snarl of their rotors receding into the distance, and wondered if maybe he was going to survive the night after all.

But then, with shouts and yells and some gunfire, pirates came pouring out of the bunker in front of him, reminding him that they were still in one hell of a tight spot.

He looked around carefully. Across the lane between wrecked and burning shelters, he could see two more figures in ghillies crouched or lying in some scant cover and concealment, their weapons still up like they were still alive and alert. Counting the other three with him, that made six. He hoped there were more survivors elsewhere in the camp, but if they didn't do something quick, that number was going to rapidly go down to zero.

Careful to stay as low as possible, and hoping that whoever was over there was paying attention and not just staring at the pirates coming out of the bunker, he gave a hand signal to move back toward the berm. At first he thought it hadn't been seen, but then a gloved hand came off of a SG 553's forearm and gave a surreptitious acknowledgment. A moment later, the two vague shapes started easing back, away from the open area.

Dan followed suit, with the other three keeping close behind him. There was plenty of smoke and shadow to take advantage of, but they still didn't dare just get up and run. If they were spotted, they'd have to shoot their way out, and that cut their chances of survival down even further.

They crawled on bellies and elbows through wreckage and carnage. Few of the shelters had escaped either the mortars or the

145

rockets unscathed; some were completely destroyed, a few were burning, some had only partially collapsed. One or two looked relatively undamaged, except for the smoke pouring out of the destroyed canvas roofs. Much of the open ground was cratered, or littered with splinters and still-smoking bits of shrapnel. How many were rocket casings and how many were bits of the crashed helicopter, Dan didn't know.

He reached forward in the flickering darkness and put his hand on something that yielded a little. He suddenly realized it was a foot, torn off by an explosion at the ankle. Bloody, jagged bone was sticking up out of it, and the foot itself was pretty torn up. He shoved it aside in disgust, and kept going.

It was only a couple hundred meters to the berm, but it felt like a couple hundred miles. They didn't dare just make a straight shot for it, either. They had to keep as much concealment between themselves and the pirates that were still coming out of their holes as possible. So they wove their way through the shelters and wreckage, trying to stay away from any that were burning brightly enough to shed any light on the ground.

With still only about fifty meters to go, Dan crept around a stack of boxes to come almost face to face with a pirate who was trying, unsuccessfully, to render first aid to one of his fellows. The pirate on the ground was missing a leg and most of his face, and was obviously dead. The other man looked up and met Dan's gaze even as he looked at him.

For a second, both of them just froze. The pirate was probably shell-shocked enough to not quite comprehend what he was looking at at first. Dan just didn't want to shoot him, since it had grown quiet enough after the raging storm of fire from above that a gunshot would definitely attract attention.

The pirate's eyes widened, as his brain sorted the picture in front of him into an unfamiliar man in a ghillie suit and camouflage face paint, his eyes obscured behind the twin tubes of night vision goggles and carrying a rifle. His mouth opened to yell as he realized that the shape in front of him didn't belong, and wasn't friendly.

Dan surged off the ground, covering the three feet to the pirate in a single lunge, his knife coming out of its sheath as he moved. He clapped a hand over the pirate's mouth as he slammed into him, almost bending the man over backward with the impact, driving the blade up under his ribs with short, vicious jabs. The pirate's hands flailed at him in pain-wracked panic, as he bore down, trying desperately to keep his victim quiet as he opened up his vitals with stab after stab.

Finally, after what felt like an eternity, the pirate's struggles slowed, weakened, then stopped. Dan lifted himself off the body, wiping his knife on the ragged, scorched t-shirt before sheathing it again and looking around to see if the violence had drawn any attention.

His heart was pounding and he could feel the adrenaline still surging through his veins, but his preternatural calm was still there. Some part of him still recognized that survival required that his emotions be shut off, and so he felt nothing as he looked down at the butchered corpse beneath him.

He would later.

Vernon, Max, and Sam had spread out around him while he did his work, weapons up and covering all directions. Vernon risked a glance back at him, and he nodded. Time to go.

They moved back into the darkness, little more than shadows slinking along the ground. The shouts and calls of the pirates, mostly in Mandarin, though a few were in Cantonese or Javanese, were getting louder as it became obvious that the attack was over. They had to move, to get out before they were discovered, but to rush at this point was to invite discovery and death. With every nerve ending screaming that they had to *move*, Dan forced himself to set a slow, stealthy pace.

Finally, they were at the berm. Now speed became essential; the berm rose high enough that there would be no concealment while they went over.

Crouched at the base, Dan looked over at the other three. They were all breathing hard; as slow as the movement had been, the sheer strain of it had been exhausting.

"On three," he whispered. "Up and over. One, two, three." Together, they came to their feet and started up the inside slope of the berm. It wasn't as steep as the outer face, and they could get up more easily, probably by design, so that the pirates could have shooters climb up and lie on the inside slope to shoot over the berm at any attackers.

Just as they reached the top, a shout froze Dan's blood. A split second later, a shot *crack*ed past his head, denying any hope that the shout had been about something else.

Almost as one, all four of them dropped to the prone on top of the berm and returned fire. It wasn't particularly aimed fire, as they each dumped most of a mag in the general direction of the bunkers. Then they were plunging down the far side and into the brush and rocks.

More shouting and gunfire echoed from behind them. The pirates were in full hue and cry now. They weren't going to be able to just slip away into the jungle. At least not right away.

At the bottom, Dan gasped, "By twos. Max, you're with me." The big man nodded, and together they turned and hit a knee, lifting their weapons back toward the top of the berm.

A figure, vaguely silhouetted against the faint glow of the fires diffused through the smoke, appeared on top of the berm, carrying one of the bullpup Chinese rifles. Dan raised his own rifle, putting the red dot on the target, but a shot *snap*ped past from behind him and took the pirate in the gut. Three more rapid shots and the dark figure dropped out of sight.

That was the signal that Vernon and Sam were in position. Dan turned and looked back, but he couldn't see the other two in the brush, so he had to hope that he wasn't about to run in front of a rifle muzzle. "Go!" he hissed at Max. The other man was already moving.

He ran, crouched over, just behind Max, stripping the nearly empty mag out and rocking another in, counting to three as he went. They had to keep their rushes short.

A storm of automatic fire roared from the top of the berm at them even as he dropped to the ground. As bad as the night might have been for everybody involved, the pirates had taken a beating and were out for blood. They knew an enemy was out there, and right at the moment, they didn't give a shit who it was; they just wanted that enemy, any enemy, dead.

Crouched behind a convenient boulder, Dan got back behind his rifle, braced the forearm against the side of the rock, and opened fire, dragging the red dot along the top of the berm as he dumped another half a magazine. A little voice in the back of his head was suggesting that conserving ammo might just be a good idea, but at the moment, they needed fire superiority just to break contact and get away.

The incoming fire seemed to slacken a little bit in response to his and Max's bullets, but it didn't die off completely. The pirates were *pissed*, and it gets harder to suppress somebody who's running on rage. The shots converging on his position, as they got a muzzle flash to aim at, made it seem like an age before Sam and Vernon opened up again. A few rounds smacked off his boulder, one skipping off the top to *buzz* off into the darkness behind him.

Finally, Sam and Vernon took up the fire again, and he turned and bounded back, his lungs heaving, every muscle protesting as he ran doubled over. Bullets hissed and *crack*ed overhead in both directions as he ran, some getting close enough that he could feel the vegetation around him getting chopped to pieces.

After another fifty meters, they were only taking a few sporadic shots anymore. Dan suspected that the pirates had pulled off the berm in order to organize a hunting party, but for the moment, he'd take full advantage of the lull in the fire to make tracks.

He and Max found Sam and Vernon just inside the treeline. "Is this it?" Vernon asked. He sounded a little shell-shocked himself.

"We'll see," Dan replied grimly. He was afraid that they might well be the only survivors. He had no way of knowing if the other two he'd seen had made it out. "Let's get to the rally point, then back to the boats." He didn't mention the fear that the boats might not even be there anymore. After the horror that had already happened that night, he wasn't willing to bet on *anything* going right.

We're dead, Dan thought. *We might still be walking and*

breathing, but we're dead. It's over.

He was crouched beneath a palm tree, barely a few meters back from the beach, watching the pirates drag their Zodiacs down out of the treeline. There were flashlights ranging over the yacht he could see further out on the water, and the cutters floating nearby were definitely not MMPR's. Nor was the frigate looming above all of them. The *Zhaotong* had come out of hiding.

He eased back carefully, trying not to make any noise. He could clearly hear the conversation as two pirates rummaged through the Zodiac they'd just pulled out from under its camouflage, even though he couldn't understand it. He worked his way back to the others, farther up on the slope.

"No getting out that way," he murmured as he joined the small perimeter huddled in a thick grove of towering trees. "The *Zhaotong* is out there. If any of the boats didn't get rolled up, they beat feet for Singapore." He grimaced, though no one could see it in the darkness. "We could call them back, but we need a safe landing site first." At least they had comms. Rex had made it out of the slaughter to the north, with all of five others that Dan didn't know, all new guys. Six survivors, out of a force of nearly fifty.

Vernon suddenly lifted a hand to signal quiet. Everyone froze, straining their ears.

The sound was faint, but only because of distance. Someone was moving through the jungle to the south, someone who wasn't all that skilled at it. Even as they listened, there was a faint crackle and thump, and what might have been a muffled curse.

Dan pointed at Max. The other man might have been big, but his size was deceptive when it came to most things, and he could move surprisingly quietly through the undergrowth. Max nodded and got up to follow as Dan led the way along the side slope.

It was tricky going, especially since the pirates weren't far in either direction. While they hadn't heard or seen anyone on their back trail in over an hour, Dan wasn't discounting the possibility that they were still being followed. After the bloodletting at the camp, they weren't going to let their quarry get away easily. Staying quiet was still absolutely necessary, and made for slow going through the thick jungle.

But whoever was making noise wasn't getting far. Dan was pretty sure he heard somebody fall at least twice more.

Dan paused as he saw movement ahead. The noise was louder, and the muttering was definitely in English, though thankfully not louder than a whisper. They were that smart, at least. "You lot need to slow the fuck down and shut the fuck up before you get us caught," he hissed.

Silence fell. He could imagine the shocked looks. Then he stepped closer and didn't have to imagine as much anymore.

There were only three of them; Jenny, Cassy, and Loren, the new guy who had been put in charge of the *Mercury Quick* for the time being. The girls were mostly kitted up and armed; Loren looked like he'd been lounging by a pool, in board shorts and not much else. He'd at least had the presence of mind to grab a pistol on the way off the yacht. The jungle hadn't been kind to his bare torso; even on NVGs, Dan could see the welts and scratches where he wasn't covered in mud.

"What the hell happened?" he asked, too loudly.

"Everything went to shit, what the fuck do you think happened?" Dan hissed at him. "Now shut your fucking mouth." He pointed back the way they'd come. "Rally point's back there. Do you know if anybody else made it ashore?"

Cassy shook her head with a shudder. "No, I think we're it." There was a quaver in her voice. "It was bad."

"I'm sure it was," he replied. "Let's go. We're not out of this yet."

Chapter 15

Shang Xiao Guo Pan faced Feng across the tiny wardroom, his face utterly impassive. The battalion commander was putting on weight with age, but he didn't appear soft in spite of the expanding belly. He looked more like a mountain, a great, immobile granite obstacle standing between Feng and his mission. The looming presence of Political Commissar Li Jianzhong at the *Shang Xiao's* elbow only served to accentuate the dire situation Feng now found himself in.

"No," the older man said. There was a finality in his voice that warned Feng not to pursue his request further. "I just lost thirty men and a quarter of my helicopter assets. Those are losses that I will have to justify to *Da Xiao* Wu Sen. What do you have to show for these losses, *Shang Wei*? I will tell you. Nothing. The deserter is still at large, and the *Zhaotong* is no closer to being recovered."

Feng fought to maintain his composure, choking back his rage at the older officer's words. He didn't dare say what he was thinking; that if Guo hadn't recalled them all the way back to the *Changbai Shan*, he and Yiti might have had a chance to regroup and re-attack. They might have salvaged the situation. Yuan might even now be lying cold on a slab in the *Changbai Shan's* hold, his damaging blackmail file under control. They wouldn't even be having this conversation.

Instead, he was now facing serious consequences for a failed mission that he might have salvaged if not for the immovable object sitting in front of him, with the single star and crossed palms on his shoulder boards.

He risked a glance at Li. The Commissar's face was as carefully expressionless as the *Shang Xiao's*, though Feng thought he saw a sort of contemptuous amusement in his eyes. The Commissar had always been strictly proper around him, but Feng had sensed the sort of self-important attitude of authority in the man that would willingly interfere with another's mission simply to reinforce his power as a Commissar.

How much do I have you to thank for this disaster? he wondered.

Apparently deciding that Feng was not going to reply, Guo continued. "While the mission remains to either neutralize or recover the *Zhaotong*, and I am sure that your orders remain in force as well, as long as there are SAMs active on those islands, I will not send my aircraft anywhere near them. There will be no second air assault."

Feng made a show of pondering that for a moment. "And if my

Jiaolong can neutralize the SAMs?" he asked.

Guo's features didn't flicker. "Then further joint operations *may* be possible. However, I will not allow you use of any more of my assets until then."

They are not your *assets, you imperious* hun dan, Feng thought savagely. *They are the People's Republic's assets.* He still kept his expression still and his thoughts to himself. Even a connected *Jiaolong* commander did not say such things to a *Shang Xiao* when he was only a *Shang Wei* himself. Instead, he simply nodded respectfully. "I shall keep you informed of my movements and progress, then, *Shang Xiao* Guo."

"See that you do," Guo said, and waved his dismissal. Feng came to attention and saluted crisply. Guo's return salute was professional enough at least. Feng turned on his heel and left the wardroom.

Shen was waiting for him outside. It struck Feng how lucky he was to still have the *Shi Zhang* with him; it could easily have been Shen's helicopter that had gone down the night before. "News from the mainland, *Shang Wei*," he said, handing Feng a tablet.

Feng took it. Most of the PLA was still using printouts, but the *Jiaolong* and the other Special Units were going increasingly high-tech. He unlocked the device and read the short report on the screen.

Finally, some good news. Hu's information had been actionable, but without the assets readily available, Feng couldn't go after the Westerners' base of operations on the Desaru peninsula himself. Direct Chinese action would probably be frowned upon by Beijing, as well. He had spent several hours trying to plan a surreptitious raid on the resort that wouldn't draw the Malaysian authorities' attention, but had ultimately passed the information on to the Second Department's office in the PRC's Embassy in Kuala Lumpur. It had taken far longer than he'd hoped to see action on the tip, but the report in his hands said that at 0400 that morning, the Special Action Unit of the Malaysian PGK had stormed the resort and captured nearly a dozen personnel, along with enough weapons and ammunition to equip a slightly understrength infantry battalion. The Americans were presently being held in an undisclosed location, likely to be transferred to Kamunting Detention Center, Malaysia's "Supermax." The Government of Malaysia would be issuing a formal, if stiff, thanks to the People's Republic of China for the information that led to the raid and the capture of the illegal operation on Malaysian soil.

Feng nodded. "One obstacle at least should be out of the picture now," he said. "The *laowai* operatives, if any survived last night, are now cut off from support. If anything, the pirates should take care of any stragglers by the time we can get back onto the islands. Then we only have to worry about the defector and his pirates."

"I'm not getting shit," Rex said, a rising note of panic in his voice. He was huddled over the small tablet and Iridium GO! that he'd brought for comms back to Desaru. "I've sent a dozen messages in the last half hour. No reply at all. What the fuck is going on?"

Dan looked over at him, resisting the urge to snap at the smaller man. The situation was bad enough without any of them freaking out. Several of the newer guys who had made it out of the pulverized hell of the northern treeline with Rex were already looking more than a little shaky, and Loren hadn't stopped whimpering since he and Max had brought him and the girls in. All it would take was for one of them to panic, and they were well and truly fucked. He'd expected better out of Rex.

"Off the top of my head, I'd imagine that something's gone wrong back at the resort," Dan replied quietly. "Either they've got some technical glitch going on, or..." he trailed off. He really hadn't meant to start down that path.

But Rex had picked up on it. "Or they're gone, and they left us here," he finished. There was a mixture of disbelief and sheer, pants-shitting panic in his eyes as he looked at Dan. "Left us on a fucking island in the middle of the South China Sea with a bunch of fucking pirates."

Dan shot him a warning glare, but it was too late. His voice had carried across the grove.

"What do you mean, they left us?" Jenny demanded. Her voice rose rapidly. "They can't fucking do that! We're fucking Americans! They can't just fucking leave us!"

"They might not have had any choice," Dan pointed out. He glanced at Vernon, who gave him a "you're in charge here, buddy," look. *Thanks, asshole,* Dan thought at him. "Presuming that that is what happened, which we simply don't know. Remember, we're not exactly out here with the full might and fury of the US Armed Forces behind us."

Jenny wasn't listening. "What the fuck is this bullshit? They had helicopters out there! Where's *our* fucking air support?" She turned on Rex, apparently deciding that he was the nearest representative of MMPR to vent her wrath on. She started hitting him. "Where the fuck is our support?!" she started screaming. "I don't care who you have to call with that fucking thing, tell them to come and fucking get us!"

Vernon stepped in at that point. Her yelling was going to travel beyond their little hideaway, even with the river close to mask as much noise as possible. He clapped a hand over her mouth to try to quiet her down, but she bit him. He yanked his hand back with a muttered, "Fuck," then wrapped her up in a triangle choke and bore down until she stopped moving. He eased her to the jungle floor far more gently than she probably deserved.

Dan glowered around at the remaining survivors. Sam, Cassy,

and Cary were pointedly looking outboard, holding security to avoid getting involved in the commotion. The sun was starting to go down again, and the grove was rapidly descending into twilight. It had been seventeen hours since they'd broken contact and gotten the hell away from Yuan's camp. After this long, he was fairly certain that these fifteen were the only ones who had made it out.

"Listen to me," he said, keeping his voice as level as possible. "Whatever is going on back on the mainland, there's not a damned thing we can do about it except keep trying to make contact. Until then, we need to stay alive, and do what we can to get out of here." He knelt next to the map of the islands that he'd had in his pack. He'd long ago decided that he'd be damned if he ever went into an AO without a map, and it looked like that habit might just save them this time. He pointed to the northern tip of Siantan. "There's a town right here on the north coast, called Terempa. It's not very big, but there will be boats there. We might be able to hire one, or if Yuan's got his claws deep enough into the community to make that a losing proposition, we'll just steal one in the middle of the night and head for Malaysia. If we can't get through to the company by then, we'll make for Singapore."

"And what are we going to do there?" Sam asked. "No entry visas, armed to the teeth...we'll be in Singaporean jail until we're old and bent."

"We'll dump the weapons and kit in the ocean before we go in," Dan said. "Along with anything incriminating. If anybody asks, we're just tourists out of a *different* resort in Desaru, who got lost at sea."

He looked around, as the rest let it sort of soak in. He still saw mostly shock, disbelief, and, most poisonously, fear. Nobody was ready for this. Like Jenny had shrieked, they were Americans, dammit. They were used to being the top dog. Dan, and he suspected, a few of the others, including Vernon and Max, had probably had enough experience in the PMC world to know that this was something that was always hanging over your head when you took a dollar to pack a gun in a foreign country without Uncle Sam's strict say-so. Apparently, not everybody on the contract had figured that out. For damned sure it hadn't been in any of MMPR's briefing materials. They probably wouldn't have gotten as many takers if it had been.

But, ready or not, this was the reality they had to face. And with Rex displaying the same mix of shock and fear as the rest, Dan realized with a sinking sensation that it was on him to make sure they held it together and faced that reality head-on.

At least he didn't have to watch his back around Lambert anymore. As faintly guilty as he felt about it, there was a sense of relief that the man hadn't made it.

He checked his watch. "Somebody wake Jenny up and make sure she stays quiet. We've got some territory to cover."

Tom Lambert had long prided himself on being a hard motherfucker. That didn't stop him from groaning and puking all over himself when he came to. Had he been a little bit more self-aware, it might have reminded him of Nong Song's awakening, but that wasn't the way his mind worked.

At first he couldn't tell where he was. That would in large part be because of the bag over his head. He couldn't see a damned thing, and the bag already smelled bad enough even without his own puke all over the inside of it. Other than that, he knew he was lying on his side, his feet lashed together and his hands tied behind his back, but that was all.

A savage kick caught him in the midsection, and he retched again, except this time there wasn't anything to bring up. He heard voices speaking in Chinese, or at least he thought it was Chinese, but he couldn't understand a word of it.

Suddenly the bag was pulled off his head, and a hand grabbed him by the hair and yanked him upright. He realized he had to have suffered some kind of TBI in the explosions at the fort. His head swam as he was roughly pulled up to his knees. He squinted painfully in the glare of several flashlights.

"What is your name?" a harsh voice asked in heavily-accented English. He tried to see who had spoken, but there was just a vague silhouette behind the harsh white lights.

It took a second for him to get his voice. His first attempt to speak came out as little more than a whisper. The hand still twined in his hair gave him a shake, further rattling his brains and worsening the pain that seemed to radiate from his head throughout the rest of his body.

"Lambert," he finally managed.

"Lambert," the silhouetted man repeated. Under other circumstances, Lambert would have found the sound of his name being pronounced "Rambert" hilarious, but he was starting to understand just how narrow the line between life and death he was presently teetering on really was. "You have trespassed on my territory, Mister Lambert, attacked my interests and killed my men. Your life is already forfeit. If you tell me everything you know about who sent you, I will make your death quick. If you insist on staying silent, I will make it last two weeks."

Lambert shook his head, as much as it hurt. "They never told us shit about who was paying for it, but my guess would be the CIA," he replied quickly. "What else do you want to know?"

"Why would the CIA be interested in my operations?" the man demanded.

"Shit, I don't know, man," he answered. "They didn't tell us that much." Whether because of his choice of words or just because the man holding him up by his hair didn't like his answer, he got a solid knee to

155

the kidneys for that one. He groaned, but managed to keep from retching again.

For a long moment, the man behind the flashlights just stood there, studying him. He thought he could see the faintest glimmer of light reflecting from the man's eyes. Finally, the man, who had to be Yuan, said, "If you truly know so little, there is no point in wasting any further time with you, Mister Lambert. Goodbye." He turned to leave, and one of the flashlights lowered as the man holding it lifted a pistol. The muzzle looked big enough that he could climb up into it.

"Wait, wait, wait!" he yelled. "Don't kill me, not yet." He was wracking his brain to think of a way out of this. He didn't want to die this way, tied up, nauseous from a concussion, and on his knees. "Listen, I'm nobody. Killing me isn't going to gain you anything."

Yuan stopped, and turned back. He paused for a moment, then stepped forward into the light of the flashlights and crouched down in front of Lambert.

While they had had a few fuzzy photos of Yuan, Lambert had never really studied them that closely. As long as he had been getting paid and getting some trigger time, he hadn't really cared. He'd figured that they'd ID Yuan from site exploitation photos when the shooting was over. But now, faced with the man himself, he realized he'd been sort of expecting a Fu Manchu sort of character, with sinister eyes and a pointed goatee.

The real *Shang Xiao* Yuan was a thoroughly average-looking Han, clean-shaven and with a close-cropped military haircut that was going a little gray in the temples. He was fit and lean, wearing a simple green jacket and black fatigue trousers. The only thing ostentatious about him was the patent-leather pistol belt around his waist, that had been polished to a high sheen.

He peered into Lambert's eyes for a moment, as the man behind him lowered the pistol. Finally, still squatting in front of his prisoner, he asked, "Do you know what I have done here, Mister Lambert?

"My former superiors doubtless call me a deserter and a pirate, but all I have done is what every warrior ultimately wishes he could do; I have conquered my own kingdom. And a kingdom has to be defended, not only against those who are attacking it at the moment, but against those who might think to attack it in the future. To that end, examples have to be made. Even if I were more mercifully inclined toward you than I am, I would *have* to kill you, as a matter of principle."

"Look, man, I'm just a mercenary," Lambert said, "a hired gun. I only came here for the money; I work for the highest bidder. If you let me live," he continued, suddenly hatching on a desperate plan, "that would make *you* the highest bidder. I won't even need any other pay, just don't kill me. I'll do whatever you want me to. Just another job to me," he added, trying to avoid *too* much abject begging.

156

Again, Yuan paused and studied him, tilting his head slightly to one side as he did so. "You are a coward, Mister Lambert," he said, "trying to preserve your own life. But, fortunately for you, I do not like to discard a potentially useful tool until I have used it up. You just may be that potentially useful tool." He stood up and turned away.

"Does that mean I get to live?" Lambert asked.

Yuan looked over his shoulder at him. "For now, perhaps." He turned back into the shadows beyond, and shouted something in Mandarin. Then he turned back toward Lambert, folding his arms in front of him. "There are still a few of your comrades in the jungle, Mister Lambert," he said. "I have cut off their escape route to the sea, but my men are certain that a few are still at large. They will be hunted down. You will assist my men in doing so."

"Sure, man, whatever you want," Lambert said. "A job's a job."

Yuan simply watched him, his expression unreadable. Lambert was sweating, hoping that he'd managed to talk the pirate into sparing him. Hell, even if he got away somehow, there was no way he was going to get paid for the job MMPR had hired them for. The job was fucked. If he survived long enough, he might manage to make a little money as a pirate. It might make up for the utter clusterfuck this job had turned into.

There was some commotion from back in the dimness behind the guards and their still glaring lights. Then they parted, to reveal two more pirates, pistols in their hands, dragging a man between them.

He vaguely recognized him as one of Will's team, the skinny kid with the nose piercings that Tackett had laid out the night of the party. Colin, he thought the kid's name was. He'd taken a beating, his head hanging down as he was dragged into the light.

Yuan stepped forward, drew his pistol, and dropped the magazine. "Show me that you can be useful, Mister Lambert," he said. He press-checked the pistol to make sure there was still a round chambered, then offered it to Lambert, butt-first.

The guard holding him by the hair reached behind him. He felt the cold of steel between his hands, then the zip-cuffs snapped free, and he could move his hands. His feet were still bound, probably in case he got any funny ideas once he took the pistol from Yuan.

He didn't hesitate. He took the QSZ-92, put the muzzle to Colin's forehead, and pulled the trigger.

"Chief?" Henson stuck his head into Lawrence's office. "You got a minute?"

She didn't, really, but she realized that Henson wouldn't be bothering her just to chat. She finished the sentence in the wire she was working up for Langley and waved him inside. He had another folder in his hands.

"Please tell me you have some good news," she said, though she couldn't say she was all that hopeful. Jemaah Islamiyah seemed to be waging a war of its own against the supposed IS affiliate in Indonesia, and had been raising the stakes over the last month, with larger and more spectacular attacks across Java and Sumatra. The *Liaoning* carrier group seemed to be playing chicken with the *Antietam* and her air cover out of Clark Field near the Paracels. It had not been a good week, and it was only Tuesday.

The look on Henson's face confirmed for her that he wasn't there to make her week any less complicated, even before he said a word. "I'm afraid not," he said. "Not really."

Lawrence sighed. "Let me have it."

He put the folder on her desk, standing nervously as he summarized. "We've got two items, probably linked. The most immediately pressing for us is the more recent. At about four o'clock this morning, the Malaysian PGK raided a resort on the Desaru peninsula, and took a bunch of Americans into custody, along with what reads like one hell of an arsenal. Not just guns, either; they had rockets, explosives, grenades, high-end comms, night vision, you name it. The Malaysian government hasn't issued a formal statement yet, at least not that we've heard about."

"Oh, hell," Lawrence breathed, burying her head in her hands for a moment. Telfried was going to raise all kinds of hell about this. Not that there was much Lawrence could have done about it; after all, her station was pretty well occupied with Islamic terrorists and Chinese expansionism. And it wasn't like the Agency was behind the group that had gotten arrested by the Malaysians.

But Telfried had some serious animosities both toward the Agency and any US military personnel. Or anyone who had been US military. She was a product of Northeast, Ivy-League, blue-blood arrogance, with the contempt for the military and the intelligence community that went along with it. And she would lash out at anyone on her list of usual suspects whenever something like this happened.

"Do we have *any* more information to indicate who these people are, and who they might be working for?" she asked.

Henson shook his head. "No, and that just leads into the next thing. There was a big dust-up on Pulau Siantan last night. Lots of explosions, gunfire, and even helicopters. It looked like somebody was trying an air assault on one of Yuan's camps."

"They had air assault assets, too?" she picked up the folder, but the overhead images were mostly thermal, and didn't show very much beyond big white thermal blooms against the black of the jungle. That must have been a hell of a fight.

Henson grimaced. "We don't think so. Again, we haven't had a lot of assets devoted to watching this particular situation; as dangerous as Yuan's bunch is, they're kind of a sideshow compared to the other sh-" he stammered to correct himself—Lawrence didn't care much for profanity, "stuff we've got on our plates. But some of the imagery people are convinced that the choppers were Chinese. To make matters worse, it looks like one of them got shot down."

Lawrence just stared at the imagery for a long moment. "And Telfried is going to find a way to lay that on the Americans who got arrested, too," she said. "What the hell is going on out here? Who the hell are these people? Why haven't we been able to track down who's out playing 'Dogs of War' in our area of interest?"

Henson spread his hands helplessly. "I don't know, Chief," he said. "Whoever it is, they've been keeping things quiet enough that nobody outside of the immediate area either knows or cares. Who was going to really give a damn about some hired guns going after pirates on some islands nobody's ever heard of?"

"They're going to as soon as they hear the news that the Malaysians arrested thirteen Americans for terrorism, or whatever they're going to get charged with," she answered, after double-checking the report to make sure she had the numbers right. "This could turn into a major international incident fast if we don't get a handle on it." She looked at Henson. "Staff meeting in thirty minutes," she said. "We need to start putting more feelers out. We need to at least know what's going on before State can start getting ahead of things."

Henson nodded and turned to leave. He paused for a second at the door. "You know, I know somebody back in Virginia who might be able to start quietly inquiring. He's been retired for a while, but he knows people all over. If anybody anywhere near Langley is bankrolling this, he might be able to find out."

"Call him," she said. "Or email him, or whatever. We have *got* to figure this out before it makes things worse out here."

Chapter 16

Dan was getting pissed. Whatever MMPR had had in mind for this op, they obviously hadn't put as much time or money into vetting and training the new guys they'd sent out with Decker. Their fieldcraft sucked ass. While the jungle growth meant that they did have to stay closer together, these assclowns were bunched together, almost nut to butt. They were also crashing through the vegetation instead of moving around it, and making about as much noise as a herd of elephants in the process.

"I'm about ready to kneecap these fucking retards and leave them for Yuan," Dan muttered to Vernon as they halted again.

"Except that then we'd have fewer guns in the fight if and when the pirates catch up with us again," Vernon pointed out reasonably.

"More ammo for the rest of us," Dan grumbled.

He realized that the current situation was awakening a particularly dark part of his character. It was an aspect that he hadn't had to deal with for a long, long time. While he had always striven to be an honest, honorable man, there was a part of him, that only came to the surface in truly dire situations, that scared him a little. That side was a cold, pitiless, remorseless killing machine, something he didn't consider to be entirely human. It would stop at little just to survive. If he stopped to think about it, it made him disturbingly like Lambert.

The difference, he told himself, was that he kept his dark side under control.

"You still think that they're going to be looking for us?" Vernon asked quietly, trying not to be overheard. "They took a hell of a shellacking, too."

"Not enough to keep them from trying to nail us on the way out. And let's not forget that they still had enough people outside of that camp that they could neutralize our maritime section while we were scrambling to get out," Dan replied. "I think Yuan's been recruiting, and has a lot more people, a lot better prepared, than we were ever led to believe. And now that he's been hurt, he's probably going to be gunning hard for anybody who hurt him, in case he loses face among his allies."

Vernon nodded slightly. "I guess that makes sense." He paused, thinking. "That also raises the question of just what kind of chance we had to do this job in the first place. If he's got that many people, trying to take him down with a reinforced company probably wouldn't have worked, even without our mysterious airborne interruption."

Dan grimaced, even as he looked around in the green dimness under the canopy to make sure that everyone was on security, rather than just rucksack-flopping and going to sleep. It had been a punishing movement in the dark, trying to get clear of any groups of pirates that might be hunting them, but they really didn't dare slack off now that it was daylight.

"Yeah. About them...I think my questions concerning Chinese involvement just got answered."

Vernon looked up at him sharply. "You think we're fighting the PLA now?"

"I don't think we're fighting anybody if we can avoid it until we get the fuck off this island," Dan replied, "but yeah, I'm pretty sure those helos were PLA. Or PLA Marine Corps, or whatever. We should have expected that the ChiComs wouldn't have taken the desertion of an entire frigate lightly."

"Maybe the extra recruiting ties into it, too," Vernon mused. "Maybe there's more going on than we're seeing."

"Oh, almost certainly," Dan replied. "None of which actually matters a damn to us at the moment. Like I said, our primary concern is getting off this fucking island alive, and making it back to the States, preferably without going straight to a federal pen as soon as we step ashore."

Vernon didn't reply to that. It didn't really require comment. Even if it somehow turned out that the operation against Yuan was officially sanctioned by the US government at some level, given how hush-hush the whole thing was, and how badly it had already gone haywire, somebody was going to need scapegoats. The most readily available were, of course, going to be the surviving contractors. Whoever was backing the op hadn't insulated themselves with so many layers of deniability just to take the fall when it went south.

They fell silent, taking the opportunity to catch their breath, listening to the buzz of insects, the cries of birds in the canopy, and the hoots and grunts of various other critters, invisible in the greenery. Visibility was only about ten yards in any direction.

Dan studied his map, as vague as it was. The Anambas hadn't really been all that important to anybody but the oil companies and a few divers until Yuan had taken them over. They had less than nine kilometers to move to get to Terempa. Under better circumstances, they might have covered that distance in a couple of hours. In the jungle, over steep mountains, and with armed opposition hunting them, it was going to take a lot longer. It could easily take three days at minimum. While a lot of Dan's experience had been in the desert, he knew enough about jungle warfare to know that under some similar circumstances, five hundred meters in a day was a good movement. At that rate, they might

161

not get to Terempa for three weeks.

Three weeks was a long time on the supplies they had. They'd probably be starving by the time they reached Terempa, and that was where they'd most likely have to fight. If Yuan had any smarts at all, and was really dedicated to catching them, he'd know that the town was the most likely choke point, and have people there waiting for them.

Of course, if the PLA was now involved, that might just act as enough of a spoiler to give them an opening to slip through. Yuan's people would be playing hide-and-seek with the Chinese as much as the contractors would be with the pirates.

He briefly considered heading back downhill to move along the coast. The beaches weren't wide, and they were rocky, but they might put some more distance between them and the pirates, and make for slightly easier movement than the jungle-covered hills. He dismissed the idea. Sure, it might make movement slightly easier, but they would also be exposed to the ocean and the *Zhaotong*'s guns. No, they'd have to stick to the jungle.

He folded the map back up and stuck it back in his chest rig, taking stock of what they had. Food and water were going to be the biggest sticking points. He had a small survival kit on him, which included water filtration, but he didn't know how many others did. It hadn't been on Decker's gear list; apparently they'd gotten a little over-confident about how quickly the op was going to go. They were already hurting from the movement they'd already made through the jungle. What water they'd brought with them wasn't going to last much longer.

As for food, he honestly didn't know what was edible in the jungle and what wasn't. Again, it hadn't been part of the briefing materials. He wasn't all that keen on experimenting, either. And hunting with unsuppressed SG 553s wasn't going to be a good idea, not when they were being hunted themselves.

We've just got to make the best time we can and get to Terempa as quickly as possible, he thought. *Time is as much our enemy as the pirates.*

With that in mind, he decided they'd rested long enough. He climbed to his feet. "Everybody up," he murmured. "We've got a long way to go."

He put Max on point. Of the fifteen of them, Max was the one he trusted the most with fieldcraft. Vernon was good, but Max was better. Sam was also decent, as much as Dan didn't like his attitude. Loren was useless, Cassy and Jenny were no great shakes, as hard as Cassy tried, and Rex and the new guys were such neophytes in the weeds that he wondered whose cousins they were to get the job in the first place.

Max led out, with Dan only a few steps behind him. Vernon would stay toward the back, riding herd on the newbies with Cary. He heard the irrepressibly cheerful Cary muttering encouragement to the rest as they got up to move out. He didn't know what kind of happy pills that dude must have brought out with him, but they seemed to be working. He found himself hoping that they rubbed off on some of the rest.

He looked back to see Sam signaling frantically to halt. He passed it up to Max, who returned the hand signal and sank to a knee.

Now what? he thought. *We've barely made two hundred fucking meters.* Granted, it had been a long two hundred meters, mostly uphill, over rocky terrain covered in jungle growth, but it was a tiny fraction of the distance they had to cover.

He moved back to Sam, who was on a knee just ahead of Cassy. The girl looked pale and exhausted, but she was still on a knee, her rifle held at the low ready, her head up and looking around. She didn't have a pack on her back, though. Both she and Jenny had come ashore with go bags, but it had taken only a short time before Dan had made them hand them off. Even with the smaller loads, they weren't keeping up to his satisfaction. Cassy had protested again, though Jenny had readily handed hers over to the biggest new guy.

"Break in contact," Sam explained quietly. "Cassy hasn't seen the others in about five minutes."

"Son of a bitch." He sighed angrily. It shouldn't have taken five minutes to report the break. "Hold here. I'll go back and find 'em."

"By yourself?" Sam asked. "Doesn't seem like all that good an idea. Pairs, man."

He glanced at Cassy. "She seems to be hanging in there, but I don't want to leave her with just one other gun. I'll be fine."

Sam shrugged. "Your funeral. But if you don't make it back in twenty minutes, we're pushing on." His voice was a study in callous indifference, which was about what Dan had come to expect from him.

Dan just nodded. That was usually going to be the plan anyway, as much as it might piss him off that Sam had said it first. "I'll be back in ten." Then he headed back down-slope, passing Cassy with a tap on her shoulder. He meant it simply as a signal that he was going by and not to shoot him, but realized she might take it as a gesture of encouragement. Which wasn't a bad thing, necessarily. He was all too conscious, even as the cold-blooded side of him came to the forefront, that he *had* to be at least somewhat encouraging. He was the leader now, if only by default. The less-experienced, less-jaded among their number were going to be looking to him to get them through, to assure them that they at least had a chance. He had to keep them from thinking too much about just how dire their situation really was.

He had covered about thirty yards through the thick growth and massive rocks when he froze.

There were people moving through the undergrowth ahead of

him. Any hope that they were his own wayward teammates was lost when he heard talking in Mandarin.

He slowly lowered himself to the ground, getting prone and hoping that the others, if they were close, had had the presence of mind to do the same. The Chinese pirates—he didn't imagine they were PLA, just based on what he could hear—were making enough noise that, provided the contractors stayed quiet, they might manage to be overlooked.

No such luck.

A roar of gunfire erupted not twenty yards in front of him and downslope. He flattened himself tighter against the rocks as bullets ripped through the vegetation overhead and smacked rock chips off the nearby boulders. The pirates were now yelling frantically, and a strangely analytical part of his brain registered the heavier rattle of AK fire over the lighter *crack*s of the 5.56 SG 553s.

He had to do something before the rest of his people were slaughtered, and he had to do it fast. The sound of gunfire was going to draw every pirate that Yuan had out combing the jungle for miles around.

He started crawling forward, his rifle held in front of him. The rocks made for slow, agonizing movement, but he didn't dare get any more upright with the amount of metal flying through the air just over his head.

At least one of the pirates was directly ahead of him. The greenery was so thick that he couldn't see him, but he could hear him, yelling to his compatriots between bursts of fire into the jungle. From what he could hear, it sounded like most of the pirates were off to his right, while his teammates were downslope directly ahead.

He was having to develop as complete a picture of the battlefield as he could by sound. The jungle was too thick to see very much, and he didn't want to put his people in his own line of fire any more than he wanted to put himself in theirs.

He crept forward some more. The rocks got bigger, and the growth sprouting from between them thinned out a little bit. He could see a little bit better.

There were two pirates immediately visible, both shooting down-slope from the massive boulder that he was peering over. Enough plants were growing out of the cracks in the boulder to obscure most of the others, but he could make out vague shapes and the occasional flicker of muzzle blast from further to the right.

They were definitely pirates, dressed in a mix of camouflage fatigues and t-shirts, with Type 56s, QBZ-95s, and Type 63s. Even aside from their lack of field discipline, these couldn't be PLA.

They were still the enemy. He'd have to make this quick.

Any noise he made was going to be masked by the gunfire, so he didn't bother to move slowly. Quickly pulling the SG 553's buttstock into his shoulder, he lined up the first pirate's upper back and fired.

He tracked along the line of pirates on top of the boulder, giving each one a quick pair before moving on to the next. It was close range, barely ten yards, so he could be fast and not worry about missing. He caught a glimpse of one round tearing up through a pirate's face with a spray of red as the man fell.

More yelling and cursing in Mandarin echoed through the jungle, and a wild spray of gunfire tore up the greenery as the pirates tried to return fire at the gunman they couldn't see who had just taken out six of their number. Dan slid painfully down the side of the rock, as much to get down the hill to his teammates as to get out of the pirates' line of fire.

The problem that immediately presented itself was going to be linking up without getting shot, by either friendlies or hostiles. He could only assume that somebody down there had panicked and opened fire, which meant that their target discrimination probably wasn't going to be at its best. He'd have to announce himself, loudly, which would probably draw fire from the pirates up in the rocks.

Nothing for it. Sliding down beside another rock, that had been split into multiple chunks by the roots of the massive tree towering above it, he got to a knee and ran toward the sound of 5.56 fire, yelling, "Friendly coming in! Don't fucking shoot me!"

Somebody took a shot at him anyway as he charged through the undergrowth, the shot splitting the air only inches from his ear. He dropped to the ground, painfully smacking a knee against another rock, his descent to a prone position turning into a nasty sprawl. He stifled a groan as his knee throbbed with pain, then levered himself up and kept moving.

"Friendly coming in!" he bellowed again, as he hobbled down the slope. The initial shock to the knee was starting to wear off, the mind-shattering pain subsiding to a dull ache. He crashed through a veil of vines and creepers to come almost face-to-muzzle with Rex's 553.

He slapped the rifle barrel away from his head. "The bad guys are up there, dumbass!" he snarled. "Or can't you fucking hear? 'Friendly coming in!' Sound a little familiar?" The truth was, he was a little shaken, the adrenaline rush making his limbs feel a little rubbery at just how close he'd come to losing his head to one of his own people. And one of the "supervisors," of all fucking things.

They were in a grove of towering jungle trees, the undergrowth somewhat thinned out by the rocks. Bullets were shredding vegetation, smacking splinters off of tree boles, and ricocheting off of rocks with loud whines. He could see Vernon and Cary nearby, huddled down behind tree trunks, returning fire when they had a shot. Somebody just beyond Vernon was ripping off long bursts up toward the rocks where he'd seen the pirates.

The volume of fire from up the slope wasn't diminishing; in fact

165

it was starting to intensify. The dogpile that he'd been dreading seemed to be starting, as any nearby pirates ran to the sound of the fight.

"Have you got everybody?" Dan demanded, grabbing Rex by the chest rig. "Sam is uphill with Cassy and Max."

"I think so, yeah," Rex replied, turning his rifle back up toward the pirates.

"You think so, or you know so?" Dan snapped. "You'd better be fucking sure." He'd rather get the info from Vernon, but right now Rex was the man on the spot, and he was supposed to have some kind of leadership skill in the first place.

"Yeah, yeah, we've got everybody," Rex insisted. "Let's get the fuck out of here."

While he was far from confident in that assurance, the fire from above was really starting to get bad. The air seemed to be full of splinters, smoke, and high-velocity bits of metal. If they didn't break contact quickly, they were going to get pinned down in the grove and die there.

"Alright, by twos, fall back to the south!" Dan bellowed. "Peel! Go!" He just hoped they could successfully link up with Max, Sam, and Cassy later. He'd set a rally point shortly after leaving their last halt, but he was far from sure that everybody knew where it was anymore.

A moment later, two of the new guys, whose names he still didn't remember, charged past below him, heading to the south. They were followed by Vernon and Cary a moment later.

Dan and Rex suddenly flattened themselves to the ground, as a long, drawn out burst of machine gun fire raked the grove, pulverizing more of their concealment, bullets and tracers spitting off of rocks and thumping into trees. The fire was close enough that the *snap*s of individual rounds were actually physically painful.

If anyone was trying to suppress the gun, Dan couldn't hear it. He had his face pressed into the jungle floor, trying to actually sink into the ground, if that was possible. He just knew that one of those rounds was going to find him soon. The tree trunk wasn't going to last forever. Even if the machine gunner didn't get him, one of the other pirates was going to get an angle and shoot him while he had his face down in the rocks and undergrowth.

The storm of bullets suddenly ceased, making the rattle of rifle fire seem almost calm by comparison. Since there really wasn't that much cover fire coming from behind them, Dan could only assume that the machine gunner had run his belt dry and was reloading.

He scrambled to his feet, ignoring the sporadic shots still cracking past him, and hauled Rex up off the ground. "Go, go, go!" he yelled, shoving the other man toward the south. They had to move or die. They might still get shot while they ran, but they'd definitely get shot if they stayed put.

Together, with Dan propelling Rex by his gear half the time, they crashed through the brush, stumbling over rocks and damned near slamming into a couple of trees along the way. A fallen tree blocked the way, and Dan shoved Rex over it, the smaller man falling to the ground on the far side even as Dan swung a leg over the log. Another bullet snapped past his head and he dropped heavily to the ground, almost falling on top of Rex as he hit.

The machine gun opened fire again, but this time the gunner seemed not to have noticed that they'd moved away. He was still hammering fire at the same spot, which gave them a bit of a breather.

At least, it gave them a bit of a breather before somebody further back started shooting again, and the gunner shifted fire to respond. It was a little bit less accurate, but they still had to get down fast as the stream of metal started chewing up the vegetation around their ears.

He got Rex's attention, and pointed south and up. "Crawl," he said. "Stay down, and don't shoot unless you've got no other fucking choice." They weren't going to be able to break contact by fire superiority in this situation. The only way they were going to get out was by being sneaky.

Rex just nodded before doing as he was told. It wasn't going to be easy going, but it was preferable to dragging their pursuit along the entire length of the island before being cornered and shot to death.

There were still rounds going overhead when he came abreast of the two new guys who were shooting in the general direction of the pirates; they couldn't see anything, so there was little hope of them hitting any of them. He grabbed the closest one, a big, muscle-bound guy with shaggy hair, as he passed and hissed, "Cease fire, get low, and follow us." He paused just long enough to make sure the dude with the screaming high-and-tight and the walrus mustache had gotten the same message, then led the way up and back.

They were missing three when the whole team finally consolidated at the rally point, in a shallow cave near the crest of the ridge.

Dan was white with fury. "You son of a bitch," he said to Rex. "You told me you had everybody." Even as he said it, he thought, *Don't try to fob this off on him. You should have gotten the fucking head-count yourself. You knew damned good and well that he wasn't up to it.*

Rex, on the other hand, didn't have an answer. He just stammered and looked shell-shocked. He was on the edge of shutting down completely.

Dan shook his head, angrier at himself than at Rex. He checked his magazines. "The rest of you stay here and hold security. If I'm not back in three hours, assume I'm dead and push for Terempa, however you can get there. There might be pirate supply caches on the way, but I'd suggest moving as fast as you can."

"Where the fuck are you going now?" Sam asked.

"I'm going back after the three we're missing," he said.

"Shit," Sam said in reply. "Nice knowing ya. Hey, why don't you leave your ammo here with us if you're going to go commit suicide? We can probably get more use out of it than you can."

"He's right," Max said. "As much as I hate to say it, there are way too many pirates on this ridge between us and where we got hit. Going back would just get you killed, too." He sighed. "Yeah, we probably should have checked before we broke contact, but as you may or may not have noticed, we might well have missed them in the chaos. For all we know, they got mowed down by that machine gun, and their corpses are getting picked over by the scavengers right now."

"It's possible," Dan allowed. "But until we know, I've still got a responsibility to them."

"And they're supposed to be professionals who know what to do if they get cut off," Vernon said. "The rally point was set before we moved. If they can get to us, they will. If they can't, trying to go back into that fucking hornet's nest after them is just going to be exactly what Sam called it: suicide."

"But hey, if you're that determined to die in this shithole, go ahead," Sam said. "Be my guest."

Dan stared out of the cave, fuming. It took him a second to see the movement down the hill, then he dropped prone.

There were three pirates working their way along the ridge, just below the cave. The net was closer than they'd thought.

Suddenly, more shouting echoed up from down the hill to the south. The three pirates immediately looked in that direction, rifles coming up for a moment, before more shouting made them relax. Dan wondered just what they were saying; he couldn't understand enough Mandarin, even if the words had been clear.

Then he saw what had drawn their attention, and his blood ran cold.

Four more pirates came out of the jungle, armed with the usual mix of rifles, except for one who was carrying a PKM. One of them, his rifle muzzle pointed up at the sky, was shoving Loren ahead of him.

Dan eased his rifle into position, laying the red dot on the pirate with the PKM, and let his breath out, his finger resting on the trigger. Could they get all seven before they waxed the prisoner?

He felt more than saw Vernon and Max on either side of him, down on their bellies and aimed in. Whether they were as set on rescuing Loren as he was, or just ready to defend the cave if the pirates decided to come uphill, he neither knew nor cared. He started to take up the slack on the trigger.

And let it off. Five more had emerged from the jungle growth to meet the seven, laughing and chatting. One gave their prisoner a cuff on the side of the head that just about sent him sprawling. The guy who had been shoving him roughly yanked him up on his feet and shoved him back toward the north again.

A few moments later, the pirates and their captive had disappeared back into the jungle, out of sight in the greenery. Beside Dan, Vernon let out a huge breath. "For a second there, I was sure you were about to start shooting."

"For a second there," Dan replied, "I was." He got up on a knee and moved to the back wall of the cave, where he pulled out his map. "This changes things."

"I still don't see how," Sam retorted. "We're still twelve swinging dicks—no, eleven swinging dicks and a split tail, no offense, Cassy—against dozens, possibly a couple hundred pirates, not to mention the fact that after the other night, I'd fully expect the PLA to start flooding the island, if only in retaliation for the pirates shooting one of their fucking helos down."

"Doesn't matter," Dan said heavily. "They've got our people now, and we know at least one of them is still alive. We're getting out with everybody who's still breathing." He glared around at the rest of them. "That means the fuckery stops now. We wouldn't be in this situation if somebody back there—I don't know who it was, and right now I don't care—hadn't fucking panicked and started shooting when they'd have been better off lying low and staying quiet.

"We're not soldiers the way you've all been trained to think of it anymore. We're not contractors. We're guerrillas. And we're going to act like it, every one of us, or we're going to die. There's no more room for error. We got the infiltration training before everything went tits-up the other night. We're going to use it. Perform, or die. It's that simple." He pointed to the map. "I made sure to note the locations of every one of Yuan's suspected camps on Siantan before we stepped off. So we've got a target deck. We'll move in on them one at a time, reconnoiter to see if any of our people are being held there, and then we'll hit 'em. In the dark, quietly. They won't even know what's going on until they're dying and it's all over but the screaming."

There was a long silence. To his credit, Sam didn't scoff. In fact, when Dan looked at him, he saw a fire in the other man's eyes he hadn't seen there before. He'd apparently chosen the right words. Sam was actually looking forward to this.

Then one of the new guys, a short, curly-haired guy with a thick New York accent, opened his mouth. "Wait a minute. Who put you in charge? Isn't Rex the top guy here?"

To Dan's surprise, it was Sam who rounded on him first. "Shut up, meat," he snapped. "Nobody asked you. If you're so hell-bent on arguing about who's in charge, leave your weapons and ammo and get the fuck out. Though I should probably just cut your fucking throat first, to make sure you don't squawk to the pirates when they roll your dumb ass up."

The little guy didn't quite get the message. He started to bow up. "You can't talk to me like that."

"Sit the fuck down and shut the fuck up," Dan barked, even as Sam started to come to his feet. "You want to know why I'm in charge? Because I'm the one taking charge, asshole. Because we don't have the time or the luxury to fuck around with who's more popular. And in case you didn't notice, nobody else here is bitching about it. So like Sam said, you either perform, or we kill you ourselves and save the pirates the fucking trouble."

The shorter man looked around at the stony, hostile stares around him, and seemed to fold in on himself a little. He subsided, sitting back down against the wall of the cave.

"You realize that you're essentially declaring war on the entire island?" Vernon said quietly, after a moment.

"Yep," Dan replied. "At least until we've got our people back and a way off. Since we still don't have any contact with the outside world, I think it's a fair bet that nobody's coming to get us." A glance at Rex, who was still looking a little punchy, got a confirmatory nod. "We're on our own, gents. Personally, given the options in front of us, I'd rather put a good hurting on the opposition before we tried to slip out from under their noses."

No one objected. At that point, it was more than likely that nobody had any better ideas. Their first try at getting to Terempa had been cut off before they'd gotten a quarter mile. The pirates were thick as flies between them and their only way off the island. It was going to be a longer haul than they'd planned on.

They may as well, as Dan had said, take their pound of flesh on the way out.

♦

Chapter 17

The weather was starting to get cool in Northern Virginia. The sky was leaden and the wind was picking up. It was probably going to rain before the day was out.

The man in the cheap suit who got out of the nondescript silver compact car was short, a little pudgy, and was pale enough to suggest that he didn't get out in the sun very much. He looked like a stereotypical accountant or IT nerd. At first glance, anyone looking at him would think that he had come to the massive stone, steel, and glass building to fix the Internet or something.

He walked into the lobby and straight up to the receptionist's desk. Placing his ID on the desk, he said, in a slightly nasally voice, "I'm here to see Price."

"Do you have an appointment?" the receptionist asked.

"Call him and give him the name on the ID," the man replied. "He'll see me."

The young woman looked skeptical, but dutifully picked up the phone and pressed the button for Mitchell Price's office. "Mr. Price?" she ventured, "there's a Mr. Steven Welsh here to see you?" She listened for a moment, then put the phone down, her eyebrows climbing toward her bangs. "You can go straight up, Mr. Welsh," she said. "Do you know where his office is?"

Welsh nodded as he started for the elevators. "I've been here before."

He opened the office door and walked into Mitchell Price's office like he owned the place. Without even saying hello or waiting to be invited, he sat down in the chair across the desk from Price and asked, "Do you have people in the South China Sea around Indonesia?"

Price simply leaned back in his chair and studied his guest for a moment. Still fit, square-jawed and handsome well into his late-forties, not a single hair out of place, his suit probably costing five times what Welsh's had, he looked the very image of the confident professional. He'd successfully leveraged both his background in Naval Special Warfare and his family's old money Northern Virginia contacts into becoming a powerhouse in the PMC world. He was as idolized as he was hated, viewed as either a super-patriot or a war profiteer. Welsh knew that the truth was actually a little of both.

"Nice to see you, too, Steven," Price said after a moment. "Come on in, have a seat. How are the wife and kids?"

"Don't play games with me, Mitchell," Welsh snapped. "I don't have the time or the patience right now, not with a possible international incident brewing in a part of the world that's already enough of a fucking tinderbox. Do you have people operating in the South China Sea or not?"

Price put his hands on his desk and met Welsh's gaze with an open, honest expression that he had doubtless practiced in the mirror for hours until it became second-nature. The man was as much a politician as he was a military contractor. "I've got any number of maritime security teams out on ships around the globe at any one time, Steven," he said. "I can't track every single one of them, but shipping lanes being what they are, it is entirely possible that yes, I do have people in the South China Sea at this moment."

Welsh's expression remained unimpressed. "Save the double-talk for your shareholders, Mitchell," he said. "I'm not talking about security guard detachments on freighters, and you damn well know it. I'm talking about an illegal paramilitary mission out of the Desaru peninsula in Malaysia."

Price's own expression didn't change, except for what might have been the faintest ghost of a smile. "Even if I had any knowledge of such an operation, Steven, do you really think I'd be stupid enough to incriminate myself or my company by admitting to an agent of the Federal government that I'm conducting an illegal paramilitary operation in a sovereign country?"

Welsh kept his face carefully impassive. "Mitchell, whatever is going on out there has already gone very, very badly for the people involved. It hasn't really gone public yet, but the Malaysians are holding thirteen Americans who were arrested with enough military hardware to supply an infantry battalion. This is very serious business."

"It certainly sounds like it," Price put in, a note of sincere concern in his voice, a faint frown starting to crease his brow.

"There will be an investigation," Welsh continued, as if Price hadn't said anything. "There has to be; this isn't something that can be swept under the rug. There has also been open combat on the Anambas Islands, and quite possibly a Chinese helicopter shot down. Which brings the PRC into the mix as well. There are a lot of people dead, and possible American fingerprints involved. If I find out that you're bullshitting me, that you or your company have something to do with this disaster, I'll make sure that you go into a deep, dark hole for the better part of a century, your money and connections be damned."

Price's face had gone cold. "You've got a lot of nerve coming in here and talking to me that way, especially after all the time we've known each other, Steven. These are very serious barely-veiled accusations you're throwing around, and I won't have it. Launch your investigation. I dare you. And when my company comes up clean, I'll see to it that your career is over. You'll be lucky to get a job in animal control by the time I'm done."

For a long moment, the two men stared each other down. Finally, it was Welsh who stood up. "I hope you're telling the truth, Mitchell," he said, his tone somewhat more conciliatory. "I really do. We've done some damned good work together over the years. It would be a lot easier if these were just some war tourist rogues out to get their kill on. But the reports we're getting of the sheer amount of materiel and ordnance the Malaysians seized suggest a major backer. I'm afraid the list of suspects gets pretty short, pretty fast."

"Maybe you should look a little closer to home," Price offered, making no move to budge out of his chair. "I've got plenty of experience being scapegoated when things went wrong over those years of 'good work.' This sounds a little more up your Agency's alley than mine. Which is something that I'm sure the FBI and a Congressional investigation would be more than happy to hear."

Welsh's expression spoke volumes about how likely he thought that was. The silence stretched on just long enough to be awkward.

"I'll be in touch," Welsh said finally. "As will the investigators."

"And I'll cooperate with them as fully as my work allows," Price replied, still not rising to offer his hand. Some of the pleasantries had gone by the wayside.

Conscious of how poorly the meeting had gone, Welsh turned and walked out. He was also entirely aware of the qualification that Price had put on his cooperation with the investigation.

When he reached his car, he pulled out his phone. It rang once before being answered.

"Well?" the man on the other end asked.

"He admitted nothing, just like I said he would," Welsh said. "I still maintain that this approach was a bad idea."

"If we'd unleashed the FBI on him without at least giving him a heads-up," the other man replied, "he would have had his pet Senators on our backs in an instant. We'd be shut down before we even started."

"So instead, we've given him advance warning to cover his tracks," Welsh retorted, "and to get his pet Senators and Congressmen warmed up to come after the investigation anyway."

"Did you get anything out of him?"

"Oh, I'm sure he's got a hand in it," Welsh said. "He's the most likely suspect in the first place, especially after the beating he's taken over his last couple little enterprises. What would look better for him than to take out a pirate kingpin with a private military force that costs a fraction what a regular military operation would? He'd be right back on the 'super-patriot' rolls in a week."

"Except that it's gone wrong." The man on the other end of the line sighed. "We're going to have to move fast, before he can make the evidence disappear. I'm afraid you may have been right, Steve. This might have been a miscalculation on our part."

"We'd better move fast," Welsh said. "Or otherwise the Agency is likely to take the blame for Price's op. And I doubt that's going to reflect well on any of our careers."

They still had preparations to make, and at least one more walk-through/talk-through to do, but Dan had given the team a break. Vernon and Sam were on security at the cave mouth—an absolute necessity given how close the pirates had gotten to their hideaway. The others were grabbing what rest they could.

All but Cassy, who was sitting up against the cave wall, staring at the ceiling. Dan went over and sat down next to her.

He hadn't really talked to Cassy that much; especially after the brushes he'd had with Jenny he'd avoided engaging the women any more than he'd had to. It wasn't just because he'd been uncomfortable with Jenny's advances, or her blatant weaponization of her sexuality. He knew what kind of damage could be done in a team through rumors about sex. Jealousy over a bird had destroyed more partnerships than he could count. Better to keep his distance and make sure no such rumors got started.

But now the situation was different. He still had to maintain some distance; there was no getting around that. But he also had to be sure that his team was on point, and that meant knowing if one of them had a problem. And it looked like Cassy had a problem. Which could lead to more problems down the road if it didn't get addressed before they went back into the jungle.

"You all right?" he asked quietly.

The sound she made was somewhere between a laugh and a sob. "No, I'm not," she said after a moment. She fell silent again, and Dan waited patiently. She seemed deep in thought, lowering her head to stare at the rocky floor between her knees.

"When I found out about this job," she said after a long silence, "and that they were actively looking for women, I thought it was awesome. I jumped at the chance. After all, I never got the 'privilege' of doing combat arms when I was in the Army. We all told ourselves that we were just as good as the grunts, but we never got the chance to prove it. This was my chance."

"What was your MOS?" Dan asked.

"MP," she replied, with the same almost-laugh, almost-sob. "Yeah, I was one of those. The female MP who was tougher than anybody around her, or at least she could talk tougher. Those infantry types weren't so great, they were just keeping women out to maintain

174

their boys' club. This job was my chance to prove that. I was out before the uniformed services started to look at taking women into combat jobs. But now I could prove I was the best, and get paid a ton doing it."

She actually sobbed a little then, and wiped her nose with the back of a filthy hand. "Boy, was I an idiot. This shit is a lot harder in real life. Hell, it's harder in training. That line about 'MPs can do everything infantry can do...' Yeah, right." She shook her head. "I should have quit in Florida. As soon as I couldn't carry one of you guys out when you got tagged as casualties...that should have been the big red flag. Sure, I can shoot on the flat range. I can even hike a little. I *know* the tactics. But I am way out of my depth here. I'm not fast enough, I'm not strong enough. It may sound petty, but the filth is really starting to get to me, and I just want to go home." She looked at him with tears glistening in her eyes. "I just wish I could have figured that out before we were fighting for our lives in the fucking jungle, cut off from extract, nine thousand miles from home."

Dan thought for a moment before replying. "To be blunt, I wish you had, too. It's a little too late for second thoughts now. I'd say I wish that I'd left you and Jenny back in Desaru, but given the comms blackout from there, that might not have been a good option, either."

He thought again before continuing. "There's not much I can say that's going to make it any better, either. We're past the point where kind words can improve the situation. Cold, hard reality is, we're in a hell of a spot, and every one of us, you included, is going to have to step up and face it. Otherwise we all die. You might even have to push past your own limits; I won't guarantee that it won't scar you for life, physically as well as mentally. It probably will. But that's the price of staying alive.

"I think that's the way it's always been, really. The stories about women warriors get glamorized and turned into these romantic legends, but I'd daresay that most of the time those stories came out of situations not too far removed from ours. Desperate times where there wasn't any other choice. None of us have the luxury of saying, 'I don't want to do this,' anymore. Not now." He took a deep breath. "Maybe if we get out of this, maybe then we can call it quits. But as long as we're still on this island, every one of us is going to need you to suck it up and drive on as best you can. We'll do our damnedest to keep you alive, and we might have to go a little slower at times, but you're going to have to push yourself. We can't do it all for you."

She nodded, her head still bowed. "I know," she said, just above a whisper. "I know. And I'll do my best. But what if my best isn't good enough?"

"Then hopefully we die quickly, in combat, instead of being tortured to death by pirates," Dan said harshly. She flinched a little at the words, and Dan found he hated himself a little for saying it. He knew it hurt, and while he'd tried to maintain his professional detachment, hurting a woman still made him feel a bit like a scumbag. He had to remind himself of the cost of trying to coddle anyone in this situation. The reality of their predicament would kill them quickly if they didn't acknowledge it. It might kill them quickly even so.

Cassy's head was still bent toward her chest. He was tempted to put his arm around her, but restrained himself. It would be rough, but she had to come to grips with what needed to be done herself. The harshness of his replies were necessary to harden her to what was to come.

He hoped. He got up and let her be, feeling like a bit like a monster as he did so. He felt like he'd just yelled at his wife, or worse, his daughter.

The conversation had also awakened another thought, that he tried to suppress as he looked at his map again, still planning. He tried to concentrate on the terrain and the contingencies and coordination of the raid on the pirate camp only a few miles away.

He didn't want to think about what Jenny, as much as he disliked her, might be going through, if she'd been taken by the pirates.

From a few feet away, Vernon murmured, "Heard most of that. Not sure I agree all the way."

"Something you'd say differently?" Dan asked.

"Maybe, maybe not." Vernon hadn't turned toward him, but was still looking out into the jungle below. "I'm just not sure she won't break as it is, is all."

"She might," Dan mused quietly. "Rex might, too. If it happens, it happens. But they both volunteered to come out with the big boys, so now they've got to play by big boy rules. We don't have the luxury of having any other options anymore."

Jenny didn't look up when she heard footsteps approaching her cage. The last couple of times someone had come over to her, it hadn't gone well; she had no illusions that this visit was going to be any better.

She wasn't sure how long she'd been in the cage. It was just big enough for her to use the bucket they'd thrown in as a toilet. There was a scrap of tarp thrown over the top of the cage to provide some shade from the sun in the daytime, but that was the only concession made to shelter, never mind privacy.

She'd avoided using the bucket for as long as she could. The cages were out in the open, and she'd balked at taking a shit in front of the other prisoners, not to mention the pirates hanging around leering at her and the other female captives, many of whom seemed to have been there longer than she had. Finally, though, the demands of nature had overridden her sense of privacy.

Of course, there hadn't been anything to use to clean herself up, so now she itched. She hadn't thought that the stink of the jungle could get any worse, but the stench coming from the bucket, particularly in the daytime heat, was making her gag.

She still wasn't sure how she'd gotten cut off and surrounded. She'd gotten fixated on one of the little bastards that was shooting at her, and then her magazine had run dry before she'd expected it to. While she'd been reloading, she'd suddenly found herself surrounded by three pirates, all pointing weapons at her head.

Maybe she'd overpenetrated. She'd certainly lost track of where the other contractors to her left and right had been.

They should have stayed with me, she thought viciously. *Fucking pussies. I was attacking; they should have come with me.*

The footsteps stopped just outside her cage. She didn't lift her head, but looked out through her disheveled hair hanging over her face.

The feet in front of her cage were wearing lightweight Merrell hiking boots, and the legs were clad in Kryptek. None of the pirates she'd seen wore that stuff. She looked up, squinting against the sunlight, to see Lambert's smirk.

"What do we have here?" he said. He squatted down to bring himself somewhat level with her. "Long time no see, Jenny."

"What the fuck are you doing here?" she croaked. She'd been given some brackish water to drink, but she was still badly dehydrated.

He shrugged lazily. "Surviving," he replied. "Something you might want to give some thought to."

"You're working for the pirates now?" She suddenly wasn't sure what she thought of that. She decided she hated him for it, especially since he was apparently free and comfortable, while she was locked in a cage with her own filth.

"And why not?" he demanded. "We're fucking mercenaries, paid gunslingers. I didn't sign up for this job for 'Mom, 'Merica, and Apple Pie.' I signed up for the money. There's no way MMPR's going to pay us after this fucking fiasco, even if we survived on our own to get home. Besides, Yuan would have killed me otherwise. Can't spend money I don't have if I'm dead."

He made it sound awfully reasonable. She still hated him. He was out there, she was still in the cage. He might have done something to get her out.

"Of course," he said, "Yuan's not looking for female fighters. I don't think he believes in 'em. And I doubt any of us are high on the ransom list. But you might have something else he could use."

Her skin crawled at his suggestive leer. She wasn't averse to sex for the sake of advancement; she'd certainly spread her legs for an advantage enough times. She'd even slept with Lambert once, during training, when it had looked like it was possible that he'd be one of the team leaders. Her failure to get in Dan's pants still irritated her, even in this shitty situation.

But this was different. She'd always slept around as a manifestation of her own power. This would be making herself powerless in order to simply survive. She didn't think she could stomach that. The very idea not only made her stomach twist, it hardened her deep-seated hate into a white-hot, burning point in her chest.

She wanted to kill Lambert at that moment. She wanted to kill everyone around her. But she knew that if she displayed that hate for a moment, before her time was ripe, that they'd kill her and she'd never get her chance to take any of them with her.

She reached back and brushed a tangled lock of hair back over her ear. "Maybe I do," she said. She knew her sex appeal was pretty low; she was filthy, dehydrated, sunburned, and crammed in a cage. But all she needed was an opening.

Lambert shook his head, though, with that same dirty grin. "Nah, don't bother with me. I already know you're a good fuck. But I'm not the one you've got to convince; Yuan's made me one of his soldiers, but I ain't in charge of shit." He stood up and waved to one of the pirates, a short, stocky Chinese still wearing his blue, gray, green, and yellow "Ocean" cammies, albeit without any insignia anymore. The man, smirking a little, levered himself up from where he'd been sitting on a log, and sauntered over.

The first thing she noticed was that he was still armed and kitted out, wearing a pistol belt and an old woodland load bearing vest, with his QBZ-95 slung across his chest. He unslung the rifle as he walked over, leaning it against the stump a few feet from the log he'd been sitting on. She tried to avoid being obvious about it, but her eyes went to the grenades hanging on his belt. They weren't in pouches, but hanging by the rings, probably so that he could just pluck and throw them, provided he didn't blow himself up when one of them caught on something and got pulled off.

"She want to make deal?" the man asked Lambert, grinning from ear to ear, in terribly accented English. Lambert just nodded.

"Yeah, I think she might," he replied. He looked down at Jenny before he turned to walk away. "Try to make it convincing. Maybe in time, we can work out something better."

She risked throwing him a glare full of daggers, but he just turned and walked off, apparently unfazed. She hoped he didn't go too far. She wanted him close enough for this.

The pirate was shedding his gear and setting it aside. "You make good time, make things better for you," he said, still grinning. "Get you out of cage, get cleaned up. Have good times."

She smiled coyly at him, throwing every bit of sex she could muster into the expression, in spite of her circumstances. She knew she still had an amazing body, and she could move it in suggestive ways that would probably drive this little bastard insane, if she had room.

He grinned even wider at her, if that was possible, and reached up to unlock her cage. He lowered the front wall, letting her out, then reached for his trousers, starting to unbuckle his belt.

"Why don't you let me do that?" she said, unfolding herself painfully from the cage, trying to make the movement look sultry instead of cramped. She wasn't sure how much she succeeded, but he must have already had all the blood going from his brain to his crotch, because he didn't seem to notice.

She arched her back, trying to relieve some of the pain, though it had the bonus effect of thrusting her breasts at his face. Her shirt was tattered enough to leave little to the imagination. He was staring at her chest, still fumbling with the belt as she stepped up to him and put one hand behind his neck, running the other down his chest.

He still didn't quite have the pistol belt off. She grabbed one of the grenades and pulled, even as she wrapped her arm around his neck and held on as tightly as she could, letting the spoon fly free with a doom-laden *ping*.

Feng figured that the quay on the southern coast of Pulau Matak had probably been abandoned since shortly after Yuan had taken over the islands. He scanned the marina and the handful of buildings under the palms through binoculars from the small rubber boat, not dissimilar to an American RHIB, that was presently quietly motoring through the strait between Matak and Siantan.

He'd wanted to get real-time overheads, but with Guo's refusal to offer any more support than absolutely necessary, his assets had become somewhat more limited. So, he was conducting his own maritime reconnaissance prior to landing.

There were no lights showing on the shore, no sound aside from the rumble of the boat's engine, the lap of waves on the gunwales, and the night noises of the jungle.

"Take us in closer," he told Cheng, who was manning the tiller. The other man nodded without a word, a vague motion of his silhouette in the darkness, and brought the boat in toward the larger quay sticking out into the strait. In the bow, Shen and Xu lay on the gunwales, their SAR-21s aimed at the shore. If Yuan had pirates waiting in the shacks, they'd have to get fire superiority quickly as Cheng pulled them off.

Feng doubted there was anyone on shore. What little he'd been able to ascertain over the last day, carefully playing hide-and-seek along the islands, led him to believe that Yuan had withdrawn most of his forces to Siantan in the wake of the attack on his fortified camp. He seemed to be going on the defensive, at least for the moment. While he almost certainly still had pirates stationed at outposts throughout the Anambas, at least the ones the Americans hadn't already destroyed, any that were likely to still be on Matak would be few, and probably easily

179

dealt with by his *Jiaolong*.

The unexpected bright side to this was that as long as most of the pirates were defending their center of power on Siantan, there wouldn't be as much active piracy against the shipping lanes heading for the Straits of Malacca. Which still didn't solve Feng's problem, but to Guo it was doubtless a victory.

At least until the *Zhaotong* started taking a more active role against targeted shipping, in which case the PLA Navy would have no choice but to get directly involved. Feng could easily see that happening, as long as Guo refused to push any harder. Yuan would decide that he'd weathered the worst the PLA had to throw at him, and he'd get bolder. But if that had occurred to Guo, the older officer had dismissed it in favor of his own risk-aversion.

Feng realized his thoughts were treading dangerously close to the kind of thing that draws the attention of Political Commissars, and gets young *Shang Wei*s sent to re-education camps. He forced himself to concentrate on the task at hand.

The boat was now close enough that he set the binoculars down on the control panel, lowered his NVGs, and slung his own SAR-21. He and his men had stuck with the decidedly non-PLA, third-party gear and equipment. If they ran afoul of Yuan's people, let the pirates think that they were somebody else, and that the PLA wasn't paying them any mind. It was probably a slim hope after the attack on the camp. The bodies and equipment in the crashed Z-8 alone would have told Yuan what he was dealing with, but there was no reason to give the enemy any more information than necessary.

Cheng brought the boat up against the quay with a gentle bump. Shen and Xu had already risen to their knees, and as soon as the gunwale made contact with the concrete, they sprang up onto the quay, rifles aimed in at the darkened shacks. Feng followed with Liu and Qiao.

Together, keeping a tight wedge, the commandos quickly moved down the quay toward the shore. They stayed quiet, scanning both the buildings and the jungle around them. Once they got to the end of the quay, they spread out and took a knee, watching and listening for any movement, any sign that they'd been detected or were about to be ambushed.

He didn't relax, precisely, but Feng was already sure they were alone and unobserved. The buildings were in poor repair, one of them visibly falling down, the others increasingly overgrown as the jungle reclaimed its territory in man's absence. While that wouldn't take long in this environment, there definitely weren't pirates present, and hadn't been for some time.

They still cleared every building and swept the perimeter before Feng got on the radio and called the other boats in. They had their base of operations, well within Yuan's territory. It was time to start hunting down his SAM caches.

And if they found what they were looking for along the way, so much the better.

Chapter 18

Inch by inch, Dan crawled along the ridgeline.

He was glad that at least most of them had saved their ghillies from the abortive assault on Yuan's camp. They were going to be absolutely necessary in the operations to come. Right at the moment, he and Vernon were working their way along the small peninsula that jutted out into the ocean on the southwest coast of Siantan. One of Yuan's caches was supposed to be out here, with a narrow trail leading down to the shore. It was probably there for quick resupply of the seaborne pirates if the heat started getting too high out on the water.

Now, provided that their intel wasn't bad again, and the cache was there, they were going to empty it out after killing everyone on site. They could use the materiel, and thinning out the herd of pirates was always a good thing.

Ten of the twelve remaining contractors were closing in on the cache in a loose circle, divided up into pairs. He'd put one of the new guys, the big, long-haired dude, who somehow had managed to avoid getting left behind in the scramble to break contact the other day, with Max. The big guy, whose name was Rich, or Rick, or something, was a blundering elephant in the bush, and Max was probably the most patient of the really reliable, bush-savvy fighters he still had left. If anybody could keep the new guy from fucking it up, it was Max.

He'd thought about putting him with Sam for about half a second. Sam would have probably just slit his throat and left him in the jungle within an hour.

Cassy was with Rex. The two of them were actually a couple hundred yards behind Dan and Vernon. He'd set them on rear security, to ambush any patrols that the pirates might have had out. If any hostiles came back down the ridge, which provided the easiest avenue of approach, Cassy and Rex could deal with them before they stumbled on one of the assault teams.

He'd justified it as a necessary security measure, which it was. The truth, that had niggled at him for a while, until concentrating on the approach banished any extraneous use of mental energy, was that he wasn't confident enough in either of them. Sure, he'd lectured everyone about how there was no holding back anymore, but Cassy just wasn't up to this.

He peered through the jungle ahead of him. The NVGs weren't

comfortable in the prone, and he'd almost knocked them noisily against rocks or trees a few times. But he wanted to *see*. They needed any advantage they could get.

A single figure was sitting next to a tree, just uphill from the cache. That pretty well confirmed that the cache was there; there wasn't any other reason for a sentry to be on that ridge. He obviously wasn't all that alert, either. His rifle was leaning against the tree, and he was smoking, the ember a brilliant point of green-white light in the night vision image. That alone would have rendered him ineffective; he didn't have NVGs on that Dan could see. The glow would have destroyed his night vision. He could be staring right at Dan and not see him in the dark.

On top of that, the faintly sweetish smell of the smoke that reached Dan's nostrils confirmed that the man wasn't smoking a cigarette. He was getting stoned, which was about to become his death warrant.

Achingly slowly, Dan turned his head to look toward Vernon. He could just make him out, a darker clump of jute, vines, and palm fronds only a few feet away. Even his gear was veg'ed up.

As was Dan's. They hadn't dared to leave anything behind, so all of them were dragging along their rifles and assault packs, even though Dan hoped to get through the night without firing a shot. He'd wrapped both his pack and weapon in as much veg as he could to further obscure their outlines, not to mention padding the steel and plastic of the SG 553 to keep from making too much noise if it banged against the rocks.

Equally slowly, the hooded lump that was Vernon's head turned, until Dan could see the twin circles of the other man's NVGs looking at him. He slowly pointed to Vernon, then made a little shaking movement with his hand. He got an "OK" gesture in return. Vernon would provide the distraction, if any was needed. Dan was going to deal with the sentry.

He eased his arm out of his pack strap, leaving it and the rifle tied to the side of it with Vernon. He still had his pistol tucked into his pants. If he ended up needing it, the night was blown anyway. He resumed his inchworm approach toward the sentry.

This is fucking crazy, a little voice in the back of his head said. He'd known a lot of guys who fantasized about slitting a sentry's throat silently, but he knew well enough that the real world didn't necessarily work that way. He'd killed a man with a knife on the way out of Yuan's camp, and it hadn't been quick, the victim's thrashing around only masked by the chaos around them. This wasn't going to be easy. There were a million ways it could go wrong. But without suppressed weapons, just shooting him wasn't going to work, either.

He concentrated on keeping his movement slow and quiet. It wouldn't be a good idea to get buck fever and start rushing. Sure, the dude was high, and probably wouldn't notice anything until it was too late, but one of his buddies might. And it was never a good idea to bank on the enemy's incompetence.

Of course if he wasn't baked, then this would be even less of a good idea.

He didn't move straight toward his target. He angled off to one side, aiming about five to ten meters away. It was still plenty close; it would have been far too close if the target hadn't been smoking hash. On the other hand, he'd sneaked within three feet of a buddy when they'd been playing around with stalking just for shits and giggles a few years back. So it wasn't impossible.

It seemed to take a very, very long time. He concentrated on regulating his breathing and, by extension, his heart rate, as he went. He avoided looking directly at his target. He had no idea if the old stories about a sentry being able to feel an enemy's eyes on the back of their neck were true, but at that point, he wasn't going to take any chances.

He moved several meters past the sentry's tree before circling back. He could see the flicker of a campfire below, now, where the cache was. At least two figures were visible near it, though they were staring at the fire. They wouldn't see shit until it was too late, hopefully. The concern at that point was whether or not they'd hear anything.

He rose up to a crouch as he crept toward the sentry's tree. The smell of the marijuana smoke was starting to get overpowering; he hoped he didn't pick up too much of a contact high.

The sentry was still sitting against the tree, smoking. That presented another problem. The tree bole was too big to reach around. He'd have to come around one side or another, which precluded getting directly behind his target.

Maybe I should just hit him in the head with a rock, he thought. *Nah, if I miss or lose my grip, it's going to make a pretty loud knock. Going to have to go with the original plan.*

Carefully treading toward the tree, he drew his knife and coiled to strike. Finally at the tree, the stink of the joint filling his nostrils, he pounced.

He plowed into the sentry, knocking the man sideways and sending the joint flying. He managed to get a hand clapped over the target's mouth and nose before an exclamation could get out, but he was still in a bad position, and the man's rifle was starting to slide toward the rocks.

He couldn't grab the rifle without letting go of the confused sentry, whose sluggish brain was starting to register that he was being attacked. It fell, but it didn't make much more than a muted *clack* as it hit the rocks, fortunately cushioned by the vegetation. Dan concentrated on the man beneath him.

The sentry was starting to struggle. Using the hand he had clamped on the man's face, he tried to knock his head against a rock, but the sentry resisted, and he managed not much more than a tap. Desperate, he dropped to the ground beside the target, wrapping one leg around him and wrapping his knife arm around the man's free arm. Of course, now he had the sentry somewhat restrained, but couldn't stab him.

The sentry was thrashing now, the desperation of his position getting through the drug-induced fog in his brain, clawing at the arm Dan had clamped around his chest. Dan held on tightly, keeping his off hand clamped over the man's face, while he tried to figure out what to do next.

He suddenly rolled on top of the sentry, letting go of the man's jaw just in time to keep from pinning his hand between the sentry's head and the tree root beneath them. He clamped that hand on the back of the man's neck, but now his knife hand was pinned beneath the sentry's body.

Taking a chance, he let go of the knife and yanked his arm free, putting his weight on the other hand, pressing the man's face into the mold and loam under the tree while he sank a knee into his back. Hastily switching hands, even as the sentry got a hand free and tried to reach back to claw at him, he snatched up the knife and plunged it into the side of the man's neck. He didn't want to slit his throat; he'd start aspirating air and blood through the wound and making a lot of noise. He just wanted to cut the blood vessels.

Hot blood pulsed out over the blade and onto his hand. His victim bucked and thrashed under him, and he shifted to pin the man's hands down with his knees, even while the sentry's feet scrabbled uselessly at the jungle floor, his soft shoes unable to get a purchase. He had to be running out of air, too, with his face mashed into the ground. Dan held on, keeping the man still while his lifeblood poured out over both of them. He'd hit the artery; it wouldn't take long.

It still felt like forever. Dan held on, both hands now clamped on the back of the man's skull, pressing him down while blood jetted from the wound in his neck, his knees now almost bending the man's elbows the wrong way. There were some muffled noises coming from the ground, as the dying man tried to scream, but Dan bore down, muting his voice in the dirt and the rotting vegetation.

Finally, the pulsing flow of blood from the sentry's neck slowed, and his struggles weakened, then finally stopped. He was gone.

Dan carefully extricated himself, his heart pounding, the adrenaline flooding his veins to make his limbs feel shaky. While he'd been doing it, he'd been the emotionless predator, focused only on doing what needed to be done. Now that it was over, he felt a little sick.

The faintest rustle drew his attention. He saw Vernon crouched nearby, with both of their packs and rifles, crushing the joint out with his boot. He saw the other man's NVGs pointed at him. Vernon gave him an "OK," which he returned, taking a deep breath, feeling the sickness and horror recede as the predator reasserted itself. It was time to hunt, not to dwell on the killing that had just happened.

There would be plenty of time for the nightmares later, if they survived.

He was soaked in the sentry's blood, but considering that he was already soaked in his own sweat, that meant little, aside from the distant fear of whatever bloodborne pathogens the pirate might have been carrying. Together, the two of them got back down on their bellies and continued toward the fire, now inside the pirates' perimeter.

Dan hadn't heard the other teams taking down any other sentries. He had no idea just how many pirates were sitting on the cache, but there didn't seem to be many. If they could stay undetected up until the last moment, with all the sentries eliminated, they might be able to finish this off quickly and quietly, and then despoil the cache at their leisure.

Of course it *couldn't* work out that way.

There was a muffled yell that was quickly cut off over to the left and down the hill, followed by a thrashing noise in the bush and a series of wet *thwack*s. Below, the pirates grouped around the fire, just barely visible now to Dan and Vernon, suddenly turned toward the noise, squinting into the darkness. They didn't seem that alarmed, not yet, but one called out a query in Mandarin. Another started to reach for his rifle, leaning against a log.

Dan reached for his rifle, about to go loud, but hesitated. A gunshot would be heard for miles. He didn't know how many pirates were around, either. They'd noticed that Yuan's people had definitely stepped up the patrols lately, apparently sacrificing crews out at sea for the sake of greater security closer to their base.

If he'd been Yuan, he might have moved everything out to the *Zhaotong*, out of reach of his enemies on the island. Of course, that might just make him a bigger target for the Chinese, or any other country's naval arm that might be out to nail him. Dan didn't know how effective a Hellfire from a Reaper drone might be on a Chinese frigate, but he imagined that Yuan wasn't in a hurry to find out.

A couple more pirates appeared out from under a shelter that Dan hadn't noticed before, carrying rifles. It seemed only a few were equipped with the more modern QBZ-95s; most were carrying either Type 56s, SAR-88s, or Type 63s.

One of the pirates was pointing toward the noise and giving orders. Four of them, reluctant and sullen by their body language, started into the jungle to investigate. That left two by the fire.

Without a word, Dan and Vernon came to a crouch and started down toward the fire. An opportunity was an opportunity.

The fire was in front of a small lean-to shelter set in the rocks. Judging by the pair that had appeared out from under the lean-to, there was a dugout or a cave back there. There might be more pirates there; if there were, they'd have to improvise.

The two they could see were both facing toward the noise, watching their comrades disappear into the dark. That made it easier.

Which was not to say that sneaking up behind an alert man to stab him to death with a knife was in any way *easy*. But it was preferable to alerting every pirate within five miles with a gunshot.

Dan was still twenty feet from his quarry when a shot echoed out over the water. It was immediately followed by a storm of gunfire. A few rounds *crack*ed past overhead, indicating that a lot of that fire wasn't coming from the pirates.

Fuck. Dan didn't even say a word, but swung his rifle off his back, put the red dot on his target and squeezed the trigger. At twenty feet, it wasn't a hard shot, even in the low light.

He'd learned a long time before never to trust a single round to put a man down, and certainly not if the round was a 5.56. He put four shots into the pirate's back as fast as he could squeeze the trigger, his hand clamped around the front end of the SG 553's forearm to keep the rifle rigidly controlled. He saw his target go down and immediately tracked to the next guy, just as Vernon shot that one in the head.

The pirate dropped like a sack of rocks, but then, incredibly, rolled over and tried to bring his rifle up. Both Dan and Vernon shot him another five or six times each, and he slumped, half in the fire, his rifle falling slack across his chest.

Leaving the dead pirate smoldering, Dan continued to sweep across the cache site. There was indeed a dugout under the lean-to, back in the rock of the hillside. There was also another pirate sitting in it, who already had his QBZ-95 pointed at them.

Only the fact that the gunman had been blinded by the fire, and couldn't clearly see the hulking, leafy figures back in the shadows saved Dan's life. The pirate took a shot at where he thought he'd seen the muzzle flashes, right at the same instant that Dan's trigger broke.

The bullet passed so close to Dan's head that he felt its passage more than he heard the hard, painful *snap*. It actually made him flinch a little, which threw his own shot, though not quite as badly. He at least winged the pirate, even as Vernon moved to get a better angle. The man in the dugout desperately flipped his rifle to full auto and sprayed the darkness past the fire.

Dan dropped to his belly, but then he didn't have a shot at the pirate. He rolled away, though he quickly came up against a tree. The pirate's long burst chipped bits of bark and splinters of wood off of the trunk above him, while he tried to get as flat to the ground as he could get. He couldn't shoot back effectively, so he had to wait the guy out.

A thirty-round magazine doesn't last long on a full-auto mag dump. In seconds, the pirate had run dry, and was fumbling to find another mag and jam it into the rifle. Dan got his knees under him and came up to shoot, but Vernon beat him to it, knocking the pirate back into the dugout with a rapid series of five shots. As Dan stood up and moved back toward the fire, Vernon moved closer to the dugout and put one more shot into the dying man's head.

The shooting off to the west had stopped. Whether that meant good news or bad news had yet to be seen. So the two of them melted back into the shadows and the weeds, waiting to see what developed. They weren't running radios for several reasons, noise being one of the biggest.

After a few minutes, a tapping noise came from the east. Three soft raps of wood on wood. They wouldn't necessarily have stood out among the noises of the jungle at night, except that Dan was already listening for them. He tapped a stick on a nearby log twice. *Clear.*

Two by two, the others moved in, signaling with discreet taps before rising off the ground like dark, leafy phantoms, and came into the cache. Cassy and Rex were the last.

"That was a little dicey," Sam whispered. He and Cary had been off to the west.

"What happened?" Dan asked.

"I fucked up," Sam admitted. "I miscalculated, and lost my grip on the sentry. Had to catch him again and then damn near chop his head off. I should have gotten closer before I hit him." Dan just raised an eyebrow, invisible behind his NVGs. Sam had tried to be cool about it, but he'd gotten buck fever and jumped the gun, and it had almost cost them the mission along with several more lives.

"We'll talk about it later," Dan said grimly. Sam just nodded. He actually appeared chastened, if that could be seen through body language while ghillied up and wearing NVGs. Dan suspected that it wouldn't happen again, but he had to address it with the other man anyway. They could not afford mistakes, particularly not those brought on by ego.

Dan checked his watch. "Since we had to go loud, we've got to make this fast," he said, just loudly enough so that the rest, most of whom had gotten back down in the prone, facing out and downhill, could hear. "Fifteen minutes. We grab what we can carry and get the hell out. Prioritize ammo, explosives, water, and chow."

Rex and Cassy dove into the cache and started quickly sorting through the rather haphazard piles of materiel. Rex hauled out two cases of bottled water immediately, and Dan started divvying them out. They were pretty low on water, even with his filtration system and careful rationing. This wouldn't last very long, but it was something.

Cassy was going through the ammo. "There's not a whole lot we can use here," she announced. "Lots of 7.62x39, 7.62x54...5.8...here's some 7.62x51...well, here's a case of grenades, we can definitely use those."

"Got it," Rex said. "Two cases of 5.56, over here."

"Break 'em open and share out the bandoliers," Dan ordered.

"Same with the grenades, and any satchels you can find."

"Found some chow," Cassy said. "I don't know why it was under the frags, but here it is." She struggled with the boxes, knocking a couple over before hauling the box of rations out with a grunt. Dan reached in to help her. "Looks like Thai field rations, but it's better than nothing."

So their diet was going to be mostly a lot of fish, rice, and peppers for the foreseeable future. "We might have some bubbly guts for a bit, but it beats starving to death," Dan agreed, lifting the case out and setting it down next to the fire to open it. "How many cases?"

She rummaged around some more. "Looks like three."

"Break 'em out," he said. "These fuckers ain't gonna need 'em anymore."

Most of them stayed on security on the perimeter while Rex and Cassy divvied up the supplies. Dan looked back to see Cassy stuffing some of it into a canvas backpack that looked like she'd pulled it out of the cache. "Just divide the stuff up into the packs we've already got," he told her.

"Dan, I've got to carry *something,*" she protested. "I can't just tag along while you guys carry everything for me."

"You are carrying something," he replied. "Your weapons and ammo. We've been over this. You won't be able to keep up with the pace we have to set with much more than that, especially after the last couple days of short food and water." He looked back at her in the dim light of the dying fire. "Your pride has to take a back seat to the necessities of the situation," he said. "Do what I told you."

She sighed angrily, but started taking the supplies out of the salvaged pack.

By his watch, they still had four minutes left by the time all of the rations, ammunition, and explosives had been shared out and they were moving. They kept to a Ranger file on the way out, rather than splitting back into pairs. Dan knew that eventually they were going to have to reduce their footprint even more, but some of their number were definitely not quite ready for that yet.

The night's work was bolstering his confidence, though. They might not be real guerrillas yet, but they were learning fast.

They'd made it almost half a klick before the remains of the cache went up in a resounding explosion, lighting the night behind them. They'd sacrificed some of the explosives to deny the pirates the supplies. They could still see the flames licking at the trees from the next ridge over for some time.

Feng was using a bit more of a brute-force approach than Dan was.

He and his *Jiaolong* had landed just around the point from the small fishing village a few kilometers east of Terempa. Some careful observation from the water had shown that the pirates had a not insignificant presence in the village; in fact, it looked like most of the locals had been run off. Several houses were noticeably empty, and there were armed pirates everywhere. He didn't know if there were SAMs present, but he was determined to take at least one of the pirates alive for interrogation to find out just *where* the SAMs were.

He was also, even if he refused to admit it, becoming determined to take Yuan down himself. Let Guo explain *that* to the Central Committee; that he'd stood by, safe and lazy, on the *Changbai Shan*, while a team of *Jiaolong* dealt with the deserter without support.

The ville wasn't large. It was essentially a single row of houses, mostly built on stilts over the shore, lining the bay. That made it that much simpler.

He had support by fire elements placed on the high ground with Ultimax 100 machine guns, spaced out where they could cover the entire ville. The rest of his men, wearing plain green jungle fatigues, plate carriers, and Western Kevlar helmets, were staged in the jungle just to the east of the village.

Feng checked his watch. The last of the gun teams should be in position. "Go, go, go!"

The lead assault team exploded out of the jungle, taking the mere ten yards to the first house in a single, fast bound. The next team pushed past the house to cover the next one, while the assaulters kicked in the door with a splintering crash and flooded inside the building.

No shots were fired, and in moments, the team was back outside, even as Feng led the third team past them. They took up outer security on the second house, while the second team breached and entered.

Gunfire erupted from inside the house, a few shots zipping through the thin wooden walls over Feng's head. It was over as quickly as it had begun, and when Shen came out, he gave Feng the "all clear" signal. Whoever had resisted had not done so for long.

Up the hill and partway around the bay, two of the machine gun positions opened fire, tracers spitting down into the town. Some of the pirates had heard the shooting and started to respond, only to be cut down by the support by fire teams.

That was fast, Feng thought. Either some of them were still up partying, or Yuan had his people on high alert after the recent attack. Either way, the village was getting cleared that night. He pointed to the next house, needlessly, as Cheng led the first team to cordon it off. Then it was his turn.

His superiors might have frowned on it, but he let Qiao kick in the door, then took the first step into the room. It was empty, and looked like it had been for a long time, as he played the light on his SAR-21 around the walls. He was fairly certain that the pirates hadn't used this house. A quick check of the other two rooms confirmed it.

The next two houses were the same. Sporadic bursts of fire from the hillside confirmed that someone was still moving around on the other side of the bay. Whether they were pirates or not, the machine gunners were making sure they kept their heads down.

As they stacked up on the next house, someone from inside fired a burst through the door. Xu tossed a concussion grenade in through the window, and Feng went in in front of the stack while the smoke was still swirling through the room.

The Chinese commandos were rather less worried about collateral damage than their American counterparts would have been. As they entered, they sprayed the room down with long bursts of fire. When the smoke cleared, two men were bleeding out on the floor, next to a pile of drugs, porn, and empty Langkau bottles. They were still breathing, but that didn't look like it was going to last long. Xu and Wen moved over to the two, kicked their weapons away from their hands, and shot each of them a couple times in the head.

House by house, they worked their way around the bay. Halfway across, there was a ferocious storm of machine gun fire from up on the ridge. Wang, who had the final fire support position, called over the radio, "They are starting to try to flee toward Terempa. We just killed six of them on foot."

"None of them escape this village," Feng reinforced. He was standing just outside the door of the latest house, breathing hard, dripping with sweat. Even relatively unresisted, house-to-house fighting is exhausting. "If they wish to surrender, we will take a few captives. Anyone else dies."

He kept expecting to reach some knot of serious resistance, but it never materialized. By the time they reached the far side of the bay, they'd killed about a dozen pirates and found a good quantity of drugs, weapons, and other goods, but little else. Certainly no SAMs, or even what he would expect to be useful intelligence.

Until Shen came up to him with a crumpled map in his hand. *"Shang Wei,* you should see this," he said.

Feng took the map and spread it out on the table in the last house, shining his blue lens flashlight on it. It had been extensively marked, and in Mandarin. His eyebrows climbed.

"If this is accurate," he said, "it is a map of every outpost the pirates have on Siantan, Matak, Mubur, and Bajau." He looked up at Shen. "This is a very good find, *Shi Zhang.* Even if we did not locate the SAMs here, we have a target list now."

"Are we staying here on Siantan, or going up to clear Matak first?" Shen asked. Feng noticed that his senior enlisted man seemed to be of the same mind as he, thinking of dealing with Yuan and his pirates without the support of Guo's Marines.

"We will still use our base on Matak," Feng replied, thinking as he stared at the map, "but as long as Yuan is based here on Siantan, we will concentrate our attacks here. I think we will strike the outer outposts and caches first, then work our way inward, tightening the noose until Yuan has no place left to go."

Shen nodded, an enthusiastic light in his eyes that Feng hadn't seen in a long time. After the setbacks and uncertainty of the early part of the operation, the night had finally gone according to plan. They had easily cleared the village and taken no casualties. It was a much needed victory.

Feng started to think that he might just succeed, after all.

Chapter 19

Lambert was awakened by a sharp kick in the ribs. Squinting up through his hangover at the stone-faced pirate standing over him, he muttered, "This is getting to be a routine, isn't it?"

The pirate snapped at him in Mandarin and prodded him with a boot again, gesturing with the barrel of his Type 56. This wasn't good. He rolled over and levered himself into a sitting position. "All right, I'm coming, I'm coming."

"*Kuai dien,*" the pirate snapped. That much Mandarin he knew. *Hurry up.* There was probably an implicit "hurry *the fuck* up" in there, just judging from the man's tone.

Lambert got his feet under him and stood up, his head pounding. That Langkau had one hell of a kick. The pirate apparently wasn't satisfied with how fast he was moving, and grabbed him by the shirt to give him a yank. He was feeling poorly enough that the little man was actually able to pull him off balance and he staggered. "Hey, what the fuck?!" he yelled, a little too loud, and he winced as the sound of his own voice lanced through his head.

The pirate wasn't having any of it. He got a fresh grip on Lambert's shirt and hauled him out of the lean-to and into the sunshine of the camp. He was a surprisingly strong little fucker.

Lambert rounded on the pirate, even though he was really in no shape for a fist-fight. Still, he was bigger than just about anyone else in the camp, or even on the whole island. The pirate suddenly pointing his rifle at his face put a quick damper on his temper. "Whoa, whoa, whoa!" he said, holding his hands out in an instinctive "don't shoot me" gesture. "What the fuck did I do?"

The pirate just pointed and barked an unmistakable command in Mandarin. Lambert followed his finger, and saw that he was pointing to Yuan's bunker.

Definitely not good. If Yuan wanted to talk to him when he was hung over, and was sending little Chang Trigger Happy after him, he doubted that he was on his way to a friendly chat.

Still, the pirate had a gun, and Lambert honestly didn't know where his was at the moment. Yuan had let him have a weapon, but he'd been too drunk when he'd passed out the night before to worry about where it was.

He probably should be a little more cautious about such things.

He might be one of the pirates now, but that didn't mean he was necessarily among friends.

"Okay, okay, I'll go see the boss," he said, sure that the Chinese pirate couldn't understand a word he said. He just tried to keep his tone conciliatory, so as not to get shot. He turned away from the pirate, acutely aware of the muzzle pointed at his back, and walked toward the bunker.

This wasn't one of the big bunkers that had been in the fortified camp they'd hit before. In spite of having beaten off the attackers, Yuan hadn't stuck around that place for long. He had other bolt holes scattered across the island, all much smaller than his fort. This was one of those, built in the jungle instead of on cleared ground. It would be much harder to find, though even an overhead search could pick *something* out eventually.

The bunker wasn't much more than a cave, reinforced to the front with logs and dirt. It had been dug out some, and there were signs of some blasting as well. Yuan had obviously put a lot of thought into building his little "kingdom," and had determined to be prepared for anyone coming to attack him.

The inside of the bunker was lit with battery-powered fluorescent lanterns, shedding a sickly, sterile glow over the room. It wasn't a good look for Yuan, lending a creepy, corpse-like cast to his face, but then, Lambert doubted that this meeting would be pleasant even out in the open sunlight.

Yuan was standing at a folding table, still wearing the plain fatigues he'd been wearing when he'd first confronted Lambert. He looked up at Lambert as the former contractor stepped into the lantern light, his face coldly impassive.

He didn't move from his position, leaning against the table over a photo-mosaic map of the Anambas. "I spared your life for you to be useful, Mr. Lambert," he said, his accent and deadpan delivery taking away none of the menace in his words. "Not simply to drink my alcohol and fuck my prostitutes. So tell me, how have you been useful?"

Lambert's mouth was dry, the light of the lanterns behind Yuan's head seemingly way too bright. "Uhh," he managed.

"I refused to allow my lieutenants to execute you after your spectacularly bad judgment regarding the woman," Yuan continued, "since you promised that you could provide a unique perspective and be a useful ally in eliminating the rest of your former comrades who are still on my island. Yet you have so far failed to act on that promise in any meaningful way. As I said, you are alive to do more than drink and fornicate."

"Well," Lambert started to say, wracking his brain for something to say to appease Yuan's anger. He was walking a finer line than he'd thought.

194

But Yuan simply raised a hand. "Spare me your excuses," he said. "You will have your chance to redeem yourself before I have you shot, or more likely simply strangled and left hanging from a tree outside of Terempa as a warning." The matter-of-fact way he voiced the threat only made it that much more ominous. "Come here."

Lambert obeyed, his sense of self-preservation overriding both his ego and his hangover.

Yuan pointed to the map as he spoke. "Last night, two of our logistics bases were attacked. Here, in the south, and here, just outside of Terempa in the north. There were no survivors in either place." He looked at Lambert with hooded eyes. "Since my sources inform me that *Shang Xiao* Guo is still keeping his station to the north and has not launched any further probes toward us, I must assume that the attackers are your former associates. Apparently, more of them escaped from the attack on my camp than we thought."

Lambert frowned at the map, trying to think past his headache. He didn't know who had survived the attack, though he knew that at least Sean and Will had been killed; he'd seen their corpses, as well as Decker's. He was fairly certain that Tackett had made it out alive, a fact that irked him, but he really didn't think that Tackett had the kind of balls to pull off a no-survivors attack. That guy would probably want to be a humanitarian about prisoners or something, and would drag along some rag-tag pirates until they slowed him down and got him caught and killed. He'd probably die thinking how unfair it was, because he was a good guy. *Moron.*

Damn, I should have asked Jenny about that, before the dumb bitch blew herself up.

Yuan was looking at him, as if expecting an answer. He shrugged, trying to buy time. "I don't know exactly how many got away," he said, "but I'd be surprised if they were able to coordinate simultaneous strikes across the fucking island. Maybe there are two groups." *Maybe Rex got away to the north. But that would leave Tackett in charge down south...nah. Without Decker backing him up, I bet Sam took over. Yeah, that's it. No survivors is more Sam's style. Too bad, he'd do well here with me.*

Yuan nodded thoughtfully, looking back down at the map. "Possible," he allowed. "It would explain the fact that we have found little trace of them since taking the prisoners on the west coast the other day, yet they were able to launch these attacks on the same night. If there are two separate groups, there might not be any coordination involved." He looked at Lambert with an unnerving intensity. "I will be reasonable, Mr. Lambert," he said. "In light of your failure with the woman, I will start you out with the lesser task. You will go with Tian to the south, to help hunt down the intruders there. If you succeed, you may have a future."

Lambert wasn't too hungover to notice that Yuan had said, "a future," not "a future with us." The implication was pretty damned clear.

The supplies they'd gotten from the cache gave them some breathing room. They weren't going to die of dehydration or starvation in the near term, and they had some extra ammunition and explosives. Dan was especially glad for the explosives; they offered some more options. Fire a shot, and your position can be somewhat localized. Sneak up through the jungle and roll a grenade into a tent, and it makes things a little more muddled for the survivors.

What they were still lacking was a good idea of where Yuan was keeping the captives. Siantan might be a relatively small island, especially compared to Borneo or Java, but at ten kilometers from north to south, it was still plenty large to hide in. Trying to comb the whole island with twelve people wasn't going to be easy. But they had no ISR, no intel support, so they were going to have to do what they could by themselves.

So they were creeping along the ridgeline toward the next camp that Dan had identified on his map. Whether or not it was still there, there might be some indicators around the site that could lead them to another camp or lay-up spot that might get them closer to their imprisoned comrades.

Exactly how they were going to bust the prisoners out was a problem that Dan hadn't quite figured out yet.

Sam was taking his turn on point, Dan behind him, Vernon taking up the rear again. The rest were in a loose file between them, at least a loose file for the jungle. Dan could look back and just barely see Rex behind him, ghillied up and camouflage-painted. Cary, behind Rex, was invisible in the greenery.

Rex seemed to have shaken off some of his shock and disbelief after the horrific reversal a few nights before. He was still subdued, quiet, always deferring to Dan, Sam, Max, or Vernon. He showed no sign of wanting to take charge, and his customary humor seemed to have disappeared.

He had, however, demonstrated a renewed tactical competence. His shock and dismay on that first night and the days after had apparently been replaced by grim determination.

Sam stopped suddenly, holding up a clenched fist. *Freeze.* Dan held his position, holding up his own fist so that Rex got the signal. He strained his ears and eyes for whatever had alerted Sam.

It didn't take long to figure out what Sam had stopped for. Whoever was out there wasn't being all that quiet.

It wasn't easy or reliable to judge numbers just by how much noise they made in the bush. One or two unskilled FNGs could easily make as much racket as an entire platoon. But he was fairly sure that this was a pretty large group, in part because he didn't think the pirates would be moving around in ones and twos after the events of the last few days and nights.

And, judging by the sound, they were coming south, along the ridgeline, right toward them.

To his credit, Sam didn't look back at Dan to see what he should do. He slowly, carefully, moved off to the right, into the hollow of a tree's roots, and slowly, quietly, lowered himself into a prone position with his rifle, still swathed in leaves and creepers except for the muzzle, the ejection port, and the mag well, pointed toward the oncoming pirates.

Dan slowly turned his head to make sure he had Rex's attention. Every movement had to be slow now, in spite of the urgency of the situation. The eye is drawn toward movement, and a quick move or gesture could give them away. This was not the place Dan wanted to get into a firefight. If at all possible, he only wanted to engage the pirates at a time and place of his choosing.

He signaled Rex that they had enemy contact imminent to the front, and to get down, off the natural line of drift, and hold still. Rex returned the signals, then turned to pass them on to Cary. Dan proceeded to look for a hollow to hunker down in.

The noise was getting louder. He'd be able to see the pirates any moment now.

In spite of the little voice in the back of his mind screaming, *Get down, you fucking idiot!* he slowly lowered himself to the ground, easing toward a tree not unlike Sam's, though further down the slope. It was growing at an angle out of a rocky outcropping that had been split and shattered by the tree's roots. He was hoping that the pirates wouldn't be quite as vigilant about checking behind them as they were looking forward. He still brought his rifle up to the ready, just in case.

His field of view had shrunk to barely a few feet. He could see the rocks, the tree above him, and the shrubs and ferns growing out of every little bit of soil. Sam was invisible behind the trees and the undulation of the hillside ahead of him, Rex having similarly disappeared behind. Except for the sound of their enemies forcing their way through the jungle ahead, he might be alone.

The footsteps and the cracking and rustling of vegetation got closer and closer. He could occasionally hear what might be a muttered curse in Mandarin, Cantonese, or Malay. For the most part, the pirates weren't being chatty, but they weren't practicing the best noise discipline, either.

While the sound helped him to track their progress, it also had an insidious psychological side effect as he lay there, trying not to move a muscle or even breathe too loudly. He could hear them getting closer and closer, always terribly aware that if even one pirate stepped too close, looked down at the wrong moment, or, worse, stepped in the wrong place, it was all over and they were all dead. Hell, a sneeze could kill them all at that point.

Closer. Closer. He thought he could see some of the bush moving with the passage of the lead pirates, though he couldn't see any of them yet. Or maybe it was just his imagination.

Then there was a figure right next to him, not even six feet away. There was still vegetation between them, but he could see the man's gray trousers and filthy tennis shoes, with glimpses of his chest rig and the orange bandanna tied around his head.

Please, nobody move, nobody make a sound, and for fuck's sake, nobody fucking shoot. He kept watching the pirate above him out of the corner of his eye, careful not to stare directly at him. Could he roll to his back and shoot the bastard in time, if he got spotted? He didn't know. He envisioned the motion fifteen times in probably as many seconds, even as he tried to keep his breathing shallow and quiet. His heartbeat felt like a bass drum in his chest, pounding all too loudly. There was no way they couldn't hear it.

The pirate kept walking, swishing against the fronds and creepers as he forced his way through the bush. Then Dan couldn't see him anymore. He heard a couple more go past, then the next one, a short man wearing OD green trousers and a black wife-beater, with two belts of 7.62x54 machine gun ammo slung across his chest and a PKM in his hands, tripped over a root and stumbled with a curse against Dan's tree.

Dan thought his heart was going to stop. The little man was right above him, his PKM barrel almost pointed at his face, his hand on the trunk of the tree only a few feet above his head. The only good part about their relative positions was the fact that Dan only had to raise his own weapon up a few inches to put a round right through the pirate.

He stayed put, motionless, willing the man to see nothing but a pile of leaves and shrubs at the base of the tree. It seemed hopeless. There was no way he wouldn't notice *something*, even if it was only the dark circle of Dan's rifle muzzle pointed at his ankles.

But with another muttered curse, the little man heaved himself back upright and walked on, barely two feet from where Dan lay. He didn't look down, didn't look back. He hadn't seen a thing.

Dan stifled a heaving sigh of relief, only then realizing that he'd been holding his breath ever since the pirate had tripped. *That was way too fucking close.*

I just hope none of the others have that close a call. I'm not sure some of them would be able to hold their fire if they did. It had taken every ounce of self-control not to blast the pirate through the sternum.

Hell, did he have the bolt back on that MG? He might have blasted me completely by accident. In which case, they probably would have found his body, and then the whole game would be blown. They'd be fucked. Not that he'd be in any position to care anymore.

They still might be fucked. The parade of pirates wasn't past the end of the file yet.

No more of them came that close, but the crackling, snapping, swishing, and cursing seemed to go on for a long time. He thought he counted at least twenty, maybe even twenty-five pirates walk past. That was a big element. *Where the fuck are they getting all these bodies? Yuan was a fucking frigate skipper. How the hell has he built a whole fucking army in this short a time?*

Finally, the racket had receded into the jungle to the south. No one yelled an alert, no shots were fired. He started to breathe a little bit easier. A *little* bit. It wasn't time to relax yet.

The run-in wasn't a good sign. They weren't on the same ridge as the camp they'd hit; he'd made sure they moved over to the next terrain feature precisely to *avoid* this kind of encounter. That told him that either somebody in the enemy camp had predicted the move, or the pirates were conducting a wide sweep to the south in order to try to roll them up.

He waited, listening to the sounds of the jungle and his own rapid heartbeat, until he heard two faint taps of wood on wood from back in Rex's direction. *Clear.* He picked a stick up off the ground and repeated the tap against the tree trunk for Sam, then slowly and carefully, still trying to stay as silent as possible, got back up to his knees, then his feet.

Sam was already up on a knee by his tree, facing north, but he glanced back as Dan came up out of the weeds, and waved him forward. Curious, Dan signaled Rex to hold his position, and moved up to Sam's position.

The other man looked over at him as he knelt alongside. Dan was struck by the fury he saw in Sam's eyes. "What is it?" he whispered.

"Did you see him?" Sam asked.

"I only saw two of 'em clearly, one close enough to smell his breath," Dan replied. "See who?"

"Lambert," Sam spat, managing to work an infinity of hate and venom into the whisper. "He was with them."

"A prisoner?" Dan asked, afraid he already knew the answer.

"Oh, hell no," Sam replied, back facing the north, scanning for any threats to come out of the jungle. "He still had his weapon and his chest rig. He's gone over." He spat on the ground. "I swear, before I get off this island, I'm going to kill him. I'll cut his balls off and feed them to him before I saw his fucking head off."

Dan said nothing for a moment. He could sympathize with Sam's bloodthirst. But at that point, he mostly just felt tired. *I thought I was rid of that son of a bitch,* he thought. *Though this certainly confirms what a complete sack of shit he is.* Not that he'd really needed any more confirmation apart from what he'd already seen with his own eyes.

"We'll deal with Lambert if and when the time comes," he told Sam. "Right now our priorities are staying alive and getting our people out of Yuan's hands. If that means killing Lambert, I'm all for it. But if you go off the reservation to go after him," he warned, "I'll kill you myself. Understood?"

"Solid copy, boss," Sam bit out. "And I hear you. I get it. But if I get the chance, provided it doesn't compromise us otherwise, I'm dumping that motherfucker in a heartbeat." His jaw worked, while his eyes stayed on the jungle. "Believe me, I wanted to blast him as he walked by. Wanted to so bad I could fucking taste it. I didn't." He glanced back at Dan. "Satisfied?"

Dan nodded minutely. "Just as long as we're both on the same page."

"Believe me, we are," Sam assured him. "But now you know."

"I wonder," Dan mused.

"What?"

"I'd just been thinking," he said, as he glanced back to the south, "that it was strange that we ran into them over here. We'd moved a terrain feature over to avoid contact, and here's a patrol, apparently looking for us, and Lambert's with them."

"You think he figured we'd circle around instead of heading north on the same ridge?" Sam asked.

"It's possible," Dan allowed. "Either that, or they're being really thorough."

"Either way, it's probably a bad idea to hang around here for much longer," Sam pointed out.

"Probably." He turned back to Rex and waved him forward. "Let's go."

It was almost dark when Sam called another halt. There wasn't much dusk in the jungle this close to the tropics. The sun had gone down, and the gray shadows under the canopy was going to be pitch black in a few more minutes.

Dan crept forward to see what was up. Sam had put up a hand and then sunk to the jungle floor, his rifle aimed forward. He'd seen pirates, or at least something that qualified as an immediate threat.

Coming up beside Sam's supine mass of jute and leaves, he didn't have to ask. He saw what had stopped them well enough.

There was a pair of armed men barely fifty feet ahead of them. One was squatting, his rifle across his knees, a glowing cigarette hanging from his mouth. The other was standing off to one side, pissing against a tree, his rifle leaning against the tree behind the smoker, a good two paces away from him.

Dan had been navigating as best he could in the thick forest ever since they'd stepped off. It wasn't easy, but he had a pretty good idea where they were. They still had a good hundred meters to go before they could get eyes on their objective.

He got Sam's attention, and pointed west, toward the draw they'd crossed earlier. Maybe they could get around the sentries that way.

Sam signaled his understanding, and together they eased back through the bush, putting a little bit more space between them and the two pirates before Sam started downhill to the west. Dan made sure Rex knew what was going on, then followed.

It soon became apparent that the pirates had a string of such little outposts set up every few dozen meters around the camp. Yuan, or whoever was making his tactical decisions on the ground, didn't want any repetition of the previous night's attack.

So Dan got the rest of the team holed up in the weeds a good hundred meters from the screening force, stripped off most of his equipment except for his ghillie, pistol, and knife, and started crawling in by himself. Better one than a dozen. It would keep their footprint small, and if he got caught and killed, the rest would have a better chance to get away.

It was a long, draining crawl through the dark. He got close enough to one of the sentry pairs that if he'd been able to understand Javanese he might have been able to follow their entire conversation. By that time he was flat on his belly, his cheek against the ground, inching forward with fingers and toes, measuring progress in meters per hour. Any quicker and he risked being heard.

He got close enough to get a good look at the camp, huddled in the shadows just beyond the light of one of three campfires. There were about a dozen crude tarp shelters strung up between the trees, with packs and duffel bags of supplies piled underneath them, but he didn't see anything that looked like a place to keep captives or any sort of headquarters. This seemed to be a field camp for Yuan's pirates and little else. He wondered what it had been before this little jungle war started; it had been one of the locations marked on his map. Maybe another distributed supply cache, much like the one they'd hit the night before. Yuan had certainly seemed prepared for a large-scale attack.

Just as carefully and quietly, he slipped back out, passing by a different pair of sentries this time. It was almost dawn by the time he reached the team's lay-up spot, and he was utterly exhausted. He told Vernon to wake him up to move in three hours, then laid back against his pack and passed out.

Chapter 20

The previous night had been a good one for Feng and his *Jiaolong*. Their target had dissolved into chaos as soon as they hit it, and any resistance had quickly disintegrated after the first group of pirates went down in a hail of 5.8mm gunfire. The commandos had taken several prisoners who promised to be cooperative, notably all non-Chinese.

Feng had executed the rest. It had eliminated the dead weight and had the additional effect of strongly encouraging the cooperation of the rest of the surviving captives.

They had returned to Feng's makeshift headquarters on Matak, where he was conducting the interrogations, though they had been, so far, surprisingly informal and easy. This particular pirate, a surprisingly large Vietnamese named Lac Quang Dung, was being particularly loquacious. Feng was taking full advantage of it, even having the man brought some tea while he took notes.

"Many of us came because Yuan promised lots of loot and women, and not much interference," Lac said. "He said that he had carefully picked the islands, and that he had insurance in place to keep all the major powers away from us, to give us free reign. That promise is falling apart. His Chinese are still staying loyal to him, but most of the rest of us, Vietnamese, Malays, Javanese, Filipinos..." He shrugged. "There are other places to go. Places without soldiers hunting us every minute of the day."

Interesting, Feng thought. *The* laowai *are ready to desert, but he still has a hold on the Han. I wonder why? Do they think that his stolen files provide him with leverage? That this is only a passing assault, that will ultimately be turned aside by the threat of revelation of the information he has? Was he really so foolish as to tell his people about it? Or is he really that charismatic?*

There had to be something more going on behind the scenes, including just how Yuan had attracted so many of Southeast Asia's underworld to come and join his little "kingdom." Of course, Feng was well aware that there was a bigger game at work; after all, *someone* had stolen the files for Yuan. Who all was involved was something he would probably never know. The *Guojia Anquan Bu* would not release the results of its investigation to any mere *Jiaolong* commander. They probably would not inform any of the PLA without the direct intervention of the Central Committee. And the Central Committee was not going to be interested in letting any more information about this unfortunate affair get out than absolutely necessary.

"How is he distributing his Han among the rest?" Feng asked, deliberately avoiding the term *laowai*. Lac was being quite cooperative; there was no need to antagonize him further with Han chauvinism. Feng knew some of his comrades who would not be so polite, but under the circumstances he saw no need to make the interview any more hostile than it needed to be. Lac knew where he stood.

"At first he was placing a few of his officers from the frigate with each group," Lac explained. "Since the attacks started, though, he has been drawing more and more of his Chinese in around him." He gave Feng a crooked grin. "Maybe he's worried that the rest of us aren't so loyal to him, hey?"

Feng squashed the flash of anger he felt at the man's friendly grin. He might be keeping the interrogation relatively soft, but that did not make him this *gou za sui*'s friend. Still, he pressed on. There were several questions that were nagging at him. "How many are left on the *Zhaotong*, do you know?"

A shrug. "Not a full crew, I know that much," Lac said. "He left a few aboard, and then he put some of the newer recruits, the ones with some maritime experience aboard with them. But I don't think there are more than fifty or sixty left aboard it."

That was barely a skeleton crew. Enough to run the ship for short hauls, but not enough for a significant cruise. Of course, it made some sense, given that Yuan had apparently kept the *Zhaotong* close, using it as little as possible. He had probably been intending to keep it in reserve for a really big target.

"Yuan's crew are sailors," Feng continued. "But his main camp was well-fortified, well-prepared, and his men fought like soldiers. Where did they get the training?"

Lac looked lost for a moment. He probably hadn't actually asked himself that question. Most of the pirates probably had little to no military experience, and had just assumed that anyone who did would know how to fight. But Lac wasn't dumb, and as he thought it through, he came up with an answer. "There are a few who seem to be his bodyguard. They are different from the rest; I don't think that they were originally part of the frigate crew. I know that the crew was on the islands for almost a month before his men started recruiting around Indonesia and Malaysia. Maybe they were training then?"

Feng thought about it. It would make some sense, but if Yuan's bodyguard weren't from his crew, who were they? He hadn't received any reports of PLA Marines deserting. It was conceivably possible that if it had happened, the Central Committee had decided to compartmentalize the information for the sake of political damage control. Losing a frigate was one thing; it could be blamed on one rogue officer. Desertions from multiple units would be much harder to explain.

There was another possibility; he knew of several Chinese PMCs working in Burma and elsewhere around East Asia and the Western Pacific. They really were PMCs in name only, for the sake of Beijing's deniability, but they had more leeway and freedom of movement than the regular PLA. If a few of them had been recruited, they could be serving as both Yuan's bodyguard and his training cadre.

"Does he have particular sites that are more important than others?" he asked, getting back to more immediate concerns. "Are there camps where he and his Han stay on any kind of regular basis?"

"There are a few," Lac replied, his face going impassive, as he figured out that he had taken Feng's politeness too far. He pointed to the map that Feng had laid out on the table in front of him. "You know about the main camp that was attacked a few nights ago. He will not be there anymore; I think it was entirely evacuated after the attack was driven off. But he has other camps, smaller camps, scattered around the island. I think he might have bunkers in most of them. He has been preparing for a long time."

Indeed he has, Feng thought. "Show me where they are."

Lac studied the map carefully, so carefully that Feng began to suspect that the man had no real idea how to read a map. But after a few moments, he started pointing out places where he at least believed Yuan had camps or caches.

Some were probably good. Some were probably guesses that were off by half a kilometer or more. Feng marked them anyway. It was a start. And if it turned out that Lac *couldn't* actually read a map, and was just pointing to random spots in order to try to prolong his life, Feng would have him shot in front of the other prisoners, to make sure they understood that lying to curry favor wasn't going to work.

Shen suddenly burst into the shelter. "*Shang Wei*," he said, "you need to come see this."

There was enough urgency in Shen's voice that Feng immediately followed him outside, telling Xu to watch Lac as he went out the door. The young commando nodded crisply, turning to block the door, his SAR-21 held low and ready. Xu was competent and enthusiastic, perhaps a little bit *too* enthusiastic.

Any thoughts about Lac or Xu were banished when he stepped outside and followed Shen's pointing finger.

The *Zhaotong* was steaming around the north coast of Siantan. And it was under attack.

The 37mm anti-aircraft guns on bow and stern were pounding away toward the north, even as a missile missed by a bare few meters, detonating just off the starboard side. But more were incoming, and the 37mms weren't up to the task. If they'd been the American Phalanx

CWIS systems, they might have had a chance. But in spite of the frigate's radar guidance, the missiles were moving too fast.

Streaking in on a gray smoke trail, a missile slammed into the *Zhaotong*'s hull in a roiling ball of fire, smoke, and flying fragments. Seconds later, the *boom* of the hit rolled across the water to the watching *Jiaolong* commandos.

"Who do you think is firing?" Shen asked.

"I think that Guo has been reading my reports, and suddenly decided that he does not wish the *Jiaolong* to have all the accolades for eliminating the deserter," Feng said. "Though I was certain that his orders were to recover the *Zhaotong* intact if at all possible." Of course, that would have involved a boarding operation, which, while the PLA Marines trained in such operations, would probably have ultimately required the involvement of the *Jiaolong*. Apparently, Guo had decided that destroying the *Zhaotong* was a fair tradeoff.

"We have to move quickly," Feng said. "If the *Zhaotong* is sinking, Guo will land Marines soon. We must get to Yuan before the Marines do."

Shen simply nodded, accepting his commander's prerogative. He wasn't going to bring up the files while the others were within earshot, anyway. He understood the sensitivity of that information. "Has the *laowai* given us Yuan's location?" he asked.

"He has given us areas in which to concentrate our reconnaissance," Feng said. "It will have to do for now."

In the distance, the *Zhaotong*, now burning, began to list to port.

Within the hour, the *Changbai Shan* and its escorts hove into view. By then there was little left of the *Zhaotong* but an oil slick and a bit of burning wreckage still floating on the sea. One of the frigates escorting the amphibious warfare ship steamed in a tight circle around the debris, then returned to the *Changbai Shan*'s flank.

Even as the frigate was circling the remains of the stricken ship, air cushion landing craft started to roar out off the *Changbai Shan*'s stern ramp, turning toward the Matak shoreline on clouds of spray. There wasn't much beach to use, and Feng would have thought that seizing the northern Matak Base airstrip would have been more urgent a task, but for whatever reason Guo was starting on the south. It might have had more to do with keeping an eye on Feng and his *Jiaolong* than dealing with the pirates, though knowing Guo, he may have simply wanted his Marines to get the extra training in jungle movement. Foolish, in a real-world operation, but Feng was fairly certain that this was Guo's first such operation. Certain habits died hard.

Feng and his *Jiaolong* were already prepping their boats to cross the channel to Siantan again. They had to move fast, and not only to preempt Guo. Feng had no illusions about Yuan's reaction to the loss of his ship. If they didn't move fast, he was probably going to find another way off the islands, to disappear into the wilds of Borneo, or, perhaps worse, into the Singaporean underworld. He'd certainly caused enough chaos to have gained a certain level of credibility in the criminal underworld.

There was one place that Lac had pointed out that Feng was determined to get to first, before Yuan could use it to evacuate. There was a marina on the southern end of Siantan. While he would have to wait for real-time imagery, he was fairly certain that a man with Yuan's already demonstrated forethought would have an escape route planned through there.

Even as the Marine transports roared in toward shore, the *Jiaolong* boats were on their way toward the east coast of Siantan, heading south.

Dan and his little band of budding guerrillas had turned west, moving down into the Terempa river valley, south of Yuan's fortified camp, where everything about this job had gone completely to hell. Dan doubted that Yuan would still be there, or even have left any people there, and Sam, Max, and Vernon generally agreed. Cary had just shrugged. "I'm no great combat leader," he'd said. "I'll cover you guys' backs, and go where you go."

Rex and Cassy had stayed quiet. Rex had just stared at the map and nodded, his face a mask. Cassy looked drawn and exhausted. She was holding it together, but Dan was sure he'd heard her crying quietly a few times when they'd halted to rest.

Most of the new guys were generally competent, if subdued. Dan was finally getting a handle on who they were, though he still mainly just pointed and signaled. At least he knew names now. Rick was the big, long-haired meathead who looked like he should be a professional wrestler. He wasn't the best in the bush; he tried, but he was big enough that he made noise every time he moved. His gear seemed to snag on every branch and creeper within a hundred yards, somehow. He made up for it by not talking. Dan didn't think he'd heard more than about ten words come out of the guy's mouth. Thom was just as quiet, though Rex had commented, in one of his rare moments of loquaciousness since that night, that the disaster at Yuan's camp had finally shut him up. The chubby, balding man with the high and tight haircut and walrus mustache had been the type to have a wildly inappropriate, poorly-timed joke for every situation, usually punctuated by what Rex described as, "the most ear-splitting, nerve-shredding, braying laugh I've ever heard." Thom wasn't laughing or talking much anymore, and the jungle was rapidly stripping away his paunch.

Bruce was the tall, lanky country boy, who didn't say much, but unlike Rick, who seemed subdued and worried, or Thom, who was obviously a little shell-shocked, quiet just seemed like Bruce's natural state. He moved like a hunter, and was probably one of the best of them at moving through the jungle. He was relaxed and alert at the same time. It seemed like this was just another hunting trip to him. He had seemed a little twitchy and irritable lately, though. When Dan asked him about it, he'd just murmured, "Ran outta Griz two days ago." Dan had been around long enough that he just nodded. Nicotine withdrawal could be a bitch.

Kieth was the other country boy; medium height, skinny, long-haired. He'd been an Army infantryman at one time. Dan wouldn't have known it by watching him. He was a neophyte in the bush. He stumbled, followed too close, fell back too far and lost contact, made noise crashing through the brush instead of slipping around it. When he was called on it, he always fell all over himself apologizing, usually too loudly. He seemed afraid of everything, especially Dan and the others.

Antony, though, Antony was a problem. He was the one who had demanded to know who had put Dan in charge back at the cave. Dan glanced back toward where he'd put the little man between Max and Vernon, the two most patient, friendly members of his team, aside from maybe Cary. He was pretty sure that even Max was about ready to commit murder. Antony obviously thought he should be in charge, and had continued to argue every damn decision made in the last twenty-four hours, in that obnoxious New York accent, until Sam had reiterated his threat to slit his throat in his sleep.

Turning back to the front, he caught a glimpse of movement through the trees at the same time Sam signaled *freeze* again. Always one to go with his pointman's call, Dan complied, though as soon as Sam relaxed a little, Dan moved forward.

"Was that what I think it was?" Dan asked in a whisper.

"If you think it looked like a mini version of the Bataan Death March, then yes," Sam replied. "I think we've found our captives."

Dan scanned the surrounding jungle. They were on the east side of the river; they'd crossed it some time before. He hadn't thought they'd gone far enough to hit the single major road running the length of the island yet, but that was it ahead of them, barely fifty yards through the trees. The captives were being herded south on the road.

"Did you get a count?" he asked.

Sam shook his head fractionally. "I only got eyes on the back end of the column, but it looked like at least five or six prisoners, tied together, with three or four guards in the rear. Couldn't tell how many up front."

Dan thought hard, visualizing the map he'd pored over so many times that he about had it memorized. If they were going south, they might be headed for another camp, or they might be going for the south coast to run to another island. If that happened, any hope of getting the captives out was going to be lost.

Their advantage lay in the fact that the pirates were moving the prisoners on the road. That gave them a defined route. The prisoners were also probably going to slow their progress.

Of course, he thought, glancing back at the rest of the team, that he could see, *we're not exactly the fastest thing moving on twenty-four feet, either*. They could go straight through the jungle, cutting the distance to the next curve in the road in half, but the jungle was going to slow them down.

Nothing for it. He pointed southeast. "You know the dogleg in the road down that way?"

Sam nodded again. "Yep. That where we're going?"

"It is. If we can get there fast enough, we might be able to get ahead of 'em and ambush 'em."

"Done," Sam replied, already getting to his feet and starting to the south. Dan got Rex's attention and pointed that way. There would be time to fill everyone in on the plan later. They had to move.

The jungle made for slow going. Cassy wasn't keeping up as well as she had been, and Rick kept tripping or getting tangled, which slowed them down even more. As much as Dan might hope that the pirates would be slowed by the bound prisoners, by the time they reached their planned ambush site, it was already too late.

Sam halted, sinking to a knee, and waved Dan forward. When Dan came up beside him, he saw the column's rear guard already going around the corner, disappearing behind a curtain of foliage.

"We could still hit 'em, and hope that the captives come to us," Sam whispered, barely a breath next to Dan's ear. They were so close that any more noise would probably be audible to the pirates.

Dan seriously considered it. But the team was still strung out behind them, and he wasn't all that confident that a seat-of-the-pants attack wasn't just going to get their compatriots killed in the process. He shook his head. "We'll trail them to wherever they stop, and hit them there."

"And if they just load them on a boat for that flesh market on Borneo?" Sam asked.

"Then we do what we have to," Dan replied. "Let's give 'em a few more yards, then we handrail the road and follow."

Lambert watched as their boat drew closer to the marina with a feeling he really wasn't used to: dread. It was finally starting to dawn on him that Yuan was actually very likely to have him killed.

He'd always been confident, both in his own smarts and in his own ballsiness. Both had gotten him through before. But now, here among real cutthroats, his confidence was starting to slip.

The sweep to the south had come up empty. There was no sign of Sam or any of the others who were presumably alive and wreaking havoc on Yuan's camps. They'd slipped through the net somehow, and after the last time they'd spoken, Lambert was starting to expect that Yuan was going to blame him for it. In the old days, he'd face an ass-chewing, maybe paperwork, court martial at worst. Here, he had no doubt that Yuan was going to be a little bit more...proactive.

He also did not imagine that when or if Yuan decided to kill him, it would be quick or painless.

None of the other pirates had engaged him much from the get go. Of course, since Tian was the only one of them who seemed to speak passable English, that was probably part of it. But since they'd left the southwest peninsula, with orders to report to Yuan at the marina to the southeast, the rest had been treating him like a pariah. Even Tian was barely speaking to him, and the Chinese pirate had actually been fairly friendly at first. That couldn't bode well.

The boat drifted up to the quay, where another pirate, with a slung QBZ-95, caught the mooring lines and tied it up. Tian just gestured for Lambert to go ashore. The sense of foreboding intensified.

The two stone-faced Chinese with rifles at the low ready waiting at the end of the quay didn't help matters any. Lambert started looking for a way out. Who could he take hostage that Yuan might not want to lose?

Then what? Maybe he could take a boat and head over to Borneo. There had to be *somebody* in that outlaw border town east of Tamjuk who could use someone with his skillset and decided lack of scruples.

His musings on hostage taking and escape were cut short by a rapped command from one of the riflemen at the end of the quay, and a firm push to the shoulder from behind. Tian might have been friendly to start with, but he was Yuan's man, and Yuan said Lambert had to move.

His heart rate starting to rise, Lambert walked toward the two gunmen, gratified at least that they hadn't taken his 553 yet. He could still defend himself, or at least go down fighting. *He wouldn't have let me keep the gun if he just wanted to kill me, would he?* he thought. *Yeah, there's no way. He doesn't want to sacrifice his own people just to take me out. So I've got nothing to worry about.* He got a little bit of his swagger back as he walked up to the two pirates. But only a little.

Neither said a word, probably because they didn't speak English, and he didn't speak Mandarin, but just flanked him and led him in toward the shore. The quay actually made a right turn and paralleled the shore of the tiny bay itself, with most of the marina's buildings on stilts over the water. There were only a couple of structures actually on the island, and the bigger one was probably where Yuan was set up.

As he'd expected, they led him inside. Yuan was waiting in the large, central room.

So was his honor guard. No sooner had Lambert stepped through the door than there was a pistol barrel being screwed into his ear.

"Lower your weapon to the floor, Mr. Lambert," Yuan said calmly, "before Ye scatters your brains all over the wall."

Lambert thought he was going to puke. His stomach twisting, he unclipped his rifle sling and lowered the SIG to the floor. As soon as he'd done so, Ye shoved him forward, hard. It wasn't quite as forceful as the man might have intended, since Lambert outweighed him by a good fifty pounds. The pistol discouraged him from pushing back, though.

"You have failed the task I set you, Mr. Lambert," Yuan said conversationally. "As per our earlier conversation, you have therefore failed to demonstrate your usefulness. Given other events that have occurred over the last day, you are therefore too much trouble to keep around. Goodbye." He waved to Ye, speaking briefly in Mandarin. Ye started to pull Lambert back toward the door. One of his escorts had already picked up his discarded rifle.

"Wait a minute!" Lambert all but screamed. He wasn't sure what he was going to say, but he had to say something. He had to find some way out. It couldn't end like this.

"You had your chance, Mr. Lambert," Yuan said. Ye continued to drag him toward the door, but even as Yuan spoke, Lambert hit on an idea.

"You've still got some of the prisoners you took after the hit on your camp, right?" Lambert said, refusing to go another step and turning back to the pirate. Ye pulled on his arm, but couldn't budge him. Desperation had nullified the threat of the pistol. Lambert didn't really have anything left to lose.

Yuan looked back at him from where he was talking to one of his lieutenants, another Chinese that Lambert didn't recognize. "Yes," he replied with a sigh, giving every indication that he thought Lambert was simply wasting his time. "They are, in fact going to be here within the hour. They will provide some capital where we are going. You might as well, but, unfortunately, I already said that I would have you killed if you disappointed me and wasted my time."

"Perfect," Lambert replied, ignoring the final comment, a plan finally solidifying in his mind. "If you've still got one of our radios that works, I can walk the rest of the contractors right in here."

Yuan simply looked at him for a long, tense moment, his heavy-lidded expression unreadable. He was probably calculating whether the time to go along with Lambert's scheme was worth more than a bullet. He looked over at the other man he'd been talking to, and quietly asked a question in Mandarin. The man shrugged and replied. Lambert felt a rising bitter anger at the fact that he couldn't understand the conversation that was probably going to dictate whether or not these were the final

210

moments of his life.

Finally, Yuan nodded curtly, and motioned to Ye. "You have bought a short lease on life, Mr. Lambert," he said. "Try not to waste it."

Lambert hadn't really thought about whether or not the rest would have had any reason to keep their comms on. After all, they hadn't really trained by the older, bushcraft rules that Dan was using. But it just so happened that Dan had split the team into two elements as they approached the marina, and they'd needed some way of coordinating. There wasn't a lot of life left in the batteries, but they hoped to make this quick.

As he peered through the jungle at the target, Dan wasn't sure anything about this was going to be quick.

There were a *lot* of pirates milling around the marina. While the whole place was fairly shallow, area-wise, and the captives were being kept on the cleared soccer field at the north end of the bay, there was no way they were going to do this without a fight, even if they waited until after dark. And he wasn't sure they had enough time to wait that long. Even though the field of view was pretty limited, it looked a lot like an evacuation was about to go down.

When the radio crackled in his earpiece, he first thought it was Vernon announcing that his element was in position. But it wasn't Vernon's voice on the radio.

"Sam?" Lambert called. "Sam, if you can hear me, it's Tom."

Dan looked over at Sam in disbelief. He and Vernon were the only ones with their radios on, mainly to preserve what batteries they had left. So Sam couldn't hear this, but he sensed Dan looking at him and met his gaze with a quizzical raised eyebrow, visible only as a crinkling of camouflage-painted skin. "Lambert's on the radio," he whispered.

There was a reflexive flash of hatred in the other man's eyes. "What the fuck does he want?"

Dan just put his finger to his lips. They were way too close to the objective to talk much. He didn't answer the radio, either.

"Sam, look, I know you're probably trying to stay quiet, so I'm just going to have to hope that you can hear me. Every one of the other contractors you left behind at the camp the other night is hoping you can hear me, too, let me tell you. I've persuaded Yuan to keep them alive for now, but he's getting impatient. If you come in and surrender your weapons in the next twenty-four hours, he'll let them live. Otherwise, they're shark food." He paused. "Look, I know you might not give too much of a shit. You're like me. We do what we've gotta do. But the rest might not like it so much if you just let the prisoners get slaughtered. I'm sure somebody else has a radio on right now."

Dan took the chance. He couldn't just let this go. Sam's eyes were boring into his, probably guessing what Lambert wanted. "Don't

211

worry, Lambert," he said, ever so quietly, into his mic. "You'll see us *really* soon."

♦

Chapter 21

Feng and Shen had been watching the marina for over an hour, from a hasty OP set up on the hill above the little bay. He had considered coming at the target from the northeast; there was a low, narrow isthmus between the marina and another small bay in that direction. But the more he'd looked at the situation, the less he liked that approach. The terrain was more permissive, making for quicker, easier movement, but it was really in the wrong direction. If they were concerned about the pirates getting away to seaward, they'd have to block the marina, and that meant going around the hill to come at the target from the southwest.

The bulk of the assault force was still en route to their staging point, only a few hundred meters from the marina. They only had about a kilometer and a half to cover, but over the hill and through the jungle, that distance could still take some time. They also had to be fresh enough to assault the objective once they got there.

Feng and Shen had accompanied Liu and Yao to their overwatch position. Liu was carrying one of the team's JS 7.62 rifles. He'd considered putting a second sniper overwatch team elsewhere on the ridge, but had decided against it. Losing Fan, Jin, Shi, and Bai in the helicopter crash had reduced his manpower enough that he didn't think he could afford to cut his assault force any more than he already had, between the snipers and the support gunners.

He and Shen would join the assault element before initiating the attack. But first, he wanted to get eyes on the objective himself.

It looked like his initial guess that Yuan would try to evacuate by way of the marina was accurate. The place was swarming with pirates, loading boats as quickly as they could. Yuan evidently felt the noose tightening.

"I think you were right, *Shang Wei*," Shen murmured. "If the deserter is still on the island, he has to be down there."

Feng nodded. "Which means we have to move quickly." Stealth would be less of a priority en route to the launch point, now. Time had just become the primary concern.

Feng got to his feet. A glance at Liu and Yao confirmed that they were set and ready, Liu already scanning the target area through his rifle's scope. Between him and the support gunners, they should be able to cover the assault force against most threats.

Together, Feng and Shen started down the hill, heading off to the southwest at first. They moved fast, not quite running, but not carefully slipping through the bush, either.

Both men were soaked in sweat and breathing hard by the time they reached the staging point. But Feng refused to take more than a few moments to catch his breath. He pointed to Xu, and then pointed toward the marina. *Go.*

Xu and the assaulters started moving. Feng took up his place in the second element. Shen would stay with the machine gunners and the two Armbrust gunners. The noncom was already moving the machine guns to better place their fields of fire on the bay. They'd open fire once the assault element fired the first shot.

The assaulters moved quickly through the jungle along the shore. The shoreline was steep, without much of any beach, and it was tough going, even for the couple hundred meters to the quay. They made a lot of noise, but at that point Feng wasn't as worried about detection. The pirates were obviously occupied, and wouldn't be expecting an attack from the south.

At least, that was what he thought up until the moment that a long, wild burst of automatic rifle fire ripped through the jungle ahead of him, right where the lead element was. A scream of pain announced that at least one of his assaulters had been hit.

More gunfire slashed through the jungle growth around them. The *Jiaolong*, Feng included, dove to the ground, a few blindly returning fire. Looking off to his left, Feng caught a glimpse through a gap in the undergrowth of a pirate on the quay that was sticking out into the middle of the bay. The man was down on a knee, dumping a mag of 5.8mm into the jungle blindly. He must have seen the movement in the vegetation and opened fire on it, either through sheer panic in the aftermath of the *Zhaotong*'s sinking, or correctly assuming that the movement meant an attack because there weren't any pirates to the south. Either way, the assault had just been significantly slowed.

Shen reacted quickly, though. While he couldn't have expected the shooting to have started so soon, in seconds the machine guns opened fire. Long bursts of fire smashed across the quay, folding the pirate in half and knocking him into the water with a spray of red.

Most of the assault element, thrown into disarray by the unexpected gunfire, were still down on their bellies on the jungle floor. Some were moaning, and at least one that Feng could see as he got to his knees was lying motionless in an attitude that suggested he was dead.

Feng got his feet under him and moved forward, grabbing men by their equipment and hauling them to their feet, kicking others that he could reach. "Keep moving!" he shouted. To stay in place now was to die; the jungle might conceal them, but it wouldn't protect them; the only thing doing that at the moment was Shen's machine gunners. They had to carry the attack through.

Yuan was *not* getting away from him.

Dan crawled closer to the soccer field. He could just see one of the pirates in front of him, with the bent, kneeling shape of one of the captives just beyond. Sam and Rex flanked him in the thick undergrowth, both all but invisible amid the foliage.

Vernon's element would be launching their diversionary attack soon, lobbing satchels of explosives onto the quay from the jungle. That was when Dan and his team would strike. They had a few minutes left to get close enough to neutralize the guards before the explosions kicked things off.

Which was why his blood ran cold when he heard what could only have been a rifle on full auto doing a mag dump off toward the far side of the bay.

A moment later, the rifle fire was answered by machine gun fire. A *lot* of machine gun fire. The pirates not twenty yards in front of him started yelling in alarm.

Vernon's dead, Dan thought, *along with everybody else.* But a moment later, Vernon's voice came over the radio.

"One, this is Two," he called. "I don't know who's hitting the pirates on the south end of the bay, but it's not us. Suggest you move now; we'll link up to the north as planned."

With a double-tap of the transmit switch to acknowledge, Dan carefully got to one knee, bringing his rifle up. Time to go loud. The others would follow suit as soon as he fired; he could only hope that they could take out all the pirates before any of the captives got wasted.

As he rose, the picture in front of him got clearer. There were half a dozen pirates and nearly as many prisoners on the field. The prisoners were on their knees, their hands still tied behind them, the pirates standing in a loose knot behind them. All eyes were presently on the south, where the gunfire was intensifying.

Rex must have heard him move, or otherwise sensed something, because out of the corner of his eye, he saw the vague green shape of the other man rise out of the undergrowth to his left. Sam was another green specter to his right.

He shouldered his rifle, put the red dot on the back of the nearest pirate's skull, and let out a breath. This would have to be quick. He was already visualizing dragging his rifle to the left to the next target, as his finger tightened on the trigger.

The shot broke cleanly, the second shot coming as soon as the red dot had settled from the recoil, a fraction of a second later. The first round had already ripped through the pirate's brainstem, the second bullet smashing up through the top of the falling corpse's skull, tearing apart a brain that was already dead.

He was already tracking the muzzle toward the next pirate even before his first target had hit the ground. The jungle had erupted with gunfire as soon as the first shot had *crack*ed out, louder than the growing roar of gunfire to the south. The next pirate was already slumping forward, red blossoms appearing in his upper back, but Dan double-tapped him anyway before dragging his rifle toward the next in line.

Only to find that that one was already on the ground, Type 56 fallen from nerveless fingers. All six pirates were down, though it looked like one had gotten a shot off; one of the captives was down on his face, blood leaking from a ruined skull.

Dan got up and moved forward, his rifle still at the ready, scanning the field and the jumbled cluster of ramshackle buildings on the quays beyond it for threats. Most of the pirates seemed to be concentrated back by the south end; none presented themselves.

In a ragged line, the green, camouflaged figures came out of the jungle and moved toward the captives.

Lambert's head jerked up as the shooting erupted at the south end of the bay. "Oh, fuck!" He had been a little surprised to hear Tackett's voice over the radio; it meant he'd definitely miscalculated something, but the sound of the attack almost made him shit his pants. He *really* hadn't thought that Tackett and the rest were *that* close. He'd figured they were hiding in the jungle trying to avoid contact until they could find a way off the island.

Even before the shooting started to the north, he was sprinting out of the compound toward the soccer field, having retrieved his rifle from Yuan's guard, though he'd only gotten to keep one magazine. Yuan was making it awfully clear that he didn't trust him. Hell of a time to send that particular message, and it wasn't like he hadn't picked up on it before...

"Come on!" he yelled to the nearest pirates, whether they could understand him or not. "They're trying to grab the hostages!"

I'm going to kill you, Tackett. Tough break for you, but the only way to make sure I stay alive is to kill you, so you've got to go down.

Coming out onto the grass, Dan checked to either side, saw it was clear, and sprinted toward the clump of hostages. Most of them looked like they were Rex's new guys, though there were a couple of Sean's teammates in with them, too. It didn't look like any of his had made it. He looked for Ty or Brad, but didn't see either one of them.

He took a knee next to Harold, one of Sean's guys. The man had obviously lost weight just in the last few days, and his head was bent to his chest, his hands tied behind his back as he knelt on the ground. He'd obviously been severely beaten; his face, what Dan could see of it, was a mass of blood and bruises.

"Hal, can you hear me?" he asked. The man stirred, looking

over at him through swollen, squinted eyes. He looked confused, as if not sure who this leafy green phantom next to him really was. "Can you move?"

Before Harold could answer, there was a shout from the door of the building nearby, and a sudden burst of gunfire. Dan dropped prone, dragging Harold down with him, as rounds *crack*ed past overhead and smacked into the ground nearby, throwing up little geysers of mud and shredded grass. He brought his rifle to bear, to see a pirate with an SAR-80, dumping the mag at the figures on the soccer field. He fired five fast shots, dumping the pirate backward on his ass, blood blossoming across his chest and neck as the bullets tore through him. But the damage was done.

Thom was flat on his face, not moving. Rex had rolled to his back, coughing and choking, red froth at his mouth. Lung shot. And at least half of the captives were also down.

Dan took his hand off the rifle's forearm, pulled his knife, and cut Harold's bonds before hauling him to his feet and shoving him toward the jungle. "Move!" he snarled. Any element of surprise they'd gained from the fight to the south was now blown. Half of the men they'd come to rescue were dead or dying. And he was starting to see movement coming toward them from the bay; the pirates were closing in.

He ran to Rex. It was bad. He'd taken three rounds to the chest, and he was already choking on his own blood. There might be a chance they could keep him alive for a little while with the limited medical supplies they had, but without surgery, he was a dead man.

That didn't mean Dan could leave him behind. Pointing his rifle at the sky, he grabbed hold of Rex's vest and started to drag him toward the trees. Sam was checking Thom; Dan looked over at him and got a grim head shake. Thom was gone. After hastily stripping off the balding man's rifle and ammo, he started cutting the surviving captives free and shoving them toward the trees.

Dan was only a few feet from the jungle when a shot smacked splinters off the tree trunk in front of him. He dropped Rex and spun, bringing his rifle down as he did so.

There were a handful of pirates coming out of the little compound off to the east of the soccer field, spraying gunfire as they came. He returned fire, a fast series of ten shots, and they scattered to the walls, trying to take cover.

One of them was almost a head taller than the rest, and had sandy blond hair.

Dan never knew whether he or Sam saw Lambert first, or which one of them shot first. It was probably down to a fraction of a second, either way. He watched through his sights as the man got smashed off his feet, bullets tracked up from his guts to his throat, knocking him down in a welter of blood, mangled meat, and flying metal.

The volume of fire from the compound and the quays was starting to intensify, however, especially as the pirates became aware that they were under attack from two directions. They had to hurry and get off the X with as many of the rescued captives as they could.

Rex seemed to be worsening. It was getting harder for him to breathe, and more blood was foaming from his mouth and nose. Dan dumped the rest of his mag at the pirates, just trying to get their heads down, and grabbed Rex by the vest again.

"Get the fuck out of here," Rex gurgled past the blood in his throat. "Just go."

Dan didn't say anything, but just kept dragging him. It was probably hopeless. There was no way they could get Rex to surgery in time. He'd die slowly and painfully in the jungle. But he wasn't going to leave him to the pirates, to die slowly and painfully for their entertainment.

Rex solved the problem for him. Dan was concentrating on getting into the jungle, and didn't feel the other man draw his pistol. He heard the report, though, as Rex put his P226 to his own temple and pulled the trigger.

Dan spun in shock as Rex went completely limp. "Damn it, you motherfucker." He knew why Rex had done it. That didn't make it any better.

He dragged the corpse behind a tree, where he hastily slung Rex's rifle and stripped his magazines. They'd need the ammo. Then he hastily reloaded, before turning and looking for the rest.

Most of the team was back in the jungle now. He could see Sam and Antony, along with Harold and a couple other captives. Sam was shooting back toward the soccer field. Dan unslung Rex's rifle and handed it to Harold. The battered man looked like he was still more than a little shell-shocked, but there was no other choice. "Get in the fight," he snapped, then suited actions to words, ripping off several fast pairs of shots back toward the marina.

"By twos, fall back to the rendezvous point," Dan yelled. There was no point in trying to be sneaky at the moment. Later, once they'd broken contact, they could go back to being quiet and stealthy. Right now, speed and volume of fire were the only things that were going to save their lives.

Their remaining lives. He'd gone in to save the rest of their comrades. Now at least two of his men were dead, along with half the men they'd been attempting to rescue.

There would be time for self-recrimination later. Right now, the cold, predatory part of Dan's mind was fully in control. He was aware of the grief and the guilt, but in a vague, academic sort of way. His entire focus was on getting clear and killing as many pirates as possible in the process.

The incoming fire was starting to slacken, at least for a moment, and the contractors took advantage, moving in longer bounds back into the jungle. The shooters often had to prod or just plain shove the freed captives ahead of them; whatever they had been put through, it hadn't left much of the men they'd been behind. Harold carried Rex's carbine, but had to be prompted to use it every time.

A ragged volley of rifle fire from behind them quickly escalated into a firestorm, and every one of them hit the dirt. Bark was chewed off tree trunks, branches were clipped off, and leaves were shredded overhead. The noise blended together into a single roaring, thunderous blast. It sounded like the pirates were trying to mow the jungle down with bullets to get at them.

The fire slackened a little, and Dan was up and moving again, pushing Harold ahead of him. The clinical part of his mind suggested that most of the pirates shooting at them had run dry at the same time, and paused to reload. Whatever the reason, they'd take the brief respite to put some more distance between them and the enemy.

He had to keep scanning the jungle to see if they had everybody. It was hard to tell; as soon as they'd gotten back into the heavy undergrowth, visibility had dropped to a few meters again. But he definitely had Sam and Antony, and three of the liberated hostages, even though the others faded in and out of sight depending on the vegetation.

Chased by what seemed like half of Yuan's army, they put their heads down and forged uphill, away from the marina and back into the jungle-cloaked heart of Pulau Siantan.

Feng rushed forward to the next house along the quay. Even leaving aside how badly the initial contact had gone, this had turned into a nightmare. Each house had to be cleared, and that usually meant moving back to the main quay, which was a deathtrap, and then into the house. Several of the pirates were set up at the far end of the quay, shooting down its long axis. Xu and Shao had barricaded themselves on the corner of one of the huts, and were keeping up a fairly steady suppressive fire, but it was still a gamble whenever they had to move forward.

This was taking too long. He didn't want to think about the fact that his own determination to cut off Yuan's escape to the sea might have been counterproductive. They had already been on the target site for over twenty minutes, though it felt like far longer. Plenty of time for Yuan to have run into the jungle while his pirates held the line for him. If Lac's intel about the Chinese pirates' loyalty to Yuan was accurate, that could very well be what was going on.

He kicked in the door, ignoring the precedence of rank or even place in the stack, and drove into the house with Hsu at his heels. It was, fortunately, empty.

219

The pirates in the last few houses had fought fiercely. He'd lost two more commandos clearing houses on the quay. It seemed as if the pirates knew that they couldn't get back to Yuan, so they were intent on selling their lives as dearly as possible.

As he and the rest of the element got ready to move back out, he noticed that Xu and Shao had stopped shooting. When they came out, he found them still in position, barricaded on the corner of the house they'd just cleared, weapons still aimed down the quay.

Xu didn't wait for the question. "The pirates stopped shooting at us, *Shang Wei*," he reported, his eyes glued on his sector. "I think they might have retreated."

Feng could still hear a lot of gunfire to the north. Something was going on up there. His sense of urgency warred with the need to proceed cautiously. It could be a trap. The pirates might be trying to get the *Jiaolong* to rush ahead, only to be attacked from the flank as they ran down the quay.

"Continue as planned," he said after a moment's consideration. "We will not be drawn into an ambush. Clear every house."

Xu and Shao dutifully rushed forward to the next house, still covering down the long axis of the quay while the rest of the assault team moved to the door. It splintered open on impact, and Hsu led the way in.

House by house, meter by meter, they cleared the marina. All resistance seemed to have disintegrated. The last pirates they saw were bailing out of the back window of a house halfway down the quay and jumping into the bay, trying to swim away. Feng and his men shot them in the water.

By the time they finally reached the compound and the soccer field at the northeast end of the bay, the evidence of a hasty retreat was everywhere. Supplies had been left in the open, ready to be loaded on the boats that were still tied up at the piers. Some half-hearted attempts had been made to sabotage both the boats and the supplies with incendiaries, but the pirates had apparently been too rushed to get away from the *Jiaolong* to finish the job. There were also a lot of bodies, not all of them pirates.

Feng was still not happy. Once they had finished clearing the compound on the northeast corner, with no sign that Yuan was still there, he ordered a thorough search of every corner, every crate, every corpse, and every pack left behind. Once security was set, with Shen's machine gun teams brought in and placed on the avenues of approach from inland, Feng delved into the search himself.

After several hours, he had to admit defeat. Yuan was gone, and had taken the files with him. His hopes for a quick, decisive end to this operation had come to nothing. He had to take some solace in the fact that he had cut off Yuan's escape. If he'd made it to Borneo, there would be no way to hunt him down before he loosed the files in retaliation. For the moment, he could hope that Yuan on the run on Siantan wouldn't have access to a satellite link to broadcast the file overseas.

Finding the tall, blond Westerner's corpse changed his calculations somewhat.

The man was armed, though for some strange reason he seemed to only have a single magazine for his SG 553 rifle. He also had a radio. And he was lying some distance away from the other Western bodies on the soccer field.

Had the Americans attacked and taken Yuan? That might account for the sudden collapse of the pirates' resistance, though he didn't imagine that they'd eliminated all the pirates, just judging from the volume of fire he'd heard to the north shortly after all resistance to the south had collapsed. If they'd taken something else that the pirates were trying to get back...perhaps hostages? Several of the corpses on the field had their hands bound behind them. That was definitely a possibility. American hostages might be very valuable. But without knowing how many such prisoners Yuan had had, he couldn't know if the pirates were after the hostages, or something else, perhaps something even more valuable.

He abruptly turned and walked down to the soccer field, where Shen's teams had dug in shallow fighting positions, their U 100s pointed up into the jungle. Shen, seeing him coming, met him halfway across the field.

"Did the pirates leave any kind of a trail?" Feng asked.

Shen pointed. "We have not looked hard, but they could only have gone north."

Feng kept his face carefully neutral. Giving vent to his frustration at this point would only make him lose face in front of his men. "We put out scout teams," he said. "As soon as they pick up any sign of the pirates, we go after them as quickly as possible."

Shen eyed him for a moment. "They have no avenue of escape left," he pointed out. "The *Changbai Shan* group will have the island completely blockaded by sunset. His one hope was to get out through this marina to Borneo. We have prevented that. What is the urgency?"

Feng took a deep breath. "Those are my orders, *Shi Zhang*," he said coldly. "Get me my scout teams."

Shen stiffened, sensing that he should not argue further. "Yes, *Shang Wei*," he said. He turned on his heel and started shouting at several of the commandos to rally up. There was work to be done.

Feng indulged in a moment's glower up into the jungle. In a way, Shen was right. Yuan should be trapped now. Every other way off of Pulau Siantan would mean abandoning a large part of his army, his supplies, and any hostages he might still have. But if the pirates had left the marina in pursuit of the Americans, who might have gotten the files?

While he was fairly confident that any American survivors were as cut off as Yuan, he could not be as certain that they were cut off communications-wise. If they got the files back to the United States, his failure would certainly kill him and destroy his family.

As it was, even if he was able to eliminate both Yuan and the Americans and secure the files, he would already have to answer for the losses he'd taken, without securing their target. At least six of his *Jiaolong* were dead or seriously wounded. On top of the losses taken in the helicopter, he had endured more dead *Jiaolong* in the last week than the unit had suffered in the last five years.

He prided himself on his professionalism, but he would make sure that Yuan paid dearly for every man he had lost.

Rendezvous was short and hurried. Dan was starting to think that Yuan must have put a lot more stock in his hostages than they'd thought. The mass of pirates was still behind them. They'd gotten some distance, but they could still hear the noise of a lot of men moving through the bush, calling out and occasionally letting off a bit of a mad minute into the jungle. One such had sent bullets uncomfortably close, clipping branches off the trees above.

Dan had already called ahead on his radio to Vernon, staying as cryptic as he could, to let him know that the RV point would be the same, but they had hostiles in pursuit. Lambert was definitely dead, but he'd still had his radio, which meant the pirates had their comms compromised. It wouldn't be a good idea to talk too much.

They'd made rendezvous, pausing and sinking to the ground near the RV point and using their tap code. Dan was fairly sure that the pirates wouldn't hear it over the racket they were making down the hill, and they had to take the chance anyway. Getting separated and staying separated at that point would simply complete the disaster that this entire job had already become. They'd be hunted down and slaughtered piecemeal.

His three taps were answered by the requisite two. He stood up and moved forward, where he met Vernon and his element.

"We can't stay here long," he said quietly. "They're not far behind us."

Vernon was looking around them. "Rex?" he asked. "Thom?"

Dan shook his head. "Both gone. Along with half the hostages."

"Fuck." He looked down the hill. "Where are we going?"

Dan pointed up and to the west. "Try and get away from these fuckers. Then we'll figure the rest out once we've got some breathing room."

Vernon nodded his understanding. Dan pointed to Sam and then up the slope. They had to move. The pirates were getting closer.

Chapter 22

Lawrence had been in a meeting when Henson had burst in with the announcement that, "All hell's broken loose in the Anambas."

By the time she reached the SCIF and got eyes on the drone feeds, the *Zhaotong* was already sinking, a plume of white fire and smoke trailing out to sea on the thermal image. She stopped for a moment, staring at the screen. It was an escalation that no one in the room had been prepared for.

"Who fired the shot?" she asked.

"It appears to have been an anti-ship missile from the north," Poole said. "We don't have imagery of the actual launch, but from the direction of the missile's flight, we can reasonably conjecture that it came from one of the *Changbai Shan*'s escorts."

Lawrence was too preoccupied with the image on the monitor to indulge in her traditional annoyance at Poole's pedantry. This wasn't a small thing. Open naval combat in the Anambas, which were actually outside the part of the South China Sea that the PRC claimed as its own territory, could completely upset the delicate balance that was still, barely, prevailing in the region. Whether the Chinese would soothe their neighbors with some kind of businesslike announcement that it was an internal matter, cleaning up a piracy problem that was—though they'd never directly admit it—the PLA Navy's problem in the first place, remained to be seen. Even if they fully justified it and convinced their neighbors that they had no further interests in the Straits of Malacca, the tensions *would* get ratcheted higher. She had no doubt that the commander of the *Antietam* was already aware of the sinking, and had put his ship on heightened alert. Same for the Air Force birds out of Clark Field. The commanders would have had no other choice, not with Chinese anti-ship missiles in the air, regardless of how far away they were.

She stayed in the SCIF for the next several hours, watching as the *Changbai Shan* group steamed into the waters off Matak and Siantan, and landed troops on Matak. She couldn't help but notice how cautiously the helicopters were flying over the island; Henson pointed it out, suggesting that the *Changbai Shan*'s commander might still be nervous about SAMs. There had apparently been several small-scale raids around the north coast of Siantan lately, that were dutifully logged whenever their limited surveillance assets observed them, but there had been no further air support, and whatever their result, it had apparently not been enough to reassure the Chinese commander that he wasn't going to lose more helicopters to MANPADS.

It was by chance that they saw the fight down at the southern marina at all. The Predator drone was focused on the PLA Marines landing on Matak, but eventually had to return to the barn. On a hunch, Lawrence had asked that the drone take a dogleg over Siantan on its way back. That was when they saw the beginning of Feng's assault.

"Wait a second," Henson said. "Look up there, on the sports field." Following his pointing finger, Lawrence saw the white blobs of human figures on the field, some apparently either sitting or kneeling, others standing above them. She wasn't sure what Henson had seen, until the standing figures started dropping.

More figures came out of the jungle, no longer masked by the canopy, and moved to what had to be hostages. Then a bunch of them dropped, returning fire to the east. In the end, only a handful got off the field and back into the jungle.

"What the hell was that?" somebody asked.

"I'd venture to guess it was a rescue attempt," Henson said.

"It didn't go very well," someone else pointed out.

"That's beside the point," Henson said, turning to Lawrence. "Those had to be some of the contractors that got shut down over at Desaru. There must have been some of them still on the ground on Siantan when the Malaysians moved in on the resort."

Lawrence kept her expression as blank as possible. "That's entirely possible," she said.

A faint frown started to form on Henson's face at her tone. "Shouldn't we do something?" he asked.

"Like what?" she replied. "Send SEALs or Marines into a combat zone where the PLA is already engaged? If this wasn't already a full-blown international incident bordering on World War Three, it sure would be then."

"But they're Americans," Henson protested.

"Who are conducting illegal military operations on foreign soil," she pointed out. She sighed. "Look, if the Chinese capture them and contact us about it, we will do what we have to to bring them back to the States to face trial, as quietly as possible. If they don't...well, hopefully they are as uninterested in sparking a new war out here over a defected PLA Navy frigate commander-turned-pirate as we are. Honestly," she continued, looking around at the rest of her people in the SCIF, "while this is ultimately State's bailiwick, our only hope of containing this is that it would be just as embarrassing to Beijing to reveal the *Zhaotong*'s desertion and activities to the world as it would be to DC to have Americans paraded in front of cameras as renegade contractors killing people on foreign soil."

Henson's expression was unreadable, but she could tell he wasn't happy. "So, we just hope they get killed in the jungle and the whole thing gets swept under the rug?" he asked.

"Essentially," she replied. "I can't say I like it any more than you do, but the facts of the situation are what they are. These people took the risk, and now they're going to have to deal with the consequences." She paused a moment, deciding whether to include the next part. "The fact is, we've gotten instructions to keep our ear to the ground for any sign of either Mitchell Price or anyone from any of his companies setting up in Singapore or anywhere nearby." When she got blank stares, she decided she was going to have to elaborate. "It is believed that Mitchell Price is somehow involved with, if not actively directing, the illegal operations in the Anambas. He agreed to cooperate fully with any investigation, but has somehow been unavailable for the last several days, and no one at his office knows where he is. Or so they say. So, we got instructions recently to keep an eye out for him or any of his people."

"As if we don't have enough else to do," somebody muttered. She looked around, but no one owned up to the comment.

In a way, she could agree. They had a possible confrontation between several navies, based entirely on the sinking of *Zhaotong*, not to mention their usual primary focus on Islamists in Malaysia and Indonesia, to worry about. The possibly illegal movements of a PMC kingpin ranked pretty far down on her personal priority list, but the orders came from fairly high up. They couldn't just be ignored.

She wouldn't devote more resources than necessary to them, either. They did have bigger fish to fry.

After three hours of trudging through the jungle, the pirates were still behind them.

They had changed direction three times, and each time, after a little while, they had needed to divert away from another band of pirates. They were being steadily forced north, with pursuers behind and to either flank. Dan didn't know if the pirates were following them, or if they just had a dragnet out for them. Either way, there were a *lot* of them, more than he'd expected to come after some foreign mercenaries and a handful of liberated hostages.

As for the freed captives, they'd quickly found that any hopes that rescuing their comrades would mean having more guns in the fight were doomed to disappointment. The men were exhausted, wounded, malnourished, and generally beaten down by what they'd endured at the pirates' hands. Ernie and Harold were trying, but they wore down quickly, and just as quickly started drawing in on themselves. They hadn't had time to slow down and get any details, but that it had been pretty horrific wasn't hard to guess. They had to treat their broken comrades like packages, rather than fighters. It slowed them down, and

Dan was dreading taking contact.

Harold was flagging again, starting to stumble, and Dan got Sam's attention, calling a halt with a raised hand. Sam looked pissed, but returned the signal and sank to a knee under a towering tree trunk.

Dan understood the point man's frustration. He could still hear shouts and the occasional broken branch down below; the pirates couldn't be more than a few hundred yards away. They were never going to lose their pursuit if they had to keep stopping every few dozen yards, but the freed captives weren't doing so hot. They just couldn't keep up.

Dan got Harold into a patch of thicker undergrowth, then started down the line to check on the rest. At least, that was what he told himself he was doing. He wasn't sure that he wasn't subconsciously positioning himself to face a contact rear if and when the pirates stumbled onto them during their halt.

The other prisoners they'd gotten out, Ernie, Gav, Aaron, and Graham, were clumped up between Max and Rick. Except for Ernie, who was sitting up against a tree, Thom's rifle in his hands, they had all gotten down on the rocky ground, lying there like dead men. Gav was actually curled up in the fetal position in the roots of a tree.

Dan was starting to guess that none of these guys had gone through military SERE, or done that well in the SERE portion of the Florida training. Or training just hadn't transferred well to real life, which, given what he'd seen of the abbreviated SERE they'd gotten in Florida, shouldn't have surprised him at all.

He considered letting it go, after what they'd been through. But then he stepped over and yanked Gav up off the ground.

"We're not out of the woods yet, motherfucker," he hissed. "If you can't pack a gun, at least you can stay up and watch for those of us who can. So pick your fucking head up and face outboard." The man groaned a little, and resisted, but Dan clamped a hand on the side of his neck, driving a thumb into the pressure point at the angle of his jaw. That got him rising off the ground. "Get the fuck up," Dan snarled. "If you think what you went through before sucked, it's gonna be nothing on what happens if those motherfuckers back there catch us again."

The others had seen and heard; they weren't that withdrawn from the real world. They struggled up to kneeling or sitting positions, facing outboard. They weren't happy, but they moved.

Cassy was further back toward the rear. She looked drawn and haggard, but she was up on a knee, facing outboard, her rifle held ready instead of leaning against a tree or dangling from its sling. She looked up at him as he passed, something approaching reproach in her eyes.

He couldn't afford to give a damn. Yes, he'd been harsh with Gav and the rest, even harsher than he'd been with her. But that hard line was what was going to keep them alive. If they made it back to the States, they could have the luxury of hating him for being a soulless monster all they wanted. He'd be fine with it. It would mean that he'd managed to get them off this hellish island alive.

Vernon was sitting on the slope, facing back the way they'd come, his rifle pointed downhill. He was utterly motionless, his ghillie's vegetation blending into the undergrowth on the hillside. Even knowing what to look for, Dan had to look hard to spot him.

He carefully lowered himself to the jungle floor next to Vernon. The other man didn't move or otherwise acknowledge his presence, except to murmur, "They're still down there. Coming uphill, too." Dan could hear them himself without much effort. Masters of bushcraft, they were not.

"How the hell are they following us?" Dan wondered softly.

"Maybe they're not," Vernon suggested, his voice just barely carrying above the noises of the jungle, even that close. "Maybe we're just going the same direction."

"We've changed direction three times," Dan pointed out. "And these assholes have been on our ass every time."

"Think about it," Vernon suggested. "If they got hit from the south at the same time we went after our guys, maybe they had to break contact and get out of there, just like we did. If they bombshelled out of there, that could be why we keep finding them behind us. They're spread out over half the damned island. We just keep finding different groups."

After a moment, Dan muttered, "That really doesn't make any of this any better, you know."

"Didn't say it did," Vernon answered cheerfully. "Just saying that it's probably why they're still behind us."

The noise from below was getting louder. The pirates were getting closer. Whether they were deliberately following or not, it was not a good idea to let them catch up. "Time to move," Dan said. It hadn't been long; barely enough time to catch their breath.

He noticed, as he labored back up the slope toward the head of the column and Sam's hiding place, that he was getting pretty gassed himself. Being hunted, sneaking and fighting, on short rations and limited water, for the better part of a week, was starting to take its toll.

Maybe we'll all be dead by tomorrow, he thought. *Then I won't have to worry about being tired anymore.*

But at that thought, for the first time since everything had gone to hell and the cold, ruthless, predatory part of him had taken over, he thought of Amy and Tom. If he died out here, they probably wouldn't ever find out what had happened. They'd live out the rest of their childhoods with their grandparents, knowing only that Daddy had left, so soon after their mother had died, promising to come back, and hadn't.

Fuck that, he thought fiercely. *I'm getting home to my kids. Even if the pay turns out to have been nothing but smoke and mirrors, I'm not breaking that fucking promise.* Even as he thought it, though, the words seemed hollow. How was he going to get off the island, cut off and apparently abandoned, and across over eight thousand miles of ocean?

One thing at a time, he reminded himself, closing off that line of thought. It would do Amy and Tom no good if he got killed thinking about them. He had to stay focused on the problem at hand.

He tapped each man as he passed, giving the signal that it was time to move. To their credit, Gav, Aaron, and Graham were still up and looking outboard, instead of having laid back down as soon as he'd moved on. They were slow getting up, even without carrying the loads the rest were, but they had apparently taken the ass-chewing he'd given Gav to heart. There would be, could be, no sandbagging, not if they wanted to stay alive.

He didn't even have to tap Sam to let him know it was time. The point man simply rose as Dan got back to his position, almost as if he had eyes in the back of his head. Of course, Dan was also fully aware of where Harold was behind him, if only by sound. They were getting more attuned to their surroundings.

Sam led the way up and to the north. They were roughly paralleling the far east ridge of the island, and would go over it soon. Maybe that would put enough terrain between them and the pirates that they could finally lose them.

After that, Dan wasn't really sure what came next. Trying to get to Terempa, or anywhere else with boats that they could commandeer that might get them to Singapore, was pretty much top of the list. Right after continuing to evade capture or death, of course.

They had made it another fifty yards when Sam put up a clenched fist.

Dan had a sudden flashback to that first miserable training op in the Florida swamp, when they'd stumbled on the objective before hitting the last covered and concealed position. *Deja vu.* Except last time, they'd had time to come up with a new, hasty plan and run with it. No such luck this time.

The pirate had seemingly just stepped out of the hillside not ten feet in front of Sam. He looked over and locked eyes with Dan a moment after Sam froze.

For a second, the pirate, cigarette and lighter in hand, just stared. He probably wasn't entirely sure what he was looking at. Then he dropped the lighter, grabbed for his SKS, and Sam shot him.

It was close range, and Sam didn't fuck around; he shot the pirate right between the eyes. The man was dead before the echoes started rolling down the hillside and off the next ridge to the west. But the damage was done.

A machine gun opened fire from only a few feet past the dead man, spraying a long burst down the slope. The gunner didn't seem to see them, but when another gun opened up with a similar mad-minute another ten yards south and downhill, Dan knew they were in trouble. They'd stumbled right into a bunker complex.

Dropping flat, he started crawling forward toward the higher bunker, hoping that there wasn't another one even higher up that was even now drawing a bead on him and Sam. There was no time to form a plan, no time to coordinate an assault. It was act or die, or worse, watch the rest of his team downslope get chopped to pieces while he and Sam huddled in the gap between emplacements.

None of this was necessarily consciously going through his mind. His focus had switched to *attack*.

Sam was moving at the same time, trying to get higher, looking for another bunker. He suddenly dropped out of sight, even as Dan got close to the firing port of the first.

The bunker had been built out of massive logs, mud, and rocks. It was nearly flush with the hillside and well camouflaged, suggesting that it had been dug deep into the ridge itself. He got right up against the flank and came up to a crouch. Flipping his selector to auto, Dan brought his rifle up, stuck the muzzle into the bunker's firing port, and blindly sprayed fire through the slot, keeping himself behind the cover of the bunker's wall. After dumping half the magazine, he let the rifle dangle on its sling, yanked one of the Australian F1 grenades they'd plundered from the cache a few nights before out of his chest rig, and pulled the pin, letting the safety lever fly free and cooking it for a three-count before hooking it hard into the firing port.

He felt the concussion through the log and dirt wall, as dust, smoke, and fragments belched from the firing port, as well as the opening upslope that the smoker had come out of. Since the port was too narrow to crawl through, Dan made for the hatch.

It wasn't a hatch, but a trench dug into the hillside and reinforced with logs. Sam was crouched inside it, just around the corner from the dogleg that led down into the bunker, his rifle pointed toward the southern bunker. "Glad I decided not to go in yet," he said. "That could have been unpleasant."

Dan dropped into the trench, facing up the other direction. A glance over his shoulder had showed him Harold and the rest scrambling up the slope in the gap he'd just opened up.

Bullets suddenly ripped down the trench, blasting splinters off the logs and the rocks and splitting the air overhead. How neither of them got hit, Dan would never know, but the pirate on the far end obviously wasn't aiming, just pointing and spraying.

Without a clear target to shoot at, Dan's return fire wasn't much better, but it suppressed the shooter enough for him to push forward, as Harold and Antony dropped into the trench behind him. Abandoning caution, he charged toward the source of the fire, hoping to get to the pirate before he could either reload or get his nerve back.

He nearly plowed into the man, who was desperately trying to rock a magazine into his Type 56, though he was shaking so bad that he couldn't get the magazine lined up. The pirate actually screamed as Dan knocked him over, dropping his rifle and holding his hands up even as Dan buttstroked him. The blow didn't put him down, and he tried to grab the rifle, so Dan put a knee in his chest and hit him again and again, until he stopped moving, his face a mask of blood and broken bone. A few bubbles of breath came out of the blood around his nose and mouth, but even that soon stopped.

The trench ended at that bunker. Slinging his rifle to his back and drawing his pistol, Dan stepped down into the bunker itself.

The man he'd just beaten to death had been the only occupant. A Type 67 machine gun was on its bipod next to the firing slit, along with several crates of ammunition, food, and water. The bunker wasn't large, being just about wide enough for three or four people, if they got close, and only about four feet high. The rocky terrain had precluded much more space than that.

Antony had been right behind him on his rush down the trench, and was waiting at the entrance to the bunker when he came out. A few shots sounded down the other direction, but the machine gun fire had stopped.

Dan grabbed Antony and pointed him toward the bunker. "There's a Type 67 in there," he said. "You've got about no time to get familiar with it. I think we're about to have company."

"Why don't we just keep going?" Antony protested. "There's no point in staying here."

"They're too close now," he replied. He could hear shouts downslope over the ringing in his ears. "There's no time. Get on the fucking gun or I'll shoot you myself and get somebody else on it."

Antony looked like he was about to say something else, but saw the dangerous glint in Dan's eyes and subsided, ducking inside the bunker. Dan hurried back down the trench toward the rest of the complex.

Vernon met him at the first bunker, which was still smoking slightly, the grenade blast having set at least one of the crates smoldering. Vernon pointed down into the pit. "This one's the deepest," he said. "Looks like it was built on top of an existing cave."

"How many bunkers?" Dan asked.

"It looks like there are five," was the answer. "Sam's mopping up the last one right now. The cave seems to be the main installation, with the other four bunkers forming outer defenses." Vernon looked down the hill, where they were starting to be able to see some movement. "Offhand, I'd say the reason we kept seeing pirates behind us is because this is supposed to be Yuan's last redoubt."

230

Dan blew a sigh past his nose. "It fucking figures," he said. "And they're right on our ass already."

"I already told the rest to start hardpointing in the bunkers and getting ready for a fight," Vernon said. "Unless you'd like to try and slip out before they get here?"

Dan shook his head. "With our luck, they'd just come after us that much faster, and we'd be fighting uphill when they hit us," he said. "Better to fight 'em here, where we can be dug in behind some solid defenses, not to mention the machine guns. Here we've got the advantage." How much of his thinking was a sort of reckless loss of hope, he didn't know. Nor did he much care at that point. He was tired of being hunted. If this was it, he'd take his chances.

He followed Vernon down into the bunker. There was indeed a cave opening up behind it, going well back into the hillside. Most of the island seemed like a massive rock pile with jungle growing on it, and this spot was no different. The cave appeared to be a gap where several huge slabs of rock had fallen together, leaving an opening between them. It went almost twenty yards back into the hillside, and had been thoroughly stocked with food, water, and ammunition. There was even a generator, several work lights, and what looked like a comm station.

The bunker itself was larger than the one Dan had cleared by himself. There were two machine gun emplacements, though one of them had suffered from Dan's grenade. The barrel of the PKM was bent; that gun wasn't working again. The other one appeared functional, and Dan went to check it himself, heaving aside the mangled corpse of the pirate who had been manning it. The blast and shrapnel hadn't been kind to the man, though his comrade was in even worse shape.

Below, through the jungle growth, he started to see the first of the pirates working their way up the hill.

Chapter 23

There was no time to coordinate the defense, and no reliable communications between bunkers. Hell, Dan wasn't even that sure who was in which bunker. He knew Antony was in the next one to his right, and was pretty sure Sam was in the far left one. Vernon and Cassy were in the big one with him.

That meant there was also no way to coordinate when to open fire. He could hope that the rest had adapted enough to the guerrilla style of warfare they'd been using to wait until the majority of the pirates had moved in to close range before opening up, but there was no way to make sure, and no time to set up any sort of signals. He just had to hope that they'd go on his lead.

It was a forlorn hope. With a ripping, rattling roar, Antony opened fire off to the right, spraying machine gun fire down the slope, bullets slashing through the vegetation and at least one pirate, who folded up with a scream as the rounds thudded into his guts. The other pirates dropped prone on the hillside, spraying fire up toward the bunkers, even as someone started screaming up the hill in Mandarin. Dan couldn't understand the words, even if they hadn't been nearly drowned out by the thunder of machine gun and rifle fire, but it was probably something along the lines of, "We're friendlies, you idiots, stop shooting at us!" Either somebody down there hadn't figured out that the bunkers had been attacked and overrun, or they thought that the noise of gunfire and explosions earlier had been the meager handful of expendables that Yuan had left manning the bunkers repulsing an assault instead of getting slaughtered.

Bullets were hammering into the logs and cracking off the rocks that formed the front of the bunker. With his hopes for an ambush blown, Dan leaned into the PKM and opened fire, keeping his sights low. Some of the tracers skipped off the rocks and plowed into tree roots, but aiming over their heads wasn't going to do much.

Vernon and Cassy had come to the firing port with their rifles, since the other machine gun was smashed and useless. Both had put a couple of bursts downrange before Dan barked, "Save the ammo. We've got lots of MG ammo in here. Don't engage with rifles unless you've got a shot." Of course, he had no way of getting that word to the other bunkers at the moment; he just hoped that they didn't burn up all their 5.56 before they really needed it.

The rounds hitting the front of the bunker had stopped. He couldn't see any more muzzle flashes downhill. It looked like the lead pirates, at least any who had survived the initial contact, had retreated back down the hill. Dan let off the PKM's trigger. The old Russian machine gun was smoking slightly, but it was running well enough.

Antony kept tearing up the jungle in front of him with long bursts for another minute, before finally figuring out that there wasn't anything out there to shoot at anymore. Dan was sorely tempted to send Vernon over there to sit on the little man and calm him down.

Before he could say anything, though, there was more movement from below. Surprisingly, Antony didn't immediately open fire this time; maybe he'd looked at his ammo supply and had second thoughts. Then the jungle erupted.

Muzzle flashes flickered dimly in the jungle down the hill, and a storm of hot lead and steel smashed through the vegetation to hammer against the bunkers. The volume of fire was easily as intense as what had forced them off the soccer field and into the jungle, except now it was more concentrated. Dan had to duck down below the firing port as several shots tore through, smacking into the logs overhead and raining splinters down on their heads. One round ricocheted with a harsh, snarling whine, to crash into one of the crates near the bunker's entrance.

The three of them huddled under the parapet, as bullets steadily chipped and chewed at the front of the bunker. Dan knew he had to get up, had to return fire. The pirates were advancing under cover of the storm of fire, and soon enough, if he didn't act, one of them was going to get close enough to lob a grenade through the firing port, and then they'd go the way of the bunker's first occupants.

Staying and fighting wasn't looking like such a good idea, now. Of course, having all those assholes down there catch up to them on the far side of the slope a few minutes later wouldn't be good, either.

Taking a deep breath, steeling himself to face the sleeting death ripping through the jungle, he put a hand on the PKM and got ready to rise.

He almost didn't hear it happen over the noise coming from below. But the sound of an explosion off to the right, near or in Antony's bunker, was unmistakable.

Grabbing his rifle, Dan pointed to the PKM. "Cassy, get ready to get on that gun if they start getting closer!" He hoped that she'd have the sand to face the suppressive fire and shoot back, but he had a nasty suspicion that the heavy fire from below was just to keep their heads down; the real attack was coming from the flank.

Staying low, his rifle tucked into his shoulder, wishing for a shotgun, he moved up into the trenchline behind the bunker, just in time to see the first pirate drop into it from above Antony's bunker. The bunker itself was still smoking a little; it looked like they'd dropped a grenade into it through the entrance, not even trying to get near the firing port. Antony had been looking downhill instead of watching the flank.

The pirate, a short, stocky, shaggy-haired man with an old Czech Skorpion in his hand, sprayed a long burst toward the bunker as he dropped down into the trench. Dan ducked back into the bunker's entrance as 9mm rounds spat more splinters off the logs and chipped the rocks as they ricocheted away with buzzing whirrs.

Desperate, knowing that the pirate was going to be on them in moments if he didn't do something, Dan stuck his rifle out and fired a fast string of six shots down the trench, blindly. The pistol rounds stopped coming, and he leaned out into the trench.

At least a couple rounds had hit the pirate, who was lying in the trench, bleeding and moaning, trying to bring his Skorpion back up, even as two more of his comrades jumped in behind him. Dan shot the foremost in the high center chest, dropping him like a rock on his wounded buddy, who screamed as the weight hit him.

The next one threw a grenade over his stricken comrades' bodies before Dan could shoot him.

Dan's blood seemed to freeze and time slowed down as the little steel sphere sailed down the trench to hit the ground in front of him with a *thump* that shouldn't have been audible over all the other noise around him, but somehow seemed louder than any of the gunfire. The frag rolled down the inside of the trench, only a foot away from the entrance of the bunker.

Vernon shouldered past Dan, scooping up the grenade as he went, almost squashing Dan against the wall of the bunker in the process. His momentum carried him into the far side of the trench, even as he fastballed the grenade back toward the far bunker, and the four additional pirates who were piling in behind a hail of bullets.

Dan heard Vernon grunt in pain, even as he grabbed the bigger man and hauled him back toward the bunker, ducking down both to avoid the gunfire and the explosion that was coming.

The grenade detonated with a bone-jarring *thump*. Black smoke boiled down the trench and shrapnel peppered the walls with deceptively soft pattering noises. If either of them had still been out in the trench, the frag would have flayed the flesh off their bones.

The smoke hadn't cleared by the time Dan was pushing out into the trench. He didn't know how badly Vernon was hit, but he could check after there was a lull. No point in checking him in the bunker while bad guys could still roll another grenade in.

He charged through the dust and smoke, his rifle up in his shoulder, trying to close the distance before any of the pirates could unfuck themselves enough to start shooting again. The first mangled body lying in the trench that materialized out of the smoke got a round to the skull. Same with the next one; he wasn't taking any chances.

The smoke had cleared enough by the time he reached the bunker to make out several more pirates on the outside of the trench, who had flattened themselves against the hillside, mostly staying out of the grenade's lethal radius, though they looked a little rattled, anyway. The first one locked eyes with him even as he swung his rifle into position and opened fire, tracking along the top of the trench, putting two rounds into each vaguely human shape that appeared on the other side of the red dot.

The first pirate took two rounds to the face at less than two feet. The next didn't even have time to figure out what was going on before the next pair tore through his body. Dan was barely even aiming, his shots so close together as he dragged the muzzle down the trench that it sounded like his rifle was on auto. At that range, he barely had to aim.

By the time he didn't have a target in front of him, the mag nearly empty, the smoke had cleared enough to see a little better. He could see some of the vegetation moving further up the ridge, where the last pirates had taken to their heels rather than face the gunfire. He sent a couple shots after them to keep them moving.

The grenade had made a mess of the bunker entrance. A couple of the pirates were downright *pulped*, little more than hamburger dressed in shredded clothing and smashed gear. The other bodies weren't in the greatest of shape, either, riven by shrapnel, squashed by overpressure, and smoking a little.

The stench was horrific.

He stepped through the slurry of mud, shit, shredded flesh, blood, and shattered bone, to duck into the last bunker. It wasn't any better in there.

Antony was slumped over the gun, his entire left side shredded and still dripping blood. The blast had thrown him sideways a little, but he had obviously been facing away from the flank, and it had killed him. It had damned near killed them all.

Movement at the entrance of the bunker made him turn suddenly, bringing his rifle up, but it was Vernon. His sleeve was bloody, but he looked otherwise all right. "I'll take this one over," he said.

"Are you good?" Dan asked.

Vernon waved at the blood on his sleeve. "I got trimmed," he said. "That's all. I'm good. Let's get back in it. We can fret over each other's health when there aren't a shit-ton of bad guys trying to kill us."

He suited actions to words, shouldering past Dan before hauling Antony's still-bleeding body off the gun and getting behind it, checking to make sure it hadn't been put out of action in the blast.

The firing from below was starting to peter out. It meant either they were running out of ammo, or they figured that the bunkers were suppressed enough to try something else. Apparently Vernon was thinking the same thing. "You might want to get back toward the

235

center," he said. "This might be the only bit of breathing room we've got."

Dan just nodded and turned back toward the larger bunker. If the pirates were about to rush the line, he doubted he was going to have time to get to every bunker to coordinate. They'd just have to wing it. He definitely wanted to be in that middle bunker when it came, though. He wasn't sure if Cassy was up to holding the center by herself.

Staying low, he rushed back down the abattoir of the trench, holding his breath as his boots squelched through the piles of offal that had been human beings only a few short minutes before. None of them smelled very good after a week in the jungle, not to mention the various stains of bodily fluids they'd picked up in close combat, but the reek of destroyed humanity was a stink that made all others seem minor.

He ducked into the bunker. Cassy was at the gun, staring hard over the sights, every muscle in her body tight as a bowstring. He could see her white-knuckling the pistol grip.

He was momentarily tempted to offer some comfort. Cassy had withdrawn even more over the last couple of days. She was drawn, exhausted, and was probably increasingly certain that she was going to die. He had no idea what had happened to Jenny, but since she hadn't been among the captives on the soccer field, he didn't imagine it had been good. If she was lucky, she was already dead.

But he couldn't bring himself to say anything, not then. They were probably about to get attacked again, and they'd need every hand, every gun. This wasn't the time to make anyone feel better. This was the time to grit one's teeth and start killing. So he just stepped up to the firing port, putting his rifle in his shoulder, without a word. She glanced over at him, and that was enough. He was there, she wasn't alone, and they'd kill all comers together.

There was more shouting from downhill. The odd burst was still rattling up toward them, but for the most part they seemed to be regrouping after their flank attack had failed.

Regrouping, or trying to run away. While the voices down below were still unintelligible, at least one had turned particularly strident, and was suddenly punctuated by a series of single shots. Dan frowned as he stared into the jungle, looking for any sign of what was happening. Was Yuan executing his own men for refusing to push forward? Or had he just heard a coup take place?

A few moments later, the gunfire from downslope resumed, and if anything it was even more intense than before. Bullets ripped through vegetation, ricocheted off rocks, and bored into tree trunks and logs. The air seemed to be full of flying metal, shredded, falling leaves, and spinning splinters. It wasn't aimed, but with that volume of fire, it didn't have to be.

Both of them were forced back from the firing port again. Dan didn't have a target, and Cassy was all but curled up in a ball beneath the gun, splinters and dirt raining down on her, biting her lip to keep from screaming. The point of suppressive fire is to suppress, and the pirates' fire was doing its job.

Dan took a deep breath, and risked getting an eye over the lip of the firing port. Bullets and fragments were hitting far too close to his head for comfort, but he *had* to see what was going on, *before* the grenades started coming in the bunker.

What met his eye was a line of pirates, screaming and yelling and firing from the hip, struggling to run up the hill toward the bunker line.

For a split second, he was a little nonplussed. He couldn't say he'd ever expected to be facing a human wave attack in the jungle when he'd signed up for the job.

He ducked back down again as another burst of 7.62 fire raked the bunker, spitting more bits of rock, metal, and wood into his face.

He crouched there, under the parapet, trying to think, as the storm of suppressive fire raged against the bunkers. They had a little bit of breathing room, only because the slope in front of the bunkers was as steep as it was, and while the suppressive fire had chopped down a lot of the jungle, there was still plenty of growth to slow an attacker trying to climb the hill. But if the pirates kept up the fire, they'd never be able to hit back before the attackers were right on them.

He looked around the inside of the bunker. He still had a couple of grenades, but he wanted more of a supply if he could find it. This might take some trial and error.

He spotted what might be a case of Russian frags back in the cave and dashed for it, keeping his head down to avoid the bullets slashing through the firing port, hoping and praying he didn't catch a ricochet somewhere vital. Cassy stayed where she was, though she did try to get the PKM's muzzle down to fire a burst blindly down the slope. The only response was an even greater intensity of fire aimed at their bunker; apparently the pirates were more afraid of Yuan at that point than they were of getting shot attacking their own fortified position.

He wrenched the crate open, and there, in little cardboard canisters, were plenty of old Russian RGD-5s. He dragged the crate behind him as he crawled back to the front of the bunker.

Pulling out one of the Russian grenades, he yanked the pin and let the safety lever fly free. He held it for about a two-count before chucking it out the firing slit, praying both that he didn't fumble the damned thing, and that the Russian fuse was as long as it was supposed to be. It would really suck to have the fucker go off right in their faces and do the pirates' job for them.

But the frag cleared the slot and bounced down the hill, detonating a couple seconds later, flaying the hillside with smoke and shrapnel.

Apparently, it still landed too short. The fire slackened a little as the pirates ducked, but the explosion was still too far up the slope to do more than pepper a couple of them.

"Less cook-off time," he muttered, dragging another grenade out and prepping it. This one he only held for a second before lobbing it and grabbing another one. Cassy had scurried over to the crate and was grabbing another one out even as he launched the third. She moved to pull the pin, hesitated, then handed him the frag.

"Not sure I could get it far enough," she admitted. "You throw it."

He took the grenade, yanked out the pin, and lobbed it. There was a certain amount of chance involved here, regardless of the length of the Russki fuses. He was tossing the things blind; either they'd open a hole that could be exploited, letting them get back up and start shooting, or he'd run out of grenades and they'd get overrun.

The two of them were getting into a rhythm, which was how they almost missed their window of opportunity. There was almost too much noise on the hillside at that point to tell who was shooting at who, much less to pick out the screams as one of the Russian grenades bounced off a rock, sailing a little farther out over the hillside to drop right at one of the advancing pirates' feet. It detonated a fraction of a second before it hit, blowing the man to pieces and spreading a deadly cloud of shrapnel for twenty-five meters around it. The boles of the towering jungle trees, that had stood solidly against the opposing storms of gunfire, broke up the kill zone somewhat, though they were nearly stripped of their bark in the process.

Dan just barely noticed the fact that there weren't bullets smacking into the front of the bunker, or at least not nearly so many. He took the next grenade from Cassy and pointed to the PKM. "Now's our chance, get on that gun!" he barked. She scrambled for the machine gun as he took the opportunity to actually look where he was throwing the last frag before getting behind his rifle. The narrow slit actually made that a more awkward throw. The frag bounced off a nearby tree trunk and careened off out of sight before exploding, adding another earth-shaking *thud* to the already deafening thunder around them.

Shouldering his rifle, he finally got a real look at the battlefield below them. A few pirates were still trying to struggle up the hill, firing as they came, but a lot more were presently hugging the rocks, trying to keep down and out of the reach of the shrapnel, and increasing volume of gunfire coming back down at them. He could just hear a few screaming moans from below, where the wounded were bleeding out their lives on the hill.

The wounded weren't his concern; neither were the ones keeping their heads down. He zeroed in on one of the pirates, a wiry man with a loaded chest rig and a wispy beard, firing his Type 56 from the hip as he labored up the hill. As much as the desperation of their situation had him itching to just flip the rifle to full auto and hose down the hillside, much as Cassy was presently doing with the PKM, he aimed, breathed, and double tapped the oncoming pirate. He'd forgotten to adjust for height, but at that range, it really didn't matter. The pirate fell backward, cartwheeling down the hill to slam into a tree. Dan was already shifting to the next target, a stocky little man who was lugging a U 100 up the hill. That one got three shots, and fell on his face, sliding down to trip the man behind him, which just put him in a position to get Dan's next shot through the top of his skull.

The tide was turning. Across the bunker line, machine guns and rifles were starting to open up, returning fire against the attacking wave, the brief breather bought by Dan's grenades opening just enough of a window for the defenders to get their heads up and start fighting back. A combination of red and green tracers outlined the deadly rain playing across the hillside, streams of bullets smashing through legs, groins, torsos, and heads, ripping their adversaries apart where they now found themselves relatively in the open, their own suppressive fire no longer enough to cover their advance.

They kept coming, though. Whatever hold Yuan had on them, they'd rather face the guns in the bunkers than Yuan's guns behind them. They kept coming, and they kept dying, smashed off their feet, all but torn to pieces by the intensifying fire from the bunkers.

In the midst of the chaos and death below, Dan started to see a few carefully dashing from tree to tree, boulder to boulder, trying to get closer. A couple of smoke grenades started to billow thick white clouds across the bloody, pulverized kill zone. In spite of the beating they were taking, somebody was still trying to take the attack on through.

Was this really Yuan's last redoubt, Dan briefly wondered, as he shot another pirate who was trying to run forward screaming inaudibly in the noise of the gunfire and explosions, his rounds going high and tearing through the man's throat, sending him spinning, a hand held to his neck uselessly, trying to stop the spray of blood. Whoever else had attacked the marina, they seemed to have cut off an attempt to escape the island. If this really was Yuan's last place to hide, it might explain his apparent desperation to retake it.

He never did know if that was the case. All he knew was that suddenly there was a knot of men in camouflage and body armor, spraying 5.8mm fire from their QBZ-95s, charging up the hill toward the bunkers, appearing through the white smoke only a few meters away.

Just as they came through the obscuring smoke, Cassy ducked back down below the parapet, yelling, "Reloading!"

One of the pirates had his rifle slung and a grenade in his hand. Dan shot him first, full in the face, then flipped the selector to auto and

239

dumped the mag, gripping the forearm hard and raking the rifle across the line. Some of the shots hit chest plates. Some hit flesh. They slowed the advancing pirates down enough for another long burst of machine gun fire to come in from the right, chopping through the attackers' flanks and laying them in the dirt and rocks in front of the bunker. The last one dropped on what was left of his face, smearing blood, bone, hair, and gray matter on the rocks, barely two meters from the front of the bunker.

Then, suddenly, it was over. A few more desultory bursts of gunfire roared out down the hill, but there wasn't any more coming toward them. He saw some movement down below, but it quickly disappeared in the jungle; probably the handful of surviving pirates running for their lives.

Cassy slumped down next to the PKM. Thinking maybe she'd been hit, he moved quickly over and started to check her for wounds. Only when he saw she was smiling weakly at him did he stop and lean back on his haunches.

"Why, Dan, I didn't think you cared," she said quietly.

"I thought you'd gotten hit," he said. She shook her head.

"I'm all right. Just...a little overwhelmed, is all. I thought we were dead."

"We still might be," he said harshly. "Don't relax yet. After we get off this God-forsaken island, then you can relax."

Her smile faded, and she got back up and behind the gun. He felt like he'd just slapped her in the face, and hated himself a little for it, but he knew that just because the attack seemed to be over didn't mean much. They were still very much in bad-guy country, and would be until they either found a way off the island or got hunted down and killed.

He wasn't under any illusions that whoever had attacked the pirates from the south was necessarily going to be friendly.

He ducked out of the bunker to check on the rest. Vernon gave him a game thumbs-up when he stuck his head in the northernmost bunker. The others were the same, with only a few minor wounds from frag and a ricochet that had embedded itself in Rick's trap. He'd be fine, if they got off the island and got him some proper medical care before the wound got infected.

Once he was reasonably certain that his people were okay, he paused by the entrance of the center bunker, looking over the lip of the trenchline at the bloodied, scorched, bullet- and shrapnel-scarred slope in front of them. On impulse, cradling his rifle, he climbed up out of the trench. He'd thought he'd seen something, or someone, in the last, desperate moments of the defense. A few meters down the hill, below the central bunker, he saw that he hadn't imagined it.

Yuan had taken a burst to the throat that had nearly severed his head, but his face was intact enough to recognize. Dan had studied his photo enough in the days leading up to launching operations to know that he was looking at the man they'd come halfway around the world to kill.

It was strange. The last time he'd studied the briefing materials felt like years ago and worlds away, but it had only been a couple hundred miles from where he now crouched in the jungle, and only slightly over a week before. The jungle and their little war had taken over their entire world, their entire lives. If they survived and got home, they would all carry the scars of this last month forever.

Without really knowing why, Dan started to search the corpse. It wasn't like he expected to ever get back to turn in any intel he found. But he looked anyway.

He found a small but high-capacity flash drive in one of Yuan's pockets. He had no idea what was on it, nor, at that point, did he particularly care, but he pocketed it anyway. Again, he had no idea why. It just seemed like the thing to do. Maybe he'd been hard-wired that way from the military. It might be useful.

Turning, he started trudging back up toward the bunkers. They had to figure out their next move. He doubted that the pirates would be that organized anymore. Yuan was dead, and most of the corpses around him looked like they were his Chinese cadre. The rest were probably running for the nearest safe haven by now.

The only question now was, who else was on the island? And were they a threat?

Chapter 24

Feng's point element had just started skirmishing with Yuan's meager rear guard when a major firefight erupted somewhere ahead, higher up on the ridgeline. Feng looked up and cursed. "Push through!" he snapped, starting to suit actions to words as he sped up himself, thrashing through the undergrowth and gaining on his pointmen. He passed Shen, and was almost up to Xu and Shao, who were still trading shots with the pirates that were barely visible in the jungle ahead. Feng flipped his SAR-21 to auto and sprayed long bursts into the jungle at the pirates, dumping the magazine in about three pulls of the trigger. The incoming fire from the pirates stopped, and Feng remembered that he wasn't supposed to be on point. He pointed up toward where the fight was happening and snapped, *"Qu ba!"*

But the jungle was not going to cooperate with Feng's haste. It wasn't long before they came up against a veritable wall of tangled creepers and large boulders, that the rear guard had apparently been using for cover while they engaged the *Jiaolong*. There were bullet scars on the rocks and the surrounding trees, and piles of casings in the leaves and creepers on the ground. Even as a series of grenade explosions resounded from the hillside above, the commandos struggled to get over the rocks and through the thick, intertwined vegetation.

The fire intensified, and then suddenly died away. Gao was still getting untangled from a mass of creepers that he'd gotten bound up in. Feng's impatience was hitting a peak. He didn't know what had just happened up there, but he was afraid that it wasn't anything good. If the Americans had beaten him to Yuan...he didn't want to consider the possibility. He had to remind himself that if they had, it didn't necessarily mean defeat. They were all but cornered. This wasn't over yet.

There were still a few scattered bursts of gunfire rattling out into the jungle, which was probably why Xu didn't hear the pirate crashing through the brush until the man cannoned into him.

Xu rolled with the impact, trying not to end up underneath the fleeing pirate, and it probably would have worked considerably better if they had not been on a rocky hillside covered in jungle growth. Instead of rolling out of reach and covering the pirate with his rifle, he just ended up tangled up with the man, trading body blows in a desperate attempt to keep him from grabbing his weapon. Feng and Shao waded in and hauled the pirate off of Xu. The man struggled a little until Shao, the team's short, stocky *Junshi Sanda* instructor, put him in a joint lock on the ground. Then the man went limp, looking fearfully up at the stony, camouflage-painted faces and rifle muzzles surrounding him.

Feng stood over him, and pointed up the hill. "What happened up there?" he asked in Mandarin.

The man just stared at him uncomprehendingly. That was when Feng realized the pirate was Javanese, and probably didn't speak more than a few words of Mandarin. He briefly wondered just how communications had been handled among the pirates if a lot of them didn't speak the same language, but when he tried Cantonese, he got a response.

"We were attacked from the bunkers," the man said, horror in his voice. "They killed the first ones to go up. Then the *Kapten* started to shoot the ones who didn't want to attack. So we attacked. They killed all of us. I saw the *Kapten* die. So I ran."

Feng looked back up the hill. "You are certain Yuan is dead?" he demanded.

"Yes," the man said, nodding vigorously. "His head was completely blown off. I saw it."

He wasn't sure whether or not to believe him; he'd seen men insist on vivid, first-hand accounts of things they'd never actually seen themselves. But whatever had happened up there was definitely over, and unless this particular pirate had simply panicked and run away, somehow avoiding Yuan's wrath in the process, then the only reason that the pirates would have broken and fled was if Yuan was dead. He could already hear more bodies crashing through the jungle nearby, lending some credence to the assertion that the pirates were broken and running for their lives.

"Tell me about the bunkers, quickly!" he snapped at the pirate. A plan was starting to form in his mind, but it would take quick action to make it work.

The pirate stammered out some details of how the bunkers and the trench line had been laid out. He knew little to nothing about the deserter's plans for the redoubt, only that it had been their destination after the attempt to escape to Borneo had been aborted by the *Jiaolong*'s attack.

Feng drew out his map and field notebook and quickly sketched in the location and the rough layout of the fortifications. Then he turned to Pan, who was still lugging the HF radio. "Contact the *Changbai Shan*," he ordered. "Tell them that the SAM threat is neutralized." He couldn't be entirely sure of that, but he doubted that the pirates were still organized enough to repel another air assault. It was possible that he was wrong, but he considered the risk to be worth it at that point. If this failed, and another helicopter went down, he was sure Guo would have his head, but if he succeeded, he would be a hero, and therefore untouchable. "Tell them that we require immediate air support and reinforcements at these coordinates." He rattled off the general area of the bunkers and what looked on the map to be a viable hasty LZ. "Stress the time-sensitivity of the request."

Pan got busy on the radio, while Feng dug the dead American's radio out of his gear. Perhaps it would be useful; if those were the remaining Americans up there, maybe he could draw them out instead of having to go into a bunker line after them.

Turning on the radio, he took a moment to think of what he was going to say. His English, while passable, was not the best. Finally, he pressed the Push To Talk button.

"To the American commander in the pirate's bunkers," he began, "I am the commander of Chinese commando forces who are here to bring the pirate to justice. You are in my Operational Area. I insist that you surrender. You will be treated well, until you can be returned to your country. I cannot allow any armed forces not belonging to the People's Republic of China to move freely on this island until the situation is stabilized. Again, surrender now, and you will be treated well. If you do not surrender, I must use any means necessary to secure the area. Even as I am transmitting this message, People's Liberation Army Marines are en route to encircle your position."

He let off the button, took a deep breath, and sent, "Do the right thing. Surrender now."

As he looked at Pan, he got an affirmative nod. The Marines were already in the air. It was almost over.

"What do we do with the pirate, *Shang Wei*?" Shao asked.

"Shoot him," Feng replied. "Then we need to get into position before the Marines arrive."

Dan listened to the stiff, heavily-accented transmission from the Chinese commando with a growing sense of despair. He had no reason to think that they were going to face anything but a Chinese prison camp if they surrendered. The crew of the EP-3 that had made a forced landing on Hainan Island back in '01 might have been treated well, if interrogated extensively, but once the Chinese found out that the Americans they'd taken were contractors, apparently written off by the US government, there wouldn't even be an attempt to return them to the States. They'd spend the rest of their lives breaking rocks in a Chinese forced labor camp.

He checked his ammunition. They couldn't stay there, not if the Chinese commander was telling the truth and the PLA Marines were inbound. Once they were surrounded, it would be all over. They had to move.

He turned to Cassy. She'd heard it as well, and was staring at him, wide-eyed, probably wondering what he was going to do. "Stay here, stay on the gun," he said. "Anybody coming up that slope still gets some love, got it?"

She nodded, jerkily. It was one more shock on top of everything else, and she had to be feeling trapped and hopeless at that point. He sure was. "We're not surrendering," he assured her as he paused just before ducking out of the bunker. She nodded one more time before turning back to the PKM and leaning into it, watching the kill zone in front of the bunker.

Dan hurried down the trench to the leftmost bunker, doubled over, not sure if the Chinese were close enough to see him and not interested in taking the chance. He called out, "Friendly!" before entering the bunker. After everything they'd been through, it would really, really suck to get shot by Vernon because he forgot to announce himself.

"We about ready to get out of here, boss?" Vernon asked, without taking his eyes off of his sector.

"As fast as possible," he replied. He told Vernon about the message from the Chinese.

The big man's shoulders slumped a little behind the gun. "We can't get a fucking break, can we?" he asked.

"Not so far," Dan replied. "I need you to get the rest ready to move. I'm going to give the comms one more try. We've got nothing left to lose. Pray that it's time for that break." He wasn't particularly expecting anything to come of it, himself, and from the look on Vernon's face as he turned away from the firing port and looked at him, neither was he.

Vernon left the gun and preceded Dan out into the trench, heading back toward the bunkers on the left flank and the rest of the men. Dan crawled back into the bigger bunker and hauled out the satcom setup that he'd taken out of Rex's pack, just in case. No messages they'd sent had been answered since the disastrous raid almost a week before, but maybe, just maybe, somebody might be listening, to hear what might as well be his last words. It would be more a cry of defiance than a message, but he felt oddly compelled to send it anyway.

It took a second to get the satellite link. He had to climb out into the trench and place the transmitter on top of the bunker's roof. Then he started typing on the little tablet.

This is probably the last transmission from the MMPR contractors deployed to the Anambas, he typed, *since you bastards decided to pull chocks and leave us to die as soon as things started to go bad. If anyone is listening, we're about to be hunted down by the PLA, and we'll probably, if we survive, go to a Chinese concentration camp for the rest of our natural lives. I just wanted to say, to whatever soft-clothed, yellow-bellied fuck sent us here, fuck you. Not that you care.*

He hit *SEND*.

Well, what the hell good did that do? he wondered. *Got a little bit off my chest, even though nobody's going to see it, and wasted a precious couple of minutes in the process.*

But as he looked down at the tablet, about to smash it against the rocks, a return message started to scroll across it.

Message received. Proceed to coordinates 48NXJ4336550030 NLT 0010L for extract. Apologies it took so long.

For a second, Dan just stared at the screen. It couldn't be real. They'd been hung out to dry. What the hell was going on? Was it a hallucination? Was it just some sick fuck still idly watching the satellite feed having a bit of a joke at their expense?

It didn't matter. If there was a hope, however slim, that it was real, that extract really was on its way, they had to take it. Better that than the certainty of death or imprisonment in China.

The sun was starting to move toward the horizon. They would still have to evade the PLA for a few more hours until midnight. He started quickly planning a route on the map, while Vernon got the rest moving up to form a hasty perimeter just short of the crest of the hill.

Sam and Cary had stayed with him, standing in the trench, rifles pointed down the hill. Dan thought he could feel the Chinese commandos getting closer, even though there was as yet no sign of them. He figured they had to be the ones who had attacked the pirates at the marina, which put them down the hill, about where the pirates had been before the ill-fated human wave attack on the bunkers.

A single shot echoed through the jungle. It didn't come anywhere near them, but Dan took it as a sign that it was time to go. He folded up the map, stuffed it in his chest rig, and hefted his rifle. "Let's move," he muttered. He found his voice was hoarse, his throat raw after the gunfight. The heat, the adrenaline, and the smoke had drained most of the moisture out of his system. He was sure the rest were hurting just as bad.

The radio crackled with the accented Chinese voice again. "I can only take your silence as a refusal. I urge you to surrender. You will be treated well. The alternative is to die in this jungle, far from your home."

Dan looked at Sam and Cary. Sam was still looking down the hillside, his rifle in his shoulder, as ready to bring the hate as ever. Even the ordinarily irrepressibly cheerful Cary seemed grim-faced and beaten down. He hadn't told them about the message yet. He was still afraid it was bullshit. He didn't want to hold out that hope only to have it snatched away.

Still, he'd have to let them know sooner or later. He would once they were away from there, and he could tell everybody. In the meantime...he lifted the radio to his lips.

"Sorry, bud," he sent. "I've already got a good enough idea of what a Commie's word is worth. We'll take our chances."

He stuffed the radio back in its pouch, already wondering how he was going to manage link-up comms with their extract. Assuming there was an extract, as soon as they got on the VHF radio to call them, the Chinese were going to overhear.

They needed to get clear first. There were still a few hours left before the rendezvous time. They could figure out the comm situation when they weren't about to be surrounded by the PLA.

He pointed up the hill, and Cary clambered up out of the trench, staying low, and started up toward the small perimeter that Vernon had set up. Sam was still looking down the hill.

"Got some movement down there," he said. "I think we're going to have company really soon."

"That's why we're leaving," Dan replied. "Let's go."

Sam didn't move, at first. "I don't know," he said, an eerily calm note in his voice. "I always kind of wanted to take a crack at the PLA before I died. Not as good as the Russians, but I'll settle for some Chinese commandos."

Dan realized he was going to have to hold out that hope sooner than he'd thought. If given the alternatives of going out in a blaze of glory in a gutsy last stand or getting eventually hounded to death in the jungle, most of them, Sam especially, were probably going to opt for the last stand.

"It may still come to that," Dan said, "but personally, I'd rather get to extract. I finally got a response on satcom."

Sam chuckled humorlessly. "You don't have to bullshit me, Dan," he said.

"I'm not," Dan said flatly. "I can show you the message when we get clear, but we've got to move *now*, before we're surrounded by Chinese Marines and cut off from any hope of getting off this fucking island."

Sam looked at him for a moment, searching his face for any sign that he was lying. "Holy shit, you're not kidding."

"No, I'm not, and we can hash it out later. Let's go. Now." Sam nodded briefly, and together the two of them climbed out of the trench and headed up the hill.

The rest were gathered in a tight circle, rifles pointed outboard, just below the crest of the ridge. Vernon had placed himself in the center, and moved aside to make room as Dan and Sam came in. "Sam's on point," Dan said. "Start moving toward the northwest. We've got to get some distance before the rest of the Chinese show up." He was already keeping one ear tuned for the sound of helicopters. The sky was quiet so far, but it couldn't last.

Sam moved out fast, the rest falling into a tight Ranger file behind him. They were making more noise than any of them might have liked, but speed was security at that point. They had to put some distance between them and the bunkers, getting outside the cordon before it was set.

They went over the top of the ridge and down the opposite slope, which was considerably less steep than the one they'd climbed to get to the bunkers. The jungle was just as thick, but they didn't have to fight the terrain as much. They weren't running, quite, but they were moving fast.

They were halfway down the slope when the faint roar of the Chinese helicopters started to build from the north. Sam picked up the pace.

The snarl of the incoming rotors was getting louder and louder as they pushed through the jungle. It was starting to sound like the helos were going to come down right on top of them, except that were still in thick jungle, where there was no place to land.

Until Sam suddenly came on a clearing that would make an excellent landing zone. At the same time as a trio of Z-8s was descending toward the ground.

Sam dived flat, and Dan quickly followed him, hoping that neither the pilots nor the door gunners had seen anything. They had come on the clearing suddenly; Sam had actually taken a step out into it before quickly drawing back.

They couldn't stay there, though. If the Chinese followed any sort of basic infantry tactics, they'd push a perimeter out to the jungle as soon as they got off the birds. They couldn't risk getting stumbled upon.

Even as the rotor wash beat at the jungle around them, Dan tapped Sam's boot and pointed down the hill when he carefully twisted his head around to look. Sam nodded minutely, then started crawling. Dan looked back to see if Harold was paying attention, realizing that the former hostage no longer had a ghillie, or much left in the way of cammie paint. There was nothing they could do about it now. They just had to stay low and move slowly. He signaled that they were continuing around the clearing, and to stay down. Harold indicated that he understood, and twisted around to pass the signal on. Dan started crawling after Sam.

The Chinese helicopters flared and landed, their back ramps dropping and the first PLA Marines running off, wearing helmets, body armor, and carrying their QBZ-95s at the ready as they ran a short way out from the birds before kneeling, watching the jungle around them. Dan could see some of it through the vegetation, he was that close to the clearing.

Slowly, carefully, they crept along the edge of the clearing, even as more troops ran off the helicopters, and their officers got them organized and moving. Dan prayed, not for the first time, that none of his teammates got nervous enough to start shooting.

With all the Marines on the ground, one of the Chinese officers raised a hand to signal to the pilots that they were accounted for. The pitch of the Z-8s' rotors changed, the roar deepening as they started to bite the air again, whipping the jungle and the grass of the clearing with a brutal wind as they clawed for the air.

Even as the Chinese Marines ducked and tried to shield themselves from the debris kicked up by the rotor wash, Sam sped up, taking advantage of the overhead movement of the vegetation to conceal his haste. Dan followed suit, coming to his hands and knees to high crawl, looking back to make sure that Harold was still behind him.

By the time the helicopters had departed and the blast of wind and debris had settled down, they'd worked their way well toward the east side of the clearing. Sam and Dan slowed again, sinking prone. Dan turned his head to watch the LZ.

There was a single squad holding security on the south side of the clearing, barely seventy-five meters away. One of the Chinese Marines suddenly pointed toward the jungle and said something to his squad leader. Dan felt his heart freeze in his chest.

The squad leader, who looked barely old enough to shave, hesitated for a moment before nodding and starting his squad moving toward the jungle. Dan cursed. They had come so damned close to getting away without a fight. He carefully turned over and pointed his rifle toward the oncoming soldiers.

But only a few paces from the edge of the clearing, the Chinese Marines stopped, as one of the senior officers in the center yelled at the squad leader. The young man answered, pointing toward the jungle. Dan couldn't understand the reply, but the tone was unmistakably derisive, followed by a barked command. The young squad leader hung his head and started his squad moving back toward the main body, which appeared to be forming up to push uphill, to come at the bunker complex from over the ridge.

Dan let out a silent sigh of relief as the Chinese Marines turned away. He stayed put, not moving a muscle, until the rest of the Marines had formed into a long line abreast and pushed into the jungle. Only once they were out of sight did he turn back to Sam, who looked back and raised his eyebrows, as if to soundlessly say, *That was close.*

They stayed low and slow for another two hundred meters, until they were on the east side of the clearing. Then Sam got to his feet, and this time they did run, intent on putting some serious distance between them and the Chinese guns.

Feng stood at the entrance of the largest abandoned bunker as rage and despair warred for mastery behind his stony expression. He didn't know how they'd done it, but the Americans had slipped through

249

the net. They weren't supposed to be able to do that; he'd been taught that American soldiers were lumbering, over-burdened, over-confident louts who depended wholly on technology over skill. Unless they had some kind of stealth tech for the individual soldier, though, they had enough skill to evade a company minus of PLA Marines sweeping the jungle on-line for them.

He thought furiously. What would be their next move? Where could they go? They had to know that trying to hide on the island was only a temporary respite; as more and more PLA Marines landed, they would eventually be hunted down. Their only hope, long-term, would be to get off the island. He turned to *Shang Wei* Yiti, who had landed with the first wave. "Did you see any sites along the coast where there might be boats moored?" he asked. "Any place that they could commandeer a way off the island?"

Yiti shrugged. "We came down from the north," he said. "All of the docks on the north coast of the island have been secured. Terempa is now in our hands, as is the village to the east of it that you raided a few days ago. We had little visibility on the eastern shore."

Feng grimaced. "That will be where they are going. There must be some private dock on the eastern shore that they will try to make for."

"But where?" Yiti asked. "I do not have the men to sweep a five kilometer wide swath of jungle, not thoroughly."

Feng thought back to some of the familiarization he had done before the mission, using overhead imagery of the islands. He pointed to Yiti's map. "There should be a small shelter and dock here, at Tanjung Momong Beach," he said. "That will be the best option."

Yiti looked skeptical, but he deferred to Feng. In minutes, the *Jiaolong* and the Marines were moving out.

Feng hoped that they were not too late. It was already getting dark.

It was thirty minutes past sunset when the Chinese force descended on the long, white-washed house that dominated Tanjung Momong Beach. The *Jiaolong* led the assault, as the Marines hurried to cordon off the dock and the tiny handful of buildings clustered between the jungle and the rocky shore.

The site appeared to be deserted. There were no lights, no generator noises, no movement aside from the Chinese troops. Feng hoped that that was because the Americans were trying to lie low, and not because they had already escaped or gone somewhere else.

He was right behind Shao as the little man kicked the door open and charged into the building.

The *Jiaolong* shone their weapon lights into every corner. The long, low building was completely empty; simply a single, vacant room without even any furniture. Whoever had been using it had cleared out long before, probably at the same time that Yuan had taken over the islands under the *Zhaotong*'s guns.

Feng cursed, but stayed in the fight. He directed his men out to the next building, while calling Yiti and telling him to push his Marines farther out into the jungle to look for any sign of the Americans. It was probably a futile gesture, however, as only Yiti's platoon commanders actually had night vision goggles.

Dan and the rest were closer than Feng knew, only about three hundred meters south, on the far side of a short point. They could faintly hear some of the noise the Chinese were making over by the dock. Dan checked his watch, carefully shielding the faint green glow with his hand. Thirty more minutes.

They had pushed several hundred more meters past the Chinese LZ before halting, at which point he'd told the rest about the incoming extract. No one had believed it, so he'd had to pass the tablet around with the message, and even then a few had probably thought that he'd fabricated it just to give them some kind of hope. But now that they were at the coordinates, Dan was finding he was starting to hope that it was real, himself. They'd been hiding out for the last couple of hours.

He was still worried about the comm situation, though. There was no way to warn any extract platform about the Chinese to the north on the tac net, since that was compromised, and any transmission would probably only intensify the Chinese hunt for them. So he set up the satcom again, and pinged the control station.

He got a prompt reply. *En route. Twenty-eight mikes.*

"If this is a trick, I'm going to find a way off this island just to wring the jokester's fucking neck," he muttered, as he typed, *Roger. Be advised, sizable Chinese force approximately three hundred meters to the north. Advise approaching from the south. VHF comms compromised, up on satcom only.*

Good copy, was the reply.

The next half hour passed in taut, nerve-shredding silence. No one dared say a word, and not only because they were concerned about getting compromised. There was a palpable feeling that to say anything was going to jinx the whole thing, that the miraculous extract was going to evaporate if any of them made a sound.

As the minutes ticked down, Dan looked to the north, trying to penetrate the thick, black jungle. Was that the sound of approaching infantry? Was there a platoon sweeping down the coast, looking for them? Or was it his imagination?

Two mikes, the screen flashed under the cover he'd made out of palm fronds. *Suggest you break down and get to the shore. Authentication by IR flash.*

"Let's move," he hissed, stuffing the comms back into his pack.

"Down to the beach, now. Two mikes."

It was a short move, only about twenty meters. The beach itself was barely worthy of the name, being a narrow, rocky strip between the jungle and the water. They stopped right at the edge of the jungle, Dan crouching beneath a towering palm tree.

He wasn't sure what he'd been expecting, but the low, angular, winged shape gliding over the water wasn't it. The thing looked like a cross between a bat and a B-2 bomber, except its wings were in the water. Even as they watched, the wings seemed to fold out, lowering the hull down to the surface of the strait between Siantan and Bajau. The strange-looking craft turned away from them, then stopped and backed water, coming only a few meters from shore. A trapezoidal ramp opened in the stern. A moment later, three IR flashes came from the darkness of the hold, or fuselage, or whatever it was.

Dan responded with two, and then pointed toward the strange craft. "Go, go, go!" he hissed.

Nobody needed any further encouragement. Sam, Vernon, and Max stayed on the shore with him, holding security toward the jungle and up and down the beach, until all the rest were aboard. Dan made sure to count each one off the beach. He wasn't going to leave any of the few teammates he had remaining behind.

Then it was time. He tapped Sam, then Max, then Vernon. Together, they waded out into the water and up the ramp. "Last man," he told the man at the ramp, fully kitted up and helmeted, his face hidden behind his NVGs. The man took one hand off the MAG-58 machine gun to give him a thumbs-up, and hit the button next to his head. The ramp started to rise.

Even before it closed, the craft's engines thrummed quietly, and they swung away from the beach, heading south down the strait.

Chapter 25

Nobody said a word as the strange stealth craft glided away from the islands. Dan might have expected the rest of the team to collapse in the hold as soon as they got some distance, but none of them did. They stayed in the jump seats, rifles still in their hands, silent and tense.

He felt the same tension. After the last week, and the certainty that they had been abandoned to die, it was simply impossible to mentally accept that it was over, that there wasn't another ambush waiting for them. Strangely, the rear gunner seemed to feel the same way; at least he didn't stow the gun and get up until they'd already been underway for almost half an hour, even though the ramp was closed.

When he finally shoved the MAG back into a small alcove apparently designed for it next to the ramp, the man stood up and turned on the interior lighting, which was still a dim green, not unlike what Dan had seen in military helicopters to avoid whiting out the pilots' NVGs. Then he flipped up his NVGs and took his helmet off.

It took Dan a few moments, in his present state of mental and physical exhaustion, to recognize the man. In most of the pictures he'd seen of Mitchell Price, the man had been wearing a suit and tie, in comfortable surroundings, talking to the media. Seeing the famous mercenary entrepreneur in cammies, body armor, and helmet, having just manned a gun on what had to be an extremely expensive stealth boat during a high-risk extract in the middle of the South China Sea, was a little odd.

Price stepped over to him. "What's your name, son?" he asked. The boat's engine was quiet enough that he didn't really have to raise his voice.

Dan just stared, hollow-eyed, at him for a moment, a little nonplussed at being called "son." "Tackett," he finally replied, "Dan Tackett."

Price put a hand on his shoulder. "Dan," he said, "you've done a hell of a job with one hell of a shitty hand. I wish I could have gotten here sooner, but there was a lot of ground work to put in to get this done after the Malaysians raided the resort, not to mention a lot of money had to change hands and more than a few favors had to get called in to get this baby." He patted the side of the hull.

That was the first Dan had heard of their base getting taken out. He didn't say anything, though. There didn't seem to be much to say.

"We've actually been trying to contact you for three days, but we couldn't get a link," Price continued. "I'm guessing that you had some rather more pressing issues than comms to deal with. Fortunately, you picked a good time to give your final defiant speech."

Dan thought for a moment, and realized that they hadn't tried to turn on the satcom more than once or twice since the resort had gone silent. They'd just sort of assumed they were on their own, and had driven on in spite of it.

"I'll be honest, there are a lot of people back home who would rather you were dead or in a Chinese prison camp," Price went on. "That was part of what I had to arrange before coming to get you; you'll all have airtight alibis as to where you were for the last couple of months. It seems I have an extremely secretive, very expensive training partnership with the Sultan of Brunei. There's a paper trail to place you there, though obviously without details, and the Bruneian authorities won't confirm anything, thanks to the secrecy agreements involved."

Dan looked closely at him, but it was Vernon who asked the question. "Why do we need an alibi?"

Price looked at him levelly. "Because this wasn't a governmental op, and certain agencies are investigating me and my companies over it," he admitted, "and just like I wasn't going to hang you out to dry on the islands, I'm not going to just turn you over to them." Looking around at the filthy, shell-shocked, bedraggled contractors, he continued. "I make no apologies; it was the right thing to do. The Navy hadn't lifted a finger, and none of the local governments were equipped to handle it. It is kind of a shame the PLA got to him first; that's only going to further bolster their aggression in the region, but at least Yuan's out of the picture."

Dan chuckled without humor. "The PLA didn't get to him first," he said, his voice low and flat.

Price heard him. His expression changed, ever so slightly. "Really?"

There were a couple of nods. "He got to us, actually," Dan said after no one else volunteered to tell the story, "and we killed him."

"You're sure?" There was an intensity to the question that put Dan a little on guard. *More* on guard, anyway.

"A burst just about took his head off," Dan replied. "I'm sure."

Even in the dim light, he could see Price's expression change. There was an eagerness in his eyes, quickly hooded by a renewed guardedness. "I'm sure, under the circumstances," he said, trying to sound nonchalant, "that you weren't able to search his body."

Dan studied him. "Why?" he asked, having noticed the change of tone in the other man's voice. Price was fishing for something. "Was there something in particular you were hoping to find?"

Price looked away. "Doesn't matter now. What's done is done."

Dan dug in his chest rig. He still had the drive. It didn't feel wet; it might have avoided the seawater on the way out to the boat. He drew it out and held it up in front of him.

"So," he said. "What's on it that's so important?"

Price's eyes seemed to flash a little in the dimness. He took a deep breath, and smiled a little. "Well, that's a long story," he said.

"We seem to have plenty of time," Dan replied, palming the drive. "It's a long way to anywhere out here."

"Fair enough," Price said, taking the seat across the hold from Dan. "You've certainly earned it." He paused for a moment, as if gathering his thoughts, though somehow Dan had the feeling that this was a long-rehearsed speech. "Yuan was planning this little adventure for a long time. He had friends, most notably in the Chinese intelligence and cyber spheres. How much they were getting in kickbacks from his operations isn't something I've been able to determine, but considering that there doesn't appear to have been any ideological component to this little crisis, there had to have been something lucrative involved.

"The files on that drive, assuming that it is what I think it is, were intended to be Yuan's insurance policy. He hoped to blackmail the PRC with the threat of releasing them, Snowden-style, if they came after him. Apparently, it backfired," he observed wryly. "They seem to have decided that the threat actually *necessitated* taking him out.

"If my information is correct, the files on that drive detail a number of Chinese operations around the world, operations that would not go over well with most of the rest of the international community. Connections with organized crime, several active insurgencies, outright terror groups...I believe there is even some reference to active partnership with North Korea's Office 39." He gave a grim little smile. "Needless to say, there is a *lot* of leverage contained on that little hard drive. *If* it is what I think it is."

Dan looked him in the eye. "So, this is why we came here. This was what you were really after."

"It was an added bonus," Price asserted. "And one that you will reap significant rewards for retrieving. I will ensure that you are all *well* compensated, I assure you." He held out a hand for the drive.

Dan hesitated. "How did you know about this?" he asked, buying time. He really wasn't sure how to approach this. This was big, national-security level stuff. Could he really turn it over to Mitchell Price? He would admit that all he knew about the man was his extremely polarized and polarizing public reputation, but he was still a private concern, and this was information that could impact global geopolitics.

"I have business connections all over," Price admitted. "Including a few with the Chinese. Some of them are more talkative than they probably should be." His hand was still out, his eyes locked on Dan.

"If he was trying to blackmail Beijing," Vernon put in, "why not

just release the shit on the Internet as soon as he came under attack?"
Dan wasn't sure if Vernon was helping him temporize, but he was
grateful for the interruption.

Price looked over at him. If he was annoyed at the delay, he
didn't show it. "It wouldn't have done him much good. Like I said, it
was an insurance policy. Blackmail hadn't worked, so I imagine his next
step would have been to try to get it to the CIA in exchange for
protection. He'd probably get it, too, regardless of what he'd done out
here." There was disgust in his voice, though Dan honestly couldn't tell
if it was genuine or a calculated act.

Price turned back to Dan. His hand was still out.

"What happens if I don't hand this over?" Dan asked.

"Nothing," Price replied. "You won't get the bonus, of course,
but the rest of the safety net I just spent the last week putting in place for
all of you will remain. Paper trail, paychecks, flights home, the works.
Of course," he said as he leaned back, letting his hand fall to his knee,
"you could try to offer that to the FBI or the CIA. But then you'd have to
explain how you got it. That could get...uncomfortable." He sighed.
"Face it, Dan, that is essentially valueless to you. It's more of a liability
than an asset."

"That's bullshit," Harold said suddenly. Dan turned a glare on
him, momentarily forgetting that the other man had been through some
serious shit himself. But to Dan, he'd been little more than baggage for
the last thirty-six hours. "That's stuff that should be going to the
intelligence community, not a private company."

"Shut up, Harold," Dan snapped.

"No, it's fucking blackmail," Harold replied.

"No it ain't," Sam said. "It's business. It seems like we've got a
choice between making some extra money for our trouble, or getting
shafted by the government for it. I'd say take the money."

There was a bit of a general murmur, though how much was
assent or dissent was hard to tell. Nobody seemed to be feeling that
talkative. Price just kept his eyes on Dan.

"You know," Vernon said into the sudden silence, "Ordinarily I
might make the speech for patriotism, and doing our civic duty by
turning this in to the proper authorities. But under the circumstances,
those 'proper authorities' were more than happy to leave us to die. Think
about it. There's a fucking cruiser in the South China Sea right now. I
know there are SOF units working the Philippines and Indonesia. They
could have intervened, gotten us out. Sure, we'd probably face some
charges, but we'd be alive. They sat on their fucking hands. And don't
even try to tell me that they didn't know what was happening."

He looked at Price. "I might not entirely care for Mister Price,
or his approach, but the fact remains, he was the only one who came for
us. And he came himself. That means something."

Dan looked down at the little piece of plastic, metal, and circuitry in his hand. Then, slowly, he held it out. Price took it.

"I hope I don't regret this," Dan said, looking Price in the eye.

"You won't," Price assured him.

Dan didn't know whether to believe him or not.

Turned out in his full dress uniform, with every medal and epaulet in place, Feng marched into the office of the South Sea Fleet Commander's office, stopped in front of the *Zhong Jiang*'s desk with a bang of his boot heels, and saluted stiffly.

His father looked up at him heavily, and waved at him to dismiss his salute. Another curt gesture dismissed the guards at the door.

"This is not good, Kung," *Zhong Jiang* Feng Caohui said. "Not good for the Navy, not good for the Party, and not good for the family."

Feng kept his gaze on the wall above and behind his father's and superior officer's head. "I had the Americans on the run," he said. "It is more than likely that they never had time to find the files." It hadn't shown up on the Internet, that he knew of, so that was a small bit of fortune.

"Without confirmation, that is not enough for me to take to the Central Committee," *Zhong Jiang* Feng replied. He leaned back in his chair and put his hands on his desk. "I have taken steps to ensure that most of the weight of this falls on Guo's shoulders," he said. "He was, after all, the ranking commander in the area, and if he had offered the kind of support he should have, you might have eliminated the deserter more quickly and positively secured the stolen files. That should keep most of the scrutiny off of you and the family. But, I cannot guarantee the higher position that you were hoping for, under the circumstances." He sighed heavily. "You will be reassigned; that is unavoidable. There is a training position opening up in the North Sea Fleet; that is where you will go. I suggest that you acquit yourself as best you can. My secretary has your orders already cut."

Feng felt the bitter pang of disappointment. Effectively, his career was over, and for a failure that couldn't even be positively confirmed.

But it was better than being stood up against a wall and shot, or sent to a forced-labor camp. He saluted again, and pivoted smartly on his heel before marching out of the office.

He would be less relieved if he knew what had happened aboard the stealth boat only a few days before.

It had been a long drive from the airport, but Dan was finally turning into Roger's and Darlene's driveway. He saw some movement in one of the windows, then the door flew open and Amy and Tom came pelting out, running to the truck before he'd even braked.

He piled out without even shutting the engine off, gathering his kids to him. Amy was crying, but Tom was just happy as could be. The little boy looked like he'd grown two inches since he'd left. He knew it was probably only his imagination, but he didn't care. He held the two of them as tightly as he could, a lump in his throat. He hadn't been sure that this was even going to happen.

It had been a few days since they'd gotten back to the States. He'd had a little time to process the horror that they had passed through, and start to mourn the ones they'd lost. It was still there, though, even as he closed his eyes, holding his children tight. He still saw the jungle, the fire, the blood, and smelled the scent of death.

He was home, he was with his kids again, but it was still going to take a long time to really come back.

Roger and Darlene came down the steps rather more sedately than their grandchildren had. Taking Amy's hand and hoisting Tom up in the crook of his arm, he went to meet them.

Darlene hugged him tightly, Tom and all. Roger just looked in his eyes. There was a silent moment of communication between the old vet and the younger. Roger sighed. "It was worse than we were afraid of, wasn't it?"

Dan just nodded. "Yeah, it was," he said. "But I made it through, and now I'm back." He gave Tom a bounce that made the little boy yell with excitement. "And I'm not going out again. I think I've had enough."

Mandarin Glossary

Shao Wei: Ensign (O-1)

Shang Wei: Lieutenant (O-3)

Shang Xiao: Captain (O-5)

Da Xiao: Commodore (O-6)

Zhong Jiang: Vice Admiral (O-8)

Shi Zhang: Chief Petty Officer (E-7)

Guojia Anquan Bu: Ministry for State Security

Jiaolong: Sea Dragon (PLA Naval Commandos)

chusheng: animal

laowai: foreigner

tongzhi: comrade

bu xu dong: Don't move.

hun dan: prick

kuai dien: Hurry up.

gou za sui: piece of shit/scumbag

qu ba: Let's go.

Author's Note

A lot of the Chinese side of this story is speculation. Very little detail of the regular operations of the PLA make it out of the PRC, so exactly how they work, their tactics and procedures, had to be guessed at. Similarly, the character of *Shang Wei* Yiti is guesswork; while there were Uighur conscripts fighting in the PLA in the past, it is presently unknown as to whether or not any are allowed in at this point in time, much less allowed to command. The Muslim Uighurs of Xinjiang are a major target of PLA operations at the moment, ostensibly under the mantle of counter-terrorism.

CPSIA information can be obtained
at www.ICGtesting.com
Printed in the USA
FSOW01n0134060616
21199FS

9 781532 775277